# ONE SECRET TOO MANY

M K Turner

## By M K Turner

### *Meredith & Hodge Series*

The Making of Meredith

Misplaced Loyalty

Ill Conceived

The Wrong Shoes

Tin Soldiers

One Secret Too Many

Mistaken Beliefs

Quite by Chance

Family Matters

Not If You Paid Me

### *Bearing Witness Series*

Witness for Wendy

An Unexpected Gift

Terms of Affection

### *The Murder Tour Series*

Who Killed Charlie Birch?

### *Others*

The Cuban Conundrum

The Recruitment of Lucy James

Murderous Mishaps

# ACKNOWLEDGMENTS

Editing by Sharon Kelly

Cover Design by www.behance.net/lwpmarshala1e9

Photography by: Gabriele Rampazzo and Katie Harp
The Victoria Rooms - Bristol

# 1

Jakub Hasek felt his muscles tense, holding his breath as the man, Josef, shuffled into view. The heavy metal chains fixed to Josef's ankles made his gait awkward, and his body swayed as if in response to some unheard tune. Jakub wondered if a sweet melody was playing in Josef's mind to obliterate the reality of his situation. The swaying stopped as a voice called out. Josef was lost from view for a few seconds as a soldier in green uniform stepped up to him. When the soldier stepped away a blindfold shielded the observer from the fear they knew would be found in Josef's eyes. Orders were barked from an unseen presence to the left of the tableau, the tone confirming authority. Jakub blinked. The words were in a foreign tongue, but it was clear enough what they meant. The blindfolded Josef fell to his knees, the crotch of his trousers darkened as his bladder emptied, and the metallic echo of the rifles being made ready filled the air.

The soldier stepped forward. His gloved hand grabbed Josef by the back of his shirt, and he grunted as he attempted to heave Josef back to his feet, but Josef's legs could no longer take the weight of his body. A large section of the shirt tore under the strain, and Josef's shaking hands grasped at the soldier for support. The voice of authority barked again, and the soldier let Josef drop back to his former position. The soldier shook his head, and Jakub couldn't decide whether it was in disgust or pity for Josef, whose body twitched involuntarily as he awaited his fate. The soldier stepped out of view, and the sound of the rifles spitting out their deadly cargo was deafening for a split second. Then there was silence.

Jakub looked at the screen of his phone for a moment longer, but, as always, stopped the recording before the now-bloodied remains of his grandfather were dragged away. He didn't need to wait for the camera to pan round to the face of the man giving the orders. He'd seen it a thousand times. He knew it better than his own.

Dropping the phone onto the bed he padded barefoot to the bathroom. The cold shower was already running, and his clothes hung ready on the outside of the wardrobe he passed on his way. They were testing the latest prototype today. Subconsciously, his fingers made their way to the remains of the large ugly bruise above his left nipple as he stepped into the shower. He gasped as the spray of ice cold water attacked his body like a million blunt needles looking to pierce his skin. Soaping his body vigorously, he smiled as he recalled the final preparations he'd made the day before, convinced the modifications would do the job. It had taken years and hundreds of thousands of pounds to get to this point, but today was the first time he had felt optimistic about the testing. He sensed the end was within reach. They would be rich beyond the imagination of most men. But he wasn't in it for the money. Not yet anyway.

After dressing quickly, he walked to the bed to retrieve his phone, wallet and car keys. Shrugging into his jacket, he opened the door and stood on the threshold with his eyes closed. The anger of Jakub Hasek was stored away for another day, and as he opened his eyes and stepped into the hall, Jake Hatton returned.

# 2

Meredith slammed the car door. Shoulders hunched, and head down against an imaginary wind, he made his way into the station and up to his office. Nodding an acknowledgement to the duty sergeant who passed him on the stairs, he assumed the words called were a greeting, and didn't offer a response, his mind still churning with the information he had been given. The duty sergeant tutted and made his way back to the front desk. He knew Meredith's expression only too well and realised that now was not a good time to ask for a donation to the retirement present they were organising.

Meredith's fingers gripped the envelope a little tighter as he pushed open the door to the incident room. Ignoring his team, he strode directly to his office.

Closing the door, he sat at the desk and removed the contents of the envelope. Having made a few more notes on the various documents, he crossed his legs at the ankle and leaned back in his chair. Lips pursed, he stared at the ceiling as he wondered whether to update the team immediately or leave it until the morning. After a few minutes, and with a sudden burst of movement, he made his decision. Scooping the envelope's contents into an untidy bundle, he made his way to the front of the incident room. Perching on the edge of a table, he clapped his hands, an unnecessary action to gain their attention. His team had been speculating about his obvious distraction following his return to the station, and had fallen silent, watching his every move, when he emerged from his office.

Meredith pointed at Hutchins. "Pa, get up here, your handwriting is neater than mine." He paused as he looked around at the members of his team. "We've been seconded to a fairly new unit at the Met. Our jurisdiction is limited to a degree, but we'll now be investigating several murders believed to be connected to a criminal group in the Russian community which has been active in the Bristol area."

Meredith handed Hutchins the first photograph. Hutchins fixed it to the blank whiteboard and stood, pen poised. He began to jot down information as Meredith spoke. Hutchins hoped he was choosing the most salient points.

"Ivor Andronikov." Meredith spelt the name for Hutchins before continuing. "Now known as Ivor Andrews, he heads up what journalists are calling the St Petersburg Faction, following the murders eighteen months ago of various drug importers, all traced back to St Petersburg. The press doesn't know about his involvement, and until this morning that knowledge remained behind closed doors, no doubt locked in a filing cabinet somewhere in Cheltenham. The murders were nationwide, but surprisingly none in, or linked to, Bristol. We're unlikely to have much to do with Andronikov. However, and this is where it becomes interesting, these two," Meredith passed across two further photographs to Hutchins, "Peter Myshkin, Russian origin, and Jan Liska, a former Czechoslovakian, have turned up in Bristol. I've checked, and they've not come onto our radar, but the boys from London assure me they are very active in drugs and prostitution, and connected to two murders that they know of. We will be reopening those investigations. They are based . . ." He stopped speaking as Louie Trump raised his hand. "What?"

"Two murders, sir? How did we miss two murders? Are they recent?"

"I was coming to that, but as you ask we'll jump forward and come back to location. Now . . ."

Meredith shuffled through the sheaf of photographs and handed two more to Hutchins. He waved his hand, shooing Hutchins further down the board. Hutchins pinned the two photographs on the far end. The first showed a white male lying naked on a mortuary slab. He had two distinguishing features: a dark hole in the middle of his forehead, and his fingertips had been crudely removed. The second was a tall, swarthy, dark-haired man, his collar turned up against the wind which lifted his dark hair, highlighting the white at his temples.

"The corpse was found in an alley behind the shops on Stapleton

Road. Found in his birthday suit at three in the morning by a local prostitute. Nothing other than his face to identify him, and he hasn't been. Well, not officially, not until this morning."

"Was this about three years ago, Gov? I think I remember it." Seaton stood and walked to the photographs for a closer look. "Central dealt with it, and this photo was circulated for months in all the papers, and even made national news. I assumed it had been solved."

"Well, you assumed wrong. Although from what I understand, certain people knew who he was within the week. His name is Jimmy Ridgeway. Born in Birmingham, and a known courier for the St Petersburg Faction. He was good at his job, up to that point anyway, and clearly did something to annoy someone. His despatch was professional. We don't know where he was murdered, but have a good idea, and Forensics believe the skin from his fingertips was removed whilst he was still alive."

Jo Adler wrinkled her nose.

"We don't know if that was torture to gain information, or torture for crossing them in some way. The blokes I've been with this morning didn't think he would know much. Perhaps he got careless." Meredith shrugged and turned to the second photograph. "The other bloke, Filipp Myshkin, cousin to Peter, is still very much alive. I'm told he was most likely responsible for killing Ridgeway. In theory, he runs a kebab stroke burger joint for his cousin, but what he actually does is oversee the packaging of large quantities of synthetic drugs made at the rear of this meat processing plant."

Meredith handed Hutchins another photograph. It showed a nondescript two-storey brick building, much like you'd find on any industrial estate. The large Perspex sign above the door, and on the side of the refrigerated truck parked outside, carried the logo of H & S Meat Products. Meredith turned back to the team.

"Legally, they produce minced beef, pork and lamb on an industrial scale. They supply to everyone from Mrs Mop at the local farm shop, to the big-name supermarkets. Both Peter and Filipp have a registered interest in that business, which surprises me. If they are as professional a set-up as it has been suggested, why would they tie themselves to the location? Something we need to work on. The business itself is whiter than white. It puts its returns in on time, pays its taxes, and has a clean bill of health from the environmental agency. It gets checked every six months or so. Payments are received via the bank, and the farm shop turnover isn't big enough to launder large quantities of cash. So where does the money go if this really is a major drugs operation? A recent inspection by Customs and Excise," Meredith used his fingers to indicate that it was unlikely Customs and Excise had arranged the visit, "showed everything to be in order. No one would have known about their enterprise, not even the London boys, if one of their van drivers hadn't managed to run over a granny on a crossing. The van was impounded, and drugs were found sealed in the walls. However, the drug squad decided to leave these where they were found. They knew the boys in London would be interested. Not shutting down the St Petersburg mob has been a thorn in their side. They hoped the drugs would lead to enough evidence to round them up."

"What happened to the drugs?" Jo Adler questioned. "Surely they didn't let them get onto the street? And you mentioned two murders."

"They followed the drugs to Plymouth, and picked them up in the English Channel from a boat scheduled to take a trip to France. That way the outfit in Bristol were free and clear, and the skipper of the boat, who swore he knew nothing about it, is currently serving time for it. We may pay him a visit. It's been the best part of three years now, so he might be willing to do a deal."

"And the other murder?" Rawlings leaned forward as Meredith passed Hutchins another photograph from the top of those remaining in his hand.

"I was getting there. That is a likeness of Veronika Biskop, or Ronnie Bishop; she changed her name ten years ago when she arrived in this country." Meredith pointed at the photograph Hutchins had pinned up, and handed Trump a small pile of photographs. "Take a quick look and pass them round. Ronnie was a former lover of Ivor Andronikov. He moved on to a younger version, but didn't like it when she turned up in Bristol and her name was linked to Filipp Myshkin."

Trump swallowed and screwed his eyes shut as he passed the photos on, and tried to remove the image from his mind. Seaton's face scrunched up in disgust as he quickly shuffled through them. He passed them on and looked at Meredith.

"And you know that's her from what? DNA? Because there was bugger all chance of recognising her face from the photographs, or any part of her, come to that. Whoever did that is one sick bastard."

"Which brings us back to Filipp Myshkin. Ronnie's DNA wasn't on record, but an engagement ring valued in excess of thirty grand was found amongst her stomach contents. The jeweller's mark led to a designer with a shop in the West End. The ring was made for her, and paid for by Ivor Andronikov. Her fingerprints were matched to a flat she shared when she arrived in Bristol; her flatmate had reported her missing months before."

Meredith jerked his thumb towards the photo of Myshkin. "He's a bad lad. Our boys are convinced he was responsible for some gruesome murders in Russia over a period of ten years or so before he came here. He headed up a military unit that was set up originally to clean up rogue factions both in Russia and throughout the former Soviet Union on behalf of the government. He got out of control, the unit was disbanded, and he disappeared. It's known he became a hired hit man, but he didn't stick to a quick shot to the head, or a quick slice of the throat. No, he excelled in slow painful deaths. He came here when he was warned that the authorities were closing in on him after he took out a minister favoured by the Russian president."

"And we simply let him come in?" Dave Rawlings demanded harshly. "I know we don't do political here, but when are we going to close the floodgates? When are we going to stick these lowlifes on a plane and sod what happens to them when they get home?" Rawlings shook his head. "I'm not talking about the average Joe, just those that we know are criminal. I'll tell you . . ." Rawlings fell silent as Meredith raised his hand.

"Like you said, we don't do politics. If we do our job right we'll be banging him up, whether here or in Russia. Concentrate on the job in hand."

"And what is the job?" asked Seaton. "It seems to me that whoever you've been socialising with knows enough to bang them up already. Why do your friends need our help?"

Meredith gave a brief smile. "Because we don't do political. This has to be a straightforward investigation into both the murders here in Bristol, and also, if necessary, the meat business. When we start applying pressure our political friends will see who gets stirred up, and this, I'm told, will give them the final piece of the jigsaw they've been working on."

"That doesn't ring true, if you don't mind me saying." Trump leaned forward, and elbows on desk, cupped his face in his hands. "That sounds to me like we only have half a story. If they —"

"Trump, I do mind you saying. Don't go chasing shadows. Simply do the job we've been asked to do. It's not complicated, it's what we're paid for, remember."

"But sir, I —"

Again, Meredith cut him off. "Enough. Do you understand?" Meredith's face mirrored the anger in his voice.

Seaton frowned. Meredith's eyes and the slump of his shoulders showed no irritation. It was clear to everyone in the room that there was more to this case than would ever be revealed to them. But what Seaton didn't understand was why Meredith had agreed to take it on. He would be effectively shackled by the blokes in London, and Meredith never jumped through hoops, irrespective of who was pulling the strings. Pursing his lips, Seaton decided to bide his time. There was a conversation to be had, but now was not the time.

~ ~ ~

Patsy and Chris watched Sharon usher the two men out of the office. When she'd closed the door she turned to them, frowning.

"That was a long meeting. Is it a juicy case? I've got my eye on a cruise up the Nile if it's a good earner." She grinned. "Come on then, what's it all about?"

Sharon Grainger was a partner of Grainger & Co, the private investigation business that Patsy had bought into when leaving the police force. The wife of senior partner Chris Grainger, Sharon only occasionally worked in the field, but kept a close eye on proceedings. She could sniff out trouble instinctively, and pick up when she was being told less than the truth by her husband, or so she thought. What she had never known was that Chris had been an SIS agent whilst working as a police officer, and, as he had recently confided in Patsy, still took on the odd case for them. This was one of those occasions, and Patsy had recently agreed to work with them too. Sharon would never have approved. It was the only secret Chris had ever managed to keep from his wife.

He shrugged. "Who can tell? They were a bit heavy on waffle and not good on detail, but they think they have a rogue scientist working locally. Patsy is going in as a personal assistant to the boss. Don't book that cruise just yet, it might be something or nothing." He made to turn away but swung back round to face her. "And the Nile? I don't think so! I want to relax when I'm on holiday not dodge bullets. Do you not listen to the news?"

Sharon's eyes narrowed. "Something or nothing took three hours? They only want a personal assistant? Why did they need both of you for that? There's something you're not telling me, isn't there?"

Sharon looked at Linda who had stopped typing away at her keyboard and was watching the exchange. "Linda, I want a full report on everything these two get up to, and how much they bill this long-winded client and for what."

She wagged her finger at her husband as he gave a heartfelt sigh and shook his head sadly. "Don't do puppy dog eyes on me, they've never worked. Spill the beans and we'll say no more."

"Light of my life, I will never understand how your brain works. I have a long meeting with Patsy and a client, and I'm up to something? You're mad as a box of frogs. Now, if you'd found out about the lap dancer last Friday I could understand your concern. Patsy, we have work to do. We need a decent CV ready for you by the morning."

Hurrying Patsy into the room he tutted at his wife before closing the door. Sharon shook her head, and walking to Linda's desk she tapped it with her fingernail.

"I was serious about you monitoring them. He knew they were coming but didn't put the appointment in the diary until this morning, and then didn't hurry them along despite this supposedly being a simple case. Keep your ear to the ground and ignore what they say."

Linda nodded agreement, eyes wide.

"What about the lap dancer?" she laughed as Sharon shrugged and sauntered back to her own desk.

"He couldn't handle more than me. I'm enough woman for two men."

Patsy walked to the window and looked out. James Benson, the agent who had recruited her, passed something to the man who would be her handler as they crossed the carpark. The second agent had chosen to be called Burt, and Patsy didn't much like him. She turned back to Chris who had taken a seat at her desk.

"How does Sharon do that? She's never far off the mark, do you think you'll be able to keep her at arm's length?"

"Yes, I've had years of practice, but you're right, she does have a nose for skulduggery. You need to give her a wide berth once we get going; maybe try and come in here when she's not in. I don't think you'll manage her at all. Now, we need to get on. You have an interview lined up with this Hatton bloke the day after tomorrow, and we need to decide which bits of your CV to tweak."

~ ~ ~

James Benson handed the card to his colleague and smiled. "Two down, one to go. That's his card for future reference, although after today, I'll handle him. You concentrate on Ms Hodge." Benson looked at his watch. "He'll be waiting so we'd better get a move on."

"Are you going to tell him? We may need to use them in the future."

"I'm not sure. Let's wait and see how things go. As to the future, they have to survive this first." Benson raised his eyebrows and shrugged. "It might never be an issue."

~ ~ ~

Meredith stepped back as his daughter hurried from the house.

"Sorry, Dad, I'm in a rush." Amanda Meredith kissed her father on the cheek. "Don't wait up." She sprinted up the drive.

Meredith heard her car door slam as he stepped into the hall.

Hearing the exchange, Patsy left the kitchen and greeted him. "She has another date. Do you know who it is yet?"

"Nope, but I will. How was your day?" Meredith pulled off his tie and dropped it on the hall table with his keys.

"Fine, yours?"

"The usual. Got two old murders the powers that be want us to re-investigate, pain in the arse. Originally dealt with by two different teams and the records are far from perfect. But, as they say, tomorrow is another day. What time is dinner?"

Patsy bristled. She and Meredith had fallen out when he had followed her to her first meeting with Benson. He'd known who Benson was and had asked her to walk away and not work with him. Patsy had not refused, but she hadn't agreed either, and as a result, to all intents and purposes, Meredith had called off their engagement. They'd not spoken about it since, and the ring she had bought him for his birthday, which had doubled up as an engagement ring, sat in the small compartment at the back of her purse intended for stamps. That had been a week ago, and stubbornly she refused to bring up the subject. To her mind, Meredith had caused the upset so it was up to him to put it right.

"Do you ever consider getting home early enough to cook for me?" She turned and walked back to the kitchen. "As I'd not heard from you, I had no idea if we were eating together. Would you like a glass of wine?"

Meredith drew in a breath, which he blew out slowly as he walked into the kitchen.

"I never say no to a glass of wine, and as to cooking, of course I'll cook. You only have to ask."

"I need to ask?" Patsy realised that she was pushing for an argument, and it was probably due to the guilt she felt at having accepted her first assignment. She continued, regardless, "Don't you think it would be nice to simply do it, and not assume I'll be here to wait on you?"

Meredith took the glass of wine she had poured him and sat heavily.

"Spit it out. Whatever it is that has wound you up. I'm too old and too tired to play guessing games." He leaned across to the fridge and pulled two leaflets from the door. The magnets that had held them in place fell to the ground. Patsy bent to retrieve them. "I'll order a takeaway. Indian or Chinese?"

"Why does something always have to be wrong with me?" Patsy replaced the magnets. "Yes, I do get fed up with being taken for granted, and with you rolling through life doing what you want to do, when you want to do it, and sod what anyone else wants. But is anything particularly wrong today? No. Life is fine and dandy, thank you."

"What do you want, Chinese or Indian? Or if you prefer I'll grab a quick shower and we can go out. That Italian was good last time."

"What, and sit there pretending to have a conversation? Are you going to talk to me, or just grunt in the right places?"

Meredith stood up, his chair scraping across the floor. "It seems to me like it's you who's avoiding talking. I'm going for a shower and we can try again when I come down."

His tone was condescending and Patsy raised her eyebrows.

"Sod off, Meredith. I'm going out." Lifting her bag from the back of the chair she brushed past him.

Meredith stood looking at the front door as he listened to her car start and drive away. Running his fingers through his hair he sighed; they needed to talk, but now was not the time. He walked back to the kitchen and refreshed his wine. Opening the freezer, choosing a pizza, he switched on the oven. He drank his wine watching the light on the oven, waiting for it to reach the desired temperature. When it did he slid the pizza onto a shelf and topped up his glass. A frown furrowed his brow, while in contradiction a smile played around his lips. This case was different from all those that had gone before. More dangerous for the team – these bad guys didn't take prisoners – and especially dangerous for him. If he did survive it, it could ruin what was, despite a few run-ins, a successful career. But it was a challenge, and he'd never been able to resist a challenge. He leaned back against the chair and stared at the ceiling. Life was going to get tough, and it was going to get messy. He didn't need aggravation at home, and he decided to put things right when Patsy returned.

~ ~ ~

Louie Trump handed Patsy a mug of tea.

"Thanks, Louie, I wish this were something stronger but I have an early start. Are you sure I'm not intruding on your evening? I had to escape Meredith or something horrible would have happened." She smiled as the sound of Linda travelled in from the kitchen. "At least I've made Linda happy."

"Of course you're not intruding. It's only a little extra pasta needed, and you're more than welcome. I'm sure things will be fine once you get home. DCI Meredith has had a long day, and these cases we've been assigned will be hard going. Especially with the boys from London looking over his shoulder. I was quite surprised that he agreed, you know, given his need to control." Trump looked wistful, "But then again, perhaps he had no choice." He smiled as Linda bustled into the room. "Don't be too hard on him."

He slipped his arm around Linda's shoulder and pulled her into a hug as Patsy leaned forward.

"What boys from London? All he said was that you'd been assigned two cold cases. He didn't mention anything about it being more than that."

Trump looked mortified for a second, and released his hold on Linda. "I've probably spoken out of turn, and you should forget I've said anything." He raised his finger to his lips. "Mum's the word."

He looked concerned, and Patsy shook her head.

"You're right, I didn't come around and don't worry, I won't mention it."

Linda looked from one to the other before clapping her hands loudly. "Right, that popped the balloon. No more talk of work; dinner is ready, come and eat. I'll tell you about this lovely little cottage I've found in Cornwall for the weekend after next. Louie is taking me away for a dirty weekend, Patsy." Linda led the way to the dining room.

"Am I indeed, and when did I suggest this, pray tell?" Louie asked as he followed her.

The three spent the next hour eating Linda's latest recipe, which turned out to be surprisingly good. Much praise was heaped on her, and they talked about the joys of weekend breaks, studiously avoiding the subject of work. The idle chatter was interrupted when Louie excused himself to take a call from his mother.

Patsy leaned forward. "How's it going with Louie's parents now they know you two are quite serious?"

She grinned as Linda batted the question away with a flap of her hand. "They love me. How could they not? They are terribly prim and proper, though. Frankly, it's a wonder Louie is anywhere near normal." She paused for a moment. "I know I said no chatting about work, but was Sharon right to be suspicious? Is there anything going on that you and Chris aren't sharing with her?"

Patsy frowned and tilted her head. "No, it's exactly what we said. Why the interest?" Her hand flew out and she pointed at Linda. "She's asked you to spy on us, hasn't she?"

Linda began to shake her head, her hands held up to show her innocence.

Patsy was having none of it. "You are the worst actress, Linda. You have red spots in the centre of your cheeks. You are after info for her! Well, there is nothing to find out. You turncoat, I thought we were friends." She reached across the table and slapped her friend playfully on the arm. "I might feed you some misinformation – that would be fun to watch. I . . ."

Patsy stopped speaking as Louie came back into the room phone in hand. He held it against his chest as he spoke.

"I was telling Mother about the cottage, and she thinks it's a wonderful idea. She thinks they should come with us because they know people down there. I told her I'd ask you – I didn't know how to refuse." Having said his piece, he held the phone towards Linda with an apologetic shrug.

Patsy laughed at Linda's expression as she took the phone and excused herself. Pecking Louie on the cheek, she told Linda she'd see her at work the next day, and made a quick exit. As she drove home she wondered why Meredith hadn't mentioned the involvement of another department, and decided it was the pot calling the kettle black with him at the moment. She decided she wouldn't mention it to him – poor old Louie's life would be unbearable if she did – but it was useful to know that Meredith was also being economical with the truth.

When she got home the house was in darkness. Going through to the kitchen she switched on the light and saw a single slice of pizza on a plate in the centre of the table. A note was propped against it.

*I hope you had something better than this. If not try to enjoy! Sorry x*

Smiling, Patsy slid the pizza into the bin, and double-checked that Meredith had switched off the cooker. Rather than go to the bedroom she went straight to the bathroom, showered, and cleaned her teeth. Picking up her clothes she tiptoed into the bedroom.

"Where did you go?" Meredith's voice was deep and slow. She'd clearly woken him up.

"Linda's. Sorry if I woke you."

"You didn't, not really, I was dozing while I waited for you."

"Why, did you want to talk to me?" Patsy climbed into bed and lay on her side facing him.

"Don't be bloody stupid, Hodge. Every time I open my mouth I get into trouble. We'll leave any talking you think is necessary until tomorrow."

Patsy smiled into the darkness. "What were you waiting for?"

"As I said, don't be bloody stupid, Hodge. Come here." He reached over and pulled her to him.

Her body immediately appreciated the warmth of his, and she pressed herself close to him.

"You're cold."

"So stop talking and warm me up."

Meredith closed his eyes as his lips sought hers, and he breathed a sigh of relief as he told himself to remember to take things one step at a time until the case was over.

# 3

Patsy opened her eyes as Meredith kissed her forehead and told her he was leaving for work. She stretched and peered at the clock: it was almost six-thirty.

"You're leaving early. It's only the second day on the case, is there that much to do? I was going to cook you a full English this morning."

"There's always a lot to do, you know that. The early bird and what have you, and I have a lot of worms waiting for me out there." Meredith put on his watch, and lifted his jacket from the hanger on the wardrobe door. "I'll take you out to dinner tonight. I'd cook, but I haven't got time to shop. Go back to sleep."

Without awaiting her response, he stepped out of the bedroom and closed the door.

Patsy closed her eyes and curled herself into a ball. Things weren't right, but at least he was trying. She waited for sleep to return, but eventually gave up, deciding she too would have an early start. As it happened it was just as well, because when she arrived at the office Chris was already there and in conversation with the man she knew as Burt. Burt jumped up and pulled another chair towards Chris's desk.

"Patsy, delighted as always. Glad you're early – I have homework for you." He tapped a memory stick on the desk as he looked her up and down. "You will also need to go home and change. You have an interview this afternoon."

"Already? I understood that would probably be tomorrow."

"It seems as though the Hatton brothers are moving faster than we thought they would." He shrugged, his hands held wide. "Nothing is ever certain in this world." He sat and indicated she should do the same. "So, from the top. Who are you, what have you done, and why are you attending the interview?"

"I'm Patsy Hodge, I'm an ex-police officer who left the force due to my relationship with my senior officer. I now work as a private detective for anyone who asks, although I have full security clearance and actually work for the government. I am tasked with providing assistance to politicians, scientists and blue-chip companies working with the government, and act as a middle woman and, depending on the job, an advisor. I can't discuss any previous assignments which are, of course, classified. And, as a bonus, I type." She screwed up her nose, indicating her displeasure.

Burt ignored her. "But if I'm to take you on, I need to have some idea what you have done before. I can't have you causing any form of issue or distraction." His face was blank as he shot the next question at her.

"I wouldn't be here if I weren't capable of assisting you. The project you are working on is important to the government." She gave a false smile. "Rest assured, I won't hamper your work, and you never know, I may even help."

Burt nodded slowly and held out the memory stick.

"I'm guessing you'll sound more sincere when you actually meet him. This will update you on all we have on the Hatton brothers and their project. Don't mess it up, Patsy, this is a very important contract the MOD are about to award. We don't want the minister to get egg on his face." He dropped the stick into Patsy's outstretched hand. "Stephen Hatton knows he has little choice but to take you on, however he is insisting on approval as they have a small, tightly knit team, and he doesn't want any problems as they near their goal."

Patsy sighed and rolled her eyes. "Well, I'd have less chance of doing that if you told me what it is you want me to find out. It's obvious I'm not going in to be a middle-woman. You are aware I'm not stupid because you wouldn't have given me the job if I were. So, why can't you be honest and at least give me a clue as to why I've been given this assignment? And no bullshit, please. If you won't tell me, fine, but don't insult me by lying."

Burt merely smiled and said, "Okay. I won't." He rubbed his hands together. "Read and watch all there is on that memory stick as soon as possible. Call me if you have any queries. Use the mobile provided."

Patsy's eyes shifted to Chris who held up a phone.

"You're meeting Stephen Hatton at four this afternoon, Chris has the details." Burt got to his feet, the meeting clearly over. He saluted them. "I'll leave you to it. As I said, change your outfit. That's too casual, but not too much leg or cleavage. You are a professional and the job's as good as yours anyway." A smile escaped briefly as Patsy raised her eyebrows. "If we don't speak before, call me once you've met him. *Adios amigos.*"

He left the office.

Patsy turned to Chris. "You know they know what I have to find, don't you? So why not tell me? Why make life so much more difficult than necessary?"

"Because they can. Because if you go in with preconceived ideas you may miss something, and when you find whatever it is that they want, you will know it. Accept that they know what they're doing and you'll feel more comfortable. You'll get used to it."

Patsy closed her eyes and drew in a deep breath, blowing out noisily, she got to her feet.

"I can't be bothered to argue. Right, you can make the coffee, and keep Linda at bay when she arrives." She brandished the memory stick. "It seems I have homework to do. And no biscuits for me – I'm putting on weight. There are far too many naughty things in this building for my liking."

She closed the door on Chris's response.

An hour and a half later she had a potted synopsis of the Hatton brothers' lives to date. Both had been orphaned at a young age and adopted by Desmond and Stephanie Hatton within six months of each other. They had spent their formative years living in Ireland on the border with Northern Ireland. There had been a minor controversy over the adoption of Jakub, as the Eastern European adoption papers were incorrect. Eventually, given the circumstances of the life to which they would be returning him, the Government had backed down and issued him with a passport.

The family settled to a near idyllic life. Desmond Hatton worked as a sales manager for a textile manufacturer and Stephanie Hatton was a teacher at the grammar school, which both boys attended. The boys were quick to learn and were always in the top sets in class. Both chose to attend Bristol University, as Stephen had been born in the city. The Hattons never kept secrets from their sons, and answered any questions about their early childhood with as much detail as they could.

Stephen had intended to find out if he had any blood relatives still living. He knew his birth mother had died of an overdose when he was four, and his father, also an addict, had left him with his paternal grandmother in Ireland and disappeared. All contact was lost with his father, and his mother's family. He'd been seven when his grandmother died. No family could be traced, and he was adopted by the Hattons a year later. As far as the records showed, Stephen Hatton had not found any family in Bristol.

Jakub had been more fortunate, and had met his uncle, his father's brother, several years before his death. The family visited Jakub's uncle on several occasions at his home in Portugal. Jakub was fifteen when his uncle learned he only had months to live and he flew out on his own to say goodbye. He was a changed boy when he returned, more serious than he had been, and the mischievous glint his dark eyes had previously carried was lost for ever. His parents put it down to the loss of his uncle. Only Stephen knew the true reason.

Stephen studied Physics and Economics, and Jakub, Chemistry and Mathematics. They were awarded first class degrees. Their adoptive parents could not have been prouder, and when the brothers decided to remain in Bristol and go into business together, they decided to sell the family home and move to Bristol themselves. Their plans were short-lived when they were killed by a car bomb intended for the security services at a Protestant bar that they just happened to be passing. The Hattons had spent what little savings they had on supporting the boys through university, and once the family home had been sold and all debts settled, the brothers invested what money was left in their business – developing and manufacturing sports clothing, and, in particular, protective sports clothing made from synthetic fabrics.

There was then a gap of some seven years in the information provided to Patsy. The brothers had received some sort of investment, although no details were given, and a scientist, Abigail Ward, began working for them. There was a list of her qualifications which meant little to Patsy. Shortly after this, the brothers had approached the MOD with their product RobusX. Information on the next eighteen months, which brought Patsy up to date, consisted only of a few emails and documents relating to their contract with the MOD.

Patsy closed the file and stared out of the window. There was nothing there to indicate what she was supposed to find. Her mind worked the information she had read, backwards and forwards, but she was none the wiser. Her musings were disturbed by Linda bursting into the room.

"Sharon's taking us for lunch; she's on her way in now. I checked the diary, and you're free until mid-afternoon." Linda clapped her hands rapidly. "She's taking us to the new Italian next to the cinema, and it's supposed to be incredible." Linda put her hands on her hips as Patsy's brow furrowed. "What?" she demanded. "Who slapped your backside? What are you looking like that for?"

Patsy leaned back in her chair and shrugged. Linda perched on the edge of the sofa, crossing her legs, and tapping her knee in exaggerated irritation as Patsy explained her reasoning.

"Call me sceptical, but it's Sharon's day off. Why the sudden urge to take us out, but, more particularly, *me* to lunch? I can only assume she wants to know about the meeting this morning, and Chris has been less than forthcoming. Is he here?"

"No, he's out." Linda rolled her eyes. "Don't be so dramatic, and don't look a gift horse in the mouth, madam. It's all perfectly innocent: apparently, the head waiter is the husband of a friend or something and she has a voucher. So put some lippy on, and grab your coat – the table is booked for twelve-thirty."

Patsy stood and lifted her briefcase. Walking past Linda, she smiled. "No can do, I'm afraid. I have to go home to change, and I have an errand for Chris before my meeting. But you enjoy, and thank Sharon for the thought."

Patsy hadn't stopped walking, and grinned as she heard Linda hurrying behind.

"What errand? There's no errand in the diary. Change into what? Sharon will be fuming . . . well, disappointed anyway. Are you sure you can't leave the errand until tomorrow?"

Patsy spun on her heel and shook her head. "You are a lousy liar, Linda. And no, I can't change the arrangements. Speak later, okay." She strode across the reception and pulled open the door. "And by the way, it's you that looks like you received a slap now."

She pulled the door closed behind her. Hurrying to her car, her eyes scanned the carpark. She hoped to make it out onto the main road before Sharon arrived. Chris could deal with her later.

Meredith walked into the incident room. Everyone was busy working and only the clicking of keyboards being struck by eager fingers and the rustling of paper could be heard. Rawlings was the only member of the team to give him a second glance before leaning forward and returning his attention to the screen on his desk.

Meredith walked over to Seaton. "Where's Trump? Find him, and I'll see you both in my office in five." He called to Rawlings, "Dave, get on the blower and book me a return ticket to Paddington," Meredith glanced at his watch, "leaving anytime between three and four-thirty, open return for tomorrow."

He turned away as Trump entered the room.

"Are you off to London, sir? Business or pleasure?" Trump asked.

"Now you're here you can find out. My office."

Meredith led the way and Trump and Seaton took a seat in front of his desk.

"I'm going to London to meet with Andronikov. Well, I say meet, it's a soirée apparently," he rolled his eyes, "but I'll get to speak to him."

"About what? Ronnie Bishop? Surely a more formal interview would be appropriate." Confused, Trump held his hands out awaiting Meredith's response.

"Trump, shut up and listen and you'll find out." Meredith doodled on his notebook with his pen as he updated the two men. "I've had a call and been given the nod on two things. First, let's deal with this meat factory. They want us to raid it, and I want –"

"Us? Why not the drug squad?" This time it was Tom Seaton who questioned Meredith.

"Because it's all tied to the murders and the drug squad have been told to back off. I want no cock-ups. By the time I get back tomorrow I want a detailed plan of when and how. You're to liaise with uniform who'll let us have the necessary men, and we'll obviously have an armed squad to go in first. Tom, you speak to Alan Peters – he'll be our liaison on that front." Both men were nodding at Meredith. "Oh yes and it will be a daylight raid. About five in the afternoon. The shop will be shut then, and the powers that be think that's when the other operation gets going. For reasons I haven't been given, this is to go ahead the day after tomorrow. I'll want chapter and verse on my return."

"No problem. What is it you're hoping to achieve in London, Gov?" Seaton slipped his notebook into the breast pocket of his shirt.

"A face to face with Andronikov, or Andrews as he now prefers. Not sure at the moment how I'm going to play that: I might try softly, softly." Meredith ignored their exchange of glances. "It's a fund-raiser at a top hotel. Andronikov is a patron of the charity, and I'm there representing the police to present a cheque from the fund-raisers we've held. Help and support for under-privileged children apparently – it sponsors play groups and youth clubs and the like."

He shrugged, "I didn't know we had been raising money, but it's a big cheque." He glanced at his watch. "I need to get a move on. I have to pack a bag and get to London in time to pick up the cheque before the dinner, which starts at eight." He turned to look out into the incident room and bellowed, "Rawlings, have you booked my tickets?" He nodded as Rawlings gave him the thumbs up, and turned back to the two men. "Right, any questions?"

"What's Andronikov – Andrews got to do with under-privileged children? When I read his bio, it didn't mention he had kids, or any affiliation with the charity," Trump remarked.

Meredith sighed noisily. "Trump, you just get this raid lined up, T's crossed and I's dotted, and let me worry about him. Perhaps he's a really, really nice bloke. Now, any sensible questions?" He nodded curtly as the two men shook their heads. "Good, get on with it."

Half an hour later Meredith arrived home. He frowned when he saw Patsy's car on the drive.

He called to her as he opened the door. "Hi, honey, I'm home. Unexpectedly, and not for long. Please tell me you're naked and have time for a quickie."

"Dad! Show some decorum, please." Amanda's voice came from the kitchen. "We have company."

Meredith mumbled his apologies as he made his way to the kitchen. Patsy grinned at him as Amanda swung round to face him. He planted a kiss on the top of her head, and smiled sheepishly at her companion. "This is Becky. We're studying, I thought it would be quieter here with you two at work, but apparently I was mistaken." Amanda waved her hand at the stacks of textbooks and notes on the kitchen table. "I take it you're not stopping long either?"

She rolled her eyes as Becky giggled.

"Either?" Meredith looked at Patsy. "Flying visit too? Come and help me pack, I have to go to London."

Patsy followed Meredith upstairs. He closed the bedroom door behind her and, taking her by surprise, pushed her onto the bed. She let out a yelp, and he put his hand over her mouth.

"Hush. We need to be quiet." He grinned as Patsy protested into the palm of his hand.

"I've just changed. Get off me, you'll crease my suit." Her eyes widened as he pressed against her. "You can't possibly be serious."

"I most certainly am."

He replaced his hand with his mouth, and Patsy surrendered.

~ ~ ~

Stephen Hatton looked up as Patsy opened the door of the coffee house. Her skirt suit with coat-length jacket, which was buttoned at the waist, flattered her figure. Her heels were high and she walked into the sparsely populated room with confidence. He knew immediately who she was. He studied her as she walked towards him. Her eyes were bright, her makeup fresh, and her hair was still slightly damp and scooped into a knot on the top of her head. He knew she had taken the time to make herself ready to meet him. He appreciated that, and smiled as she held out her hand.

"You must be Mr Hatton. Sorry I'm a few minutes late, I had a little trouble parking." Patsy returned his smile as she sat herself opposite him.

"Stephen, please, I'm still too young to be Mr Hatton, but you know that." He waited until she had settled herself, asked her what she would like and placed an order for her coffee. He turned to look at her. "Tell me, did you choose to take this assignment or was it forced upon you?" His smile was slight but his eyes became intense for a moment.

Patsy was taken aback by the suggestive tone, and inclined her head as she considered him. He was a good-looking man, but the lines etched at the corners of his eyes made him look a little older than his years. He relaxed back against the chair, his smile warm, but his eyes wary. Unlike Patsy, he was not dressed for business. The rugby shirt he wore over his jeans had started to fray on the collar, and the brown leather brogues were scuffed on the toes, and had not been polished for some time.

"I was asked and I accepted. There are only so many errant men a girl can find, you know." Patsy grinned and decided to turn the tables on him. "What about you? Were you asked to accept me, or did they insist?"

Stephen Hatton's face relaxed and he burst out laughing. "Touché, Ms Hodge. I think that you and I are going to get along just fine. You're hired." He waited until the waitress had settled Patsy's coffee on the table. "Now, what are you doing this evening? I'm speedway racing tonight, and I think you will enjoy it. There will be a good dinner afterwards too, and with any luck my brother will be paying." He raised his eyebrows as he waited for her response.

"Let's put that to one side a moment. I'm hired? You don't want to ask me any questions? How do you know I can do what you need of me?"

"I know, I can tell. I've read your CV, all I needed to know was if we were compatible. We are. All I need you to do is keep the men at the MOD updated, arrange meetings, and type the odd report. I'm sure you also have your own agenda, provided by those very secret men from whatever department they're attached to. To be honest, I'm quite flattered by the attention, and insulted by the inference that they think I might renege on the deal we have."

He shrugged, dismissing the thought. "But as I have a clear conscience it makes no difference to me. As I said, my concern was that we could work together, and I know we'll get along splendidly." He was aware from Patsy's expression that she was unconvinced, and folding his arms on the table he leaned towards her. "Patsy Hodge, thirty-four. Degree from Cardiff University, mother deceased, father living in Southampton, brother in Australia. For some reason, I can't fathom you joined the police force and have had several disastrous relationships, the last causing you to leave the force, despite having begun what was thought to be a successful career. You took a partnership with a small-time but very successful private investigator who has high-level security clearance." He smiled as Patsy raised her eyebrows. "And having been vetted and cleared by our friendly spooks, you too join the ranks of those employed to spy for Queen and country. Did I leave anything out?"

His eyes revealed his amusement as he sipped his coffee, giving Patsy time to respond. Patsy did the same. She had been unaware of Chris's security clearance, and wondered what the scale of such things was. Numbers, like James Bond? She allowed herself a brief smile at the thought. Or alphabetical? She blinked; it was irrelevant to the current situation. Replacing her cup, she too leaned forward.

"Okay, if we are to work together we need to establish two things. First, I have no agenda. I have not been asked to do anything other than assist you. I assume that is because your project is sensitive and they don't want any information going public. Second, I had one disastrous relationship, the other is doing quite nicely, thank you. I'm assuming —"

Hatton interrupted her. Drumming his fingers on the table, he observed, "Now that's interesting. You feel the need to clarify two of my details, and you put the policeman second. That suggests that even if the relationship is not yet quite disastrous, it may be heading that way." He raised his hand to halt her protest. "And even if you are going to claim that that is not the case, he still wasn't important enough to come first." He dropped his hand back to the table, giving her permission to respond.

"The importance to me has nothing to do with it. I put the job first for your benefit; after all, that is what you're most interested in. Am I to start tomorrow?"

"No, immediately. I'm sure they explained that you wouldn't be working office hours. Will . . ." he clicked his fingers and frowned as he pretended to search for the correct name, "ah yes, will Meredith be okay with that?"

A smile played around his lips as Patsy sighed. She looked him in the eye.

"Shall we stop playing games now? You know full well what his name is and you know I will do whatever is necessary to complete the assignment successfully. I can't remember the last time I worked office hours, so you can stop testing me. And for what? A display of temper or weakness? What are you trying to achieve here, Mr Hatton?"

"Stephen." Hatton emptied his cup and twisted it around on the saucer. "Only your acceptance of my invitation to accompany me this evening." He stood and held out his hand. "It's been a pleasure meeting with you, Ms Hodge. Go home and change and you can meet us at Temple Meads station at five-thirty. Jeans and something warm would be best; it's a bit messy and the forecast for this evening is for a brisk easterly."

Patsy stood to join him and he shook her hand.

"I'm not convinced that Speedway racing is part of my brief. I don't know the first thing about it."

"You should learn, because it is very much connected. Now I must hurry to ensure the bikes get off on time. Five-thirty prompt, Ms Hodge, don't be late."

With that he left her standing at the table watching him disappear as he hurried down the street.

"Well, if nothing else, he's certainly going to be interesting to work with," she muttered to herself as she collected her handbag.

"Do you want the change?" A voice from the counter interrupted her thoughts.

"I'm sorry?" She looked at the young waitress standing there.

"Your friend gave me twenty pounds when he got here. You haven't even had a tenner's worth. Do you want the change?"

"No, you keep it."

Patsy smiled as she made her way to the street. Stephen Hatton must have planned a hasty exit, it was clear he hadn't wanted to be held up paying the bill. She wondered if that was for dramatic effect, or simply to remove her ability to refuse his invitation. Tutting, she shook her head at her own vanity. It was obviously for dramatic effect; he couldn't have known whether or not she would have accepted. Why had she thought it would be about her? Did she think he was attracted to her, or perhaps she wanted him to be? Whichever it was, it was ridiculous. Angry with herself for becoming distracted, Patsy hurried to the car.

ONE SECRET TOO MANY

4

Meredith watched Boris Johnson, Mayor of London, as he pumped the hand of Ivor Andronikov up and down. It was as though Johnson were a puppet controlled by the hands of an inexperienced puppeteer. His head nodded repeatedly, his flop of blond hair lifted and fell with the movement, and, despite his smile, he seemed unable to meet Andronikov's eye. Eventually, Boris let go and turned to the microphone, slightly breathless from the unnecessary exertion. The girl who would lead Meredith to the stage beckoned to him and he excused himself from the table.

"What a fabulous donation," Johnson turned back to Andronikov. "Thank you on behalf of this very worthwhile charity, Mr Andrews. Now, who's going to give some next . . . ah yes. The British police force has many projects on the go to help youngsters. They know better than most of us in this room how important it is to give a young person a sound start in life, something to grab their attention et cetera, and here to present the cheque on behalf of the police is . . . ah yes. DCI John Meredith." Boris looked at Meredith who was walking across the stage towards him. "Come on, DCI Meredith, let's have your cheque."

Meredith lifted the poster-sized cheque so that everyone could see the six-figure sum. Boris Johnson stepped to one side, took a look at the amount as he accepted the cheque and whistled.

"Fabulous. Well done the boys in blue." Johnson inserted the cheque in the display and turned back. Meredith gripped his hand firmly and nodded politely as Boris went to work on it. "Absolutely wonderful, keep up the good work." He pulled Meredith forward, but leaned his head back towards the microphone, "And for the record, as I've supped the bubbly, I'll be pushing the bike home."

Most of the audience laughed as expected and Boris Johnson beamed. Meredith played the game and told him he was glad to hear it and went to stand next to Andronikov as the final donation was received by the ever-enthusiastic Johnson.

"Did you see his eyes?" Andronikov asked as Meredith shook his hand before taking his place in the line-up.

"I'm sorry?" Meredith faced Andronikov.

"His eyes. They show that his brain is far advanced of his mouth. I cannot understand why the man pretends to be stupid. It is unnecessary." He shrugged. "Think what he could achieve if he didn't act like an idiot. I've heard that he intentionally wears his hair like that."

"Yes, but then so much more would be expected of him. As it is, now when he achieves even a minor goal the accolades are so much greater. I think he's more than happy with his lot."

Andronikov nodded as he considered this. "You are probably right, but why go into politics? If you do something surely you must want to aim for the top?"

The audience roared with laughter at the latest joke thrown out by Johnson. Meredith and Andronikov had missed it, but both men smiled on cue.

"You are, what did he say? A DCI? I am sure you want to be Chief Constable. It is natural amongst men." Andronikov stopped speaking as the last man came to join them. Boris walked back to the microphone.

"So there, it's done. Over one and a half million pounds donated, and we still have the charity auction after dinner. I promise to try and keep up with your bids." Johnson held his hands up, as though already defeated. "Finally, may I ask for one more round of applause for these splendid people." He held his hand out towards the line of people who had presented donations, and the audience responded as requested. "Right. Good. Enjoy your dinner, and as a monosyllabic Austrian actor once said, 'I'll be back.'" Boris nodded as the audience roared again, his hair flopped back into his face, and he lumbered off, stage left.

Meredith gave a smile. "That's not the first time he's used that one. Apparently, Schwarzenegger insulted his speaking ability once . . . still, if it works…" He nodded past the others who stood in line. "After you, we're being released." He pointed at the young lady beckoning them forward, followed Andronikov off the stage, and returned to his table.

Meredith was surprised to find that he actually enjoyed the company of the people sitting around the table with him. They were a mixed bunch, ranging from a nineteen-year-old former drug addict, who had an opinion on everything, to a sixty-year-old woman who had fostered over thirty difficult children. Her humour reminded him of Peggy Green, a witness from an earlier case who now felt like a member of the family, such as it was. Meredith watched Andronikov as the evening progressed: his behaviour was impeccable, although his dislike of the Mayor showed through the false laughter at Johnson's jokes. Towards the end of the auction, Meredith followed Andronikov to the bar, but stood at the opposite end to order only his second drink of the evening. Glancing around, Meredith feigned surprise at Andronikov's presence.

He called to him. "Can I get you a drink? I can't drink anything else with bubbles in it." He smiled as Andronikov nodded and walked towards him: that had been easier than he'd expected. He ordered the drinks and the two men seated themselves on the bar stools. Meredith studied Andronikov's face. He knew that the man was in his late fifties, and although, overall, he looked younger than his age, with his muscular build and sharp suit, the deep creases across his brow and around his eyes told a different story.

"Did you do anything towards the fundraising?" Andronikov stirred the ice around in the tumbler with a small black straw. He raised his eyebrows as Meredith shook his head.

"I didn't, I'm afraid, although I have now made a contribution. I had to come to town on business and therefore they asked me to do the honours. The Avon and Somerset boys did particularly well, so they thought a local should attend. I feel a like a fraud." Meredith knocked back his drink and gestured to the barman for a refill. Andronikov followed suit and signed the tab. "What line of work are you in?"

"I have various interests. Nightclubs, restaurants, food preparation. I even have a farm, or so I'm told by my advisors." His laugh was dry. "I have been lucky in my investments, but it was not always so. I needed help as a young man, and someone kindly provided it. Now it is my turn to give someone . . . how do you say it . . . a leg up? Yes, a leg up." He laughed again. "Which reminds me, I also have shares in a racehorse." He lifted his drink and swirled the liquid around the glass. "I sometimes feel my life is too complicated and I should simplify it, but when you have had nothing but the clothes on your back, the need to build security is great."

"I think life is complicated whatever your circumstances. You should thank your lucky stars you can even consider making a change. I wouldn't know what to do if I wasn't a copper. I suppose I could dabble on the stock market in the hope I'd do well, but I don't have the cash to risk." Meredith raised his glass to salute his companion, "So enjoy your wealth, and keep doing good things."

Patting his pocket, Meredith asked to be excused. He slid off the stool, walked away from the bar and pretended to take a call. When he returned, shaking his head, Andronikov had ordered more drinks.

"Bad news?" Andronikov signed the tab again and flipped his hand to halt Meredith's protest. Meredith thanked him and perched on the barstool.

"Not bad, disappointing. I was supposed to be meeting a friend for drinks once this was done, but he's tied up on a case so it'll be an early night." Meredith sipped his drink.

"I'm going to a nice little club later. Join me, my friend, I promise you will enjoy it."

"No, no. I don't want to impose," Meredith objected. "I'll manage, but thanks for the offer." He fumbled as he attempted to place the glass back on the bar, and it fell to the floor spilling the contents. He picked it up and beckoned the barman. "Another?" he asked Andronikov, who nodded and smiled.

"Thank you. I must find the men's room, but I will be back. I like a man who, like me, likes a drink."

Meredith watched him make his way to the toilets before ordering the drinks.

"Same again for him, but make mine a diet coke."

He read his messages, texted Patsy to say he was still working and that he would call later if he could. He slid his phone into his pocket as Andronikov returned.

"I've changed my mind, if the offer's still open, I will join you. It seems my other half is going out this evening, and what's good for the goose…"

He emptied his glass and asked the waiter for the same again, and kept Andronikov engaged in conversation as his alcohol-free drink was prepared.

Twenty minutes later a band was setting up on the stage, and his companion indicated it was time to go. Meredith stood and stumbled to one side. Grabbing the bar for support he raised his eyebrows.

"Too many bubbles, I'd better slow down."

"As you like, my friend." Andronikov placed his arm around Meredith's shoulder. "This way, my car is waiting."

Meredith leaned back against the plush upholstery and whistled. "Nice. Very nice, what did . . ." He stopped speaking as Andronikov pulled the ringing phone from his inside pocket. Meredith pursed his lips, knowing that he had another phone in the pocket of his trousers. Andronikov looked at the screen before answering. He barked his name before holding what appeared to be a tense conversation in Russian. Meredith had no idea what it was about.

When the call was terminated, Meredith shook his head, feigning surprise.

"Did you say 'Andronikov' when you answered the phone?" He leaned forward, and resting his elbows on his knees, he screwed his eyes shut before looking up. Andronikov's face showed no emotion as he looked up.

"I did. Why?"

"Please tell me you're not Ivor Andronikov."

"I am. Why, should I be concerned that you have heard of me?" Andronikov looked amused.

Meredith shook his head again, and leaned forward to tap on the glass partition.

"We have to stop this car and I have to get out. I'll call you in the morning. Pull over." He called to the driver who swooped out of the traffic and stopped abruptly. Meredith shuffled to the end of the seat. "Oops." He placed his hand on the door for support. He tried the handle but the door was locked.

"Why do you need to go? Have we got a problem, my friend?"

"I'm not your friend. You're simply some bloke I met at the bar. And yes, we have a problem. I'm investigating the death of your former partner, Ronnie Bishop. I'll need to speak to you formally about that, so going out on the piss with you when I've already had enough would be stupid. Would you open the door please?"

Andronikov jerked his head at the driver who was watching the men in the rear-view mirror. The driver nodded, indicated and pulled back out into the traffic.

"Then we have no problem." Andronikov rubbed his hand over his face. "She is dead? Veronica is dead? I feared as much. What happened to her? It is clearly not good if you are investigating?"

Meredith pinched the bridge of his nose and closed his eyes. When he opened them, he leaned towards Andronikov.

"I'm serious, stop this car. I will call you tomorrow to make an appointment once I've collected the file. I don't know how things are done in Russia, but I can't socialise with a possible suspect."

"Possible? I am going to tell you now that I had nothing to do with her death." Andronikov looked genuinely moved by the news. "I once loved that girl, I thought we would have a family together. I will help you in any way I can. Trust me, DCI Meredith, you are not compromising yourself. What is the worst that can happen? You have a drink with someone you need to question formally? It will never be necessary to charge me, Meredith, you can relax." He glanced out of the car. "We are almost there, if you want to speak to me about her, join me. If not, I will get the car to return you to the hotel, but know that I speak the truth: I will tell you anything you need to know."

"But that's just it. I haven't got all the details yet, I don't know what I need to know. I've seen photographs, and they weren't pretty, if it turns out you were responsible I don't want to drink with you. In fact, I would be pushed to breathe the same air."

Andronikov's eyes flared and his features hardened. He swayed a little as the car came to a stop. Meredith's eyes moved to the door lock. The button remained static, the doors remained locked. When he looked back to Andronikov to protest he was taken aback by the expression: the man looked as though he were in pain.

Andronikov brought his face inches away from Meredith's. "I will help you. You won't mind breathing my air. I would like to do this now, but if not, we will meet first thing tomorrow morning, I have appointments after eleven."

Meredith inclined his head and considered this as Andronikov sat back. The man appeared to be genuine. Eventually Meredith nodded.

"Okay. No more drink, and basic questions tonight. I may need a further interview tomorrow once I have more information."

Andronikov nodded. The locks were released and the driver hurried to open the door. Meredith stumbled onto the kerb and

Andronikov caught his elbow and steadied him.

"This way, DCI Meredith." Meredith caught the irritation in his voice.

"Let me get some air, I'll be fine." Placing his hands on his knees, Meredith leaned forward and drew in several deep breaths. When he righted himself, he said, "Okay, let's get on with this. Which way?"

He squinted at a bright light, which flashed as Andronikov held his hand forward.

"Ignore them. This club is used by celebrities; they photograph everyone to ensure they don't miss the photograph that will earn them money." He barked something at the driver who hurried forward and spoke quietly to the photographer. Meredith had no idea what was said, but the photographer moved away quickly.

With Meredith led by the elbow, they entered a small bright lobby. Neither had coats to deposit, and the tall man in a dark suit who had allowed them access held open the doors to the main area of the club. A tune Meredith hoped never to hear again blared out at them, and a few customers were attempting to dance to the beat. Meredith watched as a young man came out of the toilet rubbing the back of his hand against his nose. He ignored him, and followed Andronikov off to the left and through a second door which led to a quieter bar. He took a seat in the alcove to the rear as invited, and waited expectantly while Andronikov ordered drinks. A young man in an expensive suit brought a tray holding several bottles, an ice bucket and two glasses. Meredith smiled his thanks at the bottle of water Andronikov lifted and held towards him. As ice was placed in the tumbler, Meredith watched the young man walk out of earshot, and stop at a respectable distance away, his back to the table, and his hands clasped in front of him. No one was going to join them without invitation.

He took the glass from Andronikov and placed it in front of him. He crossed his legs at the ankles, and sighed.

"I'm not comfortable about this. I'll simply get on with it, if you don't mind."

"Of course. How was she killed?"

Meredith thought he could see real pain in the man's eyes and he looked away briefly.

"I don't know exactly which injury killed her. I've yet to read the full autopsy report. But she was beaten. She had been tortured, and there was not enough of her face left to identify her. That was done by her fingerprints. Those that hadn't been damaged."

Andronikov closed his eyes and lowered his head a little. When he looked up his expression was blank. He showed no emotion. "I am assuming you have no idea who did this?"

"We have some suspects, and yes, you were one of them, fairly near the top of the list. The ring you bought her was found in her stomach. That would indicate it was personal. If it wasn't the man who provided the ring, it was possibly someone who was jealous, perhaps a scorned lover? When did you last see her?"

"Easter Day three years ago, although as I'm sure you will find out I did have several telephone exchanges after that. Where was she found?"

"In Bristol. As you no doubt know, that's where she went when she left you."

Andronikov's expression didn't change, but he blinked at the inference he hadn't been the orchestrator of her departure.

"She didn't leave me, not as such. We had a row over a . . ." he clicked his fingers to bring the word to mind, "an indiscretion. I told her it was such, and she should go if it was of such consequence to her. She was a fiery lady with a quick temper, and she did that. But," Andronikov pointed at Meredith, "she left to punish me. I had every expectation that she would return."

"But she didn't."

"No." Andronikov lifted his glass and poured more vodka into it. He emptied the glass and refilled it. He held the bottle towards Meredith, who dropped a handful of ice into his glass, and held it forward. He received a healthy measure which he sipped before coughing at the strength of the spirit. "Russian vodka. It is good, it does not burn the throat."

"Why didn't you try to find her?" Meredith placed his glass upon the table.

Andronikov raised his eyebrows in disbelief. He gave a short laugh. "You really don't know much about me, do you? Tell me, DCI Meredith, do you have someone special in your life?"

"I do." Meredith knew Andronikov would check, so there was no point in lying.

"And if she left you, for whatever reason, stopped returning your phone calls, would you chase after her?" He swigged his drink. "Or would you nurse your wounds, and attempt to forget her?"

Meredith held his eye. A smile played around his mouth and he nodded. Andronikov gave a laugh, rapped his knuckles on the table, and wagged his finger at Meredith.

"Ha! You see! It is not so odd. Men are proud by nature: they do things that they know will hurt them, and are powerless to take the action others might see as common sense." Andronikov shrugged. "I asked about her, discreetly, but it was for her to come to me."

He looked away for a moment. Meredith turned his head to see what had attracted his attention, and hoped his mouth hadn't fallen open. Two women had entered the bar. They were stunning. Immaculately and tastefully presented, they were both beautiful. Meredith considered this word as he watched them; in his opinion it was overused, but not in this case. The taller of the two girls lifted her hand in greeting and smiled over at them before turning away and ordering a drink. Order fulfilled, the women sat a table in the centre of the room. Meredith caught the nod of acknowledgement from the man who had brought him and Andronikov their drinks, and was still standing on sentry duty. Andronikov smiled as Meredith returned his attention to him.

"As you will see there are many ways to distract yourself when necessary. I take it you have been in a similar circumstance?"

"Yes, I can see how they could distract you. Was my circumstance similar? Only inasmuch as I didn't chase, but I didn't have such distractions: I simply waited." He shrugged at Andronikov's look of amazement. "She was worth waiting for. What was meant to be, will be. We got there in the end." His face clouded as he thought about the current state of affairs with Patsy. They had been muddling along since their disagreement, but it certainly wasn't perfect, not yet. He raised his eyebrows. "Perhaps it would have been different if I had become distracted."

"No. You are clearly a romantic." Andronikov snorted. "Maybe it was meant to be as you say. Perhaps I should try harder with this one."

"Was she your indiscretion?" Meredith took a quick glance at the women again. "I heard you moved someone in pretty quickly."

"No Sasha came later, and before you ask, those in between are all alive and well."

Meredith lifted the glass and swirled the liquid around. The ice chinked against the glass.

"If you didn't kill her, and I'll take your word on that for the time being, do you have any thoughts on who might have? I think your enquiries would have revealed exactly where she was, and who she was with. I'd like you to share that with me."

Andronikov nodded slowly. "I know that after a few nights in a hotel she went to stay with a friend in Bristol. Her friend was also from Russia and worked in a bar as a hostess. Not sexual, you understand, but the sort that welcomes guests and ensures the waiters are keeping the drinks flowing, and that the customers are happy. Veronika remained there, to the best of my knowledge."

Meredith knew that she hadn't. He knew that after a few months she had taken up with Filipp Myshkin, and that her flatmate assumed she was living with him. After too many weeks of trying to contact her, she had reported her missing to the police. He pursed his lips as he considered how much of this Andronikov already knew, and he guessed most if not all of it.

"Do you know the name of the club? What sort of club is it?"

"In your language, the Hammer and Sickle," Andronikov smirked. "It was, after all, the collapse of the old regime that provided many of my countrymen with the ability to become rich men."

"Yourself included, I take it?"

"Not so much, but it allowed me to, let's say, broaden my horizons. I was happy with my life then, I am more so now." He leaned forward as if to share a secret. "I've heard tell that there are politicians in Moscow who claim Gorbachev was a US spy and want him brought to trial." He shrugged. "Even Putin, who describes him as a friend, believes it was a political tragedy, and yet I doubt Putin would ever have come to power without the break-up of the union."

He gave a short laugh. "It is amusing that the West despised the Soviet Union, and wanted nothing less than to see its power crumble. What are your views on the arrival of so many Eastern Europeans in your country? Do you resent it, like the papers say most British do?" The amusement glinted in his eyes. "As a wise man once said, one should be careful what one wishes for."

"I don't have an opinion." Meredith raised his shoulders dismissively. "I'm not allowed to be political unless there is an election on, and even then, only in the polling booth. I am only required to make sure they don't break the law. If I had an opinion on Polish plumbers or Latvian chambermaids, I would keep it to myself."

Andronikov's nose wrinkled a little as Meredith spoke, and his words of response were sharp.

"And that is why Great Britain will never be great again. Apathy and the bleeding heart do not a strong nation build. To return freedom to the countries which once formed your empire is one thing, but to give them all passports is quite another. Then to further add to your burden you join the European Union. Your politicians had little foresight of the problems they were creating. But the greatest mystery to me," he tapped his chest with his forefinger, "is why they would want to be led by the nose by their greatest of enemies: the Germans. I have benefitted from all these errors of judgement, and I am glad, but it does not mean that I understand them."

Meredith sighed, and took a handful of ice which he dropped into his glass before adding a short measure of vodka.

"Much as I can see you would like to get into a heavy debate on the merits of dictatorship, state oppression and freedom of choice for the few, I have a murder to investigate. If it turns out one of your Eastern European brothers is responsible, then they will wish they'd stayed put. But other than that, I'll try and uphold the laws that these useless politicians pass while they're not making other bad decisions."

To his surprise, Andronikov threw his head back and laughed heartily. Pulling a crisp, freshly laundered handkerchief from his pocket, he dabbed his eyes.

Meredith raised his eyebrows. "Have I amused you?"

"Excuse me, please. It was the thought of the British police force making someone sorry in the way you indicated. I suppose the younger ones maybe," he shook his head, "but I have seen people regret coming into contact with the security forces elsewhere. To go to prison here I understand would be like a forced vacation."

He coughed and tucked the handkerchief back into his pocket. "I didn't mean to take you off track, now back to business. As I said, Elena, that's Veronika's friend, worked at the Hammer and Sickle. Veronika had enough of my money in her account not to need to work, but as I understand it, she visited regularly anyway. She also took up some course or other at a local college. I was unaware she had such interests."

"What about men? Did she take a new lover?" Meredith caught the flinch, and watched the fist, that had been made, relax, although Andronikov's face did not reveal his anger.

"I have the names of several men she was seen with. I do not know if she took them to her bed, but I know there was no one serious – not in those first six months when I bothered to ask, anyway." His eyes narrowed. "Are you going to tell me differently?" He stared into Meredith's eyes hoping to find a tell-tale trace that he did know.

Meredith blinked. "Not that I know of . . . yet. As I've mentioned, I need to get hold of the file."

"Ah yes, the file. Why would the file be here in London if she was murdered in Bristol?" Andronikov's smile held no amusement.

"Another thing I'm going to have to find out. Perhaps it's to do with you. Have you attracted police attention before?" He returned the smile he received.

"Not that I'm aware of, nor, I hasten to add, should I have. Perhaps you will let me know your findings. I like you, John Meredith. You may call me Ivor, I think we shall be friends." He saluted Meredith with the glass before emptying it.

"And I you, but I prefer to stick to Andronikov, and Andrews doesn't suit at all. You can call me Meredith. Now, point me in the direction of the gents."

An hour later, Meredith had the names of two men Andronikov had linked to Ronnie Bishop. He had also scribbled down the name of Elena's lover, her employer and brother. None of them were on file. Sometime during the latter stage of the first bottle of vodka the two women had joined them, and he was pressed to keep his mind on the job. He decided to call it a night.

"I think I've had enough. I'd better get back or I'll have the mother of all headaches when I come to see you tomorrow." His speech was slightly slurred as he attempted to stand without touching the woman who was sitting uncomfortably close to him.

Andronikov waved him back down. "You will not suffer. This is good stuff, and you are unkind, Meredith. I have told you all I know, and yet you tell me nothing. Even without this famous file, you must have some information."

Meredith swayed as he got to his feet. "Not much, all I know is that I had two major suspects, you and some bloke called Myshkin. He's also of interest to the drug squad." Meredith shrugged. "He'll be raided before I get to him; I'm not due back in Bristol until the end of the week."

"I've never heard of him, but I will ask around." Andronikov stood and held out his hand, "Until tomorrow, Meredith, I have enjoyed your company immensely. Sandi, help Mr Meredith to the car."

The woman stood and placed her hand on Meredith's elbow. His nostrils flared as her perfume assaulted his senses. He swayed again.

"No need, I'm a grown man. I'll be fine." He stepped forward, tripped on his own feet, and possibly for the first time since he was a child, he giggled. "Oops perhaps not. But seriously, there is no need for a babysitter."

He walked away, raising his hand to wave goodbye. Andronikov smirked and nodded at Sandi who hurried after Meredith. She caught up with him as he struggled to open the door.

"Here, let me." She pushed the door the other way, which allowed him to exit. Stepping into the fresh night air, she gestured at the car which rolled forward to meet them. The driver jumped out and opened the door.

"This is quite unnecessary, but if you insist," Meredith grinned at him as he climbed into the car. However, the grin fell away as Sandi joined him. "Seriously, love, I don't need your help."

"I know, but he says to make sure you get home safely, so I have to do it."

She smiled, and Meredith closed his eyes and tried not to think the thoughts that sprang unwittingly to his mind. He felt her thigh press against his, and he willed himself to be strong. Sandi watched him as he apparently nodded off on the short journey to the hotel. His eyes opened wide as the door next to him was pulled open. He fumbled with his wallet in an attempt to pay the driver, who assured him it wasn't necessary. Meredith shrugged and carefully placed his foot on the first of the steps leading to the hotel entrance. He sighed as he felt a hand on his elbow. He looked down at Sandi.

"I have to get you back to your room. Don't cause a scene, or he will think I am a prostitute."

Meredith looked up at the doorman who had already pulled the door open. The man wasn't judging her, he was appreciating the view. Sighing, Meredith allowed her to escort him. He had taken his key with him, and headed straight to the lift. Once there he pushed the call button and waved the plastic card at her.

"That's me safely escorted. Even in this state I can make it to my room."

"I know." Sandi smiled, and Meredith looked away as the lift door opened. Stepping inside, he chewed his bottom lip as she followed suit.

After three attempts and much cursing, he handed her the key. She slid it into the lock and smiled as the green light appeared, before pushing him into the bedroom.

"Sandi, this is all very nice and all that, but —"

"I know." She placed a finger on his lips and he fell silent. She slipped his jacket from his shoulders, hanging it on the back of the chair, before beginning to unbutton his shirt. Her painted nails skimmed across his skin as she pulled the shirt away. He held up his hands.

"I can do this, thank you." His hands found his belt buckle, and his trousers joined his shirt on the floor.

"I know." Sandi gave a little push and he sat on the bed. "I have to use the bathroom, I won't be long."

Meredith watched the swing of her hips as she walked away.

"Take your time, love, I can't do this," he muttered under his breath.

When he awoke the next morning, thoughts of the events of the night before filtered back into his mind. He sat bolt upright, and looked down at the bed next to him. He blew out a sigh of relief when he found it was empty. His relief was short-lived: Sandi appeared at the door of the bathroom wearing only her panties.

"Good morning, Meredith," she smiled as she lifted her dress from the chair which also held Meredith's jacket. "I was about to wake you." She stepped into her dress and pulled it up; her breasts disappeared. She walked to him and turned her back. "Please zip me up. I'm sorry but I have to go now. Perhaps we can meet again."

Meredith pulled up the zip. He watched her hop from one leg to the other as she put on her shoes.

"Listen, Sandi, I'm sorry but —"

"Hush, there is no need to apologise, you know how to contact me if you want to." Her hand was on the door knob. "I like you, Meredith, I hope you do get in touch."

She smiled as she left the room. Meredith fell back onto the bed and groaned. As if to make matters worse, his phone beeped from his jacket pocket. He stood and carried it to the bathroom with him. It was a message from Patsy. He didn't open it. Instead, he switched on the shower and reached for the soap. Before he left the room, he retrieved the file he had hidden under the mattress, and nodded as he noted the seal had not been breached.

The meeting with Andronikov was far more business-like than it had been the night before. Meredith took down in detail, which included addresses and telephone numbers, the information they had discussed the night before. A few more bits were added to pad it out, but eventually Andronikov told him he knew nothing else of value. Keen to get back to Bristol, Meredith was relieved.

Andronikov stood to show him out. "It was a pleasure to meet you, Meredith. I'm sure I can rely on you to let me know what you find out. Especially about Myshkin."

Meredith halted in his tracks and spun round to face him.

"I mentioned Myshkin?" He pinched the bridge of his nose before looking back at Andronikov. "I shouldn't have, it was indiscreet, and I'd like you to keep that to yourself."

Andronikov smiled broadly. "Of course, Meredith, my lips are sealed. But you will let me know."

"Know what? What did I say? Damn your bloody vodka."

"You said nothing other than his name had been linked with Veronika. If he is involved somehow, I must know." He watched as Meredith considered this.

Meredith nodded. "If there is anything I think you should know, I'll call." Meredith held his eye for a moment. "Do we understand each other?"

"Of course."


The rhythmic sound of the train on the track did nothing to sooth Meredith as he travelled home. He could only hope that his actions wouldn't have unexpected repercussions. With a sigh he pulled out his phone to respond to Patsy.

# 5

Patsy sat at her new desk and listened carefully as Stephen explained where various files could be found, and how to access his emails. Patiently, he told her which she should respond to, and which should be referred to him first. He opened a document he had prepared providing all the names and contact details of people she might come across. Next to each name was an icon that revealed their position and their relevance to the task in hand. Clicking on another icon which took them to the business website, he set her up as a user, before quickly running through what she might need to do. He concluded the lesson.

"I think that's enough to be going on with." Pulling a small memory stick from his pocket, he passed it to her. "I've dictated a note to go out immediately, together with one for tomorrow morning. I've given the circulation details at the end. Don't look so worried," he laughed, "it's simply an update on the latest developments."

"Then how have you already dictated one for tomorrow?"

He laughed again, and Patsy noticed the eyebrows of a small mousy woman in the corner rise.

"Because I know what they want to hear, and live updates, on a daily basis, get in the way of the day job. They are hard task masters, but I have the skill to keep them happy." He shrugged. "You don't approve?"

Patsy shook her head. "I couldn't possibly comment until I've heard what you've had to say. I'll let you know later."

Still smiling, Stephen left her to it. The woman in the corner called to her, asking if she was too important to make the coffee. Patsy bit back the response which sprang to her lips, and assured her she wasn't and asked for directions to the kitchen.

"Along the corridor, third door on the left. Irene by the way, thanks for asking." The woman tutted and looked back at her screen.

Listening to the water bubble in the kettle, she wondered why Meredith hadn't returned her call the night before, or her text that morning. While she knew the case he was working on was more than a straightforward murder, it irritated her that he could leave her bed and then forget about her until it suited him. Lifting the kettle, she brushed away thoughts that he might be in some sort of trouble. She was overreacting. If she hadn't heard from him by lunchtime she would call the station.

As she carried the coffee to the woman, she now knew as Irene, she caught her unawares. Flustered, Irene quickly shut down the screen before Patsy had time to look.

"I like having you around. Stephen has been quite chirpy this morning. When I saw how he was fussing over you, I thought you might be visiting royalty. Thanks for this." Irene sipped her coffee.

"No, not royalty, simply a temp drafted in until this project is concluded." Patsy walked to her own desk. "Is Stephen usually miserable?"

"No, that's not what I said. He's serious. Usually when he speaks to you, it's as though his mind has already left the room and is dealing with the next item on the list. You'll see: I don't think the happy chappy persona will last long, it's not natural."

Irene looked back at her screen. The conversation was over, and she had more important things to attend to. At the moment, she had no reason to like or dislike Patsy. All she had done was applied for a job and got it. What Irene was miffed about was the need for her at all. She'd wasted many hours recently wondering if she'd perhaps done something wrong, or if they didn't believe her to be sufficiently competent to continue producing the documentation on the project. Irene felt slighted, and was determined not to give Patsy too easy a ride.

Patsy, glad that the woman was now otherwise engaged, put the earplugs in and pushed the play button. She wanted to get a feel for the report before she started typing. It was a long time since she had flirted, albeit briefly, with an office job. After a few minutes, she blinked and her head fell to her chest. She understood each word, but for the best part not the sentences they formed. It was technical data about the new project. Sighing deeply, Patsy opened a blank report. The main headings had populated automatically and she typed in today's subject matter: *Shock Absorption RX123-8A*. She completed the layout and printed the document, intending to read it before she emailed it out. She needed to at least try and understand what she was writing about: it might be important to the case in some way.

"You'll get your wrists slapped," Irene called across from her desk. "They don't do waste here. Printing is a huge no-no, unless of course it is absolutely essential."

"Ah, I didn't know. I thought they might keep a hard copy to be on the safe side."

"You've got to be kidding me. Everything they do is top secret. They wouldn't have hard copies of anything lying around. I doubt anyone could penetrate their system. As you save each document it is encrypted and useless to anyone else unless it's for external use, such as those you're working on. Even then the recipient will have been given the code to access the document. On top of that, paper and ink use unnecessary resources, the cost of which could be better spent elsewhere."

"Sounds to me like that's been drummed into you. Are they mean? I hope they're not in financial difficulty. I thought they were close to completion on a very lucrative project." Patsy wondered if that was the government's interest – perhaps the Hattons were sailing close to the wind financially, or had an inappropriate investor.

"They've been in financial difficulty for as long as I can remember, and I've been with them for five years. I wouldn't say the Hattons are mean as such, just very careful. The whole building has sensor-operated lights, and they've caught me out a few times, usually in the loo. The systems also go into sleep mode after a couple of minutes of non-activity, which can be frustrating in the extreme. And, as I mentioned, there's no printing. When we have guests, I get the embarrassment of putting out a plate of rich tea biscuits." She rolled her eyes. "The supermarket's own brand, and this for very important people. I used to complain, and ask them what harm a chocolate hob-nob would do, but I was told in no uncertain terms that they are here for a meeting and not to be fed. I shut up and now I just get on with it. And you're right, there is a light at the end of the tunnel now. This will be worth millions when they're done. But for the time being, be warned: look after the pennies." Irene dropped her gaze back to her work and Patsy collected the printout.

Back at her desk, Patsy wondered if that's why Stephen had been wearing a frayed shirt and scuffed shoes when she met him, and if so, why he had left twenty pounds to pay for two coffees. She decided that a look into the Hatton finances would be necessary. But first she had to complete the reports.

A little under an hour later, and despite the occasional complicated terminology, she was done. She saved the documents before emailing them to Stephen. She didn't take a copy for herself, believing the information didn't warrant further attention. Reaching into the tray on the corner of her desk, she lifted out the file containing current invoices. Stephen had spent all of three minutes explaining the purchase ledger to her, and she hoped she would remember how to source and complete the original order. After spending far longer than necessary trying to find the file, Patsy thumped the desk and called to Irene.

"I don't suppose you know how to navigate this purchase ledger, do you? Mr Hatton did his best, but I clearly missed something."

The now familiar roll of the eyes came as Irene pushed her chair away from the desk and stood up. At least, Patsy assumed she had – Irene barely cleared five feet in height. She walked over to Patsy's desk and stood behind her.

"Double click the document icon, then work order, and put the supplier name in the box. Now scroll down and find that order number." Leaning forward she tapped the top invoice. "Fill in the amount, tick the VAT box, and . . ."

Now into the system, it was straightforward and obvious to Patsy what was necessary before Irene snapped the next order, therefore she jumped as Irene screeched. "NO!" as she was about to hit the enter key.

"Not enter, that will drag it through to the pay run." Although she couldn't see Irene's face, Patsy knew Irene's eyes had swivelled in their sockets. "Check that box in the bottom right hand screen. That gives you the current balances in the bank, and the blue text advises what the balance will be if paid, for those periods of time." Irene leaned in to see what the effect of paying the invoice would be. "Now I'm sure Stephen told you the account cannot go above one hundred thousand overdrawn. Tick ten days and see what happens." Patsy did as she was told, Irene squinted at the amended amount and picked up the remaining invoices. "No, that won't do as this one must be paid: put that one on forty days, key this one in on ten days, and the rest will have to be sixty."

Patsy did the calculation silently. If all the invoices were paid in the sixty-day period, the account would remain twenty thousand pounds below the overdraft limit. She turned to look at Irene.

"Okay, I've got that. But that will make the payment of some of those almost three months late. I can see there is income coming in, but not from where. How are they generating income?"

"By sales." This time Irene closed her eyes and sighed. "That doesn't take a genius. Are you sure you should be allowed to do this?" Snatching the mouse, she clicked away and a sales ledger appeared. "They sell suits to riders, speedway mainly, to pay the bills. And don't you dare let the balance go below twenty grand or there's a chance we won't be paid, and I'm not having that again." She did a half turn as though she were leaving. "Can I trust you to do that, or should I stay and supervise?"

"No, I think I'll be fine, I simply needed to be shown. Can you take me back to where we were before, though?"

There it was, the roll of the eyes. Patsy bit back a smile. The system was simple to navigate, now that she had been shown, and Patsy knew she was perfectly capable of finding her way around, but she knew it may come in useful if Irene thought that she didn't. She feigned surprise and delight as Irene took her back to the home page while pointing out various functions of the site.

Immediately Irene returned to her desk, Patsy went to the finance page. She opened various screens, showing account balances and customer and supplier listings. Ensuring Irene was otherwise engaged, she photographed the pages with her mobile, before returning to the task in hand. Once completed, Patsy returned to the email account, and was surprised to find she had access to all staff emails and not only Stephen's. Knowing that it was highly unlikely she would find anything incriminating or suspicious on any of them, she scrolled through the inbox and sent mail anyway. A few exchanges caught her attention and she photographed those before turning her attention to Stephen Hatton's inbox with a view to dealing with them. She was halfway through this task when Hatton returned.

"Patsy, great reports, thank you. Get today's out, keep tomorrow's in draft form and send it late afternoon tomorrow: we don't want them thinking we are reliable." He propped himself on the edge of her desk. "I've taken an order from our northern rivals; they'll be emailing confirmation shortly, and when it comes in, forward it directly to the machine room. They're paying a premium for a quick supply and as such don't mind the colours as long as the logo is prominent. I've asked them to list their sponsors and we should have the artwork on most." He smiled. "Actually, as I have to go out for a couple of hours, why don't you pop down there and choose the design for me. It will keep you out of trouble while I'm away."

"But I don't know the first thing about it! That was my first experience last night." Patsy protested, and catching Irene's expression of shock, returned it.

"You don't need to know about it, just have an eye for flair and good taste. I believe you have both, Patsy. I think you'll enjoy it."

As the door closed behind him, Irene snorted.

"'An eye for flair and good taste,'" Irene mimicked Stephen. "'You have both, Patsy.' You're shagging him! That's what this is all about – I should have realised."

"Don't be so ridiculous. I only met him yesterday," Patsy snapped back.

"How long does it take you then? Because if you're not, you will be: a blind man can see it."

"Well, if he can, it must be in his dreams." Patsy was irritated and stood to face her. "I'll tell you something, Irene, you are possibly the most tactless person I have ever met. All that huffing and eye rolling, you could do with some lessons on subtlety. I can assure you that nothing is going on between us, or ever will." Patsy had reached Irene's desk, and she picked up her mug. "Now, I'm going to make coffee, would you like one?"

"Yes, thanks." Irene showed no trace of embarrassment. "And I'll tell you this for free: that may be what you think, but I don't reckon it's what he thinks." She jerked her head towards the closed door and looked at her screen. "One sugar in mine," she instructed, effectively dismissing Patsy.

A few hours later, Patsy had visited the machine room, chosen two shades of blue for the ordered suits and had another hunt through the various email accounts. Using a basic code, she wrote the dates she had gone back to on her desk jotter. Two emails caught her attention, and when Irene wasn't looking she photographed them.

The first was from Jakub to Stephen.

*Hi, I've made formal contact. They deny knowledge but said they would ask around. I told them it paid very well. He'll be in touch, I know it.*

The second she found in the deleted file. It was from Stephen to a name unknown to Patsy, one R. Critchton at a standard Gmail address.

*Everything is progressing smoothly, we should be in a position to move in the next four weeks. Please do not contact me here again, leave it for me to contact you. Delete this address from your contacts and if you need to call use the phone provided. Thanks S.*

Patsy searched in vain for any other contact with Critchton. She wondered if Burt's IT people could resurrect deleted mail, and made a note to ask the question.

At five o'clock, Irene announced she'd done enough for one day, and was heading home. Patsy decided to join her. She needed to email the documents she had photographed, and, if she were able, try and get more information out of Burt. She walked to the carpark with Irene, and allowed her bag to be searched prior to returning to her car. She hadn't known about this procedure and decided in future she would have to email any material she collected immediately and then delete it.

She gave a sigh of relief as she pulled out onto the main road. On her homeward journey, she wondered what Meredith had meant by his text. It had been rather dramatic for him, but sweet. The more she thought about it, the more she wondered if she should be concerned.

*"Sorry I missed you last night. On the way home now, I will make it up to you. Remember, Hodge, whatever happens, I love you."*

She concluded they were too soppy for Meredith, and that he was either up to something, or something was wrong. If he hadn't gone back to the station he would be at home now. Patsy put her foot down on the accelerator: there was only one way to find out.

When she arrived, Meredith was on the phone, and pacing around the back garden. Amanda was in the kitchen.

"I cooked. I'm hoping it's edible; we didn't have the right ingredients so I had to improvise." Amanda knew from Patsy's lack of interest that her attention was elsewhere. She followed her gaze into the garden. "You are as vacant as he is. I should warn you, he's in one of his moods. He was shouting just now, poor old Trump."

"Then I'd better see if I can cheer him up." Patsy nodded towards the hob, "If that's as interesting as it sounds, you won't want him grumpy."

Dropping her jacket and bag on a chair, she walked into the garden and waved at Meredith. He held up a finger to halt her approach.

"Get it sorted and get back to me," he snapped. "It was one simple bloody instruction." He continued to rant, and fell silent as Trump presumably responded. "Yes, well tell him 'tough'. Get him to call me if he has a problem. This will happen tomorrow, I'm not being fobbed off. Call me if there are further issues." He ended the call abruptly and slid the phone into his pocket. Looking up he beckoned Patsy forward. "Come here, I need a hug. I'm away one day and it all goes to pot."

Patsy stepped into his arms. His reprimand to Trump had been sharp, and his embrace seemed urgent. Pushing herself away a little she looked up at him.

"Is everything all right? You seem to be more irritable than usual," she attempted humour, "and you've been sending soppy texts."

Meredith stared at her for a moment. "I am only irritable when idiots irritate me, and I don't do soppy. Heartfelt yes, but never soppy."

"Heartfelt? I didn't know you did heartfelt either. Should I be worried? Because when you send me a text which says 'blah blah *whatever happens*,' that is worrying."

"Blah blah?" Feigning disappointment, Meredith shook his head. "I was being dramatic. It was a long twenty-four hours, I was tired, hungry, and in need of a little loving. You read far too much into things. Blah blah being one of them." Meredith glanced at the house and lowered his voice a little, "On top of all that, Amanda is cooking. I think I'll still be hungry after dinner."

Patsy laughed to humour him. Now, she really was concerned. Meredith didn't do dramatic, ever. There was more to it, she was sure, but she would bide her time: she knew when to push him, and now was not the time.

Surprisingly, Amanda's experimental dinner was tasty, but any hope Patsy had of extracting more from Meredith was lost as he made and received numerous calls throughout the evening. The planned raid looked as though it would be called off at one point, but a few assertive calls to various senior officers from Meredith recovered the situation.

Finally, Meredith put his phone down and turned to her. "That's that done, now it's your turn."

"My turn? Really? Well, that was one of your more romantic invitations. I might not want *my turn*. Did that occur to you?"

"Nope. Come on." Meredith stood and held out his hand. "I've had to deal with Trump's Uncle David, or Chief Super to you, that bloody idiot who, for some reasons best known to others, was put in charge of the armed unit, and I have to be up at the crack of dawn. So, come sooth me."

Patsy ignored his outstretched hand. "I had a good day, thank you for asking." She shrugged. "I knew you'd be interested."

"Would you like me to sit back down and discuss your day?" Meredith's arm was beginning to ache, but he left it suspended. "We can do that if you want."

"Not worth it, it was boring." Finally, she took his hand. "But, thank you for asking." She allowed herself to be led to the bedroom.

Later as she snuggled into his chest, she knew he was far from sleep. "You're very preoccupied. Is this raid tomorrow going to be dangerous?"

"I think so."

"Do you want to talk to me about it?"

"Nope. Night, Hodge."

~ ~ ~

The next morning, Meredith grabbed his toast with one hand, and his jacket with the other. He saluted Patsy with the toast as she came down the stairs, and disappeared before she had time to wish him luck.

Amanda shrugged. "He's not said two words. Took one sip of his coffee, told me to behave and went. What's going on?"

"They have a raid today, he's preoccupied. A goodbye wouldn't have gone amiss though. I wish I'd had another hour in bed, I only got up to wish him luck." She sat at the table. "Your father can be very, very, irritating."

"Just as well you love him. Toast?" Amanda waved two slices of bread at Patsy.

Patsy nodded, and lifting her laptop from its case, she lost herself in sending the documents she had photographed the day before. She'd meant to do it the previous evening, but Meredith had distracted her. Amanda made the toast and placed it with a mug of tea next to the laptop. Patsy murmured her thanks.

"When I've caged the lion, I'll muck out the elephant; he's wearing blue today," Amanda said.

"Okay, no problem." Patsy's fingers paused, suspended over the keyboard. She swivelled to look at Amanda. "What did you say?"

"Nothing you were going to listen to. I think you two are a pair well-matched." Amanda smiled and slowly enunciated each word. "I'm going to shower now. Is that okay with you?"

Patsy laughed and took a swing at her backside as she skipped past, before returning to the task in hand.

"I'm nothing like him," she murmured as she hit the send button.

~ ~ ~

Meredith's morning briefing was literally brief – it took less than ten minutes. He gave a potted version of his meeting with Andronikov, and listened as the team updated him with the events of the day before, and the preparation for the raid on the H & S Meat Production factory. The rest of the day was a flurry of activity as all the various teams were briefed and made ready to go. Although the raid was not scheduled until five that afternoon, Rawlings and Adler were sent to monitor the activity there and keep Meredith updated from early afternoon. Delivery vans came and went, customers arrived and left with their purchases. There was no indication that it was anything other than business as usual.

Dave Rawlings called in his last report. Meredith and the team were sitting in a transporter around the corner as the armed unit approached.

"And that's it. By my reckoning we have five or six employees inside. The window display has been removed and washed down, the last customer has cleared the carpark. There are three unoccupied wagons parked up. The rest of the cars must belong to the staff."

"Thanks, Rawlings, have they put the grille across yet?"

"Negative. Two of them are outside having a smoke."

"Right, stand by."

Meredith hung up and switched to the radio. "It's a go, go, go!" he commanded.

The driver of the transporter waited until the armed unit had flown past, and pulled out behind them, the rubber screeching on the tarmac as he accelerated to keep up. Meredith grabbed hold of the dash to steady himself. Sirens blazing, the lead vehicle pulled into the carpark of the factory. Armed men jumped out shouting before it had come to a halt. The two men smoking outside dropped to the ground and covered their heads.

"They've done that before," Meredith observed to Trump as they jogged forward.

The armed team made short work of their journey through the building, securing each area as they did so. Dogs were released to aid the search. In addition to the two workers outside, five other employees were rounded up and taken to the reception area, where they sat at gunpoint while the factory was searched. All but one remained still and silent. Filipp Myshkin kept up a tirade of abuse and demands, mainly in his native tongue.

Despite the dogs indicating that drugs had been present in several different areas, none were found. The whole place was spotless, literally. Meredith was like a bear with a sore head when they completed the search of the last room.

"Every surface of every room hosed down and scrubbed – they must have worked overnight." He turned to Dave Seaton. "I don't think that's a regular occurrence, do you?"

Seaton didn't answer, he knew what Meredith was inferring, and followed him as he stormed back into the reception area where Myshkin was still creating.

Meredith rounded on him. "You! Lippy. Button it," he demanded, and jumped back as Myshkin leapt up and spat at him. The globule of spit landed on Meredith's shoe. Meredith looked down at it, and slowly raising his eyes stared at Myshkin. "Who's in charge here?"

"I am." Myshkin pulled his shoulders back and forced out his chest. His chin tilted defiantly.

"I didn't mean in charge of the cleaning, I meant in charge of the business." Meredith didn't lose eye contact, and he watched the veins on Myshkin's temple pulse.

"I say again, Mr Policeman, I am." Myshkin halted his advance as the nearest armed officer stepped forward as a warning.

"Well, I never did. No accounting for it." Meredith looked over his shoulder at Seaton. "Fancy leaving a shit-for-brains in charge." He turned back to Myshkin who was now snarling insults through gritted teeth. "Has he been searched?"

His eyes moved to the officer who had stepped forward.

"He has no weapons," came the clipped reply, the officer clearly affronted that Meredith thought they had failed to search the men.

This time Meredith turned his head. "We didn't come looking for weapons, we came looking for drugs. Get some gloves and take him to the locker room, and when you're done I'll see him in the office back there." Meredith jerked his head towards the rear door before returning his attention to Myshkin. "I'd suggest you cooperate. He has big hands." He grinned to taunt the man.

"You can't do that, it's not allowed. I know the law in this country."

"Not well enough, pal." Meredith's smile was cold. "This says we can." He slammed the warrant against Myshkin's chest. "Now, you do have a choice: we can take you down to the station or we can do it here as I suggested. What's it going to be?"

"I'll not forget this." Spittle formed at the corners of Myshkin's mouth, and his lips barely moved as he spoke.

Meredith raised his eyebrows. "Was that a threat, sir? Because you really don't want to be throwing threats around, not given your situation."

He laughed as the armed officer called to one of his team, and they led Myshkin back to the staff locker room. Myshkin continued to curse in his native tongue as he was led away.

Seaton stepped up to Meredith. "Was that wise? I know we came up empty-handed, but these boys don't play fair. Do you really think he's carrying?"

Meredith drew his head back and tutted. "You see, Tom, I thought for a moment there that you were questioning my decisions. I know that can't be true. And necessary? Of course. We have to establish who has the upper hand." Meredith turned away as Seaton held his hands up.

"You're the boss. I've never questioned that, but if he's clean you need to watch your back. That's all I'm saying."

"I'll be fine. Go and make sure they've swabbed the areas that the dogs showed an interest in. I'll go and see how they're getting on with Myshkin."

As Meredith walked away to the locker room he heard Seaton murmur something to Trump, but let it go, and a smile twitched at the corners of his mouth. By the time he reached the locker room the search had been completed. Myshkin was buckling his belt. The larger of the two officers shook his head to indicate nothing had been found.

"You were lucky this time, Myshkin. Let's hope your luck holds."

Myshkin stepped towards him. "I don't need luck. May I go?"

"You may." Meredith caught hold of his arm as he made to push past him. "And you can tell your boss this won't be the last time. We'll be keeping an eye on this little operation."

"I told you, I am the boss." Myshkin attempted to shake his arm free, and added, "There is nothing to find, your information is faulty."

Meredith kept a grip on his arm, his knuckles white with the effort.

"Well Ronnie Bishop didn't think so." He smiled as Myshkin stilled. "Oh yes, I forgot to mention I need to speak to you about her. We'll do that at the station though. Boys," Meredith released Myshkin to the two officers who had searched him, "take him to the station, I'll be there shortly. If he gives you any trouble, arrest him for assaulting an officer."

A low growl emanated from Myshkin's throat. "If I assaulted you, you would not be able to walk, so take care, my friend."

"And there you go with the threats again." Meredith stepped back a little and lifted his foot. "This counts for assault, who knows what diseases you might have." With a sudden movement Meredith twisted his foot and cleaned his shoe on Myshkin's trousers. He stepped back further as Myshkin lunged at him, and waved his finger. "Steady now, you don't want them to restrain you. They are a little heavy-handed." He gave a short laugh. "But you know that, don't you?" He turned on his heel and walked back the way he had come. "Take him away."

Meredith walked into the incident room. Trump and Seaton exchanged glances; their boss's face showed no emotion as he walked to the incident board, and that was not a good sign. Seaton looked at the two men present on behalf of the armed squad; they looked relaxed and had no idea of what was to come. The room fell silent as Meredith thumped the board with his free hand; in the other he grasped a folder. His summary of the raid was brief and brutal.

"Nothing! Absolutely fuck all, and there's a reason for that." He turned to face the room. "Traces of class A drugs were found, despite the comprehensive clean-up which must have happened overnight. Someone has loose lips or, worse, is working with, or taking back-handers from this mob." His lip curled. "Whoever it is, I hope you weren't planning a long career, because I will find you, and you'll wish I hadn't."

He focused his attention on the two armed officers. "Now, you take that back to your men, and make sure they know I don't issue empty threats. I'm going to interview Myshkin, and when I'm free I'll expect your governor to be awaiting my call."

One of the men attempted to defend his team. "With the greatest respect, I don't —"

"I don't want your fucking respect, I want answers! Now bugger off and do as I asked." Meredith strode towards the exit. "Seaton, you can sit in on this one."

Tom Seaton collected a pad and rolled his eyes at Trump as he hurried to catch Meredith. Meredith slowed as he reached the interview room. He peered through the glass panel at Myshkin, who sat with his wrists resting on the edge of the table, his fingers drumming out a tattoo as he stared at the officer who stood guarding him. His head barely moved as his eyes swivelled to witness Meredith's arrival.

Meredith sat opposite him, pushed the button to start the recorder and banged the desk with the flat of his hand. "I understand that you have refused legal representation, is that correct?"

Myshkin nodded.

Meredith spoke as if to a child. "You will have to speak." He pointed to the tape. "This is not filming, but recording you, do you understand?" He pulled his lips into a smile.

"Yes."

"Yes, it's correct you don't want to be represented, or yes, you understand?" Meredith looked smug as he watched the veins on Myshkin's temple pulse as he fought for control of his temper.

"Both." Myshkin leaned forward. His hands remained still and it looked as though he were about push himself up. He didn't. "I know I am free to go whenever I want. I would like to go now, but I have nothing to hide, so get on with your questions. I am a busy man."

"Do you have a work permit, Mr Myshkin?" Meredith smiled at him.

Myshkin had not expected that. "I do. In fact, I have applied for citizenship, soon I will have a passport."

"Not if I say no, you won't, and I have to tell you I'm not inclined to say yes." Meredith looked down at the rows of information on the sheet he had pulled out. "Not even though you celebrate your fifty-fifth birthday next week." He leaned back in his chair and crossed his legs at the ankle. "You see, Mr Myshkin, drug dealing, money laundering and murder do not a good citizen make."

"I am none of those things and you know it. What is your problem? Why am I here?"

"We both know that's a lie, don't we?" Meredith tipped the file towards him and flipped the cover open so Myshkin was unable to see the contents. "Do you know this woman?"

He placed an artist's impression of Ronnie Bishop on the desk.

Myshkin glanced at it. "You know I do. It is Veronika."

"Otherwise known as Ronnie Bishop?" Meredith tutted as Myshkin nodded. "Speak for the tape, I have explained."

"Yes, she was known as Ronnie Bishop. Why are you speaking to me about her?"

"Because she's dead."

This was clearly not news to Myshkin who continued to stare at Meredith. Meredith selected a photograph and placed it over Veronika's face.

"Did you do this to her?"

The photograph showed a mutilated hand, palm up, with only one whole finger. Again, Myshkin glanced only briefly before returning to hold Meredith's stare.

"I didn't. Why would I?"

"Because you are a sadistic bastard and would have enjoyed it." Meredith banged another photograph down as Myshkin snorted a laugh. "Do you recognise this?"

Myshkin glanced down. It was a photograph of a human head, this being evident by the bloodied mass of hair surrounding it, the general shape, and the eyeball with no socket to sit in.

"No."

"Was she alive when you did this to her face? We know she was alive when some of her fingertips were removed, but we can't be certain at what point she actually died. Did you do this to her?"

Meredith pulled out a photograph of the whole of Ronnie Bishop's remains. There was not an inch which hadn't been damaged in some way, but the worst injuries were to the head. This time Myshkin didn't look.

"Look at the photograph." Meredith tapped the desk with his fingertip.

Myshkin's eyes remained fixed on Meredith. "I do not need to, I can see she is dead. I did not do it and I do not know who did. Can I go now, or do you have more questions?"

Without warning, and causing Seaton to cry out in alarm, Meredith lurched forward, grabbed hold of Myshkin's hair and banged his face down on the photograph.

"Don't you dare fucking bleed on it," Meredith spat, and his arm trembled with the effort of holding Myshkin's head inches from the photograph. He shot a warning glance at Seaton, telling him to remain seated. "Now, I ask again, did you do this to Ronnie Bishop?"

"No." The denial was little more than a growl in Myshkin's throat. "You are not allowed to do this. I demand that you release me."

Myshkin attempted to lift his head, but Meredith's free hand joined the other to hold it inches above the photograph.

"You demand, do you? Well, let me tell you what's not allowed. You are not allowed to come into this country on a dodgy work permit, manufacture and distribute drugs on our streets, and you are certainly not allowed to get your perverse kicks by mutilating people that piss you off. Because if that was allowed, you would be in many, many little pieces, and the boys in the mortuary would be taking bets on how long it would take to arrange you in some sort of order."

Putting pressure on both hands by leaning forward, Meredith forced Myshkin's nose onto the photograph. "If you didn't do this, who did?" Without warning he released Myshkin's head and watched his body jump backwards as the pressure was removed. He looked Myshkin in the eye. "Now we've established that I don't play by the rules, tell me what you know about Ronnie Bishop. Don't bugger about, and don't attempt to lie, or I will arrest you, charge you, and when you've served your sentence, I'll make sure you're deported."

"Arrest me for what?" Myshkin sneered. He still believed Meredith was bluffing, and while he was still wary of him, he relaxed back in his chair. He became concerned as Meredith smiled and rummaged in his pocket.

"For possession of a banned substance with the intent to supply." Meredith held up a clear plastic bag containing a second bag, which held a substantial quantity of white powder. "Recovered during our body search, I'm told. I'm also given to understand that your fingerprints are all over the inner bag."

Myshkin turned to Seaton, who, despite his own surprise, merely smiled at him.

"This is a lie and you know it. Why are you doing this?"

It was Meredith who replied. "Because I thought you'd need a little encouragement to tell us how poor Ronnie met her end."

Myshkin looked from one to the other for a while before his shoulders sagged, and he stared at the photograph unforced.

"I didn't do this. If that is Ronnie, it makes me sick to my stomach." He glanced at Meredith. "I loved her."

"Why didn't you report her missing?"

"It was too complicated. I thought she had gone back to London."

"To Andronikov?" Meredith smiled as Myshkin's eyes widened. "We do our homework, you know. We know about Andronikov. I met with him yesterday, in fact. It was he who pointed me in your direction."

"Liar!" Myshkin laughed as he spat the word.

"So, here we are. Tell me why she would have gone back to London." Meredith ignored the challenge on the accuracy of his last statement.

Myshkin was staring at the space between Meredith and Seaton. His mind churned through the events of his last days with Ronnie as he tried to work out which details would not tighten Meredith's grip on him.

"I believe Ronnie had feelings for me. She was not, what do you call it, a slapper? She did not fall easily into my bed – that was some months after she came to Bristol. But I think ultimately her heart lay elsewhere. She was comfortable, but not happy." He looked at the ceiling as though to compose himself. "That is difficult to accept when you love someone. Knowing that in their head they would rather be with someone else, and we argued. That last week it was daily. On the day she left I had told her not to be there when I got home. I got home and she'd gone." He shrugged. "I assumed back to London."

"You didn't think to check?" Seaton asked. "You didn't call her, or she you? She just left, and you were happy never to hear from her again?"

Myshkin slapped his hand on his chest. "I am a proud man. I had been stupid long enough. I told her to go and she did. Why would I then chase around after her? I was glad to be free of her spell."

"And what date would that have been? We know when her body was found, and we know how long she'd been dead, give or take the odd maggot." Meredith watched as Myshkin flinched before looking at him with a coldness in his eyes that told Meredith he had made an enemy for life. "Sorry, did I touch a nerve? I didn't think you would be so sensitive. What date did she leave you?"

"She didn't leave, I told her to go."

Despite the photograph on the table, and Myshkin declaring his love for the woman, he still needed to establish it was his choice.

Meredith smirked. "The date. You said you loved her, and then you were glad to be free of her. I find it difficult to believe you don't know when this happened."

"She didn't live with me. Not properly; she lived with a friend sometimes. I thought, at first, she was there, then the friend came looking for her and I knew she'd gone back to him. It was June, I don't know the day."

Myshkin felt ashamed admitting yet again he had lost her to another man, and he stared at his hands. Meredith and Seaton remained silent, forcing him to look up. "No more questions?" Attempting to establish his lack of concern, and regain some control over the proceedings, sarcasm had returned.

"Plenty. But for the moment, we will leave it that the woman you loved disappeared without a trace, her friend came to you, concerned for her wellbeing, and you did nothing to find out what might have happened. Big, brave, strong Filipp Myshkin, content to leave her rotting in a ditch." Meredith watched the vein pulse and shook his head. "That's not love, Myshkin."

Myshkin banged the table with his fists. "I told you, I thought she had gone back to him. Why would I look?" He held shaking hands to each side of his head. "Which part of that don't you understand?"

"You didn't check whether she was tucked up in Andronikov's bed? Would have been awkward that, given your connections with him."

"I don't know him that well. Just because he is also Russian does not mean I know him. It wasn't him anyway, and if it was, he wouldn't have taken her back. We don't know who it was."

Myshkin stopped speaking abruptly. Meredith looked at Seaton to see if he'd caught the relevance of that last statement.

Seaton had, and he leaned forward, resting his forearms on the table. "We who? You said 'we don't know who it was'? Who did you discuss this with? Andronikov? Did you pass her around to see who could tame her, was that it?"

"I meant I. This is all very painful for me." Myshkin dismissed Seaton's question.

"But you don't think Andronikov did this to her?" Meredith tapped the photograph but Myshkin continued to look at him.

"I doubt it. Why would he bother? I think I have already said, I don't know and have no idea who would do this. It was probably chance – she was in the wrong place at the wrong time."

Meredith laughed. "That's true. I didn't consider the fact that we might have a random murderer wandering around out there. Do you think he might also have done this?"

He slid another photograph from the file and placed it next to the other. Myshkin looked for only a moment, but Meredith and Seaton saw the flare of recognition and surprise.

"Who is this?" he asked, his face devoid of emotion.

"This, as you know, is James Ridgeway. You probably knew him as Jimmy."

Myshkin glanced down. "I do not know him."

Meredith pulled another photograph from the file, and held it briefly in front of Myshkin's face before placing it on the table.

"But this, taken outside your official place of work, tells us otherwise." Seaton looked at the photograph he had not seen before. It showed Myshkin and Jimmy Ridgeway sitting on the window ledge of a kebab shop, smoking. Ridgeway was laughing.

Myshkin shrugged. "So, he came to my shop. That's not a reason for killing him."

"No, perhaps the other way around." Meredith smiled. "But when he dipped his hand into the till of your other business, it most certainly is."

"Are you telling me he robbed the meat factory?" Myshkin smirked. "He never worked there as far as I know. What is he supposed to have done, some shoplifting?"

Meredith pulled a final photograph from the file. It was taken in the carpark of the factory and showed the two men shaking hands, and both were smiling. Seaton hoped his expression didn't reveal his surprise

"We'll come back to your employees, but first if you don't know this man, and the meeting at the kebab shop was accidental, how do you explain this?"

Meredith watched the now familiar shrug.

"Perhaps I told him where he could buy good quality meat. Greeting customers is not a crime in this country, I don't think."

"Not as yet. But shooting them through the head and removing their fingerprints is a big no-no. I hear he was skimming at least twenty percent from each delivery and distributing it amongst his own friends. Your cousin Peter didn't like that, and you got the order to execute him. I have to say you showed great restraint, but then, he didn't break your heart like Ronnie did."

Meredith pulled back from the table as Myshkin lunged forward.

"I did not have a broken heart, I did not kill these people. I've had enough talking with you, now I would like a solicitor to get me out of here." He leaned towards the recorder. "I would like a solicitor," he repeated, and Meredith smiled.

"Interview terminated at seven-thirty." He switched off the machine and turned back to Myshkin. "No solicitor will get you out while I have this." Meredith patted the pocket containing the drugs he had said were found during the search. "And yet I haven't got enough evidence to charge you with either of these killings, so what to do? How can we help each other?"

Seaton's eyes dashed to Meredith, wondering what was coming next. The photographs of Myshkin with Ridgeway had not been shared with the team, the drugs had certainly not been found that day, and now it appeared Meredith was going to try and do some sort of deal with Myshkin. Myshkin looked as taken aback as Seaton felt.

"What do you mean?" Myshkin demanded, but the look of defiance had faded a little.

"I know you killed Ridgeway. Do I care? Not a bit. He was trash, and the world's a better place without him. Ronnie Bishop? I'm not sure. Your feelings seem genuine, but she's not missed by anyone, and her flatmate never got in touch again after the initial report. Will putting you away for killing them serve any purpose? Nah." Meredith suddenly lurched forward, his index finger inches away from Myshkin's face. "But I will, and I'll throw the drugs in too, just to round it off."

Myshkin pushed Meredith's hand onto the table calmly.

"Tell me what you want, Meredith. Then we can all get on with our lives."

"I want your cousin. I want Peter. I know he pulls your strings, but I want to know who pulls his, and why. I want you to tell me who he meets with, when and why. When I have him bang to rights, you're a free man." Meredith moved back. "But I'm not messing: you try and double-cross me, you feed me any shit and you'll not see the light of day unless there are bars at the window."

He smiled as Myshkin dropped his gaze and pondered this unexpected turn of events. When he looked back up, all his previous aggression and bravado had disappeared.

"What do you want him for? He will kill me if he finds out; he's not a man you cross."

"Human trafficking, drugs, extortion, murder . . . where would you like me to start?"

Myshkin was already shaking his head before Meredith had finished.

"You won't get near him. He is untouchable although I don't know why. He is clever and keeps all the illegal business interests at arm's length, and he makes sure he is active in the others. You won't get him, so what now?" Myshkin shrugged defeat, knowing he was caught between a rock and a hard place.

"Untouchable? No one is untouchable. If that were the case, why did he leave Russia so quickly? I hear he can't even get his wife and kids out now." Meredith gave a little laugh as Myshkin looked surprised at the depth of Meredith's knowledge. Seaton bristled a little, wishing Meredith had shared even a fraction of all this information with him. He wondered why he was even sitting in on the interview. "I have detailed information on your cousin; I know he escaped Russia before he was taken out. Now I want him shut down, and you are going to help me do that."

"But how?"

"It's simple: you keep supplying me with the information, and I will find the weakness." Meredith's tone suggested this would be simple, and again Myshkin shook his head.

"Your arrogance is misplaced. The government in Russia couldn't get him and neither will you, whatever I try and do. Tell me, what happens to me when you fail?"

"That's simple, sunshine, if you fail and he doesn't kill you, I'll be banging you up for murdering these two." Meredith tapped the photographs. "So, I'm sure you will see the importance of getting it right."

Meredith waited a beat while Myshkin considered this. "So, we'll be starting straight away. I understand he has a meeting lined up for the end of the week." He smiled as Myshkin raised his eyebrows. "Yes, I am well-informed. I want to know when and where and, most importantly, who is invited. If anything else crops up that I would want to know about, call me." Meredith withdrew a mobile telephone from his inside jacket pocket and held it towards Myshkin. "I'm speed dial one."

Myshkin stared at the phone as he considered his options. Meredith certainly was well-informed, and if he already had that level of detail there seemed little point in fighting it. He sighed as he considered going to his cousin and explaining what had happened. He wondered if he would help him set up somewhere else, a long way from Bristol. He closed his eyes as he accepted the truth. He had been told to leave Ronnie alone but he'd ignored that order and now it had come back to haunt him. Myshkin decided to play Meredith's game as, whatever the outcome, Meredith would be dead at the end of it: he'd see to that. He stretched out his hand and took the phone.

"I will do my best, but you will have to keep your distance or he will know something is going on."

"You'll do more than your best, you'll do what you're told. You just swapped one bastard boss for another." Meredith nodded at Seaton. "See Mr Myshkin out, and then meet me in my office."

Seaton returned and closed the door with a definite bang before sitting opposite Meredith without being invited.

"Are you going to tell me what that was all about?" he demanded.

"I would've thought that was obvious." Meredith looked up from the paperwork he was scanning on his desk. "Needs must, Seaton. You're going to have to trust me."

"Oh, I get the reasoning. I was wondering why I didn't know about it before I sat down."

"Because I wasn't sure what I was going to do. Let's not make an issue out of it."

"But you had photographs that the team hasn't seen, you're handing out mobile phones, but more concerning is that it appears you are letting a murderer loose without so much as a blink. I'm still at a loss as to why." Seaton blew out a frustrated breath. "What's the story with his cousin? You said he was a bad boy, but you didn't say it was catch him at all costs."

"For God's sake, Seaton, stop being such a pain in the ass. You're going to have to trust me on this. Do you trust me?"

"Of course, but —"

"No buts. What happened in that room remains between us. In fact, nothing happened; we questioned him, but didn't have enough to hold or charge him. Do you understand?"

"Yes, but . . ." Seaton held up his hands in mock surrender as Meredith sighed heavily. "Okay, okay, I get it, but I hope you know what you're doing, Gov. What are you going to do if he kills again?" Seaton allowed his arms to fall heavily onto the arms of his chair.

Meredith pinched the bridge of his nose and drew in a deep breath. Seaton could see the concern etched on his face.

"I have no idea. I'll deal with it, if and when it happens, but it's not likely, not now we have him in our sights. Now, how far are we on finding out who tipped them off?"

"We're not, but I wasn't expecting any different. It certainly wasn't one of us, if they were tipped off it will either be someone in the drug squad, or the armed boys." He shrugged. "We will have to be careful what information we share, and monitor what happens I suppose. What are your thoughts on it?"

"At the moment, we have more important things to worry about. It gave us Filipp Myshkin, but as you say, let's be careful." Meredith looked at his watch. "Let's call it a night. Tell that lot to go home and get a good night's sleep, but back here at eight in the morning."

Meredith watched as his team packed up for the night. He raised his hand to acknowledge those who called goodbye. Trump tapped on the door and opened it.

"A couple of us are going to the Dirty Duck for drinks, sir, will you be joining us?" he asked. "As we have nothing to celebrate we'd thought we'd drown a few sorrows."

"I've got a few bits to finish here. You go on, I might pop in later." Meredith nodded and Trump shut the door.

He picked up his phone, and listened as the answer message cut in. "I have Filipp Myshkin. I'll call again tomorrow."

He hung up and rubbed his hands over his face. He could do with getting drunk, but had no appetite for a session with the boys. Pulling his jacket from the back of the chair, he switched off the lamp on his desk. He was going home to drown his sorrows.

## 6

Over the next few weeks, Patsy immersed herself in the role of PA to Stephen Hatton. He wasn't demanding, but his attraction to her was beginning to grate, particularly as Meredith had become moody and secretive of late. It would be all too easy to be flattered by the attention, but she kept him at arm's length, and he didn't push. It was far more to do with what he didn't say or do, than what he did. His latest ploy was to invite Meredith to a speedway meeting, which he told her she must attend as they were testing the latest prototype and she should witness that first-hand. Patsy promised to do her best, but explained that Meredith was very busy with his workload at the moment.

"You said that when we went for pizza last week." Mischief twinkled in Stephen's eye. "I have to be honest with you, Patsy, I find it difficult to believe that he even exists. It's almost as though you've invented him to avoid certain situations." He grinned. "But, if he does and you are happy with him never being around, I can't see why you're with him."

He turned on his heel and left the room. Patsy bristled, and hoped that Meredith would come to the speedway as that would kill two birds with one stone. First, she would get to spend a whole evening with him, and second, it would stop Stephen Hatton's unwanted attention, if only for one night. She pulled her phone from her bag and texted him. Dropping her phone onto the table, she sighed and mentally crossed her fingers. She looked up as Irene snorted.

"The inevitable is getting closer, although credit where credit is due, I can see you are trying to hold him at bay. What I can't work out is why? Do you not think he . . . actually they, that both the Hatton brothers are hot? And don't give me that bullshit about being in a relationship, because you hardly mention your bloke. That's odd. I've been married for far too long, and my hubby crops up in conversation all the time." Irene glanced at the clock. "Almost five, that's me done for the day. My husband is taking me to dinner tonight, what are you two doing?"

"Irene, please. Stop trying to stir up trouble where there is none. I don't talk about Meredith because for one thing he's a policeman and what he does isn't something we can discuss," Patsy tapped the side of her nose, "need to know and all that, but also I'm paid to work, not sit here and chat." Patsy clicked her mouse a few times, closing the open documents on her computer before hitting the off button. "I think I'll have an early night tonight too."

Irene had already collected her coat from the stand behind the door, which she held open for Patsy.

"Come on, I'll walk you to the carpark." Irene's initial concerns about Patsy had abated. She kept herself to herself, was quick on the uptake, and clearly had no intention of becoming involved with the boss. "You can tell me what makes Meredith so special."

"I'll do no such thing – your blood pressure couldn't take it." Patsy laughed as Irene assured her it could. She refused when Irene invited her for a quick drink. "I can't, I'm afraid, I do have a life outside work, despite what you lot think, and you'll be wanting to get home to get ready. I'd hate to be the reason you kept the world's most perfect man waiting."

Patsy wasn't lying: she did have something to do. She had a meeting arranged with Burt, which, if it went true to form, would not be pleasurable.

Twenty minutes later, she walked into the lift of the supposedly unused office block and pushed the button for the fourth floor. She navigated the winding corridor, and having received a nod from the man sitting outside, she pushed open the double doors and looked at the two men sitting at the only table in the vast expanse of an office.

"Hello, two of you today," she observed, wondering why James Benson was present. At previous meetings, she'd met only Burt. "As I've already told Burt, this meeting is pointless; I've absolutely nothing to report. Everything was pretty much the same as yesterday, which was the same as the day before."

Reaching the table, she pulled out a chair. James Benson indicated a jug of iced water that sat on a small tin tray in the middle of the table.

"Would you like a glass of water, Patsy?" He filled a glass for her without waiting for her response.

"Thank you, though I doubt I'll finish it. There is nothing to tell."

"Give us a résumé of what happened today." Burt, her handler, seemed bored, and when Patsy turned to face him, he shrugged. "Humour us." Patsy felt the usual irritation stir.

"He made lots of calls to the government bods, 'he' being Stephen. Jake spent most of the day in the lab, I think; I don't see a lot of him. They've had a big order for suits in from Norway, and both got very excited when someone called from America asking for a sample to consider before ordering." She watched Benson's brow furrow.

"Did they send one?" His tone was harsh and Patsy raised her eyebrows.

"Not that I know of. Abigail Ward was tasked with sorting that out, but she said something about it having to be early next week. Why? Do you not want them working with the American outfit? As far as I'm aware they're a genuine bike club."

"If they are American at all. Get me the details, and when you see Stephen tonight tell him to hold off until we've checked them out."

"How do you know . . . Of course, you know. I'm not sure if I'm going yet; I said I'd try, but as the invitation included Meredith, and it's unlikely he'll come, I doubt I'll go."

"You certainly will, Meredith or not," Burt snapped.

"Why? What's so special about tonight?"

Patsy's irritation grew. She'd made up her mind not to go if Meredith said no. More to make a point to him than snub Stephen, because Meredith had been less than attentive the last few weeks. She watched Benson take out a photograph and slide it across the table to her. She gave a short laugh and picked it up. "That's whatshisname. Lyndon Ward, the guy from the internet. The one I was going . . ." A cog fell into place and she raised her eyebrows. She'd previously been asked to trace Lyndon Ward by a woman who had met him online and was convinced something sinister had happened to him. "Ward. Any relation to Abigail Ward?"

"Brother." Burt clapped his hands together twice. "Well done, Patsy, you got there in the end." Patsy ignored the sarcasm.

"Is *he* why I'm there? I'm sorry I didn't connect the two names immediately, but Ward is not uncommon, and I thought . . ." Seeing the look on Burt's face she didn't bother finishing the sentence. "Will he be there tonight?"

"Possibly. He plans to, but his paranoia may change that: he's still looking over his shoulder."

"I wonder why that might be." Patsy's irony was lost on Burt, so she added, "What do you want me to do if he is?"

"Whether he is or not, stick close to Abigail. Monitor her disappointment if he doesn't show, or conversation if he does. If it looks like you're going to lose them – they may want to talk in private – make sure you get this on her somehow." Burt pulled a small plastic wallet from his pocket and handed it to Patsy. "It's a transmitter, a bug," he added unnecessarily.

"You think they are planning something? What?" Patsy jabbed her finger at him in frustration. "If you would only tell me what you think is going on, or what you think I may discover, I may be able to bring you something more useful." The sentence triggered a memory. "Oh yes, I think Stephen may have three if not more mobile phones. I know he has two because he makes no secret of having one private and one business phone, both of which he carries with him at all times. But today, when I was in his office, there appeared to be a third in the top drawer of his desk. It could be nothing, of course." She shrugged as the two men exchanged glances.

"Now, what did you say? That this meeting is pointless? Yes, that was it." Burt shook his head. "Was there anything else you thought was pointless?" He grinned as Patsy turned to glare at him.

"I said *this meeting* was pointless. I could have told you all this over the phone. You really are the most irritating man I've ever had to work with." She turned back to Benson, who was also smiling. "So I stick with Abigail and look and listen, I secrete the bug about her person, anything else? Oh yes, I also tell Stephen to delay the deal with the Americans. Is that it, because I've got to get home and change?"

"I think that covers it. Take the phone and text if anything is urgent; one of us will be on hand."

"The phone? Why didn't I think of that?" Patsy stood and grabbed her bag, knocking the glass of water onto the photograph of Lyndon Ward. She made no attempt to mop it up. "Sorry about that, I'll be in touch."

Her phone beeped as though on cue as she opened the door. She ignored it, and made her way back to the car.

Meredith was exhausted when he got to the station. He'd not been sleeping well, and his meeting earlier had been taxing. He summoned Trump to his office.

"Tell me what's happened today, and keep it brief, Trump, I've got a headache. I'm knackered, and I want an early night."

"Of course." Trump sat opposite Meredith and flipped open his notepad. "Dave has picked up on some link between Jan Liska and Ronnie Bishop's flatmate, so he's gone to see the flatmate. We've tracked down Jimmy Ridgeway's brother: he was shocked but not upset, and interestingly Ridgeway did live in Bristol for a year or so back in the early eighties. He gave us the address where he was living. He was dealing even then, although whether it was for this mob or not, we don't know. Tom Seaton is investigating. Filipp Myshkin is still being followed by Hutchins and Jo, but nothing out of the ordinary to report. Myshkin lied about not knowing Andronikov very well. I went to the Hammer and Sickle last night, as you know, and it was full of heavy drinkers speaking in a tongue I couldn't understand, and no known faces, except . . ." He jumped to his feet and ran back to his desk, returning with a dog-eared photograph. "This was taken at a wedding reception held at the club – don't know when, or who got married – but look at the two men standing behind the bride and groom. I borrowed this from the board in the lobby."

He handed Meredith the photograph.

Meredith looked at the dark-haired couple holding up their glasses to the camera. A simple wedding cake stood on the table in front of them, and behind them stood three men, their arms around each other's shoulders. One, Myshkin, was saying something to the second, Andronikov, who was laughing. The third man had thrown back his head, and his face was not visible. Meredith peered closely; there was something familiar there, but he couldn't bring a name to mind.

"Ha! They really aren't that bright, this Russian mob. I'll call Myshkin and get him in here in the morning. It'll be amusing watching him explain that one. Do we know the other bloke?" Trump shook his head. "Well, find out, and find out who the happy couple are, it may be relevant."

Meredith stretched his arms above his head and yawned noisily.

"We need to pay a visit to that club but we'll sort it tomorrow. I really, really, must get some sleep tonight. Anything else?" Trump shook his head. "Okay, well tidy things up, call it a day, and we'll have an update from Seaton and Rawlings at tomorrow's briefing." Meredith sighed as he spotted Rawlings hurrying towards his office. "Talk of the devil."

Rawlings rapped once and entered the office.

"Not interrupting, am I?" Rawlings seemed excited.

"Get on with it, what have you got?" Meredith stared at the envelope in Rawlings' hand.

Rawlings looked at it as though he'd only just realised he had it. "Oh this, no it's not this. Desk sergeant gave me that for you on the way through." He dropped the envelope on Meredith's desk. "No, I've come from the former home of Ronnie Bishop. Elena, her flatmate, is petrified of just about everything. I pretended we knew there was a link between Ronnie and Jan Liska and she nearly passed out with fear, gabbling away in Russian. I had to take her by the shoulders and sit her. . ." Rawlings saw Meredith roll his eyes and sigh. He grinned at Trump. "Late night, Gov? So, to cut a long story short –"

"If you would." Meredith leaned back in his chair, folded his arms across his chest, and crossed one leg over the other.

Trump wondered whether he would fall asleep.

"Jan Liska is Elena's cousin. She introduced them shortly before Ronnie became involved with Andronikov. No one knew they'd had a relationship, and Andronikov took her in so to speak. Liska was heartbroken for a while, but knew they would both be in danger if Andronikov found out. Apparently, Andronikov's a proud man with a temper. When Ronnie first came to Bristol, Jan avoided her, she didn't even know he was local, and she took up with our friend Filipp. Ronnie and Myshkin bumped into Jan while out one night, their love rekindled and the two began to meet in secret. In Elena's own words, 'Filipp Myshkin is an evil man; he would have killed them both slowly. I know it was him that killed her, but he must not find out about Jan, he will kill him too.'"

Rawlings pulled out a chair. "I should add she doesn't *know* he killed Ronnie, but she thinks it could only be him. She's not Russian, she's Czech, but she speaks Russian like a native; something to do with a grandmother, and that was the only passport available." He rolled his eyes. "I wonder how many of them have legit passports."

"Don't sit, you're not stopping. But good work, Dave. Having something on Jan will be useful: might invite him to our night at the club." Meredith sat forward and fingered the envelope. It was marked 'strictly private and confidential', and had only his name printed across the front.

"Our what? Are we going out? Only I promised the missus . . ." Rawlings fell silent as Meredith waved his hand.

"Not tonight, no, we'll sort it tomorrow." Meredith nodded towards the door. "Right, let's get out of here. Anything else?" He looked from one to the other, "Good. See you in the morning."

As the two men made their exit, he opened the envelope and slid the contents onto his desk. "Bastards!" he exclaimed, causing Trump to hesitate and turn back.

"Everything all right, sir?" His eyes scanned Meredith's desk, but Meredith's hands obscured the envelope and its contents.

"Yep, night, Trump."

Meredith waited until Trump had closed the door, before sifting through the photographs and replacing them in the envelope. He slid the envelope into his inside pocket. His face was grim as he buried it in his hands. His moment of misery was interrupted by the hoot of a train, advising him he had a text. He lifted his phone and read the message from Patsy.

"Not tonight," he groaned, "not tonight."

Patsy had worded the message to hit home.

*Work do at Speedway in Swindon tonight. Transport arranged, we'll be home by eleven. I really want you to come as I can't get out of it and we've seen so little of each other lately, plus it might be fun. They also think I've invented you. I'll understand if you have something more important to do again.*

She ended the message with a sad emoticon. Meredith had turned down her last four offers of a social life for one reason or another, and he knew he'd be pushing his luck with a fifth. He tapped out his response.

*How could I refuse x*

Shoulders slouched and his frown now permanent, he left his office. He raised his hand to wave, but didn't speak to the team as he left.

"Where does he keep disappearing to?" Rawlings asked Trump, who shrugged.

"Not sure, old chap, but he'll tell us when he's ready."

Trump pulled his jacket on. Tom Seaton had told him about the information Meredith had withheld, and about his conduct in the interview with Myshkin. Trump had been shocked, but told Seaton that the boys from London would be pulling the strings, and that he shouldn't read too much into it. He wasn't comfortable though. Meredith seemed to be carrying an awful lot of secrets with him, and it seemed they were taking their toll.

Meredith and Patsy arrived home at the same time. She hadn't yet read his response, and threw her arms around him when he confirmed he would escort her to the meeting.

"Blimey, I'd have come for the pizza if I'd known that would be the response." He kissed her forehead. "I have to warn you, I've had a long, hard and very irritating day. They'd better be gentle with me."

"I'm sure they will be. They've organised transport to pick up everyone that's going, so at least we'll both be able to have a drink."

An hour later Patsy walked into the bedroom. She smiled as Meredith finished buttoning his shirt. His long legs looked even longer in the faded blue jeans, and the deep blue of the linen shirt flattered his complexion.

"You look good, a little more relaxed too. You'll need a jacket or sweater; it might get cold later. It was freezing by nine o'clock last time." She ran her eyes round the bedroom. "Have you had a personality transplant? Not only are you ready on time, but you've hung up your suit, and put the rest in the laundry basket. Only your new tie," she pointed to a red and blue polka dot tie on the end of the bed, "gives any indication you've been here. You'll have to come home early more often."

"Don't be cheeky, I can still change my mind. I'd forgotten you'd been to speedway before, was it any good?"

"That was over a month ago, and now you're asking." She cuffed him playfully. "Not my thing, but it was quite exciting when Stephen and Jake were racing."

"Hmm, I'm looking forward to meeting them. Perhaps I'll get the bug."

Meredith's words didn't ring true and Patsy shook her head.

"Don't force it, Meredith, the fact that you're coming will suffice." A horn tooted outside. "That'll be our lift, come on."

A dozen or so staff, including Abigail Ward and Clive Jenson, were already on the small coach. Clive was a cheerful soul and worked closely with Stephen Hatton. They waved acknowledgement as Patsy and Meredith boarded. Abigail was playing mother, and as soon as the coach got underway she offered them a drink. Meredith accepted the can of beer gratefully.

"Thank you, I need this." He opened the can and took a swig. "So, what do you do, Abigail?"

"I work with the development team," Abigail responded modestly. "I'm usually found hunched over a microscope, all very boring. And what do you do, John?"

"Call me Meredith, everyone else does. I'm a copper."

If Meredith was surprised that Patsy hadn't shared his occupation he didn't show it. Clive twisted awkwardly in his seat to look at them.

"She's being modest. The woman is a genius. We'd not be this far if it wasn't for her." He looked shame-faced as Abigail tutted and shook her head at him. He placed a finger on his lips. "But mum's the word. Mustn't talk out of school, walls have ears and all that." He turned back around and took a sip of his beer.

Abigail leaned towards Patsy. "Can't hold his drink. I'll have to keep an eye on him tonight."

The rest of the journey was uneventful. Meredith received and responded to a few texts, and had all but nodded off as they pulled into the carpark. As Abigail called the group together, and ushered them through the turnstiles, he wondered why he had come. Once in the noisy foyer, Abigail handed out programmes, told them where the various facilities were, and what time they should be back at the coach for departure. She led the way to the team's enclosure at the track edge. Stephen and Jake were there with the two other riders, and all tinkering with one of the four bikes lined up. Jake waved as the staff shuffled along the seating and settled themselves. Meredith and Patsy sat at the end of the second row back.

More beer was passed along the lines, and Abigail opened a small fridge installed at the front of the enclosure, and pulled out a bottle of wine. The speakers crackled into life, and the announcer boomed out that the first race would begin in fifteen minutes and riders should take their positions. The increase in noise as the bikes were fired up made any attempt at conversation pointless, and the smell of petrol fumes filled the air. Stephen looked over and smiled. He climbed over the barrier and walked towards Patsy. As he reached her he held out his hand to Meredith.

"You must be the infamous Meredith. I was beginning to think that Patsy had made you up to keep me at arm's length. Nice to meet you. I'm Stephen Hatton."

Meredith forced the return smile as he stood and shook Stephen's hand. He guessed that the handsome, thirty-something man in front of him liked to stir things up. Why else would he indicate that he had an interest in Patsy? Meredith didn't bite, nor was he sarcastic.

"No, I'm very real, and nice to meet you too. Thanks for inviting me." He nodded towards the track where the referee was calling the riders to take their position. "Are you not racing?"

"Not yet, I'm on in about half an hour. I should get suited up. I'll catch you later." He looked at Patsy. "Thanks for coming, Patsy, you look gorgeous as always." He turned and walked away.

"You didn't tell me he was a charmer, or that there was a necessity to keep him at arm's length." Meredith sat back down.

"He's not a charmer, and he's usually very focused on work," Patsy lied. "As to arm's length – he was joking, I'm sure."

"Not funny either then?" Meredith turned to look at her. He knew full well she was playing the situation down.

"As well as what?" Patsy frowned.

"He's not good-looking, and he's not funny."

A smile twitched and Patsy laughed.

"No, clearly not." She looked across to Abigail who was scanning the crowd behind. A frown appeared.

Meredith followed her line of sight. "Problems?" He placed his hand around her shoulder and gave her a squeeze. "You haven't told me what you're working on yet?"

"Mainly because you've been tied up with your own stuff, and you haven't asked. I'll fill you in later, but long story short, Abigail is sister to that bloke who was chatting Linda up online. She might have arranged to meet him here, and I have to try and get this onto her somehow."

Patsy opened her hand, and Meredith glanced at the small silver object.

"Bloke as in naughty nuclear scientist?"

Patsy felt Meredith stiffen. He'd clearly done his sums and reached the correct answer, but not the one he wanted. "Well, no wonder we haven't discussed this assignment." He glanced towards Stephen who, now suited, jumped over the barrier. "Hmm, Agent Hodge, is there anything else you want to tell me?"

"No, and I resent the question. You've not been too forthcoming yourself." Patsy patted his knee. "I'll tell you, if you tell me, Meredith. It's called simplicity, but you don't seem to like the simple life, not when you can complicate it."

She felt no guilt at not having told Meredith she'd taken the assignment; she knew there would be no way he'd ever consult her about taking a case, and he had yet to mention he was currently working with an outside team.

Meredith, however, did feel guilty. He thought about the photographs, and how much complication they would bring: there was nothing simple about them. He clasped her hand and pulled her towards him. Kissing her, he took the bug from her hand.

"You'd get bored if I was simple," he murmured as he pulled his mouth away and got to his feet. "Leave this with me."

He walked briskly across to Abigail, who was clapping frantically as Jake had won the first race and the team had been awarded the highest points. Meredith watched as the second Hatton brother pulled off his helmet and pushed his bike back towards them. Meredith draped a casual hand around Abigail's shoulder.

"I know I should have been listening, and that I deserve a slapped wrist, but which was the quickest way to the gents? I see your boy won; your hands must be sore." Meredith held her gaze and watched the flush rise to her cheeks before she smiled.

"'Our boy', Meredith, not mine." She turned, his arm still enclosing her, and pointed behind him. "Now if you go back to . . ."

She began the complicated instructions and Meredith frowned.

"I think it might be easier if I follow the signs. No disrespect, Abigail, I know you are a highly educated woman, and very bright, but you've got the female gene that doesn't allow you to do simple directions."

Patsy watched in amazement, and wished she could hear what was being said, as Abigail flushed again, and pushed Meredith in the chest playfully. Shrugging out from under his arm, she took his hand and pulled him out of the enclosure. He winked as he passed Patsy. Seeing Patsy was on her own, Stephen Hatton made his way across to her.

"One down. The pressure is on you now, you need to mirror Jake's performance," she teased as he took Meredith's seat.

"Oh, I will, and faster. I've given my bike a little tweak, but all within the regulations of course. You've lost your man, I see."

"Only for a while." She pursed her lips as Stephen leaned back in the chair, and draped his arm over the back of her seat. She shuffled forward a little. "When did you say you were on?"

Hatton laughed. "Ten minutes or so, they'll call me in a moment. Why did you move away from me? Is Meredith the jealous type?" His eyes sparkled with mischief.

"All men are the jealous type – it comes with the chest-beating. But would that worry him? No, because he knows he can trust me. I'm a one-man woman."

Hatton laughed again. "I'm very glad to hear it, and clearly you trust him too because he seemed very friendly with Abigail."

"He's a very friendly man. Even if he was interested, I think Abigail's affections lie elsewhere."

A horn hooted and an announcement came over the speakers. The next riders were asked to take their positions. Stephen ran his hand down her back before patting it.

"That's my call, wish me luck." He hurried over to his bike, pausing only to give his brother a high five as he arrived back at the enclosure. Patsy watched him manoeuvre his bike to the starting position. She jumped as Meredith appeared and reclaimed his seat.

"Mission accomplished. It's in her cardigan pocket, which was the best I could do without seriously interfering with her clothes. She will probably discover it, so you'll have to keep your fingers crossed."

Patsy leaned forward and looked around. "Where is she now?" She squinted at the huddle of people at the rear of seating area, but couldn't see Abigail or her brother.

"She went into the ladies. I see your boss is ready to go." Stephen was at the starting line. A few of the staff gave him the thumbs up, and his brother saluted him. "Why the green helmet? It clashes with his suit."

"I don't know, I wondered that last time. We'll have to ask." Patsy's eyes moved away from Stephen and began scanning the crowds again. She spotted Lyndon Ward leaning against a vending machine, and he too was scanning the crowd. Abigail approached him and he beamed at her. They embraced and made their way further back from the arena.

"I'll leave you to it, if you don't mind. I need to see where Abigail and Lyndon go, and let the powers that be know they should be able to monitor her."

Patsy was whispering close to his ear. He turned his head and kissed her.

"Don't be long. It's bad enough having to be here, but I took solace in the fact I'd be with you."

His smile fell away as she made her way through the crowd that had surged forward in anticipation of the next race. He knew he had to tell her, but where did he start? He didn't think she'd believe him; he wouldn't if roles were reversed. He sighed as Clive appeared in his line of sight interrupting his musings.

"You might want to come closer," Clive invited him. "Stephen is racing a life-time enemy, and it usually gets quite hairy. It's exciting stuff."

The two men made their way trackside, and took up position a little behind Jake. The race got underway with a squealing of tyres, and the roar of the engines. Stephen held off his rival by half a bike length on the first lap, and as they began the second, his rear wheel was tapped by the other bike. It was clear he was struggling to maintain control as he rounded the next corner.

"He didn't brake," Meredith observed. "Unless I was mistaken, he accelerated."

"The bikes don't have brakes. They control speed with the accelerator, and he wouldn't have let up with Harry on his tail, that would have been suicide," Clive remarked before shouting at Stephen to give it some.

Meredith watched the two contenders battle it out; the other two riders were not in the race at all. They rode perilously close to each other, and just as Meredith thought it was a disaster waiting to happen, the two bikes or riders, he couldn't quite make out which, appeared to have become fused. At the next bend, with all control lost, they were hurtling along the ground and heading for the barrier, which should have stopped them. It didn't; it crumpled, and the spectators behind ran for their lives. Clive had his hand over his mouth as the pair dragged a chunk of metal through the seating area before eventually grinding to a halt.

"Oh dear," Meredith muttered.

"Stephen won't like that," Clive shouted above the warning siren blaring out behind them. "He won't like that at all. I told you." His eyes widened as he watched the riders.

Stephen pulled himself away from the wreckage before helping his opponent to his feet. Both men removed their helmets and looked at the damage surrounding them as fire marshals and first aid personnel raced over to them. Without warning, Stephen turned back and punched Harry in the face. Taken unawares, Harry fell backwards. A security guard grabbed Stephen's arm, but he shook it away. Walking to the prostate Harry, Stephen leaned forward and told him exactly what he thought of him, before storming away and back towards the enclosure. Jake ran to meet him.

"I see your boss has a temper," Meredith observed.

"On occasion; he doesn't like cheats," Abigail told him as she scurried towards Stephen. Awkwardly, she climbed over the barrier and waited with Jake for Stephen to arrive. When he did, her words were few, and she ran her hands all over his body.

"She's a game girl." Meredith nudged Clive. "What's all that about? It seems she's more concerned with his suit than she is with him."

"She can see he's all right, but he's wearing the latest model and she's checking for damage."

"I can't see any, but there must be some." Meredith stepped to one side to get a better view. "Well, what can you say?" He watched in surprise as Abigail unzipped the suit and pulled it down until Stephen's torso was visible. She ran her hands over his flesh, occasionally pausing for his comments. Once satisfied, she nodded at Clive with a broad smile, and hurried away.

"Now where's she going?"

"She's meeting someone. Didn't say who, probably a friend." Clive waved to Stephen who was beckoning him. "Excuse me, duty calls."

Patsy stood to one side and smiled at Abigail. "Everything all right? I only saw the end result, not what happened."

"All fine, absolutely fine, thank God. See you back at the bus,"

As Patsy joined Meredith, she could hear Stephen cursing. She didn't catch what was said, but both Jake and Clive helped him out of the bottom half of his suit. He stood in his boxers examining the suit with Clive. Jake was shaking his head. Meredith slipped his arm around her shoulder.

"Your boss had an accident. How did you get on?"

"So I see, and all's well. The bug is working and they are monitoring her conversation." She paused. "Thank you for that, because now I'm dismissed for the day. Free," she smiled.

"If we weren't here I could think of a number of options, but as we are, is there a bar?"

"I think so, but should we not at least pretend to watch this?" She had missed the announcement about the result of Stephen's race, and the next was being called. One of the other riders took his bike to the start.

"They won't miss us. Come on, let's go."

Meredith gave her a tug and she followed him out of the enclosure. When they reached the bar, most of its customers had left to watch the next race, it was easy to get both a drink, and a table overlooking the track.

Once settled, Meredith took her hand. "Is this assignment dangerous?" He held her gaze. His eyes squinted in an attempt to gauge the honesty of her response.

Patsy shook her head. "Boring. Although I have had, or should say, am having a crash course in handling various guns. I hate it, but as they are developing body armour it sort of comes with the territory, however, when I'm working I only type about them. There are guns on the premises but I've not seen them."

"So, it's an open secret, this material they're developing," Meredith observed.

Patsy sipped her drink and nodded. "Between you and me, I think they are further ahead than they're letting on. Stephen dictates his reports in advance, and I ping them out when told to." She twirled her glass around on the coaster. "What about you? I hear you're working with some team from London. Dangerous?"

"Yep. In more ways than one, but you know the rules. If I tell you . . . and all that."

"How dangerous?" Patsy pressed.

"I don't know." He reached and took her hand, "And not being soppy, Patsy, don't lose faith in me, whatever happens."

Patsy pulled her hand away.

Meredith closed his eyes and sighed. "What?" he demanded.

"That's twice, this *whatever happens* business. I don't like it. Give me a clue as to what might?" She rolled her eyes as Meredith shrugged, and she pinched her thumb and forefinger together. "A little clue at least."

"I'm playing with some dangerous characters: people with secrets, and people who don't want me asking questions, and who wouldn't think twice about trying to bring me down in whatever way they can."

"I'm worried, Meredith, and you are doing little to dispel any concerns. In fact, they've doubled."

Meredith emptied his glass. He stood and went to the bar and ordered another without responding.

When he returned, she spoke quietly, "Tell me you're being careful."

"I'm trying." Meredith's smile was brief. "Now, let's stop talking shop, and . . . I spoke too soon."

Patsy followed his gaze. Abigail and Lyndon Ward entered the bar. Patsy waved. Abigail returned the gesture but turned her back to them as she waited for Lyndon to order their drinks. Once served, they moved to the furthest table and seated themselves.

"Must be something we said," remarked Patsy. "The smell of frying onions is killing me, shall we grab a burger?"

Meredith stood and picked up his drink. "Come on, before the crowd get there."

The rest of the evening passed without incident. Abigail's brother departed, and she returned to join the group, clearly buoyed up by the meeting. Stephen's opponent had been disqualified for dangerous driving, and the team won the overall event. Everyone had a little too much to drink. Meredith was glad that they were the first to be dropped off, and that the Hattons had not joined them on the return journey. He wasn't sure if it was simply Stephen Hatton's obvious interest in Patsy, but he couldn't take to the man. His words and gestures portrayed one thing, but his eyes held secrets. Meredith didn't like a man who couldn't look him in the eye honestly. When he put his key in the front door he was more than glad to be home.

As he lay in bed listening to Patsy cleaning her teeth, he wondered whether to ask her to stop working for whichever department it was pulling the strings. He snorted to himself, as he realised he didn't know who was pulling his, and his eyes travelled to the wardrobe which held his suit and the envelope containing the photographs. He would destroy them in the morning. He threw back the quilt as Patsy entered the bedroom.

"Come here, Hodge."

7

Patsy groaned as Meredith's phone rang. Pulling the duvet over her head, she rolled away from him as he cursed and reached for the phone. Looking at the screen he saw it was Trump calling.

"What time is it?" he snapped. He listened to Trump's apology and the reason for the call. Swinging his legs out of bed he sat up. "Who called it in?" He nodded as Trump explained. "Where is he now?" He walked to the bathroom as he continued the conversation. "Okay, keep him there. Give Sherlock a ring and tell him I'll come and see the body first, and then get over to you and speak to Mr Liska. Make him comfortable."

Meredith balanced the phone on the edge of the basin and stared at his bleary eyes in the mirror. He hadn't expected that twist, and hoped they hadn't been the cause. He took a cold shower, and rather than wake Patsy, he quietly lifted the clothes he had worn the night before from the back of the chair, and closed the door softly behind him.

Twenty minutes later he strolled into the morgue. Frankie Callaghan was examining the corpse and dictating into the overhead microphone. He obscured Meredith's view of the body.

"Morning, Sherlock, is the coffee on? I hope that's mine you're working on. I don't want to be hanging around." His tone held a cheeriness he didn't feel.

Frankie glanced over his shoulder. "Yes, to both. I'm fine, Meredith, how are you?" Frankie measured the depth of the lacerations across the breasts of the woman on the table in front of him. "When I heard this was your case I thought I'd make a start. Too awake to go back to bed now anyway. You might want to get that coffee before you look, and white with no sugar for me."

Frankie pulled the microphone closer. "Eleven separate lacerations across the left breast, cuts are no deeper than five millimetres indicating they were not delivered in haste, they are also neat and there is no tearing of the skin. Whoever did this, did it deliberately and in a controlled manner, as with the cuts to the face."

Meredith swallowed and walked back out through the clear plastic doors. He walked briskly to the kitchen area and poured two mugs of coffee. He took a large swig of his and gasped as the burning fluid scorched his throat before topping it up and returning to Frankie.

"I know you're in the middle of this, but give me the basics. I'll put yours here." He placed the mug on the corner of the tray holding the gruesome-looking appliances that were the tools of Frankie's trade, and took a quick glance at the body of Elena, Ronnie Bishop's former flatmate, and cousin to Jan Liska. His nose wrinkled and he made his way to the side of the room and sat on a stool.

"She's been dead at least five hours, and she must have over fifty lacerations, mainly to her face, chest and abdomen. Marks on her wrists indicate that she had been tethered to the chair found at the scene, but no ligature was found. I've taken some fibres from the region and should be able to let you know what it was in the fullness of time." He glanced pointedly at Meredith. "In short, she's been tortured. You'll be interested in the wounds on her right hand – some sort of symbol or lettering. Would you like to see?"

"Not until I've finished this. What killed her?"

"I've only had her an hour, but my guess is the slit that runs from ear to ear." Frankie pulled off his gloves, dropped them into a bucket, and lifted his coffee. "Give me a couple of hours and I'll confirm. I need to get the injuries catalogued before I open her up." He smiled at Meredith's expression. "You're more queasy than normal, are you off-colour? How's Patsy by the way? Sarah said they had a nice lunch last week."

Meredith gave a slight smile. That sentence would normally have ended with "we should get together" or similar, but Frankie had once been looking for a relationship with Patsy, and her involvement with Meredith had put paid to his plans. At the time, Frankie was working closely with Meredith's team, and it was he who spotted the connection that helped solve the case, and earned him the nickname of Sherlock. While Frankie was madly in love with his fiancé, Sarah, and no longer had an interest, he'd always thought Patsy could have done better than Meredith, and they all knew it.

Feeling mischievous, Meredith nodded. "She's well, thank you, Sherlock. I hear Sarah has big plans for the wedding. We should get together before the big day, less than a month to go."

He laughed out loud as Frankie choked on his coffee.

"Good God, Meredith, was that a social invitation? Is it April Fool's day?" Frankie drained his mug, pulled a fresh pair of gloves from the box, and went back to the body. "You'll have me welling up if you carry on like that."

"I can do social. I'm being trained."

Finishing his drink, Meredith stepped closer to the body. He'd not met Elena, but he'd seen her photograph. She'd been a pretty girl and now her face resembled a hideous gargoyle that bore little resemblance to the picture pinned on the board in the incident room.

He sighed. "Let's see her hand." Pulling his phone from his pocket he took a photograph of the marks on the girl's hand. "Anything on the other one?"

"No. I'm about to crack open the chest, and as I don't want this poor girl covered in vomit, did you want anything else?"

"No, just the full report ASAP. Lean back."

Frankie stepped back and Meredith took a picture of the facial injuries.

"I'll get these photos up. That'll make the team a little keener to catch the bastard. Thanks, Sherlock, don't forget to call."

It was almost six-thirty when Meredith arrived in the incident room, and Rawlings and Trump were eating doughnuts from a paper bag.

"I'll have mine with coffee. Dave, I've emailed you some photos; get them printed before the rest arrive."

Trump disappeared and returned with a coffee for Meredith, who instructed him to repeat what he already knew, then took a doughnut from the bag and bit into it.

"The station took a call from Jan Liska at around two-thirty. He didn't call emergency services, he called the station and asked for Dave because he knew Elena had spoken to him. The desk sergeant –"

"To the chase, Trump, cut to the chase. That poor bloke has been waiting hours." Meredith took another doughnut.

"Dave called me and we went to the flat. Other than the blood from her wounds, everything was neat and tidy. Nothing had been stolen, damaged or even disturbed according to Mr Liska. There was no forced entry so she had let her assailant in. The forensic team are on their way, but I doubt they'll find much. Liska says he knows who did it, but will only speak to the boss."

"That's because he's a wise man."

Rawlings handed the printed-off photos to Meredith. Meredith retained the one of the hand, and passed the other back. "No need for him to look at that twice. What do you think this is?" He held up the photograph in his hand and the others peered at it.

"It's letters, isn't it?" Rawlings tilted his head. "I reckon A, C and T. What do you think, Louie?"

Trump took the image from Meredith and studied it closely.

"Possibly, could be some form of symbol; a question mark?" Trump shrugged

"You could be right. Okay, let's get on with it. Rawlings, type up a report ready for briefing, and Trump, you come with me."

Jan Liska looked up as they entered the interview room. His eyes searched their faces. They observed his clenched fists, and saw the tension in his body.

Meredith pulled out a chair. "I'm sorry to keep you, Mr Liska, but I needed some information before we spoke." He placed the photograph face down on the table.

"You are the boss?" Liska spoke quickly and quietly.

"I am. I'm DCI John Meredith. I'm sorry about your cousin, it must have been a shock. If it's all right with you, although my colleague here will take notes, we will tape this meeting." Meredith placed his hand on the recorder, and pushed the button when Liska nodded.

"Good, because I need promises from you." Liska leaned forward, resting his forearms on the table.

"What promises would they be?"

Meredith sat back in his chair, leaving his hands, fingers linked, on the table.

"You will make me disappear, give me a new life, and I will tell you what I know. What I know you want."

"And what do I want, Mr Liska, other than to catch the murderer of your cousin Elena, and your secret lover Ronnie Bishop? Did they die because of you?"

Meredith saw the twitch of Trump's head. He knew Trump would think he was being heavy-handed, and perhaps he was, but Liska had clearly thought about this conversation and what he wanted from it. Meredith saw no reason to tiptoe around the matter.

"Ronnie did, but she didn't tell; that's why I sit here now. But Elena died because of you – you and DC Rawlings. They knew she'd spoken to him, and they needed to find out what she told him. What she knew."

He shook his head, "I didn't even know what she knew: it was our rule, it kept us safe. But she knew about me and Ronnie and may have told them. I saw what they did to her." He closed his eyes and bowed his head for a while. Meredith allowed him a moment. When he looked up he said simply, "I won't do it anymore. I will give you them. I know their secrets." He looked directly into Meredith's eyes. "But you have to tell me first, confirm for this," Liska tapped the recorder, "that you will protect me."

Meredith shot a glance at Trump, and pursed his lips as he considered his response. "If you need our protection you will have it. But for me to assess that, I need to know who we are talking about, and what your information relates to."

He watched the tension build in Liska's features. Liska sucked in his bottom lip and chewed on it. He was concerned that he would say too much.

"For starters, I know who killed Ronnie and Elena."

"Yes, you indicated that, but do you have proof? Look, Mr Liska, I know you may think you know something, and you may even be right, but without proof there is little I can do. And I certainly can't offer protection on a hunch."

Liska gave a slight nod of the head in understanding. "Okay, I see that. I can tell you about the drugs, the women, the gambling. All of it." He shrugged. "Not all in detail, but," he lowered his voice, "I know their secret, I know where the bodies are buried. Now, is that enough?"

"When you say where the bodies are buried, are we speaking actual or metaphorical?" Trump joined the conversation.

"We are talking real dead people. Why would I say so, if it were not so?" Liska looked confused.

"Because the phrase, '*I know where the bodies are buried*', is used to indicate some wrongdoing, but not necessarily actual bodies," Trump explained patiently.

"Thank you, Trump." Meredith felt excitement building inside; this could be the break he needed, and he didn't need Trump educating people and delaying that. "And who are *they*?" he pressed.

Liska tapped the recorder again. "First you promise." He sucked his lip in again as Meredith shook his head.

"No, Mr Liska, first the names." Meredith leaned back against the chair. "You have to give me more than promises to get one in return."

After a few minutes Liska pulled a pack of cigarettes from his shirt pocket. "May I?"

Meredith nodded and got him a plastic cup which he filled with a few inches of water from the water cooler. He ignored Trump's sigh.

"Ashtray," he stated, placing the cup in front of Liska. "Only the one cigarette – that's illegal now, and Trump doesn't approve." Meredith watched Liska light up, and resisted the urge to ask for one. "You were going to give us the names." He sniffed in a deep breath as Liska tilted his head and blew a plume of smoke into the air.

Taking another drag, Liska looked at him and spoke quickly, "Names only, then you promise, or I will go. Andronikov, Myshkin, and Roper. Those will do to start with." Liska blew out the smoke and dropped the cigarette into the water. He folded his arms across his chest, and drew his mouth into a thin line. He was clearly determined not to say more.

Meredith bit his lip to avoid the smile he knew was waiting to escape. "And these people are breaking the law? They have literally buried some bodies, and killed Ronnie and Elena?" He held his breath. Liska didn't speak, but nodded his head and pointed at the recorder. Meredith got the message. "Mr Liska, I'm going to leave you for a moment to find out what I can do for you. I wouldn't want to make promises I couldn't keep. Can I get you anything while you wait?"

"No thank you."

Meredith switched off the recorder and followed Trump out into the corridor, closing the door quietly. He walked several steps away from the door and punched the air. "Yes!" He hissed the word through his teeth.

Trump grinned at him. "Well, that was a stroke of luck, notwithstanding that poor girl, of course, but this should see everything wrapped up neatly, assuming he's telling the truth. He needs a solicitor now, sir, you know that."

"Sod the solicitor for a moment, we can sort that later. Find out who the fuck Roper is? We've not heard his name before, have we?"

Trump shook his head. "Not that I know of."

"Well, get back to the incident room and get onto it. Find out if we've missed something. I've got a call to make, and then we need to keep him talking before he gets cold feet. I'll be on the fire escape – I need a smoke now too."

Meredith walked off in the opposite direction to Trump. He couldn't believe their luck, he thought he'd be working this case for months. As he pushed the door open he racked his memory for any knowledge of a Roper, but none was forthcoming. He didn't mind because with Liska ready to talk, all would be revealed shortly. As he lit his cigarette a small smile lightened his features, and he tapped the phone on the railing of the fire escape, wanting to enjoy the cigarette before he had the conversation. When he did call, the phone went through to the answer service and he shook his head in disbelief. He left a message: "Meredith here. I have someone that says they can give us what we want. Call me quickly before he dries up." Knowing Trump would be some time, he lit another cigarette.

In the interview room, Jan Liska stared at the back of the photograph. His fingers slowly crept towards it. Placing his index finger in the centre of the sheet, he pulled it towards him and slowly turned it over. He looked at it and bowed his head: his worst fears had been confirmed, and he'd come too far to turn back.

Trump waited patiently while the few members of the team who had arrived searched their notes for mention of a man called Roper. When they had all given a negative response, he wrote the name on the incident board.

"When the others come in, get them to look too. It's a long shot, I know, and it may be that we find out what we want from this Liska chap." He paused. "We're dealing with some nasty individuals here. I'd like to think the fact that Liska is speaking to us stays within this office. Who knows if we can offer him the protection he will need?"

He shrugged. "And on that note, there's a duty solicitor in the building. I've asked her to wait, so I'd better go and tell DCI Meredith. I'm not sure how long we'll be, so get on with what you were already working on, and the briefing will be as and when we finish."

He left the team to their work and hurried past the interview room in search of Meredith. As he reached the door to the fire escape he heard a phone ring, and Meredith snap his name.

"Meredith. Yes, I was being serious. Jan Liska says he knows who killed the two girls. I take it you know about Ronnie Bishop's flatmate?" There was a pause. "He also says he knows where they buried the bodies. He will give me Andronikov, the Myshkins, and some bloke called Roper. What? Did that touch a nerve? Anyway, I haven't got time for idle chat, Liska might change his mind. What he wants in return is protection. I'm going to agree. If that's wrong and you have other plans for him so be it, but I need to keep him talking."

There was a long pause, and on the other side of the door Trump wondered if he should make his presence known. While he considered this, Meredith added something which caught his attention, and he stood still, his hand on the push bar of the door. "Oh yes, and one other thing, I've received some rather unwelcome photographs which mustn't go public. You'll need to deal with that, then we need to meet. I'll call you later." There was a pause as Meredith listened to the caller. "Well, I can't sort it from here, not without it getting messy. It will draw too much attention to me if Liska is genuine. I'm sure the team are already wondering."

Trump had heard enough, he pushed open the door as though he had just arrived.

"Sir, nothing on Roper . . . Oh sorry." Trump's acting was proficient.

"Got to go, I'll call later." Meredith hung up. As he did so a text arrived from Patsy. Ignoring it, he slid the phone into his pocket and smiled at Trump. "Come on, old chap, we're going to tell him what he wants to hear." He frowned at Trump's expression. "What's that look for?"

"What he wants to hear or what we are going to do?" Trump questioned, and deciding to tip the scales in Liska's favour, he added, "I've told the duty solicitor she'll be needed. Shall I go and fetch her so we can get on?"

Meredith rolled his eyes. "It's the same thing, isn't it? Why did you get the solicitor? He hasn't asked for one, and we don't know that he needs one yet."

"I know, but better safe than sorry, or we could regret it," Trump replied. "It wouldn't do to get our fingers burned."

Meredith shook his head as he followed Trump back along the corridor. Trump was such an old woman sometimes, and that did tend to complicate things.

"You go and get the brief, and I'll tell him she's coming. And don't worry, I won't do or say anything more until she arrives."

Five minutes later, Trump came into the interview room with Jane Roscoe. Meredith and Liska looked up expectantly.

Jane Roscoe smiled briefly. "Have you been speaking to my client alone, Meredith?"

There was little conviction in her question, as she knew Meredith would lie even if he had been. Meredith stared at her and smiled. Her petite frame, and wild mop of red hair, made her look more like a schoolgirl than an efficient brief. Meredith liked Jane Roscoe, despite the fact she often worked against him. She was wise enough to know when not to labour a point, and acute enough to protect her clients from themselves. She was straight down the middle, and had refused to represent several less savoury criminals as she knew them to be guilty of horrible crimes, and would not be responsible for allowing them back out on the street. Meredith respected that. He also enjoyed the fact that, when not in the interview room, he was able to fluster her.

"Ms Roscoe, Jane, I am offended. But as you look particularly lovely today, I will forgive you."

He winked and she turned away, unable to hold back her smile. Stepping neatly into the interview room, she closed the door behind her.

Twenty minutes later Jane Roscoe had taken formal instruction from her new client, and the interview began.

"You have told us that you have information about the criminal activities of men called Andronikov, Myshkin and Roper. You indicated that these included murder, and that you know where the bodies of the victims are buried. To ensure we are absolutely certain that we know who you are speaking about, I'd like you to identify them from these pictures."

Meredith began to take the first photograph from the file and he frowned. What had he done with the picture of Elena's hand? He looked to see if it had slipped from the desk. Liska pointed to the corner of the room behind the door.

"It's over there."

Both Meredith and Trump turned to look, and Jane Roscoe leaned forward as Trump went to retrieve the crumpled image. He flattened it out on the table.

"Do you know what this means?" Trump asked.

"Of course. It is the sign they use here." He said something in Russian, which none of the others understood.

"In English please, Mr Liska." Trump smiled at him. "If we need an interpreter we can arrange one, but if you can use English so much the better."

Jane Roscoe smiled as Meredith rolled his eyes.

"No, no. I'm sorry. The Hammer and Sickle, it's the sign they use to show their presence. Written on notes, painted on walls, and carved into skin. It's a warning."

"Who are 'they'?" Meredith leaned forward.

"The men you mentioned, and more. They are many."

Meredith handed him the first photo. "Do you know this man?"

Liska nodded and pointed to the recorder. "Your promise, please. First you make your promise for the recorder and the lady."

"Yes, DCI Meredith, before my client gives you what information he has, I think we should clarify what will be done to protect him." Jane Roscoe repositioned her pad, and was surprised when Meredith did as requested. No quip, no irritation, simply a statement of fact.

"Of course. Mr Liska, I confirm that should you provide us with the information you say you can, you will enter the witness protection system, and once these men have been convicted, you will be given a new identity. Is that a good enough promise for you?"

Liska looked at Jane Roscoe who nodded. She didn't always like Meredith, but knew him to be a man of his word. Liska turned back to Meredith.

"It is. That man is Ivor Andronikov. In this country, he is a businessman. His interests are many, but include drugs, prostitutes, and now, I believe, murder."

"Who do you believe he killed?" Meredith folded his arms, his fists clenched beneath his elbows, and he fought to control his reaction to the statement.

"Elena. Possibly Veronika, although most likely he wouldn't have done it himself but he would have given the order."

"So it's just a hunch? It's what you think, not what you know."

"It is with those two"

Liska lowered his head and drew in a breath to give himself the strength to talk about them. "He used to beat Veronika. At first, she came to me to protect her. I couldn't, but I gave her support, and over time we became lovers. She left him to come to me, she made him throw her out, but I knew he would never allow that, so she went to live with Elena. We continued to be a couple in secret, until Myshkin found out she had a lover."

"Which Myshkin?"

"Filipp." The name was spat from his lips as though causing him pain. "He didn't know who, but he overheard her speaking to me on the phone when she was at the club with Elena. He waited until she hung up and then snatched up the phone. He told her he had got my number and that she should be nice to him." Liska's eyes clouded. "She became his woman. I was still there, and in his arrogance, he told her many things, many secrets, which she shared with me." He paused as Meredith held his hand up.

"To clarify, did he or didn't he, know it was you?"

"No. But we only know that because nothing happened to me. I went away for a few months and nothing, so I came back. I couldn't leave her, you see."

"And Andronikov? He was okay with her being with Myshkin but not you?"

"Myshkin has something on him. He told Veronika a tale about what they did while working for a special unit of the Russian army, while they occupied Czechoslovakia. They were both young. He told her the power ran away with them, and they killed several men and one of them was important. They hid the bodies, but there was uproar at the time. The Russians were accused, but no bodies, no blame. Their unit was disbanded several months later, and the Russians eventually pulled out in 1991. My country was free, and the world had changed, finding the missing men not so urgent. Myshkin told her where they buried them, and that there would be political trouble if they were ever discovered."

"This was before 1991. I'm sorry Jan, may I call you Jan?" Meredith smiled as Liska nodded. "My history on Eastern Europe at that time is vague at best. If all this happened before 1991, surely even if the bodies are discovered, how would they connect them to that unit after all this time?"

"I don't know the exact date – it was in the late seventies I believe

– but I know Andronikov left something behind, I don't know what, but they were many kilometres away by the time he realised, and it was too risky to go back."

"Why did Myshkin tell Ronnie this? Do you have the name of the important man they killed? I'm sorry, but it seems an odd thing to do."

"I don't know his name, and if either of the two girls did, they didn't tell me. He told Veronika all this to prove he had power over Andronikov; she was convinced Andronikov would kill them. I do know that this important man they killed was an uncle to someone serving under Brezhnev. He was a young man then, and is still an advisor to the government: a clever man, a man with power. He would see Andronikov punished. He made a lot of noise at the time, but with no proof what could he do? He made sure their unit was no more. So, you see, Andronikov is worried, concerned that no one must ever know."

Liska pulled his cigarette packet from his shirt pocket and lit another cigarette. Meredith shrugged as Trump tutted.

"Okay, Brezhnev with the eyebrows, I remember him I think, and while I will look into this I can't see how it will help. Crimes committed in Eastern Europe back in the seventies won't help much with the problems these men are causing here." Meredith gave an apologetic grimace.

"Oh, but they will. I assure you, these men won't live long if the truth gets out. The man in Russia, he is old now I think, so it is important that you act quickly if you want a result."

Trump threw his hands into the air. "Mr Liska, what we want is less drug dealing, extortion, and prostitution on the streets of this country. We couldn't possibly sanction opening doors that may lead to the unlawful execution of these men." Trump shook his head. "What can you tell us about what goes on here?"

"Much, but I want them dead, not in one of your comfortable prison cells. I saw what they did to Elena and I don't want to see what they did to Veronika; I'm guessing it was as bad." He sighed as Trump nodded, unable to tell Liska it was probably worse. "Then you will understand me."

Meredith tapped his pen on the desk. "Okay, okay. We can sort out the whys and wherefores afterwards, but what we need to do now is collect as much information as possible. Let's stay with the bodies: do you know where they are buried?"

Meredith resisted the urge to tut as Liska shook his head.

"No, but I know the answer is in her flat somewhere safe. Elena told me it was her protection. The flat was tidy, they didn't find it. She probably never used it. I will find it for you."

"You're Czechoslovakian I believe, how did you become involved with these men?" Meredith moved the conversation on, but made a note to call the team working the scene.

"I was for a few years," Liska smiled, "I'm now Slovakian. I came to follow my sister and cousin. They came here and lost touch with our family. My sister returned shortly afterwards, shamed by the profession she had been forced to take. We never speak of it. Elena wouldn't go home, and introduced me to these men because they needed people to help protect their girls. I was ideal as I spoke several languages and I was family, which means I would be good at my job."

"Your job being to make sure punters don't rough up the girls?" Meredith jotted something down.

"Yes, I also treat them if they have medical issues, and am assigned the odd errand."

"Medical issues?" Trump interjected. "Why would they not see a doctor?"

"I am a doctor. I was newly qualified when I came here, and some of the injuries and diseases these girls pick up, they would not want to be seen by any official doctor."

"Where do you get the medication from?" Trump asked.

"Everything is available at a price. Even me. Clever, proud, Jan Liska. The money and life for me here is far better than at home. My family think I am a doctor here, which I am, but not in the way they think. If they come to visit I have a nice home, and lots of money." He shrugged. "I have come too far down a bad road to go back."

"You can give us detail on the prostitutes, and . . ." Meredith couldn't finish the sentence.

"No, not prostitutes as you mean. These girls are educated and bright; they are expensive and have nice homes. Escorts, I think you call them, they do not walk the street. They are clean."

Liska was clearly defending his dead cousin's memory and Meredith let it drop.

"I see. What about the drugs? How much do you know?"

"A little. I know who delivers the smaller packages. Some of the girls are users, though most not. Their clients use them though. I know where they pick them up as I've had to do it myself on occasion, and I think I know the names of some of the others involved. The girls, they speak to me."

Meredith was unsure as to whether Liska was complicit in the girls' fate or not. He could see how he was attracted to the money, and how at least they were provided with decent medical care, but he couldn't see how anyone, who would probably be able to work legally with the skills Liska claimed to have, would do what he did. Why didn't he use the information to bring Andronikov and his henchmen down himself? That way they would all be free of him. His face hardened.

"Okay, we'll get to that later, but tell me something, Liska." He saw Jane Roscoe raise her head, as he had not called him by his first name, or given him a title, she knew something had changed. "Why didn't you use the information about the burial site? Or convince the girls to if you didn't know. Why did you allow these men to continue to control your lives in such a way? I'm guessing you throw in the odd abortion."

Liska looked at his hands, and Trump shuffled in his seat. The distaste in Meredith's voice was obvious. This was not a way to get more information, as although they could stop Liska they still needed his co-operation.

After a few moments, Liska looked up. He placed his wrist on the middle of the table, his palm facing up, and unbuttoned the cuff of his shirt.

"Because I too am trapped; this information came too late." He rolled up his sleeve, and the marks from many years of drug abuse were evident. "I also use my groin, and even my feet." He stared at Meredith. "When the woman you love is forced to be with another man, you need escape to cope. This is how I coped. I now have an expensive habit, which I control, but which is paid for by others. Who else would employ me, in any capacity, and supply what I need?" His head dropped to his chest. "Let us move on, I am not proud of what I am."

"Before we do that, could we have a word, DCI Meredith?" Jane Roscoe smiled reassuringly at her client, and walked to the door.

Meredith put his hand on the recorder. "Of course. I need to do a few things anyway. Interview suspended at nine forty-five." He hit the switch to stop the recorder. "Trump, find out what Mr Liska wants to eat or drink."

Meredith stepped out of the room with Jane Roscoe, closing the door behind him.

She walked a little further along the corridor and turned to face him.

"Before we go any further, I think we need something official to protect my client. While I trust you, DCI Meredith, the information you are about to collect will put his life at risk. I fear he has said too much already, and I must make sure he is kept safe." She paused as the door opened and Trump joined them. "I suggest we take a break. You speak to whoever gave you clearance to offer protection, and let's get something in writing."

She smiled as Trump nodded in agreement. Meredith shook his head.

"Drop the title, Jane, you can call me Meredith." He winked, knowing she would flush and she did. "I'm glad you trust me, but not quite enough, it would seem. I'll make a call and see what I can do, but it could take hours with the red tape these things involve."

"Then it will be hours before I allow you to speak to my client again, Meredith." Jane Roscoe grinned as she walked back to the interview room. "I'll let my client know what's happening and make sure he doesn't speak to you before I give him the all-clear." She glanced at her watch. "I have to see another client at the office in an hour. I'll be back around two, unless you tell me that would be pointless. Don't question him, and please keep him safe in the interim."

She walked back into the room and closed the door behind her.

Meredith looked at Trump. "I like her: she's a pain in the arse, but I still like her. I must be going soft in my old age."

"I doubt that very much, sir, if you don't mind me saying. Liska doesn't want anything, says the water will do, although now you've given him permission, he'll probably smoke himself to death."

"Talking of which, I'm going for a smoke. You get on to the team at Elena's place and tell them they are also looking for something which would indicate a secret location – you know what we want. In fact, brief Jo and Rawlings, get them over there." Trump confirmed he would and as he walked away, Meredith called to him, "I know I don't need to say this, but I will anyway. Don't let on to Rawlings that Liska holds him responsible."

"Of course I won't, sir."

"Have me a coffee waiting, I'll be there in five minutes." Meredith looked at his crumpled clothes, "I'll start the ball rolling on the paperwork, brief the team, then I think I'll go home to change."

"Probably best. You are looking rather casual: smart, but casual."

"Get the coffee, Trump." Meredith smiled as he turned and made his way to the fire escape. He dialled out and got the answer machine again.

"Do you lot ever answer the bloody phone?" he demanded. "If what he's said so far is anything to go by, our boy can take them down. His solicitor won't let him give details until she sees the papers though. Get one of your boys to sort out the necessary and call me back. Sooner rather than later would be nice."

Meredith terminated the call and lit his cigarette. Noticing the message he had yet to read, he opened Patsy's text and his heart skipped a beat.

*Hope all is OK. Am going to dry cleaners later, will take your grey suit, is there anything else you want cleaned? Love you. P x*

"Shit, shit, shit." Meredith's hand trembled as he tried to punch a coherent response. Patsy had texted several hours ago, he only hoped he wasn't too late.

*Need suit, on way to change now. Nothing else thanks.*

Flicking his cigarette into the carpark below, Meredith ran back along the corridor and into his office just as Trump placed a mug of coffee on the desk.

"Change of plan, Trump. I'm going to change first, give the powers that be a chance to sort the paperwork. You can take the briefing. I'll make a few notes on what I want you to cover and I'll shoot off."

"No problem, sir."

Meredith pulled a pad out and, in handwriting he hoped Trump could decipher, listed the action points he required. As he completed the last one, his phone rang. It was a number he didn't recognise and he frowned. He answered and barked his name.

"Oh dear, Meredith, you seem out of sorts. I do hope everything is well."

Meredith recognised the voice immediately, and he snarled into the phone. "Who is this?"

"Oh, shall we play that game? I think you know full well who I am. Did you receive your package yesterday? I was half expecting a call."

"Why, what are you going to do? She was a good-looking girl, and they'll earn me brownie points if anyone else sees them. Clever though,

I'll give her that. I'm sorry I didn't get to enjoy it." He listened to Andronikov laugh, and his knuckles whitened as he gripped the phone.

"I agree. But would your partner give you points, Meredith? I hear you have a rather cosy set-up."

"Do your worst. I have broad shoulders, and have dealt with bigger problems than this." Such was Meredith's anger, he hadn't noticed Trump arrive at his door. Trump waited innocently since the door was open, which usually meant the call was not of a personal or confidential nature. "What is it you are hoping to get from me, information? Because I allowed you to ply me with drink? And I know it was you who tipped your boys off about the raid. Was there something else I can do for you?"

Meredith kept his tone level, unwilling to let Andronikov know the extent of his concern.

Andronikov laughed. "I'm sure there is plenty, and I pay well."

"You pay well, yes, someone told me that. I'm not sure I'm for sale, Andronikov; I don't have expensive habits. Let me sleep on it. I'll call you on this number tomorrow."

Meredith terminated the call and stared at his phone. That had bought him some time, but now he needed to get home. He might be able to head this off at the pass.

Noticing Trump standing in the doorway, he sighed deeply. "How much did you hear?"

"Too much, I'm afraid. Look, sir, I don't know what's going on, but . . ." Trump was now immensely concerned about Meredith's recent behaviour. He wanted to trust him, but he seemed to be digging a deeper hole for himself with each call he made.

"Precisely, you don't know, Trump. Now, here's the list, get that lot briefed. I'll be no longer than an hour, tops. And keep your mouth shut for me, there's a good chap. I know I can trust you."

Meredith tore the sheet from the pad, and handed it to Trump. Trump looked at the expression on Meredith's face. Was it fear?

"Sir, can I —"

"No, you can't. Keep your head down, your mouth shut, and follow my orders," Meredith snapped. Pausing as he pulled on his jacket, he lowered his voice as he passed Trump. "You know you can trust me."

He didn't allow Trump to answer and hurried away. Tom Seaton walked across to Trump, whose eyes followed Meredith, wondering if he really could trust him.

"What's he all het up about now?" Seaton asked.

Trump sighed and turned to Seaton. "I don't know, I really don't, but I intend to find out." He waved the sheet of paper at Seaton. "Something's going on with him, but for now, let's get on with this."

# 8

Meredith left the front door open, and took the stairs to his bedroom two at a time. The wardrobe creaked as he yanked the door open. Seeing his suit still hanging where he had left it, he felt in the pocket, and dropped onto the bed, head in hands. He drew in several deep breaths and looked up, staring at the neat row of clothes. Once he had caught his breath, he changed quickly. He had a lot to do, and he could have done without this distraction. He frowned: if nothing else he seemed to have Andronikov in tow. He swallowed. His throat was dry, probably from the fright he'd had.

Running down the stairs he headed for the kitchen, and filled a glass with water. When he'd drunk it, he refilled it and sat at the kitchen table.

The envelope in his breast pocket jabbed his ribs. He pulled it out. Unable to help himself he slid out the photographs. Shaking his head as he shuffled through them, squinting at the detail in one of them, he walked to the kitchen window. He was right. The bloke with the camera had been captured in the mirror. That might come in useful. Bowing his head, he wondered who he could trust to enlarge the image. A noise from the hall caught his attention and he spun round.

"Hello, is someone there?" Amanda's head appeared over the banister. "Oh, Dad, it's only you! You scared me half to death! Why is the door open?" Amanda's head disappeared and Meredith panicked.

The photographs were in a haphazard pile, and he had no time to straighten them or stuff them in his pocket. Scooping them up, he strode to the dishwasher and slid them on top of the machine and under the work surface above, turning to face Amanda as she came into the kitchen. Putting his hands behind him, and, using his fingers, he pushed the photographs as far back as he could. He forced a smile.

"I don't know about me scaring you, I didn't realise anyone was at home – you could have given me a heart attack. What are you doing at home?"

"Well, I was trying to sleep. I start nights again tonight, and I thought I should at least try. I think I managed a doze." Amanda removed a carton of orange juice from the fridge. "Why are you home?"

"I shouldn't be, but I needed to change. I left in a hurry this morning." Meredith glanced at the clock, and as Amanda pulled a pack of bacon from the fridge, he knew he wouldn't be retrieving the photographs until later. He sighed. "I must shoot." He kissed her on the forehead as she opened the cutlery drawer next to him.

"Okay, I would have made you a bacon sandwich, but you'll have to forego the pleasure. Have a good one." Stepping away, she bent to find a frying pan in the cupboard. Meredith moved away from the dishwasher and glanced down. There was no sign of the photographs. He drew in a breath of relief. Walking out of the kitchen he called goodbye to his daughter and cursed his own stupidity.

~ ~ ~

It was Patsy's turn to roll her eyes at Irene.

"No, Stephen didn't ask me to help him with his injuries. As I said, he was uninjured. Irene, at some point you will have to accept that I have no interest in Stephen. I-am-spoken-for," she enunciated carefully. "Now, can we get on with some work? I have a report to get out."

"But you don't wear a ring – not that that's necessarily anything to go by, I know – and I saw the way he looked at you again this morning. Promise me something?"

"What?" Patsy held up her hands in exasperation.

"If I am right, and you two get it together, even if it's only a fling, will you get me a pay rise for being right? I'm told pillow talk can work magic." Grinning, Irene looked away, not expecting an answer, and in seconds her fingers were busy at the keyboard.

Patsy pulled a face and reopened the screen that she had hidden when Irene took her attention. That morning there had been a flurry of emails exchanged between Stephen and a man called R. Critchton. They had been sent and received within the space of an hour and Stephen had deleted them instantly. Patsy had only caught the exchange as she had been working on emails in Stephen's inbox at the time. She had jotted down the exchange to the best of her memory as Stephen had then deleted Critchton as a contact, and emptied the waste basket. It appeared that Stephen and Jake were about to take a trip, but neither Patsy nor Irene had been asked to make the arrangements. Irene's teasing had been an unwelcome interruption as she might have missed the final notes. Leaving Stephen's inbox open she kept an eye on the screen as she scanned her notes. She had no idea if they were useful, and if they were, she hoped that Burt and his team would be able to access the system to retrieve the deletions.

Patsy's eyes flicked to the screen as a message appeared from Critchton in the corner. Grabbing her mouse, she clicked on it.

She made a final note wondering if she'd missed something crucial. She went over what she'd recorded.

*Hatton:*     *You're sure of the arrangements. I don't want to waste our time.*

*Critchton:*   *Positive, there is a flight tomorrow or if necessary Sunday.*

*Hatton:*     *Will Sunday be soon enough? It will be easier on Sunday.*

*Critchton:*   *Should be secure, but I'd allow a couple of days.*

*Hatton:*     *I'll speak to my brother and get back to you.*

*Hatton:*     *The sooner the better. We'll leave this evening, returning Sunday or Monday depending on completion.*

*Critchton:*   *I'll make the arrangements, flights leave at (note: I am only sure of the hour as the email disappeared too quickly for accuracy.) 21.00 – is that ok with you, or do you want to leave it until tomorrow?*

*Hatton:*     *Earlier the better, I've waited a long time.*

*Twenty minutes or so later another arrived – I have missed some due to interruption in office!!! This was final message:*

*Critchton:*   *Looking forward to it. We will also be rewarded in heaven.*

Patsy cursed silently as she photographed her notes, emailed them to her private address via her phone, then, just as Stephen had done, she deleted the evidence. Screwing her notes into a tight ball, Patsy stood and called to Irene.

"I have to pay a visit. I'll get coffee while I'm on the move, do you want one?"

"Stupid question, I thought you'd never ask."

Patsy forced a laugh at Irene's clipped response. Her eyes never left her screen, giving Patsy the opportunity of shoving the ball of paper into her pocket.

Patsy hurried to the ladies' cloakroom. Locking the door, she opened the ball of paper and tore it into tiny pieces. She flushed them away before returning to the office, collecting the promised coffee on the way. Patsy clock-watched for the next few hours. She processed various non-interesting documents, all the time wondering whether to make an excuse to find and speak to Stephen, who had been unusually quiet all day.

At four o'clock Jake strode into the office.

"Afternoon, ladies, how are things?" he asked as he walked to the tray containing documents for his attention. The two women murmured all was well. Jake sifted through his post, and, finding nothing of interest, replaced it. "Is there anything needed from Stephen or me over the next few days? We are going on a trip to look at some bikes. We're leaving early in the morning, and won't be back until Sunday, maybe even Monday, so if you need anything signed, shout now."

Patsy waved a document. "I need Stephen to sign this. I'll take it to him, shall I?" She raised her eyebrows as Jake walked to collect it.

"What is it? Stephen has already left, is it something I can do?" Taking the document, he scanned it, and lifted the pen resting on the top row of her keyboard and signed it with a flourish. "There. Done. Is there anything else?" He turned to Irene. "What about you? There's always something you want done." He smiled at Irene who slammed her eyes playfully.

"I need nothing from you, that's for sure. Not unless you want to discuss my pay rise."

"Ah, that old chestnut. That will have to wait until we get back." Jake laughed. "Okay, I'll be briefing Abigail in the lab for the next twenty minutes, if you do think of anything, that's where I'll be."

"Are you going somewhere nice?" Patsy asked as he walked away. He didn't turn to respond.

"No, afraid not. All boring bike business, but it's got to be done. Bye, ladies." He left the room only to return a few seconds later. "Actually, Patsy, you may as well take the rest of the week off. There's little to done here with Stephen away."

He gave her a knowing glance before disappearing again.

"What about me? Why don't I get a couple of days off? There is certainly favouritism going on here," Irene called towards the door, but not loud enough for Jake to hear.

Patsy laughed. "You know I'm a temp, and therefore paid hourly, why would they pay me to sit and look at you?"

"Well, there are worse things to be paid for." Irene turned back to her screen. "I understand what you're saying, but would it have hurt for me to be off too?"

Knowing Irene didn't require an answer, Patsy pulled her phone forward and texted Burt.

*Might have some info – not sure?? Can we meet tomorrow – I'm not needed until Monday. Did you know the brothers are going away?*

Patsy returned her attention to the report she had to complete for the next day. As she listened to Stephen rambling in her earphones, saying pretty much the same as the day before, she was glad that her normal day job was less boring, and couldn't understand how Irene put up with it.

Ten minutes later, she had a reply from Burt, confirming a meeting for ten the next morning. Patsy deleted the text.

~ ~ ~

Meredith had returned to the station like a bear with a sore head. He barked out his orders, and shot people down in flames if they dared ask what he thought was a useless question. By early afternoon, the team were busy carrying out their allotted tasks, and Meredith was sitting in his office awaiting the call regarding Liska joining the witness protection programme. Meredith had agreed with Trump and Seaton that they would pay a visit to the Hammer and Sickle the following evening. While he waited, he doodled on his pad, running over the events so far.

When Hutchins knocked on his door and placed a coffee on his desk, Meredith realised that he had written the name Roper repeatedly and circled it.

"Anything on this Roper bloke yet?"

"Nothing. Nothing at all, not even a sniff, but the desk sergeant has called, his brief is seeing another client, then she's all yours."

"Bugger. Thanks, Hutchins, I'd better make another call." Meredith pulled the phone towards him and hit redial. He'd already left two messages. He was surprised when the call was answered first ring.

"Meredith, you must learn to be more patient. Our chap is on his way from London now. He'll sit in on the rest of the interview. Should be with you in two hours."

"He'd better be. I don't want Liska getting jumpy and doing a runner; this could all be tied up in a matter of days. I have something else we need to discuss, but not now. I'll call you when I leave here." Meredith's thumb hovered over the end call button as he added, "And answer the bloody phone first time, every time."

Meredith left the phone on his desk and went in search of Jane Roscoe. He knocked on the door of the room she was in with her client and a frustrated-looking uniform. Opening the door, he heard the man say, "As before, no comment."

It was said with a sneer and Meredith felt sympathy for his colleague, who announced the interview was suspended and thumped the button off. He nodded agreement that Meredith could have a quick word with Roscoe, relieved to have an excuse to get out of the room for a while. He hurried away as Meredith pulled the door shut behind Jane Roscoe who had followed him out into the corridor.

"Not playing ball, I take it?" Meredith jerked his head back towards the room.

"Shoplifting and affray charge, based only on the fact he was wearing a navy hoody. No formal identification," her lips twitched into a smile, "yet."

Meredith rolled his eyes.

"I've been told that the chap with the paperwork is on his way, might be another two hours." Meredith shrugged. "Sorry, Jane, I'm sure you have suitors queuing up to take you out tonight." He expected the usual flush, but received a deep sigh instead. "Problem?"

"Possibly. As it happens, I did have an engagement tonight. I'll make a call and get back to you." She looked at her watch. "Time is moving on, Meredith. Liska is here of his own free will, and may choose to stay here, but that's unlikely. What arrangements have been made for him tonight?" Seeing the look on Meredith's face, she frowned. "I take it nothing. May I suggest you make those arrangements, and let me have the details?"

Her eyes twinkled mischievously, and Meredith grinned at her. He tilted his head. She was a very attractive woman when she smiled. It seemed to make her slight frame more alluring, and less like a girl in grown-up clothing.

"You know, Jane, you are quite lovely when you smile." The flush had returned, but Meredith didn't pass comment. "I'll check with your client and see what he wants. I doubt we'll have a safe house ready, but it's early days and I can get someone into a local hotel or B&B with him. Will that suit?"

Roscoe's eyes looked past him and he turned to see the uniformed officer ambling back along the corridor.

"I'll come with you." She glanced at the door. "That idiot can wait."

Meredith turned and walked towards the room Liska occupied.

"If I were more sensitive, I'd think you didn't trust me," he told her as he opened the door. His eyes scanned the empty room, and his pulse rate increased. "That's if I can find your client. Did you know he'd gone?" Roscoe shook her head. "Come on, let's see if we can find him."

Meredith hurried towards the custody suite. A man was emptying his pockets, supervised by the duty sergeant and the arresting officer.

Meredith banged the desk. "That can wait. Do you know where Ms Roscoe's client is? He was in room three." Meredith stared at the board behind the desk. "And get his name off there, he's not under arrest."

The sergeant exchanged a glance with the other officer, and as he wiped Liska's name from the board, he replied, "Keep your hair on, one of your lot logged him. He's in the canteen – he was hungry."

"Well, next time he moves, I want a call to the incident room; that way we all know what's going on." Meredith pulled the door open. "This way, Ms Roscoe."

The newly-arrested suspect dropped his change into the small plastic box and smiled. "I did it. I admit it. Charge me and bail me, or we'll all be wasting our time."

The arresting officer smiled. *That was easy*, he thought. Now he'd be able to catch the bank before it closed.

They found Liska on a corner table in the canteen. He was drinking coffee, his empty plate pushed to one side. He looked at them expectantly.

"We can get on?" he asked, and his shoulders drooped a little as Jane Roscoe shook her head.

"I'm afraid not, Jan. The man with the papers won't be here for some time, and I don't know how long I can stay."

Liska shrugged, unaware of what that meant to him.

"It means this will go on into the night, or possibly not start until tomorrow, although I have to tell you I favour the first option," Meredith explained. "Either way we need to know where you will stay tonight. Do you want to stay here, or should we sort something out?"

Liska looked scared. "I can't go home. I can never go home. They have been texting me, look."

He handed his phone to Meredith.

| | |
|---|---|
| 9.30 | *Sorry to hear about Elena, where are you?* |
| 9.43 | *Jan, we have a job for you, call in* |
| 10.03 | *It is a foolish man who panics* |
| 11.34 | *Jan call now* |
| 14.15 | *Disappointed. Be careful my friend. You know we will take care of you* |

"Who is this?" Meredith handed the phone back. There was no identification given, simply the numbers of the phones sending the message.

"Them. I don't know who, it could be any of them. My guess is Peter – Peter Myshkin – but it's enough they have sent a warning. What will you do with me?"

Meredith reached and took the phone back. Pulling a small notebook from his pocket he jotted down the numbers.

"You stay here until we're ready for you. I'll get someone tracing these numbers."

Liska nodded. Meredith walked away, having told the canteen manager to give Liska what he wanted, and allowing Jane Roscoe a moment's privacy with her client. She met him at the exit.

"He is terrified, and from what I hear they did to his cousin, I'm not surprised. Find him somewhere safe, Meredith."

She reached out to pull open the door, and her bracelet looped itself around the handle and snapped. It fell to the ground. They knelt to retrieve it at the same time and their heads collided. Meredith put a hand out to steady her. Their faces were inches apart.

"Steady there," Meredith took hold of her elbow. "I'm too pretty to be head-butted."

He smiled as she flushed yet again, and retrieved the bracelet before helping her upright. It was a twisted silver rope that had been held together by a heart-shaped padlock. He held it out to her.

"Very pretty, I hope you can get it repaired."

She examined the damage. "Me too, it was a present from my mother." She slipped it into her pocket. "I'll get back to my latest delightful client. You sort Mr Liska out, and I'll get them to call you when I'm free."

Meredith escorted her part way back to the interview room, before heading off to the incident room. He spoke first to Trump, setting him the task of finding a safe location for Liska.

"If it's a hotel or B&B, I want someone with him. Someone we can trust. And don't tell anyone where he's going."

"Not even you, sir?" Trump asked quietly and Meredith frowned.

"No, Trump, not even me." Meredith looked away as Rawlings and Jo Adler entered the room. "You took your time. Did you find anything?" he asked, eyeing the cardboard box Rawlings was carrying.

"Forensic did a thorough job but don't think they got much, if anything," Jo responded. "As to clues to the location, nothing obvious, Gov. We've cleared the apartment of anything that could give a hint, or that might be a code."

Rawlings placed the box on his desk.

"She kept notebooks, loads of them; she was obviously trying to improve her English. It would have taken too long to go through them all so we brought them back."

"Good, well, you make a start on that; I'll be out to help in a moment, and Jo, you get on to tracing these numbers. A pound to a penny they're pay-as-you-go untraceables, but it's worth a shot." Taring the sheet from his notebook, he handed it to her.

His phone rang, and glancing at the screen he hit the answer button and gave his name. The others watched as his head started shaking in disbelief.

"For Christ's sake! Piss ups in breweries springs to mind. When will he get here? Can he not get a cab?" He listened again. "We'll store him somewhere safe, and you sort me an alternative. Tonight would be good." He terminated the call without warning, and cursed again.

"What now?" Trump asked, and bit his lip. Having overheard Meredith's previous telephone exchanges, he didn't want to second-guess this one.

"The bloke with the papers was on a train from London. It derailed going into Reading, nothing major, no fatalities, but he has a possible dislocated shoulder and is on his way to hospital."

Meredith raised his hand as Seaton opened his mouth, "And before you ask, no, they can't duplicate the protection agreement as he wrote it and got straight on the train. They'll send someone to him, but with the railway station out of action and knowing what that will do to traffic out of London, they have no idea what time it will get here." He looked at Trump. "Get on with it."

"Yes, sir." Trump moved away from the others to begin the task of finding a safe haven for Liska.

Meredith went to update Jane Roscoe. She'd finished with her other client and was overseeing him collect his personal effects from the duty sergeant. Meredith pulled her to one side.

"Good news, I hope, DCI Meredith. Please tell me we can proceed because I can't get hold of my . . . companion to let him know I may be delayed."

"No need, it's unlikely we'll be able to get on tonight: the train carrying the man carrying the paperwork was derailed at Reading. He's on his way to hospital as we speak. It will have to be tomorrow now, unless you'll allow Liska to speak to me . . . What? Jane, are you okay?"

"Are we speaking about the train out of Paddington?" There was an urgency to the question. Meredith didn't think it possible, but Jane had become paler than usual. He placed his hand on her elbow and pulled her towards a bench at the edge of the room

"We are, was your date on it? If so, don't panic. There were no fatalities and I'm given to understand that injuries are minor to those who sustained them. Sit."

Jane Roscoe sat wearily. She smiled gratefully at Meredith. "Oh, thank goodness. I think we are fated not to be together, you know. Sam and I have tried to have a relationship for years, but something momentous always happens to stop it . . . I don't know, moving to another level, I suppose." She suddenly laughed. "I must be losing my mind – why on earth did I tell you that? Meredith, promise you won't tease me mercilessly for the rest of my life."

"I don't know why you would suggest such a thing." Meredith's eyes twinkled. "Especially if I get the odd favour." He grinned as she laughed again.

Roscoe got to her feet. "Meredith, I may have had a moment due to concern for a friend, but I have not lost my marbles. Before you ask, no, you may not speak to my client until everything is in place. Nice try though. Is he still in the canteen? I'll go and see him. I'm not in a hurry now."

Resigned to waiting, Meredith nodded acceptance.

"He is, and I wasn't going to ask," he lied, shrugging at her. "Trump is sorting him somewhere to stay. I'll tell him to keep you informed, and . . ."

Jane Roscoe's client zipped up his hoodie and called to her.

"Bye, Miss. Thanks, see you again." He sauntered out through the door held open by the duty sergeant.

Jane Roscoe gave a curt nod, and turned back to Meredith. "I'll catch up with DS Trump before I leave." She walked towards the open door, "And if I don't see you later, see you here tomorrow. Bye, Meredith."

The relief at knowing Sam was safe had clearly relaxed her.

"Does he make you smile, this Sam?" Meredith called to her, and she stopped and looked over her shoulder.

"He does. He's very funny, sweet and kind. Not unlike yourself, Meredith."

Her eyes widened; was that an attempt at humour? Meredith laughed. "Good, then make it work. You are a different person when you're talking about him. Get rid of whatever obstacles are in your way, and get on with it. I like you like this." He laughed as the flush appeared, and she hurried away, smiling.

Meredith was right, she was better with Sam. She would make it work. As she made her way to the canteen, she pulled her phone from her bag and tried to call him again.

Two hours later, a small pile of notebooks on his desk, Meredith saw her come into the incident room and speak to Trump. He glanced at the clock: it was almost seven. Trump walked towards his office as he pulled his jacket on.

"I'm off to sort out Jan Liska for the night. I take it there is still no sign of your man?" he asked as Roscoe came to stand behind him.

"None." Meredith put his pencil in the notebook as a marker and closed it. "It's been a long day, get yourself home afterwards – we'll all work better in the morning. Night, Jane, enjoy Sam."

Rather than blushing she stepped forward and smiled.

"I will, thank you Meredith. He's waiting for a coach at the moment, so it was only a blip in his journey."

Meredith rubbed his hands over his face as they walked away. He couldn't even remember what he'd read minutes ago.

Standing, he called out to the incident room. "Pack up and go home. I'll see you back here in the morning. Don't be late."

~ ~ ~

Patsy closed the lid of the laptop. Lost for something to do having finished work early and with no Meredith or Amanda at home, she'd set herself the task of finding out where the Hatton brothers were going. Jake's claim that it was to look at bikes could well be true, but if so, why the secrecy? Having scoured the internet for flights from Bristol airport, the most likely departure point, she had come to the conclusion that they would be flying to Belfast International Airport. It fit the time she had jotted down. She had added a note to her closing email to Burt.

*I may be barking up the wrong tree, but if everything is above board, why use a third person to organise the flights and delete the emails? Do you know who Critchton is yet? Can you access their emails and find out what was deleted? Finally, would you please tell me why I am there – it would be so much easier, and possibly quicker in the long run!! See you tomorrow at ten. PH.*

She looked around in surprise as Meredith opened the door. "Hello, I wasn't expecting you this early! How was your day?"

She stood and hugged him. Meredith kissed the top of her head, his eyes drawn to the dishwasher. He would have to attempt to retrieve the photographs when Patsy was otherwise engaged as it could involve dragging the dishwasher out.

"Okay, up and down. First, we think we have an informant, and we do, but red tape has delayed things, hence my earlier-than-expected appearance. So, I suppose my day was frustrating. What about yours?" Meredith hoped it would be a simple response, as he knew Patsy would see through any pretence to be interested.

"Boring. I might have something interesting bubbling, but I doubt it. Best thing that happened was the brothers announcing they were away for a few days and I could take the time off. Other than a couple of meetings, I'll be working mainly from home, which is good – it's been a while." She pushed him away. "Let's not talk about work. I don't want to fall out, and that's likely to happen. Go and shower and

I'll take you out for dinner."

"I thought it was my job to say that." Meredith cursed silently. With Patsy working from home, and his own working hours likely to start early and finish late, getting to the photographs might prove challenging. He smiled. "No, you go and shower first, I have some calls I need to make."

"Already have, I've been home a while. You make your calls. I'll wait, there's no hurry."

Thwarted at the first attempt, Meredith got a beer from the fridge and walked out into the back garden. Having no real calls to make he dialled Trump.

"Is he all sorted?"

"Yes, sir, checked with the powers that be, and got approval from Ms Roscoe. I left him with his appointed guard not ten minutes ago. I'm glad we can get on tomorrow, he's quite jumpy, you know."

"As would we be in his shoes. Thanks for that, I'll leave you to it. Patsy is taking me out for dinner."

"Lucky you. Linda is trying a new recipe, one of her own." Trump knew he need say no more as Meredith laughed.

"Oh dear. Good luck, see you in the morning. Oh, and Trump, don't forget to tell her you're out with the boys tomorrow night."

"Will do, shame it's not tonight. Ah well."

~ ~ ~

Patsy opted to take Meredith to a new restaurant that had recently opened in one of the back streets in the centre of town. They parked in the nearest multi-storey, and strolled along hand in hand. Before they reached the restaurant, they passed a pub announcing that it had live music on that night.

"That might be fun, what do you think?" Patsy nudged Meredith. "Oh, well there you go! Small world." Having walked past the painted sign, they came across a chalk board detailing that evening's live act. It was Meredith's friend, Ben Jacobs. "Shall we eat and come back to watch?"

"Let's eat and take it from there. I'm not sure I want to be in a hot sweaty bar with middle-aged women throwing themselves at my mate." He raised his eyebrows. "And I might cramp his style."

Patsy laughed and told him he was arrogant; he didn't argue.

Their meal was good, the service efficient, and the price reasonable. Meredith relaxed into the evening knowing there was little he could do until the morning. As they strolled back to pick up the car, he decided seeing Ben would be a good thing, and they stood at the bar and caught the last set of his act. He was pleased to see them, and arranged to come to dinner the following week.

It was a little past midnight by the time they got into bed.

"Well, that was an unexpectedly pleasant evening." Meredith yawned. "And an unexpectedly long day. Come here, Hodge, I need a cuddle."

Before Patsy could move closer his phone rang.

"Oh dear." Patsy stayed where she was as Meredith rolled over and reached for his phone. Other than saying his name, he said nothing until he snapped, "Meet me there in ten minutes." He hung up. "Sorry, I have to go, our witness has gone AWOL."

## 9

Meredith climbed the steps towards the open door of the Victorian terraced house. Once at the top, he was able to see Seaton talking to a man who sat on the stairs holding what looked like a tea towel to his head.

"Evening, what's happening, Tom? Any further news?"

"Nope, this is Barney. About an hour ago he answered the door and whoever it was rushed him, coshed him, and our boy is gone. The bedroom window is wide open though. I've got a team on their way now. It's possible they didn't get him, and that he heard the commotion and went out that way – it's an easy drop onto a flat roof."

"Show me." Meredith nodded an acknowledgement to the officer nursing his wound as he stepped past him. "Which room?"

"Door to your right. No signs of a struggle, and the place hasn't been searched which would indicate Liska was the object," Seaton said.

"That's bloody obvious. Anything useful at all?"

"Nope, he'd only been here a couple of hours. Trump assured me that they took the usual precautions in getting him here. Said he would bet his life that they weren't followed. He's on his way."

"Well, someone got careless. The boys in London are going to go apeshit when they hear about this. Who knew he was here?"

Meredith walked into the room allocated to Liska and looked around. A paper bag on the bedside cabinet held overnight toiletries, a damp towel lay crumpled at the foot of the sturdy wooden bed, and a newspaper was open to the television listings on the small chest of drawers. He walked to the window and, ducking down, poked his head out.

"I can't see a bloody thing; my torch is in the car. Nothing more we can do here until they tell us if that's the way he went out. Come on, let's go and await Trump's explanation."

He turned quickly and something caught his eye. He stilled and peered at the bed, which was covered in a multi-coloured duvet. There was something in the centre of the duvet, he scooped it up and squinted at it. He closed his eyes as he recognised it, and his fist closed around it.

"Fuck! No, no, NO! Get Trump on the phone – now!" he shouted already running from the room.

"What is it, Gov? What did you find?" Seaton hit the dial button and hurried after him, his phone clamped to his ear.

Trump told Seaton he was outside, and Seaton hung up and listened to Meredith's call.

"George, its Meredith. I don't suppose there's anyone around from Loy and Waterhouse is there?" Seaton frowned, wondering why Meredith needed a solicitor at this time of night. "Get them out of there, and call me back when I can speak to them."

A pale-faced Trump appeared at the front door. "Is he gone?" he asked.

"Of course he's fucking gone, don't ask bloody stupid questions. What's more of a concern at the moment is this . . ."

Meredith held his hand up, but gave no further explanation as his phone rang. He got the information he required and told the others to follow him.

Ten minutes later, Meredith pulled in across the drive of a neat nineteen-thirties semi-detached house. As he climbed out of his car, a taxi pulled up, and a suited man thanked the driver as he paid him. Casting a quick glance at Meredith's haphazard parking, he said nothing, but hurried up the path of the house.

Meredith called to him. "Excuse me sir, can you stop there please."

The man turned. "I beg your pardon?" He looked irritated.

"Police." Meredith held out his ID as Trump and Seaton hurried forward. "Can I have a word, please?"

The man pulled a bunch of keys from his pocket.

"Of course, although I don't know . . . anyway let's go inside, but keep it down, my friend will be asleep." He turned and took a step closer to the house.

"Stop. Please."

Meredith's voice was commanding and the man obeyed, but his

irritation was apparent when he strode towards Meredith.

"I don't know what this about, but let me tell you, we're not discussing it in the garden. I've had a bitch of a day, I need a drink, and a hot bath, so if you don't mind —"

"Are you Sam?" Meredith asked and the man looked startled.

"I am, but how . . . Is everything all right with . . . Oh no, where is she?"

"I don't know, sir, and everything is probably fine. This is just a precaution, but when did you last speak to Jane?"

"Two, maybe two and a half hours ago . . . why? I got stuck when my train was derailed; I've been trying to get here since mid-morning. She was fine when I spoke to her. She was at home, she said . . ."

The man grabbed Meredith's shirt, and Seaton stepped forward but Meredith held out a hand to stop him.

"A witness has gone missing. He'd only been in the safe house a few hours and only three people knew where he was." Meredith gently prised the man's fingers from his shirt and took the keys off him. "Trump here, an officer nursing a bad head wound at the house, and Jane."

Meredith looked away as the man's face crumpled.

"No, not Jane. She never would, she . . ." He swallowed, and tapped his clenched fists together in front of his face, as though that would protect him from the reality of the situation. "You're wrong." There was no conviction in the statement.

"Sam — may I call you Sam?"

Meredith didn't expect a response, but the man nodded and asked, "Do I know you? Have we met? I'm usually good with faces." He screwed his eyes shut trying to remember, and trying not to think of Jane being in danger, or worse.

"No, Jane told me about you. She said you made her happy and she was excited you were coming." Meredith put an arm around the man's shoulder and pushed him towards Seaton. "You go with Seaton while Trump and I check the house." He jingled the keys he had taken from Sam.

Seaton took Sam's elbow and Trump stepped out of the way to allow them to get past. Sam made no effort to resist as Seaton steered him towards his car. Meredith turned and led the way to the front door. He found the correct key on the second attempt, and pushed the door open slowly. As he stepped into the house, he opened his mouth to call, but closed it when he saw that the rug had been dragged along the hall and lay concertinaed against the bottom of the stairs. He glanced at Trump who drew in a deep breath as he stepped over the threshold.

"How did you guess?" Trump asked quietly as Meredith walked carefully towards the first door off the hall.

Meredith pulled the broken silver bracelet from his pocket and held it in his open palm.

"She broke it on the door at the station. I found it on Liska's bed and I knew they'd been here first."

Meredith paused at the door. It was slightly ajar, and he pushed it with his finger, opening it fully. He stepped forward and looked into the room. It was empty and he blew out a breath of relief. Trump stepped past him and went towards the second door. This one was closed, and he turned the handle and stepped into the room. Meredith began to follow but was almost knocked off his feet as Trump rushed back out, hand over his mouth. He stood retching in the hall.

"Don't you dare contaminate this house, get out in the garden," Meredith snapped, and, as Trump hurried towards the open front door, Meredith attempted to compose himself. Closing his eyes, he stepped into the room. He could smell the blood, and he stood motionless for a few seconds, afraid to look.

"Pretend it's not her," he muttered quietly as he opened his eyes and took in the scene.

A plastic sheet had been rolled out in the centre of the room, the heavy coffee table shoved up against the fireplace to make enough room for it to be fully unfurled. Without looking at the body he considered this. They had obviously planned to move the body. So, why hadn't they? Why the change of mind? Something must have happened that made them abandon her. His breath caught in his throat: perhaps she was still alive. He stilled, and forced himself to look at the remains of Jane Roscoe. She was naked from the waist up, and her eyes were open, unseeing, and dull. She was not alive.

Starting with her head, his eyes moved down her body taking in her injuries. There was a slash across her right cheek, he couldn't tell without moving her, but it appeared she may have lost a part of her ear. There was a lot of blood in that area, and her red curls had matted and stuck to her face. He swallowed back the lump in his throat as he looked at her breasts. One had had the nipple removed, and he believed it had been placed on her naval, but there was so much blood it was difficult to tell without getting closer. He hoped she had been dead before that happened. The other breast had the same markings as had been found on the hand of Elena. It was not obvious what had killed her, as, although there was a good deal of blood, it didn't appear to be enough to have taken her life. His eyes travelled back up the torso, and he examined her throat. There were no signs of strangulation. He snarled and silently promised that he would do serious damage to the man who had done this.

A noise in the hall caught his attention, and he turned to find Frankie Callaghan standing in the doorway. Frankie saw the sadness in his eyes and nodded a silent acknowledgement.

"Sherlock," Meredith greeted him. "You were quick."

"Trump called me personally, rather than the morgue: he was a little without, an easy error."

"We're all a little *without*, Sherlock. Come on in and tell me what killed her."

Frankie zipped up the paper suit that covered his day clothes, and walked across to the body. Kneeling next to it, his eyes travelled around the various injuries as Meredith's had done. He looked up and shook his head.

"Nothing obvious, unless that's blunt trauma to the right side of her head. I'll have to examine her back at base." He looked past Meredith. "Come on in, he won't bite."

Meredith turned to the fresh-faced girl standing on the threshold of the room. "Another newbie? You get through them like other people get through tea bags." He held out his hand. "Meredith."

The girl stepped forward and pulling off her glove shook his hand. "Hanson. Becky Hanson. Pleased to meet you, Meredith."

"That won't last long." Frankie gave a brief smile. "Get the camera out, and pass me a ruler."

Becky did as she was asked, and as Frankie placed the small metal ruler beneath the laceration on the cheek, Meredith turned away, unable to watch.

"Be gentle with her, Sherlock. When you've moved her, I want you – not some clodhopper, but you – to supervise the search. I want forensics on this one fast, we have to have him bang to rights."

"Noted." Frankie moved back to enable Becky Hanson to take the first photograph.

The brief flash of light spurred Meredith on. He called back to them as he left the room. "I want updates, regularly. However small the detail, I want to know about it." Meredith glanced along the hall. Several men were zipping on paper overalls in the porch. "The others have arrived; I'll let them know you're in charge."

He walked away, calling to the men, and asking them who was the senior officer. Using both his authority as investigating officer and a few choice phrases, he established that Frankie Callaghan was calling the shots. Satisfied that all would be well, he went in search of Trump and Seaton. Trump hurried over as he opened the gate and looked up the street. He was already apologising by the time he reached Meredith.

"I'm sorry, sir. Never happened before, but I've never known the victim in such a way. It won't happen again."

"It will. Where are Seaton and Sam?" Meredith dismissed Trump's apology with a flick of his hand.

"Seaton knew from my reaction that it wasn't good news, he's taken him to the station."

"Good. Is there somewhere open that sells alcohol around here? I need a drink, and I think Sam will too. It's going to be a long, long, night. Call Hutchins and Jo in, I want every piece of CCTV footage from the station to here. What time did she leave the station?"

"I'm not sure. She had one more client to see when I left her. The custody records should give us that." Trump lowered his head. "This is my fault. I shouldn't have told her where he was then she wouldn't have been any use to them."

"Don't be so bloody stupid. It probably made it quicker for her. If she hadn't known, they'd have thought she was holding out on them . . . Trust me, her knowing made it better."

Trump did not want to be consoled. "Possibly, but it was me that insisted he have a solicitor. I'll call the others and meet you back at the station. I'll pick up a bottle on the way."

~ ~ ~

Patsy rolled over and instinctively reached out for Meredith. He wasn't there. She looked at the clock and sighed. It was seven fifteen, and he'd not been home. She hoped his witness hadn't been compromised. She slid her legs over the edge of the bed and sat up, stretched and yawned. With no one home, she decided to have a bath before work and not her usual shower. Not queuing for the bathroom in the morning was a luxury of which she intended to take full advantage.

As she watched the bubbles grow and spread along the water, she smiled as she remembered she didn't have to go in to work today. She was free until her meeting with Burt. Balancing her tea on the edge of the bath, she climbed into the water and hopped from foot to foot until her body acclimatised to the temperature. Laying back, she gasped as the hot water lapped over her shoulders. Closing her eyes, she ticked off the points she needed to cover with Burt, and wondered if he knew if the Hattons were really going to buy a bike.

~ ~ ~

Micky O'Toole pushed open the door to the rear bar of The Cracked Pot, and blinked as his eyes watered at the sudden attack of cigarette smoke. The landlord, Seamus, didn't hold with the new laws on smoking, it affected his profit, so he'd kept the back room as a smoking room for locals. The surprising thing was that even those that didn't smoke preferred the company out back, leaving the main bar empty most of the time. Wiping away the unexpected tears, Micky peered into the smog.

"Can you not even open a window in here. 'Tis a glorious day out there, I don't know why you insist on killing yourselves sooner than necessary," he shouted to the barman. "A pint of Guinness, and whatever Pat is having."

He walked to the window on the opposite side of the room, and opened the small vent at the top, before going back to the bar to collect his order.

"They'll smell it outside, that's why we keep them closed," the barman offered as he pulled on the pump.

"They can smell it in Dublin – the fecking window won't be your downfall." Those within earshot laughed in agreement. "I'll buy you an air freshener. One of those that spits at you as you walk past, and stick it on the sill outside, that'll fool them." Warming to the subject, he added, "What flavour do you think we should have? Stale beer or warm farts? 'Cos take away the smoke, and that's what you're left with."

He placed the exact amount of change on the bar and carried the drinks away, laughing.

Pat Driscoll took his drink, and lifted his paper from the stool next to him to allow O'Toole to sit. "Appreciated. What brings you down this way? You're not here for a smoke, that much is clear."

The old man smiled at his former comrade in arms.

"I need work, Pat. I've run up one too many debts and I have but a couple of bob to me name. The landlady will chuck me out if I don't come up with something this week."

"What about your benefits?" Driscoll inclined his head as O'Toole shrugged.

"Already spoken for, and then some." He took a swig of his drink and smacked his lips together. "I'll be savouring this one, it'll be the last for the foreseeable. Is there nothing going, Pat?"

"Not that I've heard. I'll ask around and give you a call."

"No phone. Had to sell it to eat." O'Toole leaned forward, resting his arms on the worn, chipped table. "I miss the old days. This getting old is no fun, to be sure. I thought I might be owed a favour."

He watched Driscoll's face carefully. Driscoll nodded agreement, but his eyes were cold as they stared back at him.

"I'm sure you are by someone, but not by me surely? Who did you think owed you such a favour?"

"The lads," O'Toole looked over his shoulder, "you know who I mean. I was a good servant, I kept out of trouble and my lips are forever sealed. That must be worth something." He dipped his finger into the white froth on the top of his glass and moved it around in a slow circle.

"Ah well then, I see. I'll ask, but you know," Driscoll was shaking his head again, "I thought you were rewarded at the time, as well as having the pride of doing something for the cause. I thought the necessary money changed hands then."

O'Toole sucked his finger clean. "There was a little, but I gave up my work to serve the cause – it's been bits and pieces since. Perhaps a little pension would be appropriate."

"Times have changed, Micky lad, you know that full well. There is no money anymore. Our supporters have lost sight of the cause."

"Am I right in thinking you're telling me no?" O'Toole's face hardened, and he pursed his lips. "A faithful servant left to rot, despite his support and silence over the barren years of his old age." The threat was clear, and he sipped his pint.

"No, you'd be right in thinking that I'd ask." Driscoll rummaged in his pocket and pulled out a pen. Passing both pen and newspaper to O'Toole, he instructed, "Give me your address. I'll be in touch."

As O'Toole scribbled his address on the edge of the paper, Driscoll reached inside his pocket and pulled several notes from his wallet. He rolled them up and exchanged them for the pen. "A little to get the landlady off your back, and I mean that. I don't mean to get some tart on hers." He laughed. "I'll be seeing you, Micky."

Knowing he'd been dismissed, Micky held his glass to his lips, tipped back his head, and emptied it. Wiping his mouth on the back of his hand he got to his feet.

"A true gentleman, Pat, that's what you are." He stepped away, and catching the barman's eye, he called, "Don't forget to let me know about that air freshener. I think you should go with the stale beer myself." He laughed heartily as he left the pub.

The roll of notes held tightly in his hand, O'Toole told himself he could get back to his digs without a visit to the betting shop, and even turned left to avoid the first of those he might pass if he took the High Street. As it happened, he needn't have worried. He had ignored the black van he had passed as he left the pub, and hadn't noticed it rolling alongside him as he promised himself to pay his rent. He gave but a small yelp as he was hauled in through the side door, which slid silently shut as he was thrown to the other side. Landing face down, he closed his eyes. The smell of plastic filled his nostrils as he tried to catch his breath. He expected to be set upon and braced himself, but nothing happened as the van made its way into the traffic. That wasn't a good sign. He'd put off making the veiled threat for weeks for fear of this, but now it was here he accepted his fate, if that was what it was. Pat must have had men waiting for him, but what he couldn't work out was how they got to him so quickly, it had only been minutes.

Sweat moistened his skin. There was no airflow in the back of the van, and adrenaline pumped around his body as he weighed up his options. He could try and talk his way out, tell them there had been a misunderstanding; he was, after all, an old man now. Tell them he wasn't worth the bother, or the risk. Moving his head slightly, his face, now wet with perspiration, slid easily along the plastic covering the floor of the van. He couldn't see anything, so he rolled onto his back and sat up, grunting from the effort. The back of the van was pitch black with the exception of a small beam of light coming through a small square, cut out of the board, which separated the cab from the rear of the van. He jumped as someone close by spoke to him.

"Are you not going to speak?"

"And what would I be saying? Nice to meet you, fancy bumping into you here? I'll say my piece when I know what you want."

Despite his age, and his financial predicament, he still had his pride. He would show these fuckers what real men were made of.

"Well, shall we start with the bombing of The Spotted Cow? What would you like to say about that?"

It was a local accent, but refined. O'Toole couldn't place it.

"Depends who I'm talking to. Will you not introduce yourself?"

"Later. I want to know about the bombing."

Whoever it was leaned forward and poked him in the chest with something small and hard; probably a gun.

"What do you want to know?" O'Toole shuffled back against the side of the van and pulled his knees to his chest.

"Who did it?"

"Not me, and I'm not sure why you think it was."

"Because I'm told you were the . . . what did they call it?"

A deeper voice responded from the other end of the van, and O'Toole turned to look. He could vaguely make out the shape of a well-built pair of shoulders.

"A facilitator," the new voice said.

O'Toole turned his head towards the first voice as it spoke. Relief flooded through his body, and he allowed himself a small smile. It was the security services, he told himself, and not the others. He wouldn't be dying today.

"Ah yes. So, Mr Facilitator, what can you tell us?"

"Ha, that's a good one, unless it's a posh name for a gofer, because that's all I was. A relic, and a poor one at that, left over from the old days. One that didn't become a politician with a flash car, a big house, and conferences to attend. I ran the odd message for the new boys, but I was no real use to them, too old." He used his sleeve to mop his brow. "So, you'll see why I don't think I'll be of much use to you."

"Well, let's give it a go." There was a shuffling of papers and a small light came on overhead. O'Toole squinted at the stack of prints shoved towards him. He turned his head away from the gloved hand, and focused on the top photograph. He didn't want to see their faces; he didn't need to know who they were. "All you have to do is make two piles – one for yes, and one for no. Put those who were involved in

The Spotted Cow to the left and those that weren't to the right. We don't want to hurt people who weren't there. Although," the man sighed, "they too probably deserve a slow and painful death, but that's for others to deal with."

O'Toole held his breath for a few moments, knowing he held the power of life and death in his hands. He closed his eyes. This wasn't right. It was not for him to sign death warrants; he really had only been a messenger. He'd never got his own hands dirty, not really. Opening his eyes, he shuffled through the ten or so photographs. He knew three of the men had been directly involved. He'd taken the messages, he'd helped them get clear, and one he had even been primed to provide an alibi for, but he'd never been questioned.

"Do you recognise these men?" The first speaker leaned forward; he was very close. O'Toole closed his eyes and nodded.

"A couple of them, yes."

"Which of those men are responsible for that bombing?" The man thumped the side of the van, and it echoed as though thunder had erupted. "Stop fucking about, and make the piles."

"You're assuming I know." O'Toole flinched but kept his eyes glued to the stack as the silencer of the pistol was pressed against his forehead. He shuffled through again. Perhaps he could limit the damage he was about to do. He knew they would expect at least two, so he chose them on the basis of how much he liked them. Placing the two photographs to his left, he told himself they had been responsible, that innocents were killed, and therefore it wasn't his fault if their actions now had repercussions. "These two. I think these two were involved." He stuttered and prayed silently for forgiveness.

"We know there were four men directly involved. The police found the plan, but unfortunately it had no names, only code words. Don't mess me about, I don't want to hurt you."

The gun nudged him again.

O'Toole's stomach did a somersault and he felt sick. If he wasn't talking to the police, who was it? The army? He couldn't see that they would be doing this. It must be some Protestant outfit. He needed to play ball if he were to get out of the van unscathed. He shuffled through again. He knew five of the men had been involved in one way or another, but he liked the others. However, he needed one more. A cruel smile crept to his lips: David Jameson was there. To the best of his knowledge Jameson hadn't been involved, but the bastard had cheated him, cost him dear in the past, the arrogant shit. He pulled Jameson's photograph out of the pile and placed it with the first two, and the rest he placed to his right.

"Jameson. I think he was involved. The others weren't, I don't even know some of them. What happens now?" Still staring straight ahead, he prayed that the door would slide open, and he'd be tossed into the street like unwanted trash. He turned to face his executioner as he spoke.

"Now you die." The eyes were cold and devoid of any remorse.

O'Toole smiled at him. "And you said you wouldn't hurt me. Me, an old man collecting me pension. I didn't do it. Have you no shame?" He made one last attempt to save his life.

"It won't hurt." The finger squeezed the trigger gently, and O'Toole fell sideways, still smiling.

Over the next twenty hours, the three men identified by O'Toole were tracked down and taken from the street. Each knew why they were about to die, and all tried to deny it, except Jameson. He simply spat at and cursed the men who were to take his life, telling them he'd see them in hell.

The bodies of the four men were driven out of Belfast, and taken to a quarry. It took less than thirty minutes for the van to negotiate the rough track to the site of the next blast, and place the corpses in the low cave hacked out of the rock several days before for that purpose. As the sun rose, money changed hands, and the blast scheduled for ten o'clock took place a little early.

The Hatton brothers were sitting in the departure lounge of Belfast International Airport awaiting their flight to Bristol.

There had been a lot of paperwork to complete at the quarry, and the health and safety team worked themselves into a frenzy in an attempt to find out how the explosion had happened ahead of schedule. But it blew over quickly enough: there had been no damage that wasn't intended in the long term, no property had been damaged, and no one had sustained an injury.

10

Patsy walked along the corridor and entered the room without knocking. Burt sat alone; there was no sign of Benson.

"Nice to see you, Patsy, grab a chair." His eyes twinkled. He knew Patsy didn't like him, and it irritated her when he was pleasant to her. "You've got a couple of days off, that's nice. It's about time I found a sunny beach somewhere."

"Well, as I haven't got a sunny beach to sit on either, I won't sympathise. Was the information I sent you of any use?"

"Possibly long term, but of no consequence to the current assignment."

"Did they go to Belfast? Was I right about that?" Patsy pressed him.

"I think they did." Burt gave a slight nod.

"Think? Are they not being followed? Don't you want to know why a third person made their travel arrangements?"

"Not really. As I said, it's not related. Don't work yourself into a frenzy, Patsy, you're doing a great job." Burt smiled. "Keep doing what you're doing and we'll get there."

His smile became a grin as Patsy banged the table with a clenched fist.

"What the hell *is* related? Give me something to work on for God's sake. I don't want to type shit reports day in and day out. What I want is something that will stimulate my brain. I'm dying of boredom in that bloody office."

"That's how it goes sometimes, you know that. Would you rather be sitting in a stuffy car, eating burgers and waiting for someone in his underpants to jump from a bedroom window?"

Burt leaned forward, resting his chin on his hand. He seemed bored, despite what he said next. "What you are doing is crucial to the security of this country. When, and *if*, you find anything, you'll know, or we'll tell you at least, but the brothers going to Belfast is not of major significance."

"But it is of minor significance, yet you won't share with me."

"Need to know, Patsy. You're well aware how it works, and as I remember, being paid rather well."

"It's not about the money, you stu . . ." Patsy bit back the insult. "Tell me what's next, because other than monitoring email activity, there is little else I can do for you."

"The latest report says they are almost there. You've been there five weeks, which is nothing in the scheme of things, and if they're almost there, well, it'll be job done. You'll be free."

"Exactly what do you think might happen? They'll renege on their deal with the government? They wouldn't do that – they couldn't do that and survive. They need that contract."

"Strange stuff happens as projects come to an end. All sorts of things cloud the judgement of otherwise sensible men. Sometimes it's greed, sometimes fear, but whatever it is, things can go wrong. We're making sure everything stays on track and their side of the bargain is fulfilled. Hang in there, Patsy; don't make me eat humble pie." Burt's tone was gentle.

"What does that mean? You really are a patronising bastard, but you must have been told that before." Patsy stood and pushed her chair under the table. "Another hour of my life wasted at a meeting that meant nothing."

"What it meant, is that against the wishes of others, I said you were the girl for the job. I don't want to be wrong. I didn't intend to patronise you."

Patsy controlled the surprise she felt; it wouldn't do to let him know he had wrong-footed her.

"Well, you did, and perhaps you did back the wrong horse, or perhaps you are confused by the smoke and mirrors, but I am pissed off, bored, and I'm going home. If you have anything useful you want me to do, feel free to shout."

Patsy turned on her heel and walked briskly away. A few seconds later Benson stepped out from behind a screen at the far end of the office.

"She really doesn't like you. Sensible girl, she's got your measure. *I* said she was the girl for the job, not you, you lying bastard. I'm glad she saw through you. I knew I'd chosen correctly. She's not likely to miss anything. What news on their trip?"

"I'm awaiting an update, but two men we've been tracking have been reported as missing, and they were linked with the bombing of The Spotted Cow by the police." Burt raised his eyebrows, "But, if it was the Hattons, they've covered their tracks well. Bought two bikes which are being shipped back, and were seen out and about regularly in and around the hotel they stayed in. Do you want me to press our chaps over there?"

"Not at the moment; a few more terrorists taken off the face of the earth won't cause me to lose any sleep, assuming that's what's happened, but keep the reports coming in. They might prove useful if we need leverage against the Hattons in the long run." He nodded. "Very useful, in fact. I'm back down to London to update the minister; I'll call later unless something happens in the interim."

Burt made a call as soon as Benson left him alone in the vast office.

"Keep on it, but low key. Report only to me as soon as you have anything concrete."

~ ~ ~

Meredith sat at his desk, the notebooks from Elena's apartment piled neatly around him. He'd got through eight of the ten, but had had no joy pinpointing a possible location of the bodies mentioned by Jan Liska, nor had he any news of where Liska might be. He was now awaiting the call that would tell him another body had been found. His eyes closed and his head fell forward, his chin resting on his chest. He drifted off to sleep and was pleased when the telephone on his desk rang and woke him from visions of Jane Roscoe's body.

"Sherlock for you, Gov," Rawlings said. "When you're done, we've got a timeline, and some sightings of Jane's journey home."

"Thanks, I'll be out shortly." Meredith hit the flashing button.

"Sherlock, what have you got for me?"

"Overdose. She was killed by an overdose of a synthetic drug with similar properties to heroin. I guess that was to loosen her tongue. I found a small puncture wound in the crook of her arm, and have had the blood results back from the lab. There was only one puncture mark and the dose was huge. I'm not convinced she could have talked with that in her system, but if they found your man, I guess she did."

"And . . ."

"And what? You saw the other injuries, the injection of drugs was the only thing to add."

"And was she conscious when they carved her up? Don't piss about, Sherlock, I need to know what I'm dealing with."

"Judging by the blood loss, she was alive, yes, but I doubt very much whether she was conscious. I'm not familiar with this drug, but from the composition I'm guessing five to ten minutes of disorientation, and another five comatose, then death." Frankie paused, "Look, Meredith, if it helps, even if she was conscious she would have been as high as a kite. The pain would not have registered."

Meredith cleared his throat. "What about forensics? Do we have anything?"

"A few fibres, and a shoeprint at the rear of the house in a large plant pot. Looks as though they came in through the conservatory window. But no fingerprints, no alien DNA. I'm sorry, Meredith, this was very professional."

"That's what I thought. They were clearly going to take her somewhere, I wonder why the change of heart?" As an afterthought he added, "You've printed the whole of the plastic sheeting I take it?"

Frankie bit back a sarcastic retort and confirmed that the whole house had been examined with a fine-toothed comb. Meredith thanked him and ended the call. He tapped the receiver on his desk, and screwed his eyes shut in an attempt not to think about Jane's last moments. With a sudden roar, he swiped at the pile of notebooks with the receiver, and they toppled off the desk. Replacing the receiver, he stood and went to update the team. They had heard his response to the call, and they fell silent as he walked slowly towards the whiteboard. He studied the photograph of Jane Roscoe which had been taken from her firm's website. She smiled shyly, and her pale innocent face caused a lump to rise to his throat. Not speaking, he swallowed and picked up a pen. He wrote two words on the board: 'Overdose' and 'Conscious'.

He underlined the second three times before he turned to face them.

"She was given a massive overdose and was probably out of it when they carved her up, but she was alive. Catching the man or men that did this takes priority over the other murders."

He glanced at Seaton, who had raised his hand.

"They are one and the same, surely? The hammer and sickle was on both Elena and Jane, so if we can tie up one we'll have the other."

Meredith gave a slight shrug. "Possibly, but I want the actual person. The symbol is not unique to one man, it's not a personal signature." He half turned and pointed to Jane's photograph, "But that was personal. Unnecessary carnage, and I will find him . . . Sod the rest, I want him. Am I understood?" The team murmured their agreement. "Good. Now we've established that, what news on her movements? And those of us going to the bar tonight will finish here at two, unless anything else happens. We need to catch up on some sleep to ensure we don't miss anything. I also think we should split into two groups and go in separately. Those of you not at the raid will attract less attention."

Rawlings stood and lifted an A4 notepad from his desk. He walked to the whiteboard and Meredith handed him the pen.

"Jane didn't leave the station until seven-thirty. She saw another client after Liska. Trump had already dropped Liska off by the time she left. This other client's name was false. It was Eastern European, but he didn't have ID on him. The address he gave turns out to be a launderette, and the flat above is empty."

"Hang on a minute, how did we let someone without ID go?"

"It was an affray. The man got into an argument around the corner with a shopkeeper for taking an apple. When the shopkeeper complained he manhandled him a bit, and his wife called us. He was only brought here to allow them both to calm down – it would never have got to court. Then he held his hands up to it and gave a full confession with Jane present. The arresting officer was going back today to see if the shopkeeper wanted to press charges." Rawlings held his finger up, "And before you ask, the shopkeeper had never seen him before. We have good shots of him while at the station, but the face recognition software can't identify him. He's new to us."

Rawlings lifted a photograph from his desk and positioned it underneath Jane's. He drew a question mark next to it.

"What time was he booked?" Meredith snarled. "I was there, with

Jane. Liska's name was on the board . . . he must have known she was representing him, shit! I can't remember what was said, except telling the duty sergeant to wipe Liska's name off." He ran his hands through his hair. "I bet he got arrested purposely. I bet he simply wanted to get inside and see if he could find out anything of use." He shook his head. "We dished her up to them on a fucking plate." Pulling out the nearest chair he dropped his weight onto it. "Carry on."

Rawlings stepped back to the board and started listing times and making bullet points as he spoke.

"She left here at seven-thirty, her car turned left and we picked her up again as she left Broadmead and headed along Gloucester Road. The last sighting of her car was at seven forty-nine, near the leisure centre on Horfield Common. She lives two minutes away from there, and her car was in her garage when she was found. Her car was caught on camera seven times in total. From the timings, it appears she didn't stop on the way home."

"That's because she was in love." A few glances were exchanged, and Meredith shook his head, "Sorry, she was rushing home to see Sam. Poor sod. Is he okay?"

"Gone to stay with a friend. He gave a formal ID about an hour ago. He's pretty messed up." Jo shrugged. "He thinks it's his fault for being held up."

Rawlings resumed his commentary. "We've watched the cars following Jane's through all seven cameras, and only two were the same. One was a taxi, the other a blue Volkswagen Golf." He wrote down the registration on the board. "False plates, but we have boys out looking for it, and we're asking neighbours if they saw it in the area. It was pretty dark by that time, though, so no joy as yet."

He stepped sideways to Liska's photograph. "Our bloke guarding Liska was taken by surprise at approximately eleven-thirty. A guy dressed in black held him at the bottom of the stairs, while the other searched the house. He remembers nothing after that. He came around at eleven forty-five, and called it in. He has no idea if they got Liska, or if, as is possible, Liska heard the commotion and got out of the window."

Having jotted the events on Liska's section of the board he went back to Jane's.

"Frankie says she'd been dead for no more than ninety minutes when we found her. Which puts the approximate time of death at ten-thirty. It only takes ten minutes to get from Jane's house to the safe house, so there was a good hour between the two events. They may have stayed at Jane's or they may have organised some sort of meeting elsewhere. The results of the door-to-door are in: no one knows anything, and most were awoken by our lot coming and going outside." Rawlings shrugged. "That's it, I'm afraid. Not much to go on."

"You've circulated his photograph?" Rawlings nodded. Meredith stood and rescanned the board. "Good. Who knows, with any luck we'll bump into him tonight." He looked around his tired team. "Anything else before we disband?"

"Not much." Trump shook his head, "Hutchins tracked down Jimmy Ridgeway's sister. She hadn't seen him since he left for Bristol, although she didn't know that was where he was headed. She said he'd been involved with a girl here as a teenager. The girl had a kid, and later the sister heard she'd died from an overdose, nothing of interest there."

"Nothing on either of the two girls. How did you do with the other notebooks? I've still got two to go through." Meredith sighed at the negative response. He clapped his hands. "Right those of you working tonight, pack up. I'll meet you back here at seven-thirty. The rest carry on, and call if anything new comes in."

Seaton made sure everyone was working on something relevant, and pulled his jacket from the back of the chair. The others attending the bar that night had already left, all except Meredith who remained in his office. Slinging his jacket over his shoulder, Seaton tapped on Meredith's door and walked in.

"Gov, you really should . . ." He stopped speaking as Meredith was on his mobile. Meredith beckoned him forward.

"So, sod what happens? Yes, I'll take the money." Meredith listened for a while. "Yes, it's clear." Dropping the phone on the desk, his weary eyes looked at Seaton. "Are you off, Tom?"

"Yep, and you should be too. I've sorted the rest of them out. You'll be no good tonight if you don't get some shut-eye."

Meredith flipped the notebook shut. "I know. Come on, I'll walk with you."

~ ~ ~

Patsy called out quietly as she heard Meredith open the door.

"I'm in here. Don't make a noise, Amanda is sleeping." Meredith put his head around the living room door, "Oh boy, you look rough."

"I feel rough. Come to bed, and don't expect a reward, I need a hug."

Assuming she would follow, he went upstairs.

Allowing his clothes to crumple at his feet, he was in bed within minutes of arriving home. Patsy looked at the huge piles of CDs and DVDs she had removed from various shelves and cupboards and decided to leave them. She crept into the bedroom. Meredith lay naked on the bed, his hands behind his head, and his eyes shut. Patsy lay next to him.

"You have clothes on," he observed as he pulled her closer.

"Because I'm not staying. If you have to go out tonight, you need to sleep and I don't want to disturb you. I've heard it's not good news. I've had Linda on, but that's a conversation for later. What time do you need to be up?"

"Six-thirty, or thereabouts. They killed her, Jane Roscoe. She was representing our witness. God knows what they've done to him if they caught up with him. She was one of life's nice people." He sighed, and rolling onto his side he pulled Patsy into the crook of his body. "Trump thinks it is his fault. It's not, but you can't tell him."

"Go to sleep, you can tell me later."

"Thank you, Hodge."

"You're welcome."

Ten minutes later, Meredith was snoring softly. Patsy set the alarm in case she forgot him, and tiptoed out of the bedroom. Louie Trump did indeed think it was his fault, and she worried for him because if Meredith was this upset by this latest turn of events, Louie would be beside himself if he thought he had in any way caused it.

Returning to the sitting room, she threw herself back into her clearing and cleaning. She had called Chris for guidance regarding the Hatton case but he was in a meeting with a new client, which left Patsy to mull over her frustrations alone. She decided to spring clean, albeit autumn had arrived. Linda had promised she would get Chris to call her back. That was before launching into her concerns about Louie; his distress had been obvious, and Linda had been considering taking the day off. She'd phoned Patsy for advice. Patsy had told her to check she wasn't needed, and make the offer. She warned Linda to listen to Louie's response, as sometimes people needed to be alone. Knowing they were working that evening, she didn't want Linda winding him up into a frenzy.

Several hours later, shelves, cupboards and drawers had been cleared, cleaned and reorganised, pictures polished, and the rug rolled back. Patsy would attack with the vacuum when Meredith and Amanda awoke. Attempting to move the sofa to enable her to vacuum under it later, she jumped violently when Meredith appeared in the doorway.

He laughed as she yelped and held her hands to her chest.

"You seem busy. Do you want a hand?"

"You shouldn't creep up on people. I almost had heart failure. Grab that end for me, I want to clean underneath." Patsy renewed her grip on the end of the sofa.

"Underneath the sofa? Do people really do that?" he joked, as he helped her complete the task.

"Idle hands. I had to do something, or I'd go mad." She bent down, and, after retrieving a lost earing, she held it up triumphantly. "You see, it's always worth moving the sofa."

"Point taken. Do you also need a paperclip, a ten pence piece and a pound of dust?" Meredith asked as he turned to leave. "What have we got to eat? I will probably have a drink tonight, and should line my stomach."

Patsy caught up with him and nudged him out of the way.

"Your stomach is always lined – I doubt it's ever been empty. Pork chops and salad or pizza. Everything else will take too long."

"I had cardboard pizza the other night. I'll go for the protein in the pork, but what about a few chips?" He sat at the kitchen table and gave her his most charming smile.

"Only if you go shopping – no potatoes. We have some fresh bread though." Patsy wondered whether he would complain, but he didn't.

"Bread it is then." Remembering the conversation earlier in the week, he added, "Can I do anything to help?"

"What are we having, I'm starving?" Amanda now appeared in the doorway rubbing her eyes. "I have to be in work in a couple of hours, feed me please. What?" she added as Meredith jumped to his feet.

"I'm getting in the bathroom first. You help Patsy, I'll get ready." He ruffled her hair as he slipped past her. Amanda took his seat.

"What can I do, and what's happened to the sitting room? It looks like we've been burgled."

"I'm bored so I'm spring-cleaning." Patsy placed a chopping board on the table, and began collecting salad from the fridge. "Any cheek and you'll starve. Be grateful I didn't vacuum."

Amanda made a large salad while Patsy grilled the chops and sliced the bread.

"Dad isn't singing. He usually sings in the shower," Amanda observed as they listened to the sound of running water overhead.

"He has a lot on his mind. There was a particularly horrible murder yesterday, a solicitor he was fond of, and tonight he's going to a club probably frequented by the men who did it."

Amanda grimaced. "And there was me thinking I had it tough. I'm on geriatrics tonight, always makes me sad. Mind you, I'd rather that than accident and emergency – that's a nightmare at night. You wouldn't believe the way in which people can damage themselves."

"I think I have a pretty good idea." Patsy opened the cupboard to get some plates, and shook her head. "Look at that – everything everywhere. You can always tell when your father has emptied the dishwasher. I think I'll attack the kitchen next."

"Well, any money you find under the dishwasher is mine. I upset my purse the other day and couldn't be bothered to pull it out. Cobwebs lurk behind there, or at least they did in my last place. Did you know Dad was frightened of spiders?"

"I am not." A fresher-looking Meredith returned to the kitchen buttoning his shirt. He had missed the beginning of the conversation. "Why are we talking about the horrible, creepy crawly things anyway?"

"Patsy has a cleaning head on. I've told her any money she finds is mine."

"Including the tenner, she found down the side of the sofa?" Meredith sat next to his daughter. "I had that, it'll buy my first round."

"First drink, more like. Do you know how much drinks cost in clubs?"

The conversation carried on in this vein until their plates had been emptied, and Meredith had also made himself a banana sandwich in place of a sweet. Amanda told him he was a heart attack waiting to happen as he spread the bread with liberal helpings of butter. As she stood to leave the kitchen, the doorbell rang.

"I'll get it." She opened the door to Dave Rawlings. "Hi, Dave, they're in the kitchen. How's Ellen?"

"A little monkey, but well, thanks." Rawlings' daughter had been abducted earlier in the year, and although she had been unaware of her predicament, her parents were now very protective. Amanda told him to send her love, and left him to find his own way to the kitchen. He passed Meredith, who was coming the other way.

"Thanks for the lift, Dave, I'll be two minutes."

He left Rawlings greeting Patsy. He refused her offer of a drink, explaining that although he wasn't sure if he'd be fit to drive home, he needed to pace himself for the night ahead.

"Good man." Patsy chewed her bottom lip.

"What? I can see you want to say something."

"Between you and me, I had Linda on earlier. Trump is really cut up about what happened to your witness and his solicitor; he blames himself. Will you keep an eye on him?" She smiled. "And Meredith, come to that, but for all sorts of different reasons."

"I hear you, I'll do my best."

"Best at what?" Meredith asked as he reappeared.

"Will you stop creeping around, please? Dave's going to keep you on the straight and narrow. Now go, be safe, be careful and keep in touch. I have cleaning to attend to."

As soon as the men had gone, she loaded the dishwasher before attacking the living room with the vacuum. Amanda came back downstairs and Patsy called her in for assistance in putting the furniture back into position.

"There you go. Do you want me to get the dishwasher out for you? There is a knack, and I have a vested interest."

"I'm not sure I'm . . . Oh, come on, I have nothing better to do."

Amanda went ahead to the kitchen as Patsy unplugged and wound the lead the vacuum. Hearing Amanda gasp, and pushing the vacuum in front of her, she made her way to the kitchen.

"Did you break a nail, or was there more money than you . . ."

She stopped speaking as Amanda made a clumsy effort to hide something behind her back as she spun to face Patsy. Something fluttered to the floor, and Patsy stepped neatly around the vacuum and picked it up. It was a photograph. She frowned, sucked in her bottom lip, and held out her hand.

Amanda shook her head. "Patsy, I'm sure there is some perfectly innocent . . . Oh bollocks, there isn't, is there?" Amanda pulled her hand forward and held out the other prints. Patsy barely looked at them as she shuffled through them. "Say something." Amanda put her hand on Patsy's shoulder.

Patsy looked at her. "What?"

"Anything. Patsy, I'm so sorry . . . Why on earth were they on top of the dishwasher?"

"I have no idea, but it would appear your father is being blackmailed." Patsy placed the stack of photographs next to the sink. "Now, move out of the way, I have cobwebs to attack."

Amanda began to protest. "But Patsy, don't you –"

"Amanda, this has been a shock for both of us. I don't want to talk about it. I want to clean the kitchen. This is between me and your father. Now get yourself off to work, there are pensioners waiting for you."

Patsy took her by the shoulders and turned her to face the hall, demonstrating a calmness she didn't feel. Her heart thumped in her chest, and her lungs appeared to have lost the ability to draw in breath. Amanda turned as though to speak but Patsy shook her head. "Leave me, please, Amanda. Call me later when you're on your break. Off you go, I need to see how much money I can find."

She watched as Amanda collected her bag from the hall table and opened the door.

"Amanda," she called and Amanda turned, her eyes filled with tears for the pain she knew Patsy must be feeling. "Not a word to your father. I don't want him rushing home until I'm ready. I'll deal with this in my own time."

Amanda nodded, and unsure of what to say, she simply raised her hand. Patsy returned the gesture, and standing absolutely still, she waited until she heard the whine of Amanda's car indicate she had pulled off the drive. Content she was alone, Patsy lifted the photographs and shuffled through them once more. It took all her resolve not to make that call and tell Meredith exactly what she thought of him. Biting back tears, she slammed the photographs onto the table.

"Bastard! Total, absolute, cheating, fucking bastard," she cursed, and plugged in the vacuum.

Patsy spent the next three hours cleaning the kitchen. Every cupboard emptied, cleaned, and reorganised. The food cupboard and fridge were relieved of out-of-date jars and packets, and every surface was polished until it gleamed. Amanda was never going to be rich – Patsy only found four pence under the dishwasher, and surprisingly no cobwebs.

Every twenty minutes or so she picked up the photographs before slamming them back down. She wanted to kill him, she wanted him to face her and tell her why. She never wanted to see him again, but most of all she wanted him to hug her and tell her it would be all right. Eventually, she stood on the threshold of the kitchen, wrung out the mop for the last time, and eyed the photographs from afar. A glistening wet floor barred yet another look through, which she thought was just as well. It didn't get any easier.

She jumped as the phone rang behind her. Turning, she saw the flashing screen of the mobile on the hall table and walked over. Amanda was calling; she ignored it. Instead, she went upstairs and pulled out a suitcase from the bottom of the wardrobe. She collected her toiletries and make-up, and enough clothes to last her a few days and packed them. Leaving the suitcase to the bottom of the stairs. She looked in the kitchen. Staring at the mop, still in its bucket, she wondered whether to put it away. Deciding against it, she went back upstairs and showered.

Applying fresh make-up to her face, she stood looking at herself in the mirror. She had no idea where she was going to go. She didn't want to go to Chris and Sharon's, and she certainly didn't want to give Linda and Louie any more to cope with. It would have to be a hotel. She hated staying in hotels alone. Going to visit her father crossed her mind, but she dismissed it quickly. He'd probably come up and punch Meredith on the nose. She smiled at the thought.

When she returned to the hall, she found she had missed two calls: one from Chris, the other from Amanda. She listened to Chris's message and decided it could wait until tomorrow. She dialled Amanda.

"Hi, Amanda, I'm sorry you had to see those photographs."

"You're sorry? Why? I'm going to give him such a hard time. He's a stupid, selfish . . ."

"I'm leaving tonight, Amanda, I won't see your father. You take care, I'll be in touch."

"What did he say? How did he explain that?" Amanda demanded. "Why should you go? Kick him out, it's his fault!"

"It's also his house, and I've not spoken to him."

"Not even a text?"

"Not even a text."

"But don't you want to give him what for? Patsy, please don't go, stay there, I'll say I'm ill and come home," Amanda pleaded.

"I'm leaving right now. You finish your shift."

"Well, you might not want to speak to him, but I'm bloody well going to."

"Amanda, leave him. He's working, and it could be dangerous. Leave it until tomorrow. I'll write him a note."

"A note? Patsy, you can't deal with this with a note."

Patsy raised her voice. "Amanda! I need to deal with this in my own way, now please, let it alone."

"I'm sorry. Call me tomorrow, please. Let me know you're okay."

Patsy assured her she would, and hung up. She walked into the living room and collected a notepad and envelope. Taking it to the kitchen, she sat at the table and arranged them next to the photographs, and for the next twenty minutes she tried to work out what to say. Picking up the pen, she made three false attempts before finally finding the words. Folding the note, she slid it into the envelope, and picked up the pictures. Her hand hovered over the open envelope, as she wondered whether to include them. In a decisive mood, she shoved them into her jacket pocket and left the note in the centre of the table. She surveyed the kitchen; at least she was leaving a clean house. Walking past the mop she went to collect her case. As she drove off she noticed she'd left the lights on but shrugged her indifference.

~ ~ ~

Meredith and his team had split into two groups. Three people who hadn't attended the raid were to go to the club first on the pretence of celebrating a birthday. Meredith took the others to a bar close by, and bought a round of drinks.

"Right, this is the first. We'll have another at the club when we get there, but that's the lot. They know we're coppers and they should leave us alone, but I might wind things up a little depending on what happens, which means I need you lot on your toes. Hopefully, tonight we will be able to get photos of those frequenting the club, and find out who the bloke with Andronikov and Myshkin in that photo was. I want you acting as though you're already pissed when you go in. Any questions?"

While they drank, they mused over possible links between the various faces that they had dug up during the investigation so far, but the biggest question mark hung over the unknown Roper. Meredith finished his pint and carried the empty glass back to the bar. The others followed suit, and they walked the couple of streets to the Hammer and Sickle. There was much merriment as Meredith instructed them all to do their best drunk impression on the way so they would be ready when they hit the club. This was a good move as they were being watched as soon as they turned into the street where the club was located.

"It's not very nice round here, is it?" Trump lifted his arm and waved his finger around in a circle.

Seaton walked sideways into him, his finger held to his lips. "SHHHH. Don't be such a snob, they'll hear you."

"I'm not a snob," slurred Rawlings, "how dare you?"

"Because I can." Seaton tripped on the curb.

Meredith turned and walked backwards, facing the three men.

"We're being watched. White transit on the other side of the road. Keep it up, but don't overdo it."

They made it to the entrance, where a large muscular man with cropped blond hair and piercing blue eyes stood looking at them. He had biceps so large it appeared as though his tee-shirt sleeves would cut off the circulation to the rest of his arms. He held out his arms blocking their entry.

"Gentlemen, this is a members' only club. I don't think you are members." His accent had a slight Eastern European twang. He gestured up the street, indicating that might be the path they should take.

"No, it's not, pal, I checked." Meredith's left foot collided with his right, and he took several steps towards the man who smiled.

"It is tonight, sir, I think you should move on."

"We're coming in, pal, so step aside if you'd be so kind." Meredith grinned like a naughty schoolboy.

"I think you may have had a little too much to drink. I don't think we want a stag party in tonight." He pointed to a sign above the door that stated that the management reserved the right to refuse entry.

Seaton stepped forward and placed a finger on the man's chest.

"Now, I might have had one too many, but I know you're not management, and nor am I. Now, do as the Governor says and let us in." He gave an additional prod for good measure.

"Take your hands off me. That's assault and I don't want to have to defend myself. When I do that, people tend to get hurt."

Louie Trump bellowed out a laugh, causing the others to turn and stare. He laughed as though he were unable to control himself, eventually ending up leaning forward, his hands on his knees, and Rawlings patting his back.

"What's wrong with you?" Seaton grinned at the doorman. "I don't think he's all there." He tapped his temple. Turning back to Trump he asked again. "Are you going to be there all night, or are you going to tell us what's so funny?"

Trump pulled himself upright. Putting his other hand into his pocket, he pulled out his ID.

"Now you, good fellow, are preaching to the converted. We know the law, and we jolly well want a drink." Holding his ID open he swung his hand around to enable the others to see, "Show him chaps or we'll be here all night." He hiccoughed for good measure.

"Mad and posh. I don't think I mentioned posh, did I?" Seaton also produced his ID, shortly followed by Meredith and Rawlings.

The smile had fallen from the doorman's face. Snarling, he stepped to one side.

"In you go, but any trouble and you're out. I don't care if you're royalty."

Trump patted him on the arm as he stepped into the dimly lit lobby. "Good chap. Can I buy you a drink, old man?"

The doorman followed him in. "No thank you." He looked over their heads at the girl in the cloakroom. "Let them through, no charge." He squeezed past them and held open the door to the bar. "Behave please."

He watched them weave through the tables and make their way to the bar, where a skinny dark-haired woman smiled at them. Turning back to the girl in the cloakroom, he shook his head. "I don't need this. Keep an eye on them and shout if they cause any trouble; I have a call to make."

Pulling his mobile from his back pocket he opened the door to the street. The girl nodded and looked at the small monitor under the desk. The men were lined up along the bar, and the tall good-looking one was trying to climb on a stool. She shrugged; there were a lot of strangers in tonight, but that was good for the tips. Perhaps she should give Yolanda a ring, she might get some business.

As the barmaid attended to their order, Meredith leaned towards Trump. "I saw the board with the photos as we came in. The gents are out there, and I'll go and have a better look later. I see our lot are enjoying themselves."

Trump nodded and smiled, before casually turning around and scanning the room. Back to the bar, he leaned on his elbows as though to steady himself. He spotted Hutchins, Jo Adler and Bob Travers laughing together. They were seated at a table at the far end.

"It's busier tonight than the last time I came in. What's the plan? I assume you have one?"

"Not really, I . . . Hello, there's the groom." Meredith nodded towards the entrance door.

"The what?" Trump caught on and peered at the man who had entered. "Really? I can't remember him that well. Did you bring the photograph?" He paused as the door opened again, "The bride I take it?" He watched the well-built woman follow the man, and struggle to clear the gap between the tables. The coupled seated themselves in the centre of the room. "That's odd, they haven't bought a drink . . . Oh, spoke too soon."

The barmaid carried across a tray holding a bottle of vodka, a stack of shot glasses, and a dish of nuts.

Meredith slid from the stool and patted his breast pocket. "I have a plan now, and I'm putting it into action."

He walked across to the couple and bent to say something to them. Trump raised his eyebrows as Meredith pulled out a chair and joined them. Trump watched Meredith spend the next fifteen minutes laughing and joking with the couple. He downed several shots, and Trump sighed: so much for keeping in control. After the final shot Meredith slammed down his glass, and leaning awkwardly over the table, he kissed the woman on the cheek. Collecting his half-full pint glass, he returned to Trump.

"I can see you enjoyed that, but did you get anything?" He smiled as Meredith winked at him.

Meredith climbed onto a bar stool and drained his glass. He ordered two more from the barmaid. Once she was busy further along the bar, Meredith murmured, "They confirmed it's a bloke called Roper. Apparently, he gate-crashed their reception. They were introduced by Andronikov, and he put one hundred quid behind the bar as a present. They honeymooned in Croatia, and Andronikov is an old family friend."

Trump wondered how Meredith had extracted so much

information in such a short time.

"Myshkin is a cousin. I take it? How on . . ." He stopped speaking as the barmaid returned. She placed his fresh pint next to the one he had yet to finish. "I thought we were only pretending to get drunk?" he asked lifting the glass and taking a sip.

Meredith looked sideways at him.

"We are. It's only a couple of pints, Trump. And in answer to your earlier question, we didn't get as far as Myshkin. Oh God, they're going to have music. I hope that doesn't mean Cossack dancing and smashed glasses."

Two men in baggy trousers and white shirts open to the waist, pulled low stools into the corner of the room, and arranged sheet music on small wooden stands.

"I never could get the hang of that."

His attention was drawn back to the barmaid who had called "Sir?" several times. She held a phone towards him, and he tapped his chest. "Me?" She nodded and passed him the receiver. He gave Trump a shrug as he spoke his name, and listened to the caller. He uttered only two sentences during the three-minute call: "The photographs were unnecessary, they won't cause me an issue." Then, at the end of the call, "Of course we can do business, I'm not stupid." Hanging up, he passed the phone back to the barmaid, and pursed his lips, scanning the optics as he considered the call.

"Are you going to tell me, or do I have to guess?" Trump asked as the musicians started their warm up.

"I'll brief you later," Meredith glanced round as the customers began to clap in time to the first tune. "It's too noisy in here."

The next hour or so was of little use to their investigation. Seaton had little luck trying to get any information from the cloakroom attendant about either Ronnie or Elena. Rawlings had scanned the pin board and found that Trump had secured the only photograph of anyone related to their enquiry, and the punters singing and clapping to the music made it impossible to have anything other than a shouted conversation. Meredith had given Travers' team permission to stand down when he came to the bar to order fresh drinks, and he was thinking of calling it a day when Seaton came with news.

"Myshkin has arrived. He's in the lobby speaking to the doorman."

"Good. I was starting to get bored." Meredith gave a small smile, and, like Trump, he looked towards the door as Myshkin swaggered in. His shoulders back and chin up, he smirked as he nodded acknowledgement. Meredith ignored him.

"That's the way, Gov. Don't you dare start on him in here, it'll start a second Cold War."

The three men observed as Myshkin greeted several of the other customers enthusiastically. There was a lot of back slapping and bear hugs.

"You see? He's showing the level of support he has," Seaton warned.

Myshkin had a brief conversation with the groom, slapped him on the back and said something in his ear, causing the groom to roar with laughter and bang the table before sharing the joke with his bride. Finally, Myshkin stood a table's depth away from the three men, and, looking at Meredith, he jerked his head towards the lobby.

Meredith grinned. "Seems like he wants to speak to me." Meredith stepped forward, pushing Trump back towards the bar. "Stay here, it won't take two of us."

"Hands in pockets, Gov," Seaton reminded him as Meredith walked away.

Myshkin held the door open for Meredith. The doorman stood on the other side.

"Should we ignore his order to stay put?" Trump wondered.

"Give him five minutes. He can't get in too much trouble in that time." Seaton glanced at his watch as the door closed behind Meredith.

Meredith followed Myshkin across the small lobby towards the gents' toilets, aware that the doorman had fallen into step behind him.

He turned, wagging his finger. "I can hold my own, thanks, you stay here and look menacing." He was surprised when the doorman smiled and stepped back. "That was easier than I thought it would be," he muttered.

Rawlings zipped his trousers and turned to pull the flush. He hunched his shoulders instinctively as the door into the toilets slammed back against the ceramic-tiled wall. He heard Meredith's voice hissing out a warning, and placing his hand on the bolt, he slowly slid it back in case he should be needed.

Meredith had shoved Myshkin forward as he opened the door, and now had him pinned against the wall.

"You piece of shit. How dare you summon me with a flick of your head? I don't know who you think you are, but to me you are nothing but the shit on my shoe that needs removing. Now what do you –"

Meredith grunted as Myshkin flattened his hands against the wall and pushed back forcefully, causing Meredith to lose his balance. Meredith stumbled and grabbed onto the basins to steady himself. The two men now stood nose to nose: had they been dogs they would have been snarling, teeth bared. Instead, they stared at each other, both awaiting the other's next move. It was Meredith who broke the silence.

"What do you want? Spit it out – I have better things to do with my time."

He flinched as Myshkin reached into his pocket. Myshkin laughed as he pulled out an envelope. He slapped it against Meredith's chest and held it there with the palm of his hand, causing Meredith to step back until he rested against the basin.

"Compliments of Ivor Andronikov. Why he should pay you I have no idea. But you are now to leave or the deal is off." Myshkin leaned forward. "Do you understand, Mr Policeman?"

"I understand you." Meredith took the envelope and slid it into his pocket. "Tell Mr Andronikov I'm obliged. But you," Meredith punched his finger into Myshkin's chest, "you can go back to whichever stone you hide under, and wait for me to come get you. Because I will get you."

Meredith was unprepared for the head-butt Myshkin delivered to the bridge of his nose. He groaned as he heard the loud crack as it made impact, and felt the blood flow. He made to swing a punch but Myshkin was too quick for him. He grabbed Meredith's arm and twisted it up behind his back.

"You will never have me. You know it, I know it, so don't play that game. When Andronikov has finished with you, I will finish you, but first I might pay a visit to that pretty girl of yours."

"Like fuck."

Meredith leaned forward before throwing his body back with as much force as he could muster. Myshkin lost his grip on Meredith's arm and the momentum carried them across the small room. The door to the cubicle behind Myshkin flew open, and Meredith forced him backward and, as a consequence, Rawlings too, until Myshkin ended up sitting on Rawlings' lap. Rawlings locked his arm around Myshkin's neck as Meredith turned, growling and spitting blood out of his mouth. His eyes briefly registered the surprise he felt at seeing Rawlings before he aimed a kick at Myshkin's crotch. Myshkin roared in agony, and kicked out at Meredith as Rawlings clung on to him.

"Cheers Dave." Meredith turned his head to spit again, and dodging Myshkin's flailing legs, he stepped between them and grabbed Myshkin's chin. "You go within a mile of her, and I will kill you. I will inflict more pain on you than you have ever dealt out." His blood dripped onto Myshkin's face. "I know what you did to those girls, and I will do it to you, one way or the other, so be warned. I'm not planning on locking you up, I'm not that kind." Meredith jumped back. "Now get out of here, and warn chummy outside that his presence is not needed."

Meredith nodded permission for Rawlings to release his hold. Myshkin staggered to his feet. One hand caressed his throat, the other rearranged the crotch of his trousers. He didn't look behind at Rawlings, his eyes remaining fixed on Meredith. He spat out what Meredith assumed was a curse in Russian as he walked backwards to the exit. Pulling the door open he lifted his hand, and, fashioning a gun from his fingers, he shot Meredith before disappearing.

"What the bloody hell –"

"Shut up and watch the door, I need to clean up a bit." Meredith turned and looked at his reflection. His nose had swollen, and was already beginning to change colour. He had blood everywhere. He cursed fluently as he turned on the tap and splashed water over his face.

"Clean up? That horse has bolted, Gov. I think you've just lost a friend."

Meredith walked to the paper towel dispenser and pulled several sheets out to dry his face with. He walked back to the mirror and dabbed at his nose, wincing with each touch.

"I think we've outstayed our welcome. Let's round up the others and –"

He turned quickly as the door opened. Rawlings pulled his arms into a fighting stance, and blew out a relieved breath as Trump came in.

Trump looked back over his shoulder. "What did you say? Can't get in too much trouble in five minutes?"

Seaton's head appeared over Trump's shoulder.

"What happened to hands in pockets?"

"I slipped." Meredith spat bloody spittle into the basin. "Let's call it a day. I doubt we'll get much more from tonight."

There was no sign of Myshkin or the doorman as they made their way out of the club. They waited a little way down the road until the others had also made a safe exit. As the state of Meredith became known, many questions were asked but went unanswered.

"Enough," Meredith said finally. "For some reason, I've developed a headache. Get yourselves off home, because that's where I'm going. I'll want doughnuts with my coffee in the morning. Eight sharp. Dave, take me home, I won't be allowed in a taxi in this state."

Calling his thanks to Rawlings, Meredith started down the drive. He smiled as he noticed the lights were on. Patsy had waited up and could attend to his needs. He opened the door.

"I'm home, and don't panic, it's only a nosebleed," he called, slipping out of his jacket and unbuttoning his shirt. "I could do with a drink."

He walked to the kitchen and filled the sink with cold water. Dropping his shirt in, he watched the water turned pink. Patsy hadn't answered, and assuming she had fallen asleep he went in search of her.

Myshkin's threats had not fallen on deaf ears, and he was wondering how to word his warning to her. As he walked back towards the hall, he noticed the mop standing in its bucket. He'd never had Patsy down as a housewife. As this thought occurred to him, he remembered the photographs and his head turned towards the dishwasher. Catching sight of the envelope on the table with his name neatly printed in the centre, he knew instinctively it was not good news, and collected a glass and bottle of wine before seating himself at the table. He poured the wine and fingered the envelope. Perhaps he should ignore it, take a shower, and go to bed, it would still be there in the morning.

Curiosity got the better of him and he slid the note from the envelope.

*Meredith,*

*I found the photographs and quite frankly I am at a loss for words. Nice ones anyway. I have no idea why they are in our home, or indeed who your companion is, but I guess that doesn't matter.*

*We've had a bumpy ride, you and I, and right at this moment I don't think I can cling on. Please don't call me, I need to deal with this in my own way.*

*Patsy*

The note was short, and Meredith turned the page over to ensure he hadn't missed something. Finding nothing he screwed it into a ball and dropped it onto the table. Picking up the glass of wine, he switched off the lights and went to the bedroom. He looked at the open wardrobe doors and kicked them shut.

"You couldn't speak to me face to face? Well, fuck you, Hodge! I'm too old, and I'm too tired." He emptied the glass in one gulp, hit the light switch, and fell onto the bed. Kicking off his shoes, he turned his back on her side of the bed. "Fuck you, Hodge."

# 11

Peggy Green grumbled as the doorbell rang. She'd only just settled to watch her favourite reality show. Walking through the hall, she was tempted to go back as she heard the commentator say, *"What Jeremey doesn't know is that a surprise is awaiting him when he opens that door."*

Peggy wondered if there was a surprise awaiting her too. There was.

When she opened the door, Patsy Hodge stepped forward and burst into tears. Wrapping her arms around her, Peggy kicked the door shut and led her to the living room. Jeremey had opened the door, and was now screeching his disgust. Peggy switched off the TV, and pushed Patsy to sit on the sofa.

"What is it, Patsy?"

Peggy crossed the room to the cabinet in the recess. Taking two tumblers and a bottle of whiskey from it, Peggy poured generous measures into each. She held one out to Patsy. "In your own time. I'll wait."

Following the loss of her husband and daughter, Peggy Green had opted out of society for a while. She had met Meredith and Hodge when she became a witness to a crime, and later the victim of a mugger. Peggy's straight-talking, no-nonsense attitude had endeared her to the couple and Amanda, and she had been adopted and become part of their family unit. She sipped her drink patiently as Patsy took control her emotions.

"Sorry, Peggy," Patsy sniffed, "I didn't know where else to go. May I stay here tonight?"

"Of course. What's Merriwinkle done? Are you going to tell me, or should I mind my own business? I can, you know."

Peggy had purposely called Meredith by the wrong name at their first meeting, and as it amused her she'd never dropped the practice.

Patsy considered this for a moment. She wanted someone to tell her that the photographs weren't real, but knew that with Peggy she was more likely to get the blunt truth. Fishing in her pocket and found a tissue and blew her nose.

"Not at the moment." She gave a little shrug. "Is that okay? I need to sort my own head out first."

"That's fine," Peggy held her glass up. "Take a sip, it will help. But if you need to sort your head out, as you put it, whatever it is that's got you into this state can't be straightforward and two heads may be better than one." Peggy pursed her lips. "But if you are going to be here, you do have to speak to me." Standing she placed her glass on top of the television. "I was going to get some supper. Do you want anything to eat?" Patsy declined the offer. "Okay, but you can come and keep me company while I prepare it. It's nice to have someone here, even in these circumstances."

"When do Antonio and Paul get back?"

Antonio was Peggy's lodger, and Paul his son by Meredith's late ex-wife. They had come to know each other via Patsy, and Peggy had taken them in.

"A couple of weeks, but I don't know for how long. His mother has sold the house in Spain, and is talking about buying here. I suppose I was hoping they would stay here." Peggy lifted a block of cheese from the fridge and made a face. "Bet that makes you laugh. Miserable, solitary old Peggy wanting all that noise around her. It does get on my nerves sometimes, but the good outweighs the bad, so we'll see."

"Have you told him that? He might think he's outstayed his welcome." Patsy sat at the small kitchen table and, taking the breadknife offered by Peggy, she sliced the loaf. "How many slices?"

"Just the one, unless you've changed your mind; these hips have got enough of a wobble already." She smiled as Patsy cut an additional slice. Hoping she wasn't pushing her luck, she added, "Where is Merriwinkle? He's not going to come banging the door down, demanding your return, is he? I'd hate to have to punch him on the nose, although given the state you're in I probably will anyway."

Her eyes twinkled, and Patsy gave a half smile.

"He's working. I doubt he'll even know I'm not there until sometime tomorrow."

"Bit late to be working, isn't it? Is he staking someone out? I don't know what he was thinking about leaving you in that state. That's the first thing I'll be dealing with when I see him." Peggy hoped that her way of extracting more information from Patsy wasn't too obvious. "Cheese?"

"He doesn't know, and yes please."

"What do you mean, he doesn't know? How can you get yourself into a state, and Merriwinkle be oblivious? How can he upset you when he's at work?" Peggy put the cheese back into the fridge, and turned, hands on hips. "He is working, is he? You're not using that as some sort of euphemism." She bent towards Patsy. "Look, I know I said I didn't need to know, but I do. Come on girl, spit it out, because at the moment I'm mentally cutting off his dangly bits."

She hoped that might raise a smile, if not a laugh. It didn't. Peggy was well aware of how much Meredith thought of Patsy, and was sure that cheating on her would be the last thing that would cause such upset. When Patsy ignored her and bit into the cheese, Peggy tutted in irritation.

"I'll do a deal with you." She didn't say what and Patsy's eyes narrowed.

"Go on, what?"

"You tell me what Merriwinkle has done, and I'll not phone him and tell him to get his arse round here to sort it out." Peggy bit into her sandwich.

"You wouldn't, I know that."

"I certainly would, oops . . . sorry." Peggy retrieved the piece of sandwich which had flown out of her mouth. Swallowing, she pointed the sandwich at Patsy. "Don't ever call my bluff. I was always up for a dare."

"Of that there is no doubt." Patsy forced a smile. "Can we do this again in the morning? I'm tired and once we get started, it could run for quite a while."

"Nope, not if you've snuck out and he doesn't even know what he's done. That's not fair." Peggy stood and wandered into the other room, giving Patsy time to consider this. She returned, bottle in hand. "And, if we're not going to have the conversation, we might as well have a tipple."

"You're taking his side?" Patsy shook her head. "I don't believe that, and of course he knows. How could he not know? Do I strike you as some hysterical teenager?" The tears were long gone, and Patsy was now becoming angry, not least because Peggy, with no knowledge of the dispute, appeared to be supporting Meredith.

"You do at the moment, yes." Peggy took a gulp of her drink and smacked her lips together, "That hit the spot. Now, look at it from my point of view. You turn up here weeping and wailing. You refuse to tell me why, and even admit Merriwinkle doesn't know why."

"Don't be bloody stupid, he knows, and I left a note." Patsy blew out a breath. "I'm sorry, Peggy, I shouldn't have snapped, and I probably shouldn't have come. I'll make a move, but thanks for the offer."

Peggy shrugged. "Off you go. I suppose a note is better than an explanation for whatever it is he's done. I thought my logic was off-centre, but not even demanding he explain himself . . . well, that's a matter for you I suppose." Peggy suppressed a grin when Patsy didn't move. "Are you going soon? Only there's a programme I wanted to watch after the news."

"I think he slept with someone else. There were photographs on top of the dishwasher."

"On the dishwasher? Why would anyone, particularly Meredith, keep photographs on top of the dishwasher? It doesn't make sense."

"It's the location that bothers you?" Patsy rolled her eyes. "He had clearly been caught short and had to put them somewhere."

"But how did you find them? Why were you looking?" Peggy looked bemused. She wasn't, but she wanted to keep Patsy talking.

"I wasn't, I was cleaning. Look, Peggy, the why and where is irrelevant, surely? It's the content that's the issue."

"Were they saucy?" Peggy raised her eyebrows, a stern look on her face.

"No, Peggy, they were of Meredith as a baby. Of course they were saucy!"

"Don't get sarcastic with me, I'm guessing most of this." Peggy folded her arms across her chest.

"There are five photographs, all of which show Meredith with an attractive naked woman in a . . . I was going to say 'compromising' position, but it doesn't seem appropriate. Needless to say, they were both having a good time."

"When were they taken?"

"What?"

"When were they taken? The man has been around the block, Patsy. I doubt you were a virgin when you met either." Peggy held her hand out. "Let me see."

"NO! Peggy, really!" Patsy fell silent. She hadn't considered that they could be historic photographs. She would still rather not have seen them, but that would be a better explanation. Closing her eyes, she wondered if Meredith had read her note yet. She drummed her fingers on the table. They were itching to take the photographs from her pocket. "I didn't think about that."

"Then I suggest you do." Peggy refilled her glass. "Check."

Getting to her feet, Patsy took several strides away from Peggy, and slid the photographs from her pocket.

"Stay. You're not looking." She held up the flat of her hand as Peggy made to join her.

"I'm not a dog." Peggy sat back in her chair, tutting.

Peggy's comment was lost on Patsy who was scanning the photographs. Meredith's hair, such as she could see, looked the same. But it hadn't changed for the best part of twenty years judging by other, less graphic photographs she had seen. His face was not in focus on all of them, but he looked pretty much the same as he did now. Then she saw the tie. Her face crumpled, but this time in anger. She turned the photograph to face Peggy, although it was too far away for Peggy to see. Peggy squinted, craning her neck forward.

"It's recent. There's his tie over the back of the chair. It was a birthday present. I was right, what a bastard." She passed the photograph across to Peggy.

Peggy's pursed lips were back.

Meredith lay naked on a bed, his eyes closed, straddled by a naked woman. It was clear from the woman's expression that she was enjoying the experience. On the other side of the bed was a dressing table, in front of which sat a chair with the incriminating tie hanging over the back.

Peggy lifted it closer to her face. "He doesn't seem to be enjoying it as much as she is. A birthday present, you say?" She held the photograph towards Patsy. "Well, now I can see why you're upset, and I agree it appears he's been a total bastard . . . if, of course, that's the tie you think it is. The question is, what are you going to do now?" She sighed as Patsy put the photographs back into her pocket. "Merriwinkle has let us down."

Patsy patted her on the shoulder. "I know. Still, there's lots left in that bottle. Let's get drunk and forget about him for a couple of hours."

Patsy woke several hours later with a start. She had fallen asleep in the armchair, and Peggy had left her there, having thrown a blanket over her. Stretching out her legs, she leaned forward, arching her back. Her hand flew to her mouth as nausea kicked in. Keeping perfectly still she tried to remember where Peggy's bathroom was. Seconds later, she cursed Meredith as she rushed to the bathroom. Unable to take the time to close the door, she emptied the contents of her stomach. Kneeling in front of the toilet bowl she ran her hands over her face. Her skin felt cold and clammy, and, afraid to leave the vicinity of the toilet, she leaned against the wall, grateful that she didn't have to work the next day. She closed her eyes; perhaps she could sleep here. The vision of Meredith with the woman entered her mind, and try as she might, she couldn't erase it.

Hearing Peggy moving next door, she hoped she wouldn't get up. While she had been kind to Patsy, it was clear that she wanted to hear Meredith's excuses before passing final judgement. 'It looks like she's enjoying it more than Meredith.' What sort of observation was that to make, given the circumstances? Resting her head against her knees, she blew out a sigh of relief: Peggy hadn't appeared.

Then the realisation hit her. Using the towel rail, she pulled herself to her feet, her hand searching for the light switch. She found the cord and pulled it, blinking against the sudden harsh glare. Putting the lid down, she sat on the toilet, pulled the photographs from her pocket, and skimmed through them quickly before going to Peggy's room.

"Peggy, I'm going. Thank you so much for being there for me. I'll call you later."

"What? Where are you going?" Peggy lifted herself on to one elbow.

"Home, I need to see Meredith."

"Halle-bloody-lujah." Peggy peered at the red numbers on the clock. "It's four in the morning, could you not wait until daybreak?"

"Nope. Bye, Peggy, I'll call you." Patsy was already running down the stairs.

Meredith pretended to be asleep as she tiptoed into the room. He was knackered, pissed off, and the last thing he wanted was a fight. That could wait. Patsy knelt to the side of his feet and patted his leg.

"Wake up. I need to speak to you."

"I won't, and you don't. Not now anyway. I'm in no condition. You won't believe a word I say, so hands up, I did it. Does that help?"

"No, seriously, Meredith, wake up."

"Why? Call me all the names you can think of, work out what you're going to do, and let me know tomorrow. I can't do this now."

Patsy gave a frustrated grunt as she jumped from the bed. She immediately regretted the action as her stomach lurched, and her head thumped. Ignoring this, she flipped the light switch.

"For Christ's sake." Meredith pulled the duvet over his head.

Patsy grabbed the bottom of the duvet and yanked it. Meredith cursed as it flew off the bed. He turned over and looked at Patsy, who gasped in horror. Running to him she took his face in her hands.

"What happened? You look awful," Gently she touched the pad of her finger against the huge swelling which had closed his left eye. "Does that hurt?"

"Of course it fucking hurts! Get off." With a flip of his hand he brushed her away and walked naked to the bathroom. Lifting the lid of the toilet he relieved himself. Patsy followed him. "It's no use following me, I'm not doing this now."

He closed his eyes, it was less painful.

"I know you didn't do it." Patsy announced simply.

He snapped his head towards her, opening one eye. "What?"

"Careful, or you'll clean it up." Patsy warned, a laugh in her voice.

Meredith turned away, and concentrated on finishing the job in hand. "Explain," he commanded, attempting not to frown as that caused his whole face to throb.

"It was something Peggy said when she saw the photos."

She laughed as Meredith groaned.

"Peggy? Why has Peggy seen them? Have you gone mad? I'll never be allowed to forget this." Pulling the flush, he walked to the basin and snorted as he caught sight of his reflection. "The last twenty-four hours have not been good. I need you to explain and explain quickly, because I need to sleep."

A smile twitched around his mouth, a smile of relief, which he held back until he was sure he was home and dry.

"Come back to bed – I feel quite delicate myself – and I'll tell you."

As Meredith allowed himself to be led back to the bedroom, he wondered how, given the circumstances, his luck seemed to be changing. With his good eye, he watched as Patsy undressed, leaving her clothes where they fell before hitting the light switch.

"I was enjoying that view," he grumbled as she climbed in next to him.

"Not so fast, Romeo, you still have some explaining to do." Patsy smiled into the darkness. "Shall I go first?"

Meredith slumped back on the pillow. "Please."

"I'm sorry I doubted you. It was seeing the tie, the one you had for your birthday." That was a lie, Patsy had taken in little of the detail until her discussion with Peggy, but now felt the need to justify her reaction. She was pleased Meredith couldn't see her face.

"Can we cut to the bit where you know I didn't do anything?" Meredith wanted the matter to be closed. He didn't care why she believed him, he only wanted to have one less thing to worry about.

"When Peggy looked at the photograph," she ignored Meredith's grunt of disbelief, "she said you didn't look as though you were enjoying it as much as she was." Patsy drew in a breath as the image flashed into her mind. "And when I thought about that, I wondered why the photographs at all? If you were going to have sex with someone, why on earth would you allow photographs? I looked again, and if you look closely, you can see the person taking them. Did you know that?"

"I did. I was trying to work out who I could trust to enlarge it, or enhance it, or whatever it is they need to do. Go on . . ."

"Well, obviously that told me you were not a willing participant. It was staged. Even you are not arrogant enough to invite someone to take photographs of you in the act. So, I'm sorry I doubted you, but I'm sure you will understand my shock on finding them."

"Arrogant? Is that fair? Some bastard has put me in compromising photographs, attempted to blackmail me, and you call me arrogant! I'm offended." Meredith relaxed, and thanked whoever it was who was watching over him, "Come here." He reached over to pull her close.

"Not yet. I want to know how DCI sharp-as-a-tack John Meredith got himself into that position? Were you drunk? Did you know her?"

The tension returned to Meredith's shoulders. "Will you marry me?"

Patsy gasped and turned to face him. "What? We've been there and done that – it didn't last long. Are you avoiding answering me?"

"No, but I've been stupid, only trying to protect you of course, but I want it put right. I love you, and I have no idea why you put up with me, but I want to keep that love. So, will you? The sooner the better, no fuss, no fanfare, just our commitment to each other."

Patsy fell on top of him, only to be pushed away as he shouted in agony as her nose found his.

"Watch the face! Was that a yes?"

"Yes."

"Good, come here and be gentle with me."

Meredith's scream of agony had broken the spell. Whilst Patsy was elated, she wanted an answer to her question.

"Let's finish the conversation first. Who, how and where? Then we can see about other things."

Meredith pulled her to nestle in the crook of his arm. "When I was in London. I met a bad Russian who sent his girl back to the hotel with me. Supposed to be a gift." He pushed Patsy back down as she attempted to challenge him, "Clearly a set-up. She told me she would be in trouble if I didn't let her take me back to the room. I was pretending to be drunk: I admit I'd had a few, but I wasn't plastered. Once there she did the 'let me stay an hour and they'll not think anything of it'. I agreed and told her I wasn't capable anyway. And before you ask why I agreed it was because I wanted to talk to her. I was there investigating a murder, remember. We sat down, she on the chair, me on the bed, and she poured the drinks. I honestly remember little after that until I awoke the next morning. They'd also searched my room, but didn't find the file because I was sleeping on it. So, that's it. I was set up, and you, you wonderful woman, could see that. Now, can we celebrate getting engaged . . . again?"

Patsy had many more questions, but decided to save them. She was home, they were together, and she was happy to accept that.

"Yes. It'll be a small party."

She laughed as Meredith gave a shout.

"I wasn't talking about inviting others!"

"I know. I was being humorous. Come here, Meredith."

"Not funny. I'm already here, Hodge."

## 12

Patsy frowned as she greeted Chris Grainger. Although he smiled, his face was pale and he looked fatigued. There were beads of perspiration on his brow.

"Morning. Are you okay? You don't look well." Patsy pulled out the chair and sat opposite him.

"Feeling a bit rough as it happens. Must be something I ate, but thanks for noticing. How's Meredith?" Chris leaned back in his chair and yawned.

"In what way? Was that a general friendly enquiry, or an 'I know something's going on' question?" Patsy lifted the envelope from her bag.

"Both. Bring me up to speed on everything, I may be off again later." Chris shrugged. "I could do with going to bed, not chasing around the country, but a man's got to do et cetera."

"I wondered why you didn't return my call yesterday. But we'll come to that later. Why the sudden interest in Meredith?" Patsy's eyes narrowed.

"Not sudden, he's one of my best friends. I'm simply interested."

"As it happens he's got himself into a bit of bother, and I was going to ask for your help." Patsy tapped the envelope on the desk. "But, as you will discover, the fewer people that see these the better. I'm hoping you can assist and I don't have to go to Linda."

"What is it you're after?" Chris folded his arms and shivered as though he were cold. He glanced at the clock. "We've got about thirty minutes before anyone else arrives, get on with it."

"Meredith is well, except for a suspected broken nose, a spectacular black eye, wounded pride and some pornographic photographs in which he plays a starring role. Not a willing one, I hasten to add. And yet," she tilted her head, "something tells me you know that, or most of it. Is there something you want to share with me?"

Chris jutted out his bottom lip. "Nope. What is it you need?" He pulled his head back as Patsy jabbed her finger towards him.

"Liar! You're not shocked? Do you not want to know how he could have been an *unwilling* participant? What's going on?" Patsy slumped back in her chair. "I'm worried now, Chris. Someone is playing games with my life, and it's not funny. I know you were some superspy." She held her hand up. "Okay, I know I exaggerate, but how can it be that you know anything about Meredith and his problems? Ahh." She allowed herself a smile. "Meredith told you."

Chris rolled his eyes. "What do you need? We're wasting time."

"Meredith wants an enhanced view of whoever took the photographs. He was caught by the mirror. Well, we think it's a man." Patsy handed the envelope over, and watched as Chris examined the photographs. She ignored the smile he tried but failed to suppress.

"Drugged him, did they? Who's the girl?"

"Does it matter who she is? Some tart connected to one of the men he's investigating. And yes, they drugged him. Can you enhance that or not?"

"I'll give it a go, but it would be easier if we had the digital copy. Go and put it on the scanner." He shuffled through the pile and passed the correct photograph back.

Patsy did as she was asked, and waited while Chris tapped away at his computer. He beckoned her over. Collecting the photograph, she went to stand behind him. Pulling the mouse across the image, he framed the reflection in the mirror and, clicking a few buttons, he enlarged the image. Patsy leaned forward and squinted at the face.

"It's not brilliant, but you'd recognise him if you knew him. I don't suppose you do?" She gave a laugh. "I think Meredith could do with some luck at the moment . . . don't worry, it's only wishful thinking."

Chris didn't answer her question.

"Where does he want me to send it?"

"His private email address. Meredith wants this kept quiet until he knows he can prove something. He also wants this man, whoever he is, to continue to think he's got something on him."

Chris saved the enhanced image and attached it to an email. He asked for coffee, and as Patsy walked away, he quickly typed a note and hit the send button. Ten minutes later, the photographs were stored safely in Patsy's bag and they sipped their coffee. Patsy looked at Chris over the rim of her mug.

"I know you know why I'm working for the Hattons, and I want to know too. If you won't or can't tell me, pull me out. I'm losing the will to live there, and I'm going to miss whatever it is you want me to find because I'm bored and I won't see the wood for the trees."

"You know this job is boring, tedious, downright crap sometimes." Chris pulled a handkerchief from his pocket and mopped his brow. "But it's not like you to be precious. What's going on?"

Patsy dropped her chin and considered this for a moment. Lifting her head, she shrugged. "I want to do something that helps. When I was a copper, it was boring and humdrum sometimes, but it all had a purpose. I suppose what I'm after is something that makes me feel I'm not simply clocking enough hours to earn a wage. I want to do something of value."

"Everything we do has a value. Maybe not to us, but certainly to someone, or we wouldn't be able to charge the fees we do." Chris massaged his temples. "I've got a shit headache, and tons to do. Do you want this assignment or not?"

His words were clipped and the frown on his forehead set. Patsy knew he had far more he wanted to say about her attitude, but his anger was well controlled.

"Tell me it's important. I know you're pissed off with me, and I can understand that, but you could put a temp in there for all the good I'm doing."

"It's of national importance, and far more so than simply getting this body armour perfected." Chris pushed himself out of his chair. "Conversation over, are you going back or not? It's a simple enough question."

Patsy confirmed that she would. She didn't ask any further questions, and Chris nodded curtly. Lifting his briefcase from the side of his desk he walked away.

"Good, keep a clear head: there are secrets to be uncovered. Share your pain with me if it helps, but I would have thought you were old enough to cope." He pulled open the door. "I'm off. I'll be on my mobile."

Patsy gave a grim smile as the door closed behind him. She felt like she'd let her father down and been reprimanded. Sighing, she walked to her own office. With nothing better to do she decided to check her emails and have a catch-up with Linda and Sharon. Quickly and efficiently she answered or deleted the few emails and circulars in her inbox, and opened the spam folder. Scrolling through the emails offering cheaper life insurance or sexual aids, she hit the delete button in irritation. She pulled her hand away from the keyboard as her eyes scanned the preview of the email headed, *'For the good of your health'*. Patsy had expected it to be another wild claim about some potion or lotion, but the word 'Meredith' sprang out at her. She opened the email.

*For the good of your health*

*We are sorry to have to contact you in such a manner, but your man Meredith is a renegade. His high and mighty attitude has no foundation. Do not trust him, do not believe him, support of him could be dangerous.*

It was unsigned. Patsy glanced at the sender's address but it was simply a series of numbers at a popular mail server. This was clearly connected to the photographs. She hit the forward button and typed a note for Meredith. In it she asked if he had any thoughts on the identity of the photographer. Quickly deleting the remaining spam, she opened a Word document and typed in the word 'renegade' and moved the mouse to the Thesaurus function. It was an odd word to use in a threat; surely cheat or liar would have been more apt. Hovering the mouse over the synonyms, she read the alternatives aloud.

"Apostate, traitor, rebel, turncoat, betrayer, defector, deserter. Betrayer I could understand, but traitor, or turncoat?" she mused.

Meredith had said the men he was investigating were Russian, so taking that into consideration she should be quite impressed with their English. She shut down her computer as she heard Linda come into the main office. She was singing. Walking to her door, she watched as Linda went through the same routine as she did each morning: kettle on, coat on hook, computer on, bag under desk, check in-tray, rearrange keyboard and mouse mat which the cleaner always insisted on moving, log into computer, and remove something sugary from a bag.

"How many calories does that cake have?" Patsy laughed as Linda jumped, and sugar granules sprinkled all over her desk.

"PHPI, how many times? If you are in, leave some sort of signal."

Linda placed the cake on her mouse mat carefully, and swept the granules from her desk. "That scare almost put me off my cake. And probably a million calories, but I don't care."

Patsy walked forward and perched on the edge of Linda's desk. "Firstly, the alarm was off, so you should have known someone was in. Secondly, I thought you were going on a strict diet, or have you decided against fitting back into the dress you wore to your first date?"

Patsy's amusement was evident, and Linda put her nose into the air.

"You can laugh, but it's a classic. You'll eat your words when you see me in it." Linda logged into the system. "Tea or coffee?" she asked as she pushed herself away from the desk and went to the kitchen. Looking back over her shoulder, she asked, "How's Meredith?"

Patsy's head jerked towards her. "Fine, why?" She followed Linda to the kitchen.

"Because Louie is a troubled man, he's gone all moody on me." She waved a teaspoon at Patsy. "In fact, if he wasn't Louie, I'd think he was having an affair."

"Don't be silly, it's probably this case he's working on. Anyway, what's that got to do with Meredith?"

"Probably nothing," Linda shrugged, "but when he arrived home last night he didn't come straight to bed. I went down to see him and he was on the phone. I have no idea who he was speaking to as he walked out into the garden. It was obvious he didn't want me to hear the conversation. When he finished that call, he made a couple of others. I did ask, but he told me it was work." She pouted. "When we went to bed, I got a peck on the cheek, no cuddles or pillow talk – a peck and a turned back." She handed Patsy her tea. "I was less than impressed. He was gone before I woke this morning."

"You see, it was only work. Linda, you can't expect him to share everything; it's not possible, and could compromise the case. You're not the most secretive of people, you know. But I still don't see what that's got to do with Meredith."

She tried not to smile at the look of incredulity on Linda's face.

"I can keep a secret. I have many things stored up here," she tapped her temple, and walked back to her desk, "which I haven't told anyone because I know they're confidential. Many!" She sat at her desk and huffed. "I am offended. Seriously offended. All I wanted to establish, out of friendly concern, was what was going on with Meredith that made him the topic of so many conversations? I'll not bother in future."

Looking away, she picked up her cake in one hand and mouse in the other, and taking a bite of her cake, she pretended to concentrate on the screen in front of her.

"What conversations?" Patsy returned to sit on the corner of the desk. "In what way was Meredith the topic?"

She rolled her eyes as Linda gave a shrug.

"All those Louie had last night for starters, pacing around on the patio, trying to keep his voice to a whisper."

"Meredith is his boss, of course he's going to mention him." Patsy's eyes narrowed. "Unless you heard more than that . . . What exactly did you hear?"

"Nothing really, anyway, it could be confidential and I've probably already said too much." Linda took another bite of the cake.

"Ha! So you are being dramatic." Patsy tutted and stood up. "You should calm that imagination or it will get you in trouble."

Patsy walked towards her office, a frown creased her brow as she mentally crossed her fingers. Linda clearly knew something, but didn't know what it was herself, getting it out of her would be a painful process.

"I am not being dramatic," Linda called after her. "The reason I heard his name is because Louie raised his voice. He never raises his voice." She looked smug as Patsy turned to face her.

"And he said what exactly?" Patsy stood arms akimbo, a look of disbelief on her face.

"'DCI Meredith wouldn't do that.' Then he lowered it again so I heard blah, blah, blah, he got cross but before he paced to the other end of the garden, he said, 'If Meredith is up to something I will take action, but hold your fire for a couple of days.'"

Linda smirked as Patsy's mouth opened a little. "You see, I knew it was odd. What with that and Chris . . ." Linda's face fell and she shut her mouth firmly. Putting her cake down, she placed her fingers on the keyboard. "Now, I have work to do. Sharon will be here soon, and she was in a foul mood last week." She looked up as Patsy strode back to stand in front of her desk. "What?"

"Oh no, lady, that's not the end of this conversation. What about Chris? Come on, spill the beans." Patsy resumed her position on the corner of Linda's desk.

"It was nothing." Linda gave a dismissive flick of her hand. "There's nothing to tell."

"Tell me." Patsy attempted to catch Linda's eye, but she had busied herself with the removal of a few errant sugar granules. "Linda, look at me." Reluctantly Linda raised her head. "Tell me what you heard, and I'll decide if it's nothing. Meredith came home in a right mess last night – got into a fight while they were out, which is not like him. Anything to do with him could be important."

"Oh. Louie didn't say, is he all right? I hope he didn't put Louie in danger."

"Wounded pride, probably a broken nose, and a seriously black eye. What did Chris say?"

Linda pouted, and her head moved from one side to the other as she considered her answer. "Not much, actually; at the time, I thought he was speaking to you. It was last night when Louie was also angry about Meredith that I wondered, you know, if something was going on."

Patsy sighed. "Because Chris said . . ."

She began the sentence for Linda, and held out her hand waiting for the information.

"Oh, bloody hell. Right, if I tell you, you mustn't let on to Chris that I did. I don't want the sack for gossiping."

"You won't get the sack –"

"I mean it. Promise, or I won't tell you."

Patsy drew a cross on her heart. "Cross my heart, hope to die. What, are we teenagers again?"

Linda looked genuinely concerned, so much so she had replaced the cake on the mouse mat. "Chris was so angry – I could tell by his face when I took him his coffee. He was listening to whatever was being said when I went in, but as I left he said something like, 'Bloody Meredith, sort him out. We can't have him turning renegade on us, tighten the strings.' So, you see," Linda's eyes were wide and she nodded solemnly, "it could get me the sack. He wouldn't want me to be passing that on."

Seeing the look on Patsy's face she paused. "That means something, doesn't it?" She tutted as Patsy shook her head. "Don't try and deny it. I can tell by that look. Oh no, here comes Sharon. Don't say anything, promise."

Sharon bustled into the office carrying several shopping bags.

"Promise what? That little boutique on Princess Victoria Street in Clifton has a sale on, I couldn't resist bringing my bargains in to show you." She dropped the bags at the entrance to the kitchen. "I'll put the kettle on first."

As she turned her back on them, Patsy looked at Linda and put her finger to her lips.

"Can I take a peep?" she called to Sharon as she collected the bags, placing them on Linda's desk she pulled out a cashmere sweater. "This is gorgeous." She looked at the price tag, which had been marked down by half. "Ouch! Even at half price, that's more than I would pay." Looking over her shoulder as Sharon returned, she added. "Just because they say it's a bargain, it ain't necessarily so."

"It is. Feel the quality. Now, you were going to tell me what promise?" She looked from one to the other.

Linda bit into her cake, knowing she would be unable to lie to Sharon.

"Linda wants me to go around tonight. I think I might have promised Amanda I would go to the cinema, but she's insisting."

"Girls' night, is it? I'm up for that, what time?" Sharon pulled a blue dress from the largest bag. "Look at this baby. Absolutely perfect for the dinner. Chris . . . Oh damn. Sorry, ladies, I can't make tonight, we have a dinner at some bloody golf club."

"Never mind, another time." Patsy checked the clock. "I must be off. Linda, I'll be with you about seven-thirty." She stroked the dress in Sharon's hands. "Great fabric."

Collecting her things from her office, she left the other two examining the remainder of Sharon's bargains. Once in her car she chewed her lip as she considered what Linda had told her. Why would Chris be speaking to someone about Meredith in such a way, and who could possibly pull Meredith's strings? Had Chris been speaking to one of the team in London, and if so, what was his involvement? Twice that day Meredith had been referred to as a renegade, which was too much of a coincidence.

"I have to get to the bottom of this," she murmured, pulling out of the carpark.

When she arrived home, she did something she'd not done before: she went through Meredith's things. She checked the pockets of all his suits, and riffled around in his underwear drawer. She searched the bedside cabinet, and even looked on top of the dishwasher, given that

that was where he had hidden the photographs. When she found nothing unusual, she began to feel guilty for checking up on him when she had no real foundation to do so.

Deciding she would definitely discuss it with him that evening, she texted him asking what time he would be home for dinner. Twenty minutes later she received a reply advising he was on his way to London, but would be catching the last train home and could do with being collected from the station at ten forty-five. Patsy pursed her lips as she confirmed she would do that. Something was going on, and she needed to see how much more information Linda might have.

She texted Linda and arranged to meet up for a pizza. Patsy didn't want Louie around for the conversation she intended to have, particularly if he too was questioning Meredith's behaviour. She needed to think, and to relax. She could feel the muscles of her back getting tighter by the minute. Her thought processes worked well in the bath, and it would help her unwind, not to mention fill some time until she had to meet Linda.

Patsy had one foot in the bath before she remembered she had taken the towels to wash them. Hopping to the airing cupboard, she pulled a towel from the stack. An envelope hit the carpet with a thud by her foot. As she bent to retrieve it, she knew immediately what it was, but she opened it anyway. As she suspected, it was cash. She counted it and found five thousand pounds in used fifty-pound notes. Resealing the envelope, she placed it under the top towel and went back to her bath. Many thoughts and scenarios ran through her mind as the warm water lapped around her body. Each one left her more frustrated than the last.

"Meredith!" she shouted, releasing her frustration before dunking under the water.

~ ~ ~

Trump tapped on Meredith's open door. "Sorry to interrupt, sir, Dave tells me you're off to London again."

"I am." Meredith looked back at the papers on his desk and picked one up. "Did we ever find out who Ridgeway was shacked up with in Bristol? Was there anything there?"

"No, sir, not top of the 'to do' list as you will appreciate. History now, and it's unlikely to be related to the case, is it? About –"

"How do you know that?" Meredith demanded in disbelief.

"Know what?"

"That it won't be relevant to the case! Have you got a crystal ball now?"

"No, but it's not likely. Not given the circumstances."

"Who knows? Not us. Apparently, we do police work on the balance of probabilities now, not fact. Get it looked into. Put Hutchins on it, he's got a good nose for that sort of thing. Today."

Trump kept any further opinion to himself. He didn't want to irritate Meredith any more than he already had. He wanted to go to London with him.

"Yes, straight away sir. This London trip, I don't suppose I could tag along, could I?" His smile was hesitant.

"What for?" Meredith's frown had deepened.

"No real reason, I thought it might help me get a better handle on the case if I knew more about the faces involved."

"Really? Well, you'd know more about them if you investigated them instead of making assumptions. So no, you can't come for no real reason. Get on with the job in hand, Trump."

Meredith returned his attention to the papers on his desk, and Trump walked back into the incident room without further comment. Meredith glanced up as the volume of sound from the room fell momentarily: all eyes were on Trump who gave an almost unperceivable shake of the head. Meredith went back to his paperwork.

An hour later he picked up a file and headed to the door.

"I'm off. I'll see you first thing for the briefing. Anything comes up, call me." He turned to leave.

"Do you want a lift to the station, Gov?" Rawlings called.

Meredith didn't turn back. "Nope. Got a taxi waiting, thanks." Meredith pushed open the door and disappeared.

Rawlings waited until he was sure that Meredith wasn't going to return. "Told you," he said knowingly to Seaton.

"Told him what?" Jo Adler looked at Rawlings.

"Something's going on. The Governor is up to some —"

"Enough said, Dave," Seaton interjected quickly. "Keep it to yourself until tonight."

"Why, what's tonight? Sounds to me that you lot are up to something concerning Meredith that I don't know about. Tell all."

Seaton jerked his head towards the side of the room and Jo

followed him across.

"Not much to tell, bits and bobs. We're meeting at Louie's tonight for a drink, you coming?"

"I am now."

~ ~ ~

Meredith stormed into Andronikov's offices and, ignoring the shouts from the receptionist, strode towards his office door. Before he got there, it was blocked by a broad-shouldered man with a shaven head. His front tooth was gold, giving him a menacing aura when he smiled at Meredith. Meredith pulled out his warrant card and pressed it against his nose, but not so hard as to cause the man to move.

"Get your arse out of the way or I'll have a team of blokes in here, and you'll be the first one they bang up," Meredith growled.

The door behind the man opened and Andronikov grinned at Meredith.

"Making an entrance, I see. There is no need to be so . . . so bullish, Meredith. Step aside, Andre, Mr Meredith must have something important to discuss." Andre did as he was asked, and Andronikov swept his arm flamboyantly. "Meredith, come in, do."

Crossing the threshold, Meredith paced to Andronikov's desk. He pulled a sheet of paper from his inside pocket, unfolded it, and slammed it on the desk.

"Is this your work?" he demanded.

Andronikov walked over slowly and picked up the paper. He scanned it quickly. His lips remained tight but his eyes revealed his amusement. He refolded the sheet and held it towards Meredith.

"It is not. I'm insulted that you think I would work at this level. It seems to me you have upset someone, but not me. Is there anything else I can do for you? You seem to have more than just that to worry about." His smile emerged as he regarded Meredith's facial injuries, and Meredith fought to contain his temper.

"Do you know who wrote this? Is it that slimy bastard Myshkin? He may have a little trouble with the ladies for a while." Meredith smirked briefly before his eyes returned to the cold glimmer. He pointed at Andronikov. "Whatever our deal is, he's not part of it. When we're done, which had better be sooner rather than later, he's mine."

Andronikov shrugged. "As you please. Now, as you're here, tell me the latest news."

"Not much to tell, but we will get there." He pulled the file, which had been rolled into a cylinder, from his pocket and dropped it on the table. "Full and gory detail of how Veronika Biskop died. That autopsy report spares little detail of the pain she must have endured, and for what?"

Meredith watched Andronikov's expression closely. There was no change: he didn't grimace, he didn't smile, but a stillness had come over him. "My money is on Myshkin, but what are your thoughts?" Meredith had relaxed a little and, uninvited, he took a seat.

"I have no thoughts, I want proof. I want to know everything that you know." Andronikov snorted a short laugh. "I have been told you are good at your job, and therefore, Meredith, I think you may be holding something back."

He raised one eyebrow and his head tilted to one side, as though he were dealing with a naughty child. "But I hope you have more sense than that. I am not funding your retirement for the good of my health. Are you sure you have no further information?" Walking to the other side of the desk, Andronikov slid open a drawer and removed a well-stuffed envelope. He tapped it on the edge of the desk. "I hope I am not wasting my money."

Meredith held out his hand and took the envelope. "Nope. But I can only give you what I've got. You know the deal. You walk away from anything I might find, and everyone else goes down." He stood and tucked the envelope into his inside pocket. "And I mean that: no last changing of the rules." Meredith got to his feet.

"I have no intention of changing the rules, Meredith, and I only hope you and I are playing the same game."

Meredith walked to the door. Pulling it open he turned back. "I'm not playing, pal, this isn't a game."

"And yet you've taken the money, placed your bet, and allowed the wheel to spin."

Meredith shrugged. "You're right, I suppose. But I only back certainties, and I always win."

He closed the door behind him, giving a cheery wave to the receptionist. Once outside the building he checked the time. There was an hour until his next meeting, assuming they turned up. He decided to walk, and hopefully find a pub on the way where he could grab something to eat.

# 13

Patsy pulled up outside Linda's house. It had been a pleasant enough evening, but Linda had nothing further to tell her with regard to Meredith and what he might or might not be up to. Now she had an hour to kill before she was due to collect him from the station.

"Hush when we go in, I expect he'll be in bed," Linda whispered as she put the key in the lock. "Go through to the kitchen and put the kettle on. I need the loo." She began to tiptoe up the stairs.

Patsy nodded a silent acknowledgement and made her way along the hall. As she reached the kitchen she heard voices and slowed her pace.

"All I'm saying is, that when it's all added together it doesn't look good." It was Dave Rawlings' voice. "I'm the first to champion the Gov as you know, but if he doesn't at least let one of you two in on it, there's something fishy going on."

"I'm not sure, Dave," Trump replied. "If DCI Meredith is keeping secrets, I'm sure there will be a good reason for it. I do agree it's frustrating. I think that perhaps the best course of action is to ask. Tell him that we know something's not quite right."

"Good luck with that," Jo Adler snorted. "The Gov will be offended and tell us where to go! What are you going to say? 'Look, Gov, you were violent against a suspect being questioned after telling him you're going to set him up for possession, you're taking calls from the Russians, you were seen taking a backhander in the gents, and then you kicked the shit out of someone. Oh yes, and you keep disappearing to London with little or no feedback. Now, please tell us this is all above board.'" Jo shook her head. "Can't see that being accepted gracefully."

"Actually yes, that's exactly what I would say. When he has it all laid out like that he'll understand our concern, surely?" Trump's voice had lost any conviction.

"No, Louie, he'll be as pissy as hell that we doubted him and, like Jo said, make our lives hell." Seaton paused, "Or, worst case scenario, he'll make something up to keep us quiet, and if we know it's bullshit, what then?" He held out his glass, "I'm getting depressed, top me up, Louie." He sighed. "When I was unsure as to what to do when I was younger, my mother used to say 'What's the worst that could happen?' Then you'd weigh up the possible outcome and choose the course of action least likely to cause you bother."

"No, that's not right. Surely it would be the one where you gain the most but with consequences you're prepared to accept," Dave Rawlings challenged.

Jo Adler stood and yawned. "Whichever it is, the worst that can happen is not having Meredith on side. I vote we keep quiet and watch carefully." She took a pace towards the door. "Now, I have a husband to get home to, so I'll powder my nose and I'll see you lot back at the ranch tomorrow."

"But what do we do if this odd behaviour escalates?" Trump asked.

"Have another meeting. That was a fine bottle of Scotch." Tom Seaton also stood, "I'd best make a move too. We're agreed, no one is going to challenge . . ."

Patsy could hear they were on the move, and not wanting to get caught eavesdropping she pushed open the door and gave a shout, her hand on her chest.

"Oh boy! I didn't think there was anyone here. Linda told me to be quiet because Louie would probably be in bed." She surveyed the table which was scattered with empty pizza boxes, glasses and an almost empty bottle of single malt. "Are you celebrating something?"

"No, letting off steam, that's all." Seaton stepped forward and pecked her on the cheek. "Shame the Gov isn't around, not the same without him. You look good, Patsy, how's everything with you?"

Patsy smiled at him, but her eyes didn't reflect the warmth of the smile; her brain was in overdrive processing what she'd heard.

"All good, thanks. A catch-up in a kitchen? You lot must be getting old, or have they got a new landlord at the Dirty Duck?"

"Ha! No, we didn't want a late one, and Louie offered to do the honours." Jo hugged Patsy and stepped into the hall. "Lovely to see you, we need a night out soon. I must dash – Aaron will be getting moody, I promised to be home by nine."

Patsy was amazed at how easily the lie left Jo's lips, and was disappointed there was not a hint of guilt in her expression. As they all collected their things and departed for home, there was none of the usual banter, and Patsy could understand why. With all she'd heard, there was nothing to be jolly about. Now she was placed in the difficult position of whether to discuss what she'd heard with Meredith and risk the probable backlash that would cause for his team, or continue to monitor developments. She didn't want to keep secrets from him, but neither did she want to cause such an upset, and after all it seemed Meredith had a few secrets of his own. It was with a heavy heart that she left to pick him up.


Navigating her way around the Bristol blue-coloured taxis, Patsy reversed into a parking space at Temple Meads railway station. She looked at the crowd hustling through the exit, and hoped it was Meredith's train that had recently arrived. Tired men in suits and youngsters with backpacks joined the orderly taxi queue, and the blue snake of waiting vehicles moved slowly forward, collecting their fares. The bulk of the crowd dispersed and there was Meredith, clutching a bouquet of flowers. He spotted her car and waved them at her. Patsy couldn't help but smile; he looked crumpled and weary, but still cut a dash as he sidestepped the stragglers. She climbed out of the car and went to greet him.

He pulled her into his arms and kissed her. "Thanks, Hodge." He handed her the flowers, "These are for you."

"Why thank you, kind sir, what have I done to deserve these?" Burying her face in the cellophane wrapping she breathed in their fragrance. "They are lovely, but it's not like you to be spontaneous, what's the catch?" She poked him in the ribs before opening the rear door and placing them carefully in the footwell.

"You don't need to do anything, simply being you is enough. Now take me home, I need a drink, and anything else that might be on offer."

Opening the passenger door, he cursed as he folded his body into the compact space. Patsy had not changed her car since they met, and yet he still complained about the lack of leg room on each journey he had to suffer.

As the engine roared into life, Patsy turned to him. "Good day? You're in a surprisingly pleasant mood considering the time. I take it no one took advantage of you today?"

"Nope, they tried, but I resisted. I knew what was waiting for me at home. On a more serious note, it was a reasonable day, no more, no less. What have you been up to?"

"Me? Is that a serious question or are you being polite?"

"Both, but let's not start that conversation again. Did you have a good day?" Meredith grunted as he repositioned his legs. "I know what I'm buying you as a wedding gift – a decent-sized bloody car."

"My day was interesting. I was at the office, but I won't bore you with the detail. So, the wedding is still on?" There was a lightness to her tone, and Meredith grinned. Patsy was not going to do or say anything until she had something of substance to say. She returned his grin.

"It is, same rules, and I want my ring back." He nudged her with his elbow.

"For keeps or just until I piss you off again?" She gave a cough as though embarrassed.

"Where is it?" Meredith nudged her again. "I'd turn and look at you, but I can't bloody move."

"In my bag, in the footwell next to the flowers." She laughed as Meredith reached his hand back and muttered and complained until he managed to lift the bag onto his lap.

"What the hell do you keep in this? How can you need this all with you, at all times? When I leave the house, it's wallet, keys, phone, and any loose change."

"That's because you never ladder your tights, never reapply your lipstick, never brush your hair, and the battery of your phone is always running out." She glanced down as Meredith rummaged in the bag. "It's in my purse in the little stamp compartment."

Meredith found and pulled out the ring. He slid it onto his finger and waved his hand in front of the steering wheel.

"For keeps. Now put your foot down, and let's get home."

An hour or so later, Patsy returned from the shower. Walking to the dressing table she pulled her hair into a ponytail and reached for a band. Next to the small ceramic pot that held her bits and bobs she saw the envelope. She didn't comment but completed her hair, and pulled on her robe.

Walking back out of the bedroom, she called to Meredith. "I'll get you a fresh towel ready. Don't fall asleep, that pizza will be cooked to a crisp." Meredith grunted something incoherent.

Patsy lifted the top towel and there was the envelope she'd found earlier. Its twin remained in the bedroom. She took the towel to the bathroom and placed it next to the shower before taking the envelope back into the bedroom.

"Is Amanda saving for something? I've found an envelope stuffed with fifty-pound notes in the airing cupboard." She waved the envelope at him. "But why on earth would she hide it in amongst the towels?" She turned to the dressing table, paused, and lifted the other envelope with her free hand. She turned to face him. "Oh, there are two of them. Not Amanda's?"

Meredith sat up and stretched. "No, mine." Yawning he swung his legs over the side of the bed. "I didn't want to leave them lying around, but you distracted me before I could deal with the second one."

Patsy made a pretence of opening the second envelope, and pulled her fingernail across the bundle of notes.

"There are thousands of pounds here. Have you started a sideline I don't know about?" She tried to make the smile natural as Meredith walked towards the door.

"It's not mine, don't get planning a huge wedding. I'm looking after it for someone."

He went to the bathroom and Patsy heard the shower come on and followed him in, still clutching the envelopes.

"Why? Have they not heard of banks? Sounds fishy to me."

Meredith had stepped into the shower cubicle and pulled the curtain. She sat on the toilet lid.

"It is fishy, so don't ask questions and I won't have to ignore you."

"You mean, lie to me." Patsy's false smile had become a frown.

"No, I mean ignore you because I won't answer your questions."

"Meredith, have you gone mad? You're a police officer, why are you holding money for someone? Who is so important that you would risk your career?"

"Is that pizza going to be edible?" Meredith, as promised, ignored the question.

"Shit. This conversation isn't over. Do you want wine with it?" Patsy called as she placed the envelopes in the basin and hurried away.

"Of course." Meredith peeped out from behind the curtain, and seeing she had left the room stepped out of the shower and wrapped the fresh towel she had left for him around his waist.

Down in the kitchen, Patsy cursed as she removed the barely edible pizza from the oven. Placing it in the centre of the table, she collected two glasses and opened a bottle of wine. She called to tell Meredith it was ready. A piece of charred crust flew across the kitchen as she attempted to slice the pizza.

Meredith stooped to retrieve it as he came in. "That looks appetising. We should have stayed in bed." He pulled out a chair.

"The middle is okay, I hope. Who is this friend you're babysitting thousands of pounds for?"

Meredith raised his eyebrows. "Not a friend, it's work. Drop it, Patsy, let's not start a conversation that'll end in a fight."

"If you're not doing anything wrong, why would it end in a fight?"

"That's not what I said. Drop it." Meredith bit into his pizza.

"So, the money is from someone at work? Is that okay?" Patsy held her slice of pizza poised as Meredith's jaw struggled to chew the large bite he had taken.

"It'll do. Might need a few fillings tomorrow." He reached across the table and took her hand. "Don't do this. Trust me, I know what I'm doing, but I won't talk about it. When are we going to do the deed? I think sooner rather than later; it can't all blow out of control then." He squeezed her hand before releasing it to pick up his glass. He sipped his wine. "The wine's good, if nothing else."

Patsy studied him for a while. It wasn't in her nature to let things drop, but her instinct was to take him at his word for the moment. He didn't appear to feel any guilt, and he wasn't angry – yet. All of which indicated he was not up to no good. She smiled.

"I'll speak to Dad in the morning. He's got a holiday booked, so we need to avoid that but I can't remember when it is. Quite frankly, if it's only the four of us that'll be just fine by me." She nibbled the end of the pizza.

"Four?" questioned Meredith. "What about Amanda?"

"That included Amanda. Why, who have I forgotten?" Patsy

frowned as she replaced the slice of pizza on the plate.

"Your father's intended . . ." he prompted, and Patsy grimaced.

"Oh boy, I still can't get used to that. I'll rephrase: I'll be happy if it's only the five of us." She took the slice of pizza from Meredith's hand and dropped it on the plate. "Don't eat that, it's disgusting. Come on, let's go back to bed."

Never one to waste food as a rule, this time Meredith didn't argue, and five minutes later he was switching off the bedside lamp.

"I'm trusting you not to do anything stupid, you know that, don't you?" Patsy nudged him in the ribs.

"I do. Goodnight, Hodge."

"That's it?"

"It is, yes. Now go to sleep."

Meredith snuggled deeper under the quilt and was asleep in minutes.

Patsy stared towards the dressing table and wondered if the envelopes were back in the airing cupboard. She hoped she had made the right decision to leave the matter alone. She couldn't bring herself to believe that Meredith was involved in something dodgy, but was that because she wanted it to be so, or because the wedding was back on? She was still awake, an hour later, a gurgle of disquiet in the pit of her stomach keeping her from sleep.

## 14

Meredith scanned the report on his desk, his surprise evident. "Small world," he muttered as he completed the report. He looked at Trump who raised his eyebrows.

"Someone you know mentioned in there?"

"Someone I've met – no use to us – but it seems that I'm destined to have cases that are connected to Hodge's in some way." He tapped the report. "Stephen Hatton, Althorpe as was –Patsy is working for him. He races bikes among other things."

"Really? The lad that was adopted? Now, that is a coincidence." It was Trump's turn to look surprised.

"Isn't it just. No use to us, he was only a tiddler when his grandmother gave him up for adoption. Who's Terry Dumas? Have we tracked him down?"

"Tom's going over to see him later. He's living in a hostel in Bath. Good friend of Ridgeway, but a major addict apparently, not sure how much help he'll be, but I suppose it's a shot."

"Little acorns, Trump." Meredith shrugged. "I appreciate that it might be a waste of time but no stone unturned, and all that."

"You're right, sir. Did Patsy get to you on time last night?" Trump asked as he walked to the door.

"Yes, why?"

"No reason. She came in to have a coffee with Linda after their meal and wasn't expecting us to be there, and ended up rushing off."

181

"Us?" queried Meredith.

Trump cleared his throat. "Yes, a few of us had drinks, nothing major. You would have been invited, naturally, but you weren't around."

"So why are you embarrassed?" Meredith scrutinised Trump. He was out of his comfort zone when lying; he looked constipated and started to fidget. Meredith had an inkling he wouldn't have been welcome.

Trump forced a ridiculous grin. "Why would I be embarrassed? Right, I'd better get on, some CCTV footage Jo has been looking at might be of use regarding Veronika Biskop."

Meredith threw his hands out. "Why don't I know about this?" he demanded, getting to his feet.

"Because you wanted that report, and I was going to tell you once you'd read it. Jo only told me minutes ago." Trump now sounded offended, and added defensively, "You know, sir, I can't win with you sometimes: if I'd told you about the sighting, you'd have complained about not having the report."

Meredith tried to hide his amusement. "As I told someone only yesterday, I always win. Don't pick the wrong side, Trump."

He strode out into the incident room, leaving Trump to ponder the deeper message in that retort.

"Where's this film?" Meredith asked no one in particular, as Jo Adler wasn't at her desk.

"Next door." Seaton put his hand over the mouthpiece of the telephone. "She's getting it ready for us now. Take a pew." He nodded towards the small television in the middle of the room.

Jo was back a moment later and walked briskly to the television and slotted a disc in the side. Picking up the remote, Jo moved the film onto the section she wanted and pushed the pause button. Looking at Meredith, she asked, "Do you want to see this now, or wait until the others are free?"

"Now," Meredith snapped as though it had been a stupid question.

He sat at the closest chair to the screen and leaned forward. Jo hit the play button. Seaton terminated his call and joined Trump, who was now standing behind Meredith. Jo started her commentary.

"Veronika's remains were found on the seventeenth of October two years ago. She had been dumped in a small copse in Ashton Court, but she hadn't died there. Her flatmate, Elena, first reported her missing in late June, and then again in July when she had not heard anything. After that, as you know, she gave up."

"Myshkin said she left him in June, so that fits." Meredith signalled to Jo to continue.

"This is the footage collected by the boys investigating the first report after a barman who worked at – yes, you've guessed it – The Hammer and Sickle, reported he'd seen her in Broadmead walking away from the Holiday Inn and towards the Galleries shopping centre. There were hours and hours of it: I have no idea how thorough they were, but I struck lucky on the fifth. I've still got forty or so to do, but I think this is the only one that's going to help us."

Jo fast-forwarded the recording to ten-fifteen on the night of tenth of July. She pointed at a woman sidestepping a homeless man setting up his bed on the pavement for the night. "I think that's her."

The men leaned forward and Seaton mumbled agreement. They watched the woman, dressed in jeans and a flowing floral top, put her hands in her pockets and walk slowly towards the shopping centre. Her head was bowed as though she were deep in thought. She didn't look up until she reached the pedestrian crossing, and then moved out of vision.

"We lose her here for three minutes, but before I show you where she disappeared, look at this." She took the recording back three minutes and froze the frame at the rear of a car driving past the woman. "Look at this car. The number plate isn't clear enough for full recognition, but it starts with AA. What make do you reckon that is?"

"It's a Lexus, Adler, get on with it," Meredith urged, and Jo moved the recording on.

"This was taken by the camera at the entrance to the Galleries carpark, much better quality as it's lit properly at night. This is less than a minute away from the car passing her, and if she crossed the road at the crossing she would have passed this entrance." The Lexus was shown driving into the carpark. The full registration was visible, and the car had two occupants. Jo moved the recording on again. "This is the exit. Ten twenty-two, seven minutes after she passed that poor homeless chap, and the Lexus isn't stopping in the carpark."

The group watched the Lexus appear at the barrier. A hand came out of the driver's window and inserted the card to raise the bar. As it pulled away, Jo stopped the recorder.

"What's different?" she challenged them.

"Three people in the car, and one is wearing a floral shirt." Meredith clapped his hands. "Well done, Jo. Good work. So, come on, tell us. Who's the registered keeper?"

"Peter Myshkin." Jo grinned. "It was almost new at the time, and the good news is it's still registered in his name. The bad news is that unless we find something on the other tapes, we have no clear view of the original two occupants, and even if we did, there is nothing to say they were responsible for her demise. But still, it's a start."

"Bloody right it is." Meredith stood. "Let's shake 'em up again. Trump, get a warrant to search that car; Seaton, you and I will pay our friend Peter a visit. Jo, get Rawlings and Hutchins on to those tapes with you. I want to know who was in that car."

"Are we going to see him before or after we get the warrant?" Seaton asked Meredith's retreating back.

"Now! Find out where the car is, and get someone to guard it until Trump gets the warrant." Meredith looked over his shoulder. "COME ON, MOVE IT!" he shouted, and added quietly, "Or are you all still hung-over from your little get-together last night?"

Meredith knew they would all be wondering who had told him, and his smile was brief at the stunned silence before they dispersed to follow his orders. He had no doubt their meeting was about him, and he didn't know whether to feel let down that they were beginning to distrust him, or pleased that he had trained them well enough to doubt him.

~ ~ ~

Patsy pulled into the carpark and returned the wave from Stephen Hatton. He beckoned her forward as she climbed out of the car. Patsy joined him at the white van as the first bike was wheeled down the ramps.

"New toys to play with?" she asked as the second bike followed.

"Certainly are! This baby is quite rare; I've been dying to get my hands on one of these." He saw Patsy's sceptical look and laughed. "It needs work, but give me a couple of weeks and you'll see what I mean."

"I'm sure. Did you buy them on your trip?"

"We did. We weren't sure if it would be a waste of time, but we came up trumps. Two for the price of one – the dealer threw that one in for free." Stephen waved towards the second bike.

"What a bargain, did you have to go far?" Feigning interest, Patsy leaned forward to look at the bike.

"No, only a couple of hours away." He looked at his watch. "Now we must crack on, we have two MOD chaps in this morning. Damn pain, but what can you do?"

He gave instructions to the men unloading the bikes and walked into the main building with Patsy. There was a spring in his step as he strode through reception and towards their offices, and his smile and greetings were freely distributed to anyone who caught his eye.

"You're clearly pleased with your purchases, you're very buoyant today," Patsy observed, adding quickly, "not that you're not usually happy, of course."

Stephen threw his head back and laughed. Placing his arm around her shoulder, he pulled her to his side, and his eyes searched her face, his smile infectious.

Patsy grinned at him as she wriggled away to a more comfortable distance. "A bike can really make you this happy?" she asked.

"It can, but it's not only the bike. Everything we have worked for is coming together. Boxes are being ticked, and," he lifted his shoulders, and, for a moment, looked vulnerable, "I can't explain it, but what goes around comes around, and freedom is within reach."

He stopped walking as a frown creased her forehead. "Ignore me, I'm being dramatic. We are close, and . . ." He looked along the corridor as Jake Hatton approached. "And this genius is going to give us the cherry on the cake! Good morning, Jake."

"Morning. The bikes have arrived, I hear." Jake clearly didn't share his brother's enthusiasm. He nodded at Patsy. "Good morning, Patsy, I trust you are well." Returning his attention to Stephen he pointed to the door to Stephen's office. "A word please, Stephen."

"Why so serious, Jake? It's a glorious day, everything is falling into place. I've spoken to Abigail, she told me."

"Abigail is always optimistic." Jake shrugged. "But, if all goes well today, then tomorrow we can make arrangements for the final test before we call the MOD in."

"It will go well." Stephen slapped his brother on the back. "Have more faith." He turned to Patsy. "Get ready to light the touch paper, I'll be along shortly."

He pushed open the door to his office and held it for his brother who rolled his eyes as he stepped in. As the door closed, Patsy heard him add, "I'm going for it. I'm making the calls – I'm bringing the men in tomorrow."

She didn't catch Jake's response, and as she made her way to her own office, she wondered which 'men' he was referring to and decided it was probably the MOD people. Stephen's euphoria clearly wasn't shared by Jake, and she was irritated by yet again only having a vague inkling of what was going on.

Patsy kept a close eye on the email accounts, and saw little of Stephen for the rest of the day. Every time she took him coffee or paperwork, he was using a mobile phone to make calls and the conversation paused until she left the room. At one stage, it appeared Stephen was bartering over a rate for staff, but to the best of her knowledge they hadn't been planning on hiring anyone. One thing was sure, from the snippets she picked up, something had the brothers fired up. Stephen Hatton was animated in all he did, and Jake was buzzing with nervous energy. Something was going to happen the next day, the arrangements of which were private, much like the trip to Belfast.

Late afternoon, Stephen put his head around the door, told Patsy he was off to the bank, and asked her to be on time the next morning. She had been early every day since she started, and he knew that, but such was his distraction he missed the look of irritation that momentarily creased her features as he called a cheery goodbye. Patsy ignored the snort of amusement from Irene and noted the salient facts she had picked up during the day. Once out of the grounds, she pulled into the carpark of a builder's merchant and called Burt to update him. He listened in silence as she reeled off the list, and sighed as she ended with a question.

"Do *you* know what's happening tomorrow? Is it only me in the dark?"

"They are nearing the completion of the product, they're probably hyped up about it." His tone was flat.

"So why all the private conversations and phone calls? Surely that's what everyone wants to know?"

"I don't know." Burt sounded much like a patient schoolteacher. "That's why you're there, isn't it?"

He tried not to sigh, but Patsy heard it none the less.

"Okay, okay. Because I know you know more than you are letting on, I thought you might go mad and share. Not to worry, I'll carry on solo regardless." She terminated the call and threw her phone on to the passenger seat. "Prick!" she cursed and hit the horn as a flatbed truck almost reversed into her, its load of timber stopping inches away from her windscreen.

~ ~ ~

Meredith looked up as Trump rapped his door.

"You must have someone smiling down on you, or friends in high places. Warrant is being printed as I speak."

"Good, grab your coat, let's go meet Mr Peter Myshkin and see if he's as charming as his cousin." Meredith pulled his jacket from the back of the chair and strode into the incident room. "Seaton, you and Travers get that car. I'm assuming someone has arranged transport?" He turned back to Trump. "You're driving. Now, grab the copy of that recording. It'll do until Jo comes up with something else."

Trump turned into Mariner's Drive and Meredith let out a low whistle.

"Not bad for someone who runs a meat factory and a kebab shop." Meredith leaned forward and looked through the large iron gates suspended on substantial brick pillars. He took in the huge property beyond. "Bloody electric gates. Wait here, I'll get the intercom."

He walked to the stainless-steel panel and pushed the button. The camera mounted on one of the pillars turned towards him. He waved and showed his teeth in a mock smile. A male voice with an Eastern European accent answered.

"Hello, what can I do for you?"

"Well, if you're Peter Myshkin you can open the gates and speak to me about your cousin Filipp, who may be charged with murder later today. I'm DCI Meredith." He held his ID towards the camera. A few seconds later the gates began to open.

"Come in, please."

Meredith rejoined Trump in the car.

"Arresting Filipp now, are we?" Trump enquired.

Meredith ignored his sarcasm. "We might be, and I'm sure Peter wouldn't have co-operated if I'd told him we were investigating him. Drive on."

As they approached the front of the house, Peter Myshkin appeared on the top step, and waved.

"Smug bastard, can't wait to wipe that smile off his face." Meredith glanced around, no sign of the car. "Do we know if it's here?"

"Parked outside a hair salon in Westbury. His wife must be driving it."

"Good, we'll keep him busy while the boys pick it up."

Meredith was out of the car and walking towards Peter Myshkin. His hand held out, he thanked him for seeing them, and introduced Trump.

Myshkin held the door open for them. "Come in, please. I'm most concerned. My study is first door on the right."

He made no comment about Meredith's face.

Meredith pushed the door open and walked into the oak-panelled room. He took a seat on a red leather Chesterfield sofa, and indicated Trump should sit next to him. Myshkin smiled and asked if they required refreshments. Meredith shook his head.

"Let's get straight down to business. I take it that plays DVDs?" He pointed to a small flat-screen TV on the wall. Myshkin confirmed that it did and Meredith passed him the disc. "Good. Stick this on, I've got a film to show you."

Myshkin inserted the DVD and, rather than sit behind his desk, he sat on the sturdy wooden coffee table, his back to Meredith and Trump.

"What is this?"

"I'm glad you asked," Meredith replied as the Holiday Inn appeared, followed seconds later by Veronika. "I know you'll know all this, but I'm going to talk you through it anyway." He leaned forward and pointed at the screen. "That is the last sighting of Ronnie, or Veronika Biskop. You can see she's walking away from the hotel. I suspect she had a liaison of some sort. And here we are, at the Galleries shopping centre. That is your car. Ronnie crosses to the carpark entrance, your car drives in, only two occupants you'll note, and . . . here it is leaving. Important this, because you'll see there are now three occupants, and the latest is Veronika. We know because of the pattern on her blouse. But you already know that – you were driving."

Peter Myshkin sat perfectly still, his hands gripping his knees.

"I thought this was about Filipp? I know nothing of this . . . who is this woman?" Only his lips moved, and he remained staring at the screen despite the fact the recording had stopped.

Meredith lunged forward and grabbed Peter Myshkin by the scruff of the neck. He pulled him back until he was almost flat on the table. He released Myshkin's neck and placed his hand on his chest, pinning him to the table.

Myshkin was struggling to get up, but Meredith simply placed his other hand on his chest and applied more pressure. The veins in Myshkin's temples bulged, his face became a darker shade of red, and his whole body was shaking with the effort of freeing himself.

"Don't fuck about, pal. I'm not in the mood. I've seen the photographs of her remains. We're . . ."

"Sir, I –" Trump thought Meredith should back off but he was shot down by Meredith's snarl.

"Shut it. Mr Myshkin is going to tell us why."

He looked at Myshkin who stopped struggling, closed his eyes, and chuckled.

"Arrest me or get out of my house. You are wrong. You are clutching at straw. I know it, you know it. You have crossed the wrong man, my friend." Myshkin held Meredith's gaze; his expression would have caused most men to question their actions, but Meredith merely laughed. Myshkin smiled at him. "Laugh well, Meredith, it may be the last time."

"Why's that?" Meredith wanted to wipe the beads of perspiration from his forehead, but was determined to keep the man pinned to the table. He looked across to the desk as a mobile phone vibrated before it started to ring. "That'll be your wife. Probably standing in the street with her hair half done. We've got the car, and however good a job you did cleaning it, we'll find traces of her. Steady now."

Myshkin had jerked the top half of his body forward in the hope of catching Meredith off guard. Meredith simply changed his position a little, allowing himself to be able to place his knee in Myshkin's groin. Myshkin lay still.

"That's better. As I was saying, when we find that trace, I will have you, and probably Filipp too. If not, I'll find another reason, but one way or another I'll have you both."

Myshkin spat out a snort and shook his head slowly as he spoke. "No, my friend, you are already dead." He moved his head to look at Trump. "Take your boss away. Take him far away. The longer you watch this ridiculous show, the more you place yourself in danger."

Despite believing that Meredith was totally out of order, Trump merely raised his eyebrows and said quietly, "Is that a threat, sir?

189

Because it wouldn't do to be threatening two police officers, very unwise."

To Trump's surprise Myshkin started laughing. He was genuinely amused. When he brought himself under control he looked back at Meredith.

"I think I might kill you myself. I'd like to hear you scream. Your friend here needs to be taught the facts of life." He snorted again. "Police officers. What does that mean in this country? Nothing! You are powerless, no good for anything other than issuing parking tickets. Even though you think you have protection, do you think he is more powerful than I?" He lifted his head and looked towards Meredith's knee. "You have me at a disadvantage, but for how long? You have now started something you can't stop."

It was Meredith's turn to snort.

"You reckon? I can put a stop to you anytime I like." He raised his eyebrows. "I don't play by the rules. I haven't given anyone a ticket for a long time."

"Why, because you are in Andronikov's pocket? Don't be fooled into thinking he is bigger than me, it's not true. Do you know the only way you can put a stop to me?" He paused as though expecting an answer but Meredith didn't respond. "Kill me, before I kill you."

Meredith bent forward until his mouth was next to Myshkin's ear. "I will, don't worry," he whispered. Then, pulling his head back a little, he quickly moved his hands to Myshkin's shoulders, pulled him into a sitting position, and formally arrested and cautioned him. He gave a little grunt as he dragged him to his feet.

"You silly policeman, I will be free within hours," Myshkin taunted as Trump secured his arms with a plastic tie. As Trump pushed him towards the door, Myshkin leaned in close. "You heard him tell me he was going to kill me. I will make you say that in court, if he lives that long."

Trump shook his head. "I heard nothing of the sort, I do, however, have you recorded as threatening to kill DCI Meredith." Trump pulled his phone from his pocket and turned the screen towards Myshkin so he could see it was still recording. "This way, sir."

Myshkin walked confidently out of the study and through the hall towards their car.

Trump caught Meredith's eye, a look of disgust on his face.

"Do your job, Trump, no more, no less," Meredith advised quietly and patted him on the shoulder.

"I intend to, sir. I'm more concerned about you doing yours at the moment." Trump looked away, unwilling to enter into further discussion.

Meredith pursed his lips as he watched Trump guide Myshkin's head into the rear of the car. From Trump, that was an open challenge, but he didn't respond despite knowing that his silence would plant further doubt in Trump's mind.

They drove back to the station without further comment. Once there, Myshkin's lawyer was called, and while they waited Meredith used the time to bark at Jo Adler, telling her to get more evidence. He also tried to charm Frankie Callaghan into supervising the search of the car.

"I know it's not really what you do, Sherlock. I'm sure I can supply a body given time, but someone may have died in that car. We know how she died – you've read the report – but what we need to know is where, and who did it. Now, I know with your skill and determination, despite the passing of time, you will make sure that nothing is missed."

Meredith rolled his eyes at Seaton who didn't appear amused at Meredith's newly-found charm. He'd listened to the recording Trump had made, and while whatever Meredith whispered to Myshkin wasn't clear, the pause in proceedings made it clear it was probably a damning threat, and Myshkin was under the impression that Meredith was closely linked to Andronikov. That wasn't good; not good at all. Seaton was worried for and about Meredith. It was clear he was trying to bring down the Myshkins, but his motive for doing so was not so obvious. He perched on the edge of Meredith's desk as his boss hit the speaker button.

"Meredith, your flattery is all well and good, but the inference is that the forensic team assigned to the car will do less than a thorough job, and that is simply not true. I have three post-mortems booked today, and whilst I am willing to make a phone call, I can't just drop everything. It's not even my case," Frankie responded.

"Then I'll get it transferred to you. Now we know who she is, I'm assuming the family will want the body for burial or repatriation. Before that happens, I'll need a second PM, so you can do that. Little whatsit, the ten-year-old that works with you, can do the others. All probably natural causes anyway." Meredith sighed. "So, will you do it, or do I have to make you?" He ignored Seaton who groaned and rubbed his hand over his face. "You know mine is bigger than yours. I'm trying to be polite here."

"You are a total pain in the arse, but you know that. You go and pull your strings, Meredith. If I get given the case I'll look at it tomorrow, but for now take your flattery, and your threats, and sod off!" Frankie terminated the call.

"He'd have done that if you'd not tried to bully him," Seaton observed. "What's going on, Gov? I've heard Trump's recording, and that wasn't very sensible, was it? If you use it you're in shit up to your nostrils. You took that one step too far."

Meredith's eyes narrowed, and he released a sigh. "When I need advice on what to do, I'll ask for it. Are you hovering for a particular reason, or have you come with the specific intention of pissing me off?"

"Both." Seaton stretched his lips into a smile. "Jo has the evidence that Peter Myshkin was driving that night. She hasn't got a clear shot of the other man, but is working on it." He shrugged. "I thought you might want a prompt update given his brief is on the way. And I also wanted to offer an ear if you needed someone to talk to – you know, about whatever is going on with you at the moment."

Meredith stood and stretched. "Thank you for that, get me the recording. And as to the other, I've got two of my own thanks." He walked past Seaton. "I'm going for a smoke, get it set up."

Seaton wondered if his mouth had fallen open as he watched Meredith make his way towards the fire escape. Meredith had always been awkward to deal with, but this was a whole new level of arrogance. Surely, he must be a little concerned about the allegations made by Myshkin, and the damning evidence on Trump's phone? He seemed to be on a collision course and enjoying the ride, and try as he might Seaton couldn't see the benefit – unless Meredith really was on the take, as had been suggested. He shook his head to dispel that thought, but it returned not ten minutes later when, having watched Veronika apparently pleading with Myshkin while leaning through to him from the rear of the car, he saw the man smash her in the face with the back of his clenched fist.

Meredith all but ran to the interview room and shoved the disc into the machine.

"Watch this," he commanded Peter Myshkin.

Seaton entered the room as Myshkin closed his eyes.

"I am waiting for my solicitor," he drawled. "I will do nothing until then.

Meredith negotiated the table awkwardly and grabbed Myshkin's hair, forcing his face towards the small screen.

"You will do what you're told." With his free hand Meredith knocked Seaton's from his shoulder, and used it to tilt Myshkin's chin up. Thrown by this level of violence, Myshkin opened his eyes and watched his fist collide with Veronika Biskop's face before she fell back onto her seat.

"You are a fucking coward. Who told you to do this, and why did she have to die?"

"You make it sound personal, Meredith." Myshkin's previous bravado had gone. "This has nothing to do with you, walk away."

"What, before or after you kill me?" Meredith released him by pushing him forward forcibly. "It's you who's a dead man walking, mate, but we'll go through the niceties with your brief first. I will have justice for Jane Roscoe, and I think I'll dish out some the way you do." With that he stormed out of the room, yelling back to Seaton, "Get him a glass of water, and call me when the brief gets here."

Seaton ran his fingers through his hair. He didn't like this turn of events at all. He paled when the duty sergeant called down the corridor that Myshkin's solicitor had arrived. A few minutes earlier and Meredith would already be out of a job. As he walked slowly back along the corridor to collect him, he pondered Myshkin's words. Meredith *was* acting as though it were personal, and although Meredith had a soft spot for Jane Roscoe, it couldn't be that, so what was his motivation?

Myshkin had a twenty-minute meeting with his solicitor, who summoned a now much calmer Meredith.

"Are you going to charge my client based on one small film showing him defending himself?" He paused, and when Meredith didn't respond, added, "If not, release him now. You have no evidence he murdered this woman, so he'll not be answering questions, even with 'no comment'. I'll be filing a full report of your actions and threats. It's unbelievable that in this day and age the police are still treating people in this manner."

Meredith ignored him and turned to Seaton. "Get Trump, I need an interpreter: I don't do posh bullshit." Pulling out a chair opposite the two men, he sat and hit the record button, announcing those in the room. He leaned back in the chair and stared at Myshkin, a smile dancing around his lips.

The solicitor waited a moment or two, and when Meredith didn't speak he tutted in exasperation. "DCI Meredith, I would like to speak to your superior. Now."

"Feel free," Meredith waved his hand towards the door, before pointing at Myshkin, "because he stays here." Finally, Meredith turned his attention to the solicitor. Without notes, he began listing the injuries found on the body of Veronika Biskop: it took several minutes before his memory failed him. He tapped his pen on the table. "I know that he and his cousin Filipp Myshkin are responsible for those injuries. In addition, I believe they are responsible for the torture and murder of Jimmy Ridgeway, Veronika's flatmate Elena, and someone you may know since she worked in the same field: Jane Roscoe?"

Meredith gave a small smile as the solicitor jerked his head up. "Thought that might get your attention. She was, as you are now, simply doing her job. Helping someone who claimed to be innocent, and trying to get them out of this station." He jabbed his finger at Myshkin, "He didn't appreciate that, or I suppose it could have been cousin Filipp, but he," again his finger punched a hole in the air, "was pulling the strings."

Meredith drew in a breath. "In addition, he is probably responsible for the kidnap and murder of Jan Liska, who hasn't been seen since Jane Roscoe was tortured and eventually murdered to give up his whereabouts." Meredith's voice cracked. "So, you see, *sir*, you can go and speak to whoever you like, but I'm having him."

The four men sat in silence for a while as Myshkin's solicitor processed this. Eventually he cleared his throat.

"And the evidence for all these spurious allegations is where? It seems to me, DCI Meredith, that you are hurt by the loss of Jane Roscoe, which may or may not be linked to the others you listed so eloquently, and you are clearly desperate to have someone to blame. But it is not my client. Now, are you going to ask any questions – none of which will be answered – but we can go through that charade if you wish?"

"Nope, he can go." Meredith smiled menacingly at Myshkin. "If he feels he'd be better off, be my guest." He stood and opened the door.

The solicitor jumped to his feet and hurried past, beckoning his client.

As Myshkin passed him, Meredith leaned forward. "Until the next time," he said quietly.

Myshkin paused. "Indeed," and waiting until the solicitor was out of earshot, added, "Ridgeway? Who is this man?" He smirked at Meredith before hurrying away behind his solicitor.

Meredith turned to Seaton. "You see? He's just told me that he did the others but not Ridgeway." Shoving his hands in his pockets, he stepped out of the room.

"Hang on one minute." Seaton jumped to his feet. "Are you going to tell me what the hell that was all about?"

"We have nothing concrete as yet, so let him sweat. Let's see what we've stirred up."

"A whole load of shit, that's what. Why didn't you question him? Why all the dark looks and knowing remarks? Gov, it's getting like you're under some sort of self-destruct spell. You need to step back and refocus." Seaton's voice revealed his concern. He stopped abruptly as Meredith spun to face him.

"I'm doing what's necessary. You should do the same. Now, if you'll excuse me, I have things to do tonight. I'll see you in the morning."

He turned and walked away, leaving Seaton shaking his head.

## 15

Stephen Hatton looked at his watch. It was a little before six in the morning, and he glanced at the monitor on the left of his desk. His lips twitched as the small red car approached the security gate. He looked away realising it would take a few minutes for the guard to run through the security checks. Stephen headed to the coffee machine and flipped the switch, knowing that in five minutes Jake would be with him. He drew in a breath and held it for a few moments, his eyes closed in silent prayer and his crossed fingers tapping the wooden table holding the coffee machine. He didn't want Jake to know how nervous he was, but the money was running out. They had to bring a finished product to the table to make sure the government maintained their interest and, of course, their contribution to the funding. They had wanted an exclusive deal, but he had only agreed to three years' exclusivity: it was one of the few things he and Jake had ever disagreed on.

Opening his eyes, he pulled his hand away from the table and blew out a breath. Pulling the sleeves of his sweater away from his wrists, he prepared the coffee. Mugs in hand, he had not reached his desk before Jake entered the room. Stephen smiled at him, and to his immense surprise, Jake smiled back. Stephen slopped the coffee as he lifted his hands in mock disbelief.

"You smiled. You never do that on testing day. What's happened?" A slight frown creased his brow as he placed the drinks on the desk.

"I have a good feeling about this one. Anyway, I'm allowed to smile, aren't I? I always do. Are you trying to tell me I'm miserable?"

"Not all the time, no, but always on test days, yes." Stephen leaned forward, scrutinising Jake's face. Jake dropped into a chair, and as he lifted the coffee he put his feet on the desk.

Stephen's smile became a laugh. "You've done it, haven't you?" Stephen clapped his hands together before pointing at Jake. "You've bloody done it. Admit it." He pushed Jake's feet from the desk playfully. "Come on, for once in your life let go and enjoy the moment." His slight Irish accent always became more pronounced when he became excited, and he roared with laughter as Jake nodded solemnly before sipping the coffee. "My God, Jake, we'll be rich again! And not before bloody time my friend . . . my brother."

His features softened, and eyes flicked to his watch. "What time do we begin the test?" He already knew, but with success seemingly within their grasp he was keen to get on. He waved his arm at Jake. "And I'll tell you this for bloody nothing: this will soon be a Rolex, or one of those other expensive timepieces. No more scrimping and bloody saving."

"You hate people who define themselves by labels, and testing begins at nine, as well you know, my friend, my brother." Jake suppressed his smile. "How easily your head can be turned. I'm disappointed." He looked down and shook his head in mock disappointment.

Stephen walked to him and slapped him on the back, his smile gone, his face serious. "We are going to get our reward, Jake, our reward for the hand we were dealt as children, for what happened to our parents, and most of all for what we have sacrificed over the last few years. Has it gone to my head?" Stephen's and Jake's eyes met. "No. I've always been there, up here," he tapped his temple, "I've simply been waiting to collect." His smile returned. "Now get down there and get set up. I'll join you at nine. I'll have the emails ready to go as soon as you give the green light. And whatever you do, don't start without me."

Jake nodded and paused, his hand on the doorknob. "If this is it, and I believe it is, don't forget what we have to do before we start this new life you have planned," he raised his free hand to halt any response, "otherwise, it will mean nothing."

His hand fell to his side and he opened the door. Without looking back, he made his way along the corridor to the lift. Once there, he placed his index fingers on the small glass screen to the left of the door;

a green light flashed and the door opened. Once inside, it closed behind him, and a pad cleansed his prints from the screen in readiness for the next person with appropriate authority.

The lift completed its short journey to the basement. Jake walked purposefully past the laboratory, the workshop and the small office area, and entered the testing room. The reinforced walls of the cavernous room were whitewashed. Various areas had been sectioned off for the different types of testing, and a row of overlarge tailor's dummies were draped with dull metallic-coloured tunics. His fingers found the key in his pocket as he approached the strong room. Behind the huge steel door was a myriad of weapons that would be needed soon. Inserting the key into the lock, he punched half of the numerical code on the pad that was revealed as the locking mechanism was activated, then he turned the key ninety degrees clockwise before completing the code. His head gave an involuntary nod as he heard the brief, shrill beep that signalled the door was unlocked. As he placed his hand on the bar to pull open the door, he heard someone enter the room behind him and turned to face them. He smiled as Abigail Ward waved at him.

"Hi, Jake. I bought cake to celebrate." She held up a supermarket carrier bag. "Today is the day, and we shall eat cake!" She walked to the refreshment area and placed the bag on the counter, laughing. The Hatton brothers enjoyed a healthy lifestyle. Both were at the peak of physical fitness, which was hard-won due to their punishing exercise regime, and a very healthy diet. Any form of sugar or fat was avoided, and only on rare occasions would they veer from their chosen lifestyle. Abigail believed today was one of those days. She had briefly thought about buying champagne, but knew Stephen had had an alcohol problem when his adoptive parents died, and she didn't want to be the one to lead him back down that road.

Abigail had worked with the brothers since they had started their quest to develop the most advanced and effective synthetic fibre, which they had named RobusX. Although it had the potential to be used for many things, and no doubt would be in the fullness of time, the Hattons were focused purely on its use to provide body armour for the armed forces, and, as a personal side-line, for protective suits for racing and speedway drivers.

"Do you know, Abigail, I think you're right. I'll be having a large slice." Jake smiled as Abigail beamed and began to unpack the bag.

Abigail was less than a decade older than the brothers, but had taken it upon herself to mother them, almost from the first day she had started working with them. Stephen was aware she had a soft spot for Jake, and although he knew she was far from Jake's type, he repeatedly warned Jake against giving her any form of encouragement of a romantic nature. It wasn't needed. Jake was only too aware of Abigail's importance to their success. He watched as she removed her coat, and being barely five feet two, had to raise herself on the balls of her feet to reach the coat hook. Her sweater rode up revealing a layer of dimpled skin spilling over the top of her trousers. Abigail was not fat, but she certainly carried too much weight for a woman of her height. Knowing his nose was wrinkling at the thought of her naked, Jake quickly pulled his eyes away and returned his attention to opening the strong room. Buttoning her white lab coat, Abigail hurried to join him.

Upstairs, Stephen Hatton began to dictate the message that would be sent to announce their success once it had been confirmed. At eight forty-five he walked into the administration office, his excitement barely under control, and held out his hand to Patsy.

"Come with me: you are about to witness history in the making. One day you will tell your grandchildren about today." He smiled as her eyebrows questioned this since she was fully aware of what they hoped to achieve.

"Me? Why? I'd love to, but surely . . . that is, this is totally unexpected." Despite her words, Patsy Hodge stood and walked towards him. She wondered if today she would find out whatever it was they were after. What she believed Burt already knew. Willing herself to remain calm, she hoped she looked confused rather than excited.

Stephen Hatton placed a casual arm around her shoulder, a habit that was becoming rather too frequent, as he led her towards the lift. She bit back her irritation, and tried to step away from his grasp. Knowing they had probably completed the project, she had become Stephen Hatton's latest challenge.

He tightened his grip, and his eyes glinted with amusement as he spoke. "Hurry now, Jake will be clock-watching." His hand squeezed her shoulder as he increased the pace. "Do you know, Patsy, I might let you join us for the final test – I know you can handle a gun."

Patsy's head jerked towards him but her step didn't falter as she continued at the brisk pace he set. She hadn't been expecting that.

"That was a long time ago, and it wasn't for me. Guns are not my thing, I'd be no use."

This wasn't true. Whilst Patsy hated guns and the carnage they caused, and she had opted out of armed duties once she had completed her basic firearms course, following her recent training she was now able to use several different types of weapon proficiently.

Stephen removed his arm and placed his two index fingers on the screen.

"We'll see. Give it a go, you can't do any harm." He laughed as he followed her into the lift, which automatically began its journey to the basement once the doors had closed behind them.


Patsy raised the rifle to her shoulder. When it had steadied she looked down the barrel and, moving it a little to the left, she found the small red circular target. She hesitated.

"Do it!" yelled Jake Hatton. "I promise it will be fine."

Still in a good mood, Jake encouraged her, although he would have words with Stephen later. He was pleased he had taken an interest in the woman, but even Stephen couldn't believe this was the way to a girl's heart, and on any other day he would have been irritated by her presence. But today was a good day, and nothing could blight his high spirits.

Patsy closed her eyes for a second, and wondered for the umpteenth time why Stephen had involved her in this. Much like Jake, she couldn't believe he thought it would win her over. Opening her eyes, she realigned the sight to the target and pulled the trigger. A sharp crack rang out and she lowered the rifle to see the result.

Jake Hatton flinched as though he had been slapped, and clapped his hands. He turned his back to her, knowing that the movement of his body upon impact was because he had been waiting for the bullet to hit. "Again!" he commanded.

Patsy raised the rifle. The target mark in the centre of Jake's shoulder blades was bright against the dull metallic tunic. Her finger tightened on the trigger, she squeezed it gently and another shot rang out. Jake's head jerked slightly and he took a half step forward. He spun around.

"A light punch, no more. Let's check the damage before we move on."

He hurried up the range towards Patsy. Patsy lowered the rifle and smiled at him. She didn't want to be doing this, but at least all was going to plan, both for the Hatton brothers and, she hoped, for herself. She had been allowed into the restricted zone of their premises for the first time. As she turned to face Stephen and Abigail, who were grinning at the rapidly approaching Jake, she wondered how much quicker it might have been if she had welcomed his advances. She blinked as Meredith loomed large in her mind, and looked at Stephen. He held out his hands and took the rifle from her. He replaced it in the holder in the large rack that had been wheeled out of the strong room.

"I hope you've bought enough cake."

Jake had reached them. Abigail helped Jake remove the tunic, which they laid on the table opposite the rack of weapons. As he pulled off his tee-shirt, Abigail's fingers traced the line of his rib cage, pushing firmly into his flesh every inch or so, her eyes darting to meet his after each prod. She avoided the existing bruise.

"Nothing." Her voice was barely a whisper, and her eyes glistened with excitement. "Turn around," Abigail instructed curtly and Jake obeyed. Abigail leaned forward and inspected the area between his shoulder blades closely. Her nose was almost touching the unblemished skin, and she drew in a breath before she began the examination.

Stephen laughed as she began prodding. "Abigail, it worked! It actually bloody worked. You are a genius. See, Patsy, I told you that you would witness history in the making."

Stepping past Patsy, he moved Abigail to one side, and placed his hands on his brother's shoulders. "Are you sure you're ready for this, my brother?"

Jake's smile was broad. "Never more so." He turned to Abigail. "Bring the full suit."

Patsy watched Abigail hesitate, her brow creased with a concern she didn't voice. Jake had been shot with several different calibres of hand gun and a high-powered rifle. They had had little impact on him: RobusX had worked as expected. Patsy wondered what could possibly cause Abigail to worry. In the short space of time Patsy had worked there, Abigail's affection for Jake had been more than apparent, and she had only minutes ago shot at him with a semi-automatic pistol without hesitation, yet now she hesitated.

Patsy jumped as Stephen slapped Jake on the back.

"Good man. Abigail, make the call." Stephen's voice betrayed his emotion as he slung his arm around Jake's shoulder and they started towards an unmarked door behind the gun rack.

Abigail pulled a phone from her pocket. "Make ready. Ten minutes to live test." Abigail closed her eyes in silent prayer. When she opened them, Patsy was standing before her.

"What's happening? Are you all right, Abigail? You seem concerned." Patsy reached out and touched Abigail's arm.

"She's fine," Stephen called. "Abigail, take Patsy to the tower so she can watch."

"Watch what?" Patsy asked as Stephen pulled the door open.

"A little cat and mouse," he called, stepping out of the room. "Go with Abigail."

The door closed behind him, and Patsy turned to Abigail for more information.

Abigail shrugged. "The ultimate test. Those tunics were the final dummy run; now they're going to try the suits. They are going to face automatic fire from the world's deadliest weapons." Abigail headed towards a door in the corner and Patsy followed her. "They have four men, all famed for their accuracy as snipers. Three are ex-military and one is simply . . . I don't know what to call him, let's settle for mercenary. He's reputed to be the best. They will enter an arena, much like you would if you went paint-balling. The difference being there is no paint, only bullets looking to find their targets. They won't know where their enemy is or what direction the fire will come from. It will be as close to natural warfare as we can set up. Except they don't fire back." Abigail held the door open for Patsy. "This way. We will watch and record from the tower. Hurry now, I want to make sure they suit up properly."

"Is that necessary?" Patsy asked as she hurried up the metal staircase behind Abigail. "Surely the military will carry out those sorts of tests? What are the men's orders? What's the point? They have proved RobusX works, is there any question of that? Have I missed something?"

Patsy's questions tumbled out one after the other. She knew this was why she was here, but had no idea what she was supposed to achieve. Drawing in a deep breath as she cleared the final flight of steps she waited for Abigail to punch in a code before pressing her index fingers on the glass panel. Abigail didn't respond to her barrage of questions.

The door slid open and Patsy looked around the room. Lit only by two small panels in the ceiling, a vast bank of screens filled the wall in front of them, and to their left a floor-to-ceiling window overlooked the grounds surrounding the building. She tried to remember how many floors they had climbed.

Abigail sat in front of the screens and pulled a microphone towards her. Her fingers flew across the keyboard on the expansive desk, and one by one the twelve screens illuminated the room. Four of them had a large yellow dot flashing in the corner. Patsy studied them; all there was to see was foliage and woodland. A movement on the screen to the bottom left caught her eye and she stepped closer. Stephen Hatton's muscular frame came into view, and his hand reached out and hit a button. He turned to face the camera.

"Are you ready for us, Abigail?" he asked, as Jake came into view. Both men, naked with the exception of their boxer shorts, looked into the camera. Patsy watched Abigail flip the switch at the base of the microphone.

"I am. I have the system setting your route now. The others have taken their chosen positions. Now, dress in front of the camera, I want to make sure you get this right."

A man Patsy hadn't seen before, wheeled a rack forward, hanging from which were four suits. Two looked much like all-in-one underwear, the others similar to those worn by racing drivers, but without logos from sponsors. And rather than bright team colours, the suits had a camouflage pattern. The man handed each of the brothers the underwear. They stepped into it quickly, before each accepting the outer suit which took a little more effort to don. Finally, they pulled on what appeared to be a rather cumbersome balaclava helmet. All but their eyes were now hidden from the world.

Abigail leaned forward. "Switch on communications, please. Terminate loudspeaker." Her voice was tense as she watched the brothers simultaneously press their hands to their ears.

"The handsome Hatton brother checking in. Do you copy?" Stephen's voice filled the room.

"Really? I hear you, Stephen. Jake, everything okay?"

"Perfect, Abigail, perfect. Have the cake ready for our victorious return." He took something from the man who had helped them dress and strapped it to his arm as Stephen did the same. Patsy leaned forward; they looked like large divers' watches. Jake tapped a button and lifted his arm to check the reading. "Destination coming through in 5, 4, 3 . . . Okay, coordinates in, all set."

"Me too. Let's get this show on the road. See you in thirty minutes, ladies." Stephen turned his back to the camera and lifted an arm in salute.

Abigail ran her fingers through her hair as the two men disappeared from view, her eyes scanning the screens. Two pulsating dots appeared on the map filling the far screen – one blue, one green. They slowly separated.

"You call 'abandon' the minute you feel anything. No chances, you hear me?" Abigail never took her eyes from the screens as the blue dot moved south and the green southwest.

"I take it that's them." Patsy observed, "They have different routes?"

"Silence, please. Abigail, switch off your mic." Stephens's hoarse whisper caused both women to jump. Abigail switched off the microphone and turned to Patsy.

"Yes, different routes, but both will be taken the full circuit, so the weapons will be tested on each suit. Most of the area is covered by cameras so you will see them in a moment." She pointed to a screen, "There's Jake now, and any minute . . . there's Stephen. If they are not on camera you will see only the dots."

Patsy watched the two brothers set off on their mission. Both walked steadily, occasionally glancing at their watches.

"I'm not sure I understand this. The men with guns are not visible, but Stephen and Jake are. How do they know where the others are? They'll be picked off easily."

"They are supposed to be. We are testing the suits, not playing a game." Abigail was tense and snapped her answer.

"Then why all this soldier crap? They could have just stood there as they did with us? Sorry Abigail, I'm missing something here."

"Apologies, Patsy, I didn't mean to be rude. We have tested, and tested again, the resilience and reliability of the material. It's too difficult to explain to you in full, but think of it as a liquid in a solid skin. To the touch, it feels firm and unyielding to a degree, but its strength is its ability to move within its skin. Put simply, it deflects and absorbs impact by sending the liquid shock waves out around the structure of the garment which then settles back to where it began. What would have been the bullet hole is repaired. Our modifications have also stopped men being knocked over or even bruised by the impact of bullets or shrapnel for the best part. But, each impact absorbed causes the material to heat up a little: it's not been a major issue, however, it has never been tested under rapid gunfire with a human inside the suit. We don't know what will happen then. We know the material won't fracture, but we have only done tests on fairly large pieces, and so far, so good. It got quite hot, but didn't hinder the wearer. We have shot pigs in the head – they survived – but we don't know how the human brain will respond to the impact, and to the increase in heat caused as the material absorbs and settles, absorbs and settles and so on."

Abigail turned to Patsy. "What we do know is that when a man braces himself for the impact, his heart rate increases, his body temperature rises, and the impact is felt a little more. We don't know why. We have tried heating the material from the outside in laboratory conditions, and then applying impact, and all tests have been positive inasmuch as the material remains intact, the wearer unharmed, but the body temperatures reached would hinder the wearer, particularly in warmer climates. The pigs responded well and showed no sign of anything but irritation when shot at, and while their body temperature did increase, they carried on as normal. One male continued to mount its mate while under fire. *But*, when you're making a product like this, eventually you have to test it on humans. The suit they wear under the body armour has qualities similar to a wetsuit: it keeps the body temperature inside constant, but does not increase in temperature itself. In principle, it should neutralise the effect of the outer suit getting hot. If they knew when they would be shot, they would brace themselves and it would affect the trials. They are on their guard, exactly the same as a serving soldier would be in a war zone. There is danger, and you know it's coming, but you don't know when or where." Abigail shrugged. "It's our final test."

"Why do they test it themselves? I'm sure there are lots of heroes out there willing to be paid to test this? In fact, I'm surprised the MOD hasn't offered a few squaddies. If they have this right, this is huge, why would they put themselves at risk?"

"Because that's the way they were brought up. I've tried to reason with them on many occasions, but the old 'do unto others' thing wins out every time. If they do not trust it to work, why should they expect others–" Abigail stopped speaking as Jake's voice came over the speaker.

"Ten percent in, and something poked me in the back several times. Grid co-ordinates twenty-fifteen. Moving forward."

The room fell silent and the two women watched Stephen hunch forward and move into some undergrowth. Patsy's eyes travelled to Jake, and she blinked as several leaves fluttered to his left. He took a step to the right.

"Wow! I've taken a head shot and I think several to the left shoulder. All good. Grid co-ordinates ten-thirty-one. Not even flushed! I'm going to step up a pace." Jake had been kneeling beside a tree to check his position. Having reported in, he jumped up and began to run, zig-zagging as best he could through the dense foliage in front of him.

The two women watched the remainder of the exercise. Each man reporting in when they believed they had been hit, Jake walked straight into the rapid fire of a DSR 50 sniper rifle and reported a mild discomfort on his torso. As the two men made their way to the final destination, Abigail relaxed. Blowing out a breath she turned to Patsy with a broad smile.

"Two minutes and it's done. We can get the data analysed and the reports done ready for the big guns. The boys are home and–"

"Arghh! Bastard! I've been shot in the foot. We didn't do shoes! Have a medic standing by." Stephen's voice was harsh.

Abigail's hand flew out and hit a black knob sitting in the centre of the desk. The sound of the alarm filled the room, its wailing punctuated by a robotic voice telling everyone that the exercise had been aborted. In the background, Patsy listened to Jake calling for confirmation that his brother was okay. If Stephen responded she didn't hear it. She turned as Abigail jumped to her feet.

"I need to see them but I can't leave you here, you'll have to come. Hurry now."

Abigail was already punching in the release code for the door. Patsy reached her as she placed her index fingers on the glass panel and followed through the door which had yet to open fully.

They took the stairs down at some speed. Abigail quickly opened the door at ground level, then, keeping to the contours of the building, jogged away to the left. Patsy hurried to keep up. They reached a wooden building on the edge of the wooded area. It reminded Patsy of a chalet she had stayed in on her one and only skiing holiday. They passed quickly across the small lobby and through the open door of a room to their left. Inside, Jake was being assisted in the removal of his suit by two men in pristine white lab coats. Stephen was already stripped to his boxers, and sitting with his leg outstretched and supported on a chair. A third man with a first aid bag was inspecting a bloody wound.

Stephen smiled at the two women. "It's only nicked. Stings like hell, though. I'll live, don't look so worried, Abigail." He called to the man assisting Jake, "Clive, pass me that tracksuit, and get the men and their weapons to the ops room. I want a debrief now." He raised his hand as Abigail began to speak. "I know we'll get the data shortly, but I want to hear it from them."

Stephen dismissed the paramedic and pulled on the tracksuit. Patsy followed the group into a larger room. It was light and airy with full-length windows that looked back onto the main building. A large, sturdy table held a projector, and much like a schoolroom, several small tables, their chairs tucked in neatly, faced the front of the room. Patsy took a seat on the far side as Abigail and the Hatton brothers huddled over a desk examining the suits. When Abigail was satisfied, she asked the brothers to reveal their torsos which she inspected closely before running her hands over their heads, Patsy assumed looking for signs of damage. She only caught the odd sentence, but they were clearly high-spirited, and Patsy noted Abigail spent more time examining Jake than Stephen.

They fell silent as the door opened and four men filed into the room followed by Clive, still wearing his lab coat and clutching a sheaf of papers. Jake gestured to the desks in front of the table as several weapons were wheeled in on a trolley.

"Gentlemen, please take a seat," Stephen invited.

Patsy studied the men as they sat. Two were pretty much as she expected them to be. Dressed in camouflaged combat trousers and tight black tee shirts, they were broad-shouldered and thick-necked, and tattoos adorned their muscular arms. Chins forward and backs straight, they were clearly ex-military. The third man was smaller, both in height and stature, and dressed in black trousers and a black polo-neck sweater. His red hair was cropped short and the sprinkling of freckles on his nose stood out against his pale skin. As the fourth man entered, he caught sight of Patsy, and his thin lips curled into a smile revealing yellowing teeth. He ran his fingers through his thick, dark hair which was greying at the temple, and nodded an acknowledgement. Dressed in trainers, dark jeans and a black zip-up fleece, he was by far the most relaxed of the four men.

Patsy returned the nod and looked away. She knew his face: his photograph had been repeatedly projected onto the screen in the briefing room. *He* was why she was here. Filipp Myshkin was of interest to Burt and his department, and Patsy wondered if they knew he had merely been hired to take shots at the brothers.

Stephen quickly scanned the sheaf of papers he had taken from Clive before handing them to his brother. By this time the men were all seated, each having chosen a separate table, and eyes front, they waited to be addressed. Stephen's face remained impassive as he gave them his full attention, his eyes settling on the last man to enter.

"Filipp, perhaps you'd like to explain why you shot at my feet? As it happens the wound was superficial and no harm done, but you didn't follow orders."

Despite Stephen's relaxed demeanour Patsy caught the edge in his voice and saw Jake's shoulders stiffen. There was a rustling as the other men turned to look at Filipp Myshkin.

"I did follow orders. I did exactly that." The words were spat out. "I was told to shoot to kill, the only no-go zone being the eyes. I knew I couldn't kill you, I know why we are here. I am not stupid." His tone was challenging and he held Stephen's gaze.

Patsy wondered if that was hatred burning in the dark eyes.

Filipp held up a finger, "But that didn't stop me maiming you. In a warfare situation, I would have shot both feet properly, you would be down, and I would come and finish you off face to face. That suit would merely be an inconvenience." Filipp shrugged and forced a smile. "As it happens I was kind, and I merely pointed out your weakness. You should be grateful: I did the job I was hired to do."

There was arrogance in his voice and Jake stepped forward, shoulders braced, his fists clenched. Patsy saw the slight movement of Stephen's hand that stilled Jake. It was Stephen's turn to force a smile.

"And I thank you for that. We will put that right within the week. I see your choice of weapon was a Heckler Koch and you fired over fifty rounds. Did you observe any response from us after we'd been hit?"

"When I shot him in the head," Filipp Myshkin nodded towards Jake, "his head moved and recoiled from the shot, but other than that very little. He has a weak neck, no doubt."

Filipp snorted in amusement as he moved his gaze to Jake, his nose wrinkling as though inspecting something unsavoury. He looked away, blowing a short blast of air through his nostrils to demonstrate his lack of respect.

Patsy looked at Jake's neck, it was like a tree trunk growing from his torso, she very much doubted it was weak.

Jake controlled his response by leaning forward, resting his fists on the table before him. Tearing his eyes away from Myshkin, Jake looked at the other men. "And what about you three? Did you notice any response from us?"

For the next thirty minutes the brothers questioned the men and extracted as much information as they could on every shot fired. Clive jotted down their answers. When they were content that they had collected enough data, the men were dismissed. Patsy watched as Clive handed envelopes to each man as they exited the room. The envelopes were thick, and Patsy guessed they were full of cash. She made a mental note to check the bank accounts that she had access to when she returned to the office.

The door closed behind the men and the Hattons and Abigail fell into conversation with Clive. All were animated, and their grins displayed their pleasure. Patsy realised she had been forgotten. She stood and told the others that she needed to get back to the office.

Stephen smiled. "Patsy, we are ignoring you. We have to finish up here. I'll arrange to have you escorted to the main building." He placed a call.

Minutes later there was a rap at the door and Patsy was shown to a car waiting outside. She started to protest, "I can walk back, it's only minutes away. Please don't worry."

"Sorry, Miss, this is a live zone. You have to come with me." The chauffeur smiled as Patsy climbed into the car. "I've opened the windows to let some air in; the air con won't kick in by the time I get you there."

Patsy thanked him for his consideration, and in the event was grateful she had been taken a different way back to the front entrance. Her driver had to wait for a Land Rover to pass. In the vehicle were the four men. Patsy grimaced as Filipp Myshkin lifted his hand and gave a regal wave as they came level with her car. He opened the window as far as it would go and leaned out.

"Tell him I know you now," he called, and grinned as the car pulled clear.

Frowning, she wondered who she should tell as she watched the vehicle making its way along the drive leading to the main gate. Stephen Hatton, Meredith or Burt? Her instinct told her it would be Meredith. She also wondered if Burt would now tell her who Filipp was, and why they were interested in him.

"Did he say something, Miss?" Her driver turned to look at her.

"Not that I understood." Thanking the driver, Patsy slammed the car door and hurried into the building. She barely smiled at the receptionist as she passed, so keen was she to get back to her desk and resume her search for information on the four men.

~ ~ ~

Meredith was weary, and he sighed as his keys clattered onto the hall table. He knew Patsy wanted to go out to dinner, but he had neither the energy nor the inclination. He looked at her as she appeared at the top of the stairs, and held up his hands.

"I know I said we'd go out, but I'm knackered. I doubt I could lift the fork to my lips. But on the bright side, I'll order the takeaway; all you have to do is choose." He pulled his tie from his neck and hung it on the newel post. He stood watching her descend, and added, "And if you're going to have a go, get it over and done with: I know I'm the worst bastard that ever walked the earth, inconsiderate et cetera et cetera, but if it makes you feel better, give it your best shot."

Patsy smiled as she reached him, and stopping a few stairs up she pulled his head to rest on her chest.

"Forgiven. You look pretty much like you feel, and I don't really want to be seen out with you." She kissed the top of his head. "Go and jump in a bath, I'll order the food, and we can have an early night. You look like you could do with it."

Meredith smiled into her cleavage. "Now that is what I call a good night. You realise the bath will revitalise me, don't you?" Wrapping his arms around her, he pulled her closer.

"That's what I'm hoping." Patsy pushed him away.

"So hurry up and get in. You never know, depending on how long the takeaway is going to be, I might just join you."

Meredith grinned, and placing his hands on her waist, he lifted her down the final few stairs.

"In which case, don't order quite yet. I'll even have bubbles for you." Slapping her backside, he started up the stairs. "Switch all the phones off – I don't want any interruptions," he instructed as he reached the top.

Patsy was about to answer when the front door behind her opened. She turned and smiled at Amanda, ignoring Meredith's groan.

"You look as worn out as your father," she observed. "Tough day?"

"I don't want to talk about it. Are you two still eating out, and if so, do you mind if I join you?" Amanda dumped her bag on the hall table. "I hate all men, particularly good-looking men, and I feel the need of company. I could. . ." She paused as her father groaned again and shut the bathroom door. "Is Dad okay?"

"Tired." Patsy put her arm around Amanda's shoulder. "I'm about to order a takeaway, you can choose. Are you sure you don't want to talk about it?"

"No. Chinese please. We're ordering the banquet by the way, I need comfort food."

An hour later the kitchen table was strewn with mostly empty food cartons, and Meredith opened a second bottle of wine. Amanda declined the offer and left her father and Patsy alone.

"I'm sure you'll join me," Meredith smiled as he refilled Patsy's glass. "Let's bin this lot and have an early night."

"What a splendid idea." Patsy cleared the table in seconds. "You put the plates in the dishwasher and I'll take the cartons out to the wheelie-bin; the kitchen will smell in the morning if we don't do it now."

She walked to the back door and turned the key, but pausing in the open doorway she turned back to Meredith.

"I don't suppose you know a Filipp Myshkin, do you?"

She watched Meredith freeze as he lowered the dishwasher door. Still bending forward, he turned his head to face her.

"Why? Have you come across him?" He tried but failed to keep the tension from his voice.

Patsy frowned and stepped back into the kitchen. "I met him today . . . who is he? I can see that you know him."

She flinched as Meredith banged the plates onto the work surface.

"He's a nasty, dangerous piece of work is who he is. What do you mean, you met him?"

"I can't say too much, Official Secrets Act and –"

"Fuck the Official Secrets Act. This is me, Patsy, you can trust me. Tell me how you met him!"

Patsy pictured in her mind the fat envelopes nestled between the towels in the airing cupboard.

"I'm sorry, I didn't mean to offend. He was at work today, and when he left he said something like, 'Tell him I know you now.' I had no idea who the *him* was, hence the question. So, how do you know him?"

Her heart beat a little faster as a look of fear passed briefly across Meredith's features before being replaced by anger.

"This is no game, Patsy. Just what is a Russian bad boy doing at a factory manufacturing bikers' suits? What did he do there?" he yelled.

"Calm down, will you! It's clear you're frightened but shouting at me won't help, will it?" She rolled her eyes as Amanda hung over the banister to ask if everything was all right.

"You see where it gets you? Now we'll have Amanda down here too."

Walking quickly to the hall, Patsy assured Amanda all was well, it was only her father over-reacting as usual. When she went back to the kitchen, Meredith was sitting at the table with a large glass of wine in his hand. He pursed his lips.

"I am frightened, yes: frightened for you, as it happens. He is a dangerous man, and guilty of some cruel and horrific crimes – the murder of Jane Roscoe being one of them. So, I ask again, calmly, what was he there for?"

Patsy joined him at the table, her eyes wide.

"He's a sniper. The Hattons have developed a fabric, much like Kevlar, but better. They've named it RobusX. Don't ask me for the science, but as well as making suits for bikers they've developed a suit of body armour far superior to anything else on the market. They will have a major contract with the MOD. Today they tested it in as close to the conditions in which it will be used as possible. Filipp Myshkin was hired, for cash, to take pot shots at the Hatton brothers." She drew in a deep breath. "I've now told you more than I should have, and I know you won't share that information. Now it's your turn. Are you certain he killed Jane and others?"

"Positive."

Meredith sipped his wine and closed his eyes, his head tilted towards the ceiling. Patsy knew he was joining up dots. Unaware of what vision he would come up with, she left him to it and completed her journey to the bin. She too began processing the information she now had to hand. Meredith had obviously pissed the man off in some way if he now feared for her safety, but if he did think Myshkin responsible for more than one murder, why hadn't he arrested him?

In the kitchen, knowing he was alone, Meredith rubbed his hands over his face and groaned. He knew he might be responsible for putting Patsy in grave danger. He needed Filipp Myshkin out of the picture, and quickly. He also needed to look at the history of the Hatton brothers in more detail. It was too much of a coincidence that Jimmy Ridgeway was connected, albeit loosely, to Stephen Hatton, and now here was Myshkin working for him. How did they know each other?

He smiled as Patsy returned. "I'll not beat about the bush. I need you to tell me what you know about the Hatton brothers. Myshkin is not the first link to the case I'm working on, and Patsy, believe me when I say time is of the essence."

Patsy held her hands out helplessly. "I don't know much. Stephen was given up by his grandmother as a baby and later adopted by a couple in Ireland, and Jake was born in Czechoslovakia, and also adopted, although not so neatly, as a young boy. They were raised in Ireland, went to Bristol University, and stayed here to work. Mother and father have no background, other than to be normal. They were killed by a bomb – wrong place, wrong time, pure fluke they were anywhere near it."

Meredith had inclined his head.

"What? What did I say that helped?"

"Jake Hatton is Czech?"

"Originally, yes. Why is that relevant? I thought you said Myshkin was Russian." Patsy shrugged, "Help me here, Meredith, I can see you've made some connections but you have to show me the full picture."

Meredith didn't respond immediately: he was now wondering if there was a connection between Jan Liska and Jake Hatton. Liska had told of Czech townspeople being killed by the Russians, and Myshkin could well have been involved in that, but why would Jake Hatton hire him if there was bad blood? He shook his head.

"No, I haven't managed to join the dots." He raised an eyebrow. "But a picture is forming. There is something, I know it – I simply have to find it. Where did Jake Hatton grow up? Do you know?"

"I had to get rid of their bio once I'd read it and I've forgotten. I know someone who will know, though. Shall I make a call?" Patsy reached across and lifted her phone.

"Not at the moment, I don't want anyone else jumpy about this." Suddenly he grinned. "I bet his bio is online; perhaps that will tell us. Google him, you'll be quicker than me."

Meredith was right: the Hattons' website did have a potted history of the staff, and named Jake Hatton's birthplace as Horovice.

Meredith covered his face with his hands. "I know that name, I know it. Why do I know it?" His voice was muffled by his hands.

Patsy was about to say something encouraging when her phone beeped indicating a text had arrived. It was from Linda.

*Sorry, PHPI, I forgot to email you. A Phillip called and said he'd see you tomorrow. He was most insistent I get the message to you. Who is he?*

Patsy tapped Meredith on the shoulder. Pulling his hands away from his face, he took the phone from her.

"I don't have an appointment with anyone called Phillip. In fact, I think the only 'Phillip' I know is Filipp Myshkin. I think Linda has spelt it incorrectly?"

Meredith remembered what he had been trying to bring back to the surface of his mind and he jumped to his feet.

"I have to go out for a couple of hours. You stay here: don't answer the door or go out." He strode out to the hall.

Patsy hurried after him. "What? Why? What have you . . ."

Meredith stopped abruptly and turned to face her. "I'm not his favourite person. He made a threat about you to me before and I thought it was hot air. It still might be but I'm taking no chances. I have to sort him out."

He ignored her response and, collecting his keys, hurried out of the house.

Amanda appeared on the stairs. "What's going on? Is this about the photographs?" she asked.

Patsy stood looking at the front door and shook her head. "No, I think it's something far worse. I think there's a chance your father may have got himself in over his head."

## 16

M eredith hurried into the incident room and pulled out the evidence log. Running his finger down the page, he found the reference he needed, wrote it on his hand, and made his way to the basement, where he forced himself to talk amiably to the duty officer. Thirty minutes later, he unlocked the door to Elena's apartment and climbed through the crime scene tape. He found the apartment to be in much the same condition as he remembered, although it was clear that items had been moved about and not put back as tidily as they had been before. Walking around the spot where Elena had spent her last moments, he dropped into the armchair and looked around. It was here; he knew it was.

Moving his eyes from the left of the door he scanned each item intently. He passed the bookcase which, if necessary, he would tackle later, but he hadn't touched it on his previous visit and therefore he didn't think it would be there. He studied the painting of a wooded glade, and peered at the signature. Not obvious enough. After an hour he gave up, and still ignoring the bookcase he moved into the kitchen. He opened drawers and cupboards, but knew as he did so that it was pointless. He entered the first bedroom and sat on the unmade bed. Inspecting the photographs on the dressing table and hanging on the wall around the mirror bought a sadness to him he wasn't expecting, and his anger towards the Myshkins grew a little deeper. The photographs didn't hold the answer. He pulled open the drawers and half-heartedly rummaged through the contents, knowing it wouldn't be there either. He repeated the process in the second bedroom. As he lifted the shoebox from the bottom of the wardrobe he caught sight of his watch; he'd been there three hours and, with only the bathroom to go, he believed he may have got it wrong. His anger multiplied.

~ ~ ~

Patsy groaned in frustration as her fourth call to Meredith was directed to his answer service. He'd been gone for hours without a word, and she was now concerned for his safety. Despite knowing it would make him angry, she called Tom Seaton. Seaton was with her within ten minutes, his hair still wet from the shower she had interrupted. She gave Seaton all the information she had, and her concern grew when he called Trump to join them. The looks exchanged between the two men once Trump had been updated released the final thread holding her in check. Opening her hand, she allowed the glass she was holding to fall. The two men were duly startled as it shattered at their feet.

"Right! Now that I have your full attention perhaps you'd let me know exactly what's going on. You are Meredith's trusted friends and colleagues, and yet he has chosen not to ask for your help in tracking this Myshkin person. Why is that? If he's as dangerous as Meredith suggested, surely it would be better if he wasn't working alone. Now stop looking at each other, look at me, and tell me why."

"Patsy, calm down it may be nothing, and –" Seaton attempted to pacify her.

"Tom, don't treat me like an idiot, you know better. Tell me!" Patsy had raised her voice and, hearing a movement above, stepped over the broken glass and shut the kitchen door. "Amanda is upstairs. She is already suspicious because of Meredith's reaction to my meeting with Myshkin. Start talking now, or I'm going over your heads. Meredith won't like it, but he should answer his bloody phone."

She smiled as Trump jumped to his feet.

"Patsy, don't do that, not yet, there are . . . well, let's just say a few things DCI Meredith has been a little secretive over. I don't know exactly what is going on, but he's not doing it by the book, and he seems to have someone other than the Super telling him what to do. If you go to the top now, you could land DCI Meredith in deep water.

Leave it to us – we'll find him, I'm sure, and perhaps even be able to talk some sense into him."

Patsy's heart stopped for a moment. Things appeared to be worse than she had imagined. Could Meredith be corrupt? She stared at the broken glass for a while.

"How bad is it?" she asked, her eyes on Trump whom she thought she'd be able to read the easiest. He looked away and gathered his thoughts. While he did so, Seaton boiled over.

"About as bad as it can get! He's taking orders and backhanders from some Russian Mafia-type in London. He disappears without so much as a by-your-leave. He's planted evidence on suspects, Filipp Myshkin as it happens, and has threatened to injure or worse, two suspects who should have been held yet he let them go. If you want to call the top brass feel free, because I can't give you an explanation for this one." He looked at his colleague. "And nor can Louie. If Meredith indicated he was taking this bloke out, let's try and stop him adding murder to whatever he's up to. Come on, Louie."

Louie mumbled his apologies and went through to the hall with Seaton.

Seaton turned back to Patsy. "I have to tell you, Patsy, if he's crossed the line, I'll have him." He added, his voice thick with emotion, "It will break my heart but I will."

"And so you should, Tom. Wait there." Patsy rushed past him and went to the airing cupboard, where she collected the two envelopes. When she returned she shoved them into Trump's hands. "He said he was looking after it for someone." She gave a laugh. "Never said who, but keeps telling me to trust him. And I do," she sighed and gave a shrug. "But if he is or was being blackmailed, I have no idea by whom, and the SIS are interested in him." She brushed away Trump's question with a flick of her wrist. "Don't ask, I've already said too much. Just get out there and find him. Bring him back safely, and for God's sake stop him doing anything else stupid."

The two men didn't speak. They simply nodded and left the house. Patsy returned to the kitchen where she collected a dustpan and brush. A solitary tear dripped from the end of her nose as she began sweeping up the glass.

"One secret too many, Meredith; you can't see the wood for the trees."

Meredith's shoulders were slumped as he left the bathroom of Elena's apartment. He'd give the bookcase a cursory once-over, but either he had it wrong, or whatever it was he knew held the key had been removed and was stored in the evidence box. At least he hoped so. There was always the chance someone else had been and worked out what he couldn't remember.

As he pushed open the door to the living room, a broad grin spread across his face. There it was. He was sure this would hold the answer. Lifting the calendar from the wall he hurried to the table in the corner of the living room and flipped the pages. It took him less than fifteen minutes to work out where the bodies were buried. Rolling the calendar into a cylinder, he slid it into his pocket and switched off the light.

"Got you, you bastard. I'm coming to take you out."

Once in the car he pulled out his phone. He had numerous missed calls from Patsy, one from Amanda, and the last, a few minutes before, from Trump. He didn't bother to open his texts because they might distract him, and his focus had to remain on finding Myshkin.

Filipp Myshkin knocked back the remainder of his drink but his frown lingered as he listened to the message again. Picking up the bottle, he topped up his glass, and glanced at the clock. He still had ten minutes, so he beckoned the barmaid forward and arranged to meet her at the end of her shift. Her smile and enthusiasm were false, but she had been on the wrong end of his bad temper in the past and had no intention of going there again. Grinning, he handed her the half empty bottle.

"Keep this on ice. I have a meeting, but I'll be back for it," he instructed as he slid his phone into his trouser pocket. The girl's hopes soared – perhaps the meeting would be long, and her shift would end before his return.

"Okay, I will. Is your meeting nearby?" she asked. She maintained her smile as Myshkin shook his head.

"The meeting is here. I don't know what it is about, but don't you worry, I will be ready for you when you've finished." He grabbed his crotch and thrust his hips forward with a grunt. "You won't miss out." Winking, he walked away.

Once in the lobby, rather than take the front exit, Myshkin opened a door to the left of the cloakroom and walked along the short corridor to the yard at the rear of the building. Standing on the threshold, his eyes scanned the shadows to ensure all was well. Other than the empty barrels and crates of bottles there was nothing there. He walked to the gate and slid back the two bolts holding it in place, then stacked two barrels in front of the door through which he had entered the yard. He had no idea what this meeting was about, but there appeared to be money in it for him and he didn't want to be interrupted. Resting against a stack of crates, he checked his watch again: it was almost time. This guy had better be punctual, because that barmaid was good. Pulling a cigarette from behind his ear, he cupped his hands around the flame of the lighter, and as he drew the first draft of smoke into his lungs, the gate opened. He blew the smoke into the air and nodded.

"You are on time." He raised his eyebrows indicating that was a surprise. "What do you want? Whatever it is, it had better pay well. I don't like you, but I'm happy to take your money."

~ ~ ~

The doorman rolled his eyes as Trump and Seaton hurried into the club foyer. He shoved his hand against Trump's chest and halted their progress.

"Oh no, not again. I don't care who you are unless you have the paper."

"He means search warrant," the cloakroom attendant added.

The doorman nodded. "Yes. Unless you have this, you are not coming in."

"Is Filipp Myshkin here?" Seaton asked over Trump's shoulder.

"Why? Do you want to beat him up again?" The doorman snorted out a laugh. "I don't think so."

"Is he here or not? His life is probably in danger and it's imperative that we speak to him," Trump attempted to reason with the man. "If we're right, and you don't tell us where he is, you will regret it one way or another."

"Leave please. I have no idea where he is." The man walked forward, his hand still on Trump's chest and his bulk forcing the two men backwards.

Seaton called to the cloakroom attendant.

"Take note, love. We tried to help him: if Filipp or Peter ask, we tried. But this fucking idiot wanted to play the hard man. I'm not getting the blame for what happens."

The man stopped pushing.

Trump tried again. "Is he here? If he is, I only need two minutes of his time, that's all." He looked at the cloakroom attendant. "Is he here? Because if he is, and you don't do something to help, you could be complicit in what happens."

The girl had no idea what Trump meant, but it sounded bad and her eyes darted to her left and the door which Myshkin had gone through not fifteen minutes before.

Trump nodded his thanks. "Look, old man, I'm going to give you two options. Either you let us in to see Mr Myshkin, or I'm calling the station and getting every officer we have on duty in here following the tip-off we've had about drugs. Accompany us if you're worried . . ."

The doorman sighed and his shoulders sagged a little. "I will go first. If he will see you so be it, if not you will go, or I will make you."

"Good man, now get a move on."

The doorman hurried to the end of the corridor where he turned and held his hand up to stop them coming closer. They did as required, and he pushed the bar to release the door. It opened less than an inch and he put his weight on it.

"It's blocked," he said simply before taking several steps towards them, turning and hurling himself at the door. The barrels on the other side scattered, and the metallic racket they made as they rolled away and bounced off the walls of the yard caused the three men to wince. Stepping into the yard, the doorman stopped dead in his tracks as he took in the scene. "You?" he said simply, and fearful for his own life he turned to Trump and Seaton. "This is what you meant?" He tried to step behind them.

"Stay where you are," snapped Seaton and the doorman froze. Seaton held his hand forward. "Give it here, Gov. Don't make this any worse than it already is."

Meredith was kneeling beside the bloody corpse of Filipp Myshkin. Using the hand that wasn't holding the gun, he pushed himself to his feet.

"Don't be bloody stupid, Tom." He looked at his free hand as he stepped forward; it was covered in blood, and he wiped it on his trouser leg.

"Gov, the gun. Give me the gun." The tension Seaton felt was evident, and Trump stepped forward.

"Sir, if you don't mind, may I check to see if he's alive? We can do the 'who's going to hold the gun' thing later."

"He's dead, I've made sure of that. Do you think I'm stupid? Now get on –"

Meredith was interrupted as Seaton screamed at him. "GIVE ME THE FUCKING GUN!"

Meredith was visibly shocked and he held the gun forward. Although it was pointing at him, Seaton knew he was safe. He took hold of the barrel and pulled it into his custody.

Meredith had regained his thought process. "As I was saying, what we need to do . . . what?" Meredith looked at Trump who had stepped forward. With a quick and subtle but forceful movement, Trump grabbed Meredith's arm, twisted it behind his back and pushed him against the wall. Meredith grunted as his already damaged nose met the brickwork. "What are you doing, get –"

He was silenced momentarily as Trump spoke.

"John Meredith, I am arresting you for the murder of Filipp Myshkin, you do not –"

"Don't be fucking stupid. Get off me." Meredith attempted to move his shoulders, but Trump leaned forward, pinning him against the wall. Meredith called over to Seaton. "Tom, sort this idiot out before I'm forced to do something we'll both regret."

"I think that door has shut, Gov," Seaton said quietly, and spinning towards the doorman who was backing away, he pointed the gun at him. "Stay where you are. In fact, sit down. I said DOWN."

The man hit the ground like a sack of potatoes, his arms wrapped around his head in a vain attempt to deflect any bullet that might come his way.

Seaton said nothing to allay his fear, instead he turned back to Meredith. "I'm sorry, Gov, but this is too big to turn away from. The money, the phone calls, the threats – all doable, but not this." Seaton pointed at the body with the gun.

"I didn't do that." Meredith laughed, and Trump felt his body relax. "Really? You both think that?"

"To be quite honest, sir, I don't know what to think. But you've not helped yourself, have you?" Trump said with a sigh.

"You pompous prick. You could have just asked."

"I have asked. We've all tried, one way or another, but you've lied about lesser things. For what it's worth, I'm sorry, and if you are innocent I'll understand if you want me to move on." Trump unwound a little as Meredith shrugged.

"You're right, it looks bad. I've had a few secrets I needed to keep, and I should have shared them with you. I know you can both keep secrets. I know you're discreet." He sighed. "Let's get this over with. Finish the caution, and let's get back to the station."

Trump flashed a smile at Seaton and began to complete the caution. Totally trusting Meredith's words, he freed his arm. Meredith turned to face him, rolling his shoulder to loosen the muscle. He nodded at Trump as the familiar words were read out. From the corner of his eye, he saw Seaton drop the gun into his jacket pocket. Taking this as his cue, he let out a loud roar and rushed forward, pushing Trump backwards until he tripped over the corpse. Stunned, Seaton didn't move quickly enough, and before he had reached Trump, Meredith was away through the open gate at the end of the yard.

Trump held his hand towards Seaton.

"Pull me up, I believe I'm sitting in a pool of blood." He looked around him. "There's an awful lot of it."

As Seaton heaved him up, careful not to contaminate the scene with any more footprints, he shook his head.

"Do you think he really expected us to keep quiet about this too? I think he must be having some sort of breakdown."

Trump wiggled his buttocks, grimacing. "I think he did, you know, but this is one secret too many." Trump shuddered. "I can feel the blood soaking onto my skin now. Make the calls."

17

Meredith drove sedately along the M32 and exited before it joined the M4. Pulling over as soon as he could, he stopped the car, jumped out and threw up into a waste bin. Wiping his mouth with the back of his hand, he walked back to the car and lit his last cigarette. He pondered for a moment on whether he should call Patsy. Deciding against it as they might already be with her, he wondered on his best course of action. What he wanted to do was to drive to London and give Andronikov a little of what he deserved, but he was probably being watched now, so it was too risky.

Meredith switched off his phone, removed the SIM card, and blew a smoke ring, watching it break up against the windscreen. Andronikov would get his in due course, he would make sure of that. He thought about Trump sitting in a pool of Myshkin's blood and a grim smile emerged, albeit briefly.

"I told you to choose the right side, Trump," Meredith mumbled to himself, and realising Trump had good cause not to choose him, he shrugged, resigned to the fact that he may have lost that friendship for good. He thumped the steering wheel in frustration. He needed somewhere to go, but all those that would offer him safe haven under normal circumstances wouldn't come near him now. His considered calling Ben Jacobs, but dismissed it quickly: he had a new girlfriend in tow, and the fewer people that knew his whereabouts the better. Then it came to him. Starting the engine, he pulled into the traffic and headed towards Peggy Green. She was on her own – the Spanish contingent were away, Patsy had mentioned that – and if anyone would help him, he knew Peggy would. At least, he hoped she would. He muttered a silent prayer.

When Peggy opened the door, she tutted and rolled her eyes. "What is it with you two turning up on my doorstep in the dead of night?" She leaned forward and squinted at his clothes. "Is that blood? It is, isn't it? Well, you're not coming through my hall in that mess. This is a new carpet, get yourself round the back."

"Thanks, Peggy. I'm fine, thank you for asking. Chuck me your car keys first."

"You're not getting in my car either. Have you taken leave of your senses, man?" She closed the door, repeating, "Get round the back."

Meredith sighed, wondering what on earth had made him think this might have worked. He hurried to the back door where Peggy made him strip off any clothing with even a splash of blood on it. As he obeyed, Meredith asked her to move her car out of the garage to enable him to put his in. Peggy shook her head as she supervised the removal of his clothes. Normally his discomfort would have amused her, but the seriousness of the situation was clear and she worried about the man who had given her the courage to come home.

"Why do you want to hide it? What have you done? Whose blood is this? Merriwinkle? If you're making me a whatsit, an accessory, I'll bloody brain you."

"I'm not, so you won't need to. Come on, Peggy, just move the damn car."

Huffing, Peggy turned away and collected her keys from a drawer in the kitchen. "Give me yours," she demanded upon her return.

"Why?"

Peggy rolled her eyes. "Because, Merriwinkle, should anyone come asking, and the neighbours report a half-naked man moving cars about in the middle of the night, I think suspicions might be aroused. As it is, if that nosey cow in number eleven sees me doing it she'll be over here before you've had time for a drink."

Meredith handed over the keys and, as promised, waited in the back lobby until Peggy had completed the changeover. She dropped both sets of keys onto the table and looked at him.

"Get your arse in here before you freeze to death." They went into the front room where she opened a cupboard and poured two measures of whiskey into glasses. "Sit there and drink that. I'm not sure I'm ready to question you yet."

She sat and took a large swig from her glass. Smacking her lips together blew out a breath. "That's better," she jerked her finger towards his discarded clothes. "Am I burning them or washing them? I assume you've done something stupid."

"I have, but it's not that simple." Meredith emptied his glass and stretched over to collect the bottle. He poured them both another, more generous measure. "It's a very long story, Peggy, and the less you know the better."

He sighed as her hands flew to her hips.

"Really! You think that will work? First, I have that poor long-suffering girl in floods of tears, showing me photos of you getting your rocks off. Then you arrive covered in blood and ask me to hide you and your car. So I didn't think it would be simple. But you're going to tell me, or you can take your blood-stained clothes, get your car out of my garage and sod the hell off." Peggy muttered, "It's a long story, I'll give him long story." She pulled in a deep breath and smiled at him. "Now, as I understand it, the best place to start is the beginning." She glanced at the clock: it was almost midnight. "We've got all night."

~ ~ ~

"I don't believe it. He wouldn't." Amanda looked at Patsy for support. "Tell them, Patsy. I know Dad can be a total bastard and not think of the consequences, but murder?" Amanda shook her head. "No, not murder."

"I agree," Patsy said quietly. She turned to Seaton. "Do you honestly think that, Tom? I know everything looks like it is, but I'm with Amanda: even Meredith isn't that stupid."

"I understand your hesitation, and a couple of weeks back I wouldn't have thought he'd take backhanders. But he did, he's made it worse by running. He knows the score better than anyone. Why would he run? After all, if –"

He was interrupted by the phone ringing in the hall. Patsy flew to answer it.

"It might be him." Amanda stated the obvious.

They listened to the one-sided call.

"No, he's not." Patsy wasn't given the opportunity to greet the caller. "Why, what did he say? Well, Meredith isn't here either." She listened a little. "No, no. What good will that do? I'll get him to call if he turns up, I . . . SHIT!"

Seaton had walked into the hall.

"Who was that?" he asked. "Clearly not Meredith."

"Sharon. Chris got a call, muttered some obscenities about Meredith and left the house. She wants to know why, if Chris was here and what's going on?"

"He called Chris Grainger," Seaton nodded. "Makes sense, I suppose. His options will be limited until he turns himself in."

Patsy simply nodded an agreement. She wasn't so sure that it had been Meredith who'd called Chris, given the tale Linda had told her the day before and Chris's interest in Meredith. Knowing she needed to speak to Burt or Benson, and quickly, she had to grab a moment of privacy to make the call. While she remained loyal to Meredith, he needed help. He would be the last to admit it, but she failed to see who else could provide it. She sat at the table and held her head in her hands.

"I think I'm going to be sick."

"That's the shock." Amanda walked over and rubbed her back. "Hold your head lower and draw in some deep breaths."

Patsy did so for a while, then jumped to her feet. Hand over her mouth, she left the room at speed. Once in the bathroom she filled a glass with water and groaned. She slopped the water into the toilet bowl as noisily as possible, hoping it would sound like she was throwing up.

Amanda called from the hall. "Drink some water and I'll put the kettle on."

As Amanda returned to the kitchen informing Seaton that she would kill her father when she saw him, Patsy dialled out and pulled the flush as she filled the glass again. Willing the call to be answered quickly, she sat on the edge of the bath. James Benson answered as the doorbell rang and she heard Amanda greet Sharon.

"I haven't got much time, so keep the answers short," she whispered. "Do you know what's going on with Meredith?"

"I've heard," Benson replied simply.

"How, who told you?" she demanded harshly.

"Does it matter?"

"Yes, no, I suppose not," she stammered. "Did he do it?"

"Well, I wasn't there, but I doubt it." She heard the yawn.

"I'm sorry, did I wake you? Tough fucking shit. Do you know where he is?"

"No, we have people looking. If we locate him I'll let you know."

"People? What people? You tell me what the hell is going on, what Chris Grainger has to do with it, or I'm going to blow this wide open. It seems to me you're playing both ends against the middle and that's not acceptable. He's a good man, and you are not going to stitch him up."

"How do you know that?" Benson sounded distracted.

"Know what?" she hissed, and hearing footfall on the stairs, she groaned and pulled the flush again.

Benson sighed again. "Are you in the bathroom? Look, Patsy, I'm monitoring the situation. Everything will come out in the wash, but for now keep your mouth shut and do your job. Don't go all girly on me. Meredith is a grown-up, and he knows what he's doing . . . I hope. I'll be in touch."

Benson hung up as Seaton banged on the door.

"Patsy, are you okay? Are you speaking to him?" he called. He sounded agitated. Patsy pulled the flush again.

"I'll be out now. Give me some privacy, for God's sake." She picked up her toothbrush and made a meal out of cleaning her teeth. Once done she opened the door and glared at Seaton. "Tom, we're on the same side. I was calling Linda, look." She held out the phone and Seaton checked the call history. The last call had been to a contact called Linda three minutes before. Patsy snatched the phone back. "As if I haven't got enough on my plate, I've now got to deal with Sharon."

Without a second glance, she hurried down the stairs. Sharon was waiting at the bottom and threw her arms around her.

"You poor girl." She patted Patsy's back as though she were a child. "Amanda has told me. I'm sure it can't be true. Chris must be out trying to help him as we speak. I came around to give Meredith a piece of my mind. Chris has been poorly, he shouldn't be out, but he's such a good man he's clearly putting Meredith before himself."

Patsy untangled herself and bit back a caustic comment about Chris. "He didn't do it. I've no doubt he's been stupid and put himself in a difficult place, but I won't believe he killed the man, however horrific the murders he committed were. Meredith's seen that and worse before, so why would he suddenly want to deliver some form of justice himself?" She waved her hand. "No, it's too ridiculous."

Seaton and Sharon both looked away, as though embarrassed. Patsy coughed out a short laugh of derision.

"Why can't you meet my eye? Because you think he was paid to do it? Bollocks! Now get out of my home, the lot of you! Now, please."

Tom Seaton sighed and began to explain he'd been assigned to watch her, but she shouted over him.

"Search the house, be content that he's not here and stand on the doorstep if you want, but you are not welcome in my home. Now get out!" To reinforce the message, she moved quickly to open the front door. As Seaton stepped over the threshold, he opened his mouth to say something. "Save it, Tom. You're the last person I'd tell if he called."

Seaton pulled his phone from his pocket as he stepped out into the chilly early morning air. He didn't hear what Sharon whispered into Patsy's ear as she gave her a second unwanted hug.

"I don't blame you for kicking us out. I promise I'll find Chris and make sure he sorts this out, somehow. I know he knows people."

Patsy stiffened and pulled out of her embrace. "You know nothing, Sharon, absolutely nothing."

Sharon frowned and opened her mouth to ask what Patsy meant, but Patsy had already taken her by the shoulder and turned her to face Seaton. Sharon held her tongue: she would speak to Chris first. Her instinct that he was keeping secrets from her had obviously been correct – there should be no secrets between a husband and wife – and she would get to the bottom of this if it killed her. She murmured goodbye, and Patsy closed the door behind her.

Patsy leaned her forehead against the door and screwed her eyes shut, still trying to make sense of the situation.

Amanda had remained silent throughout the exchange, and now placed her hand on Patsy's shoulder. "Thank you for defending him. I know it looks bad."

Patsy spun to face her. "It's bad. It's about as bad as it gets without him actually having killed someone. If he calls you, Amanda, you must tell me. You have work tomorrow, get yourself off to bed and try and get some sleep."

Amanda knew from Patsy's tone that that was the end of the conversation, and although she knew that sleep was unlikely she made her way to her bedroom.

Outside, Seaton answered his phone. Trump told him Meredith's phone had been switched off but the last location had been near the M4/M32 interchange.

"Probably on the way to London and his new-found friend Mr Andronikov," Seaton observed.

"I'm sorry to say it seems that way, yes. The Super tells me men are already watching Andronikov. I hope DCI Meredith sees sense and gets in touch with us before he gets in any deeper." Trump sighed. "I've got to go, Dave is waving to me. I'm guessing something has happened, I'll keep you posted."

"If you would. Patsy's kicked me out – she knows more than she's letting on. I have to say, Louie, can't see how it could get any worse. I'm coming back to the station. Even the Gov is not stupid enough to come back here."

Seaton walked to his car. As he opened the door, he saw Patsy watching from the bedroom window. He raised his hand and waved, and she drew the curtains.

~ ~ ~

Meredith's clothes sat in a black plastic sack on Peggy's kitchen table. Freshly showered, Meredith had raided her lodger Antonio's wardrobe, and he was now wearing a pair of pyjama bottoms and a sweatshirt that was a little too small for him. He topped the glasses up for the third time.

"Okay, I'm with you so far, but what I don't understand is why you ran? If you're telling the truth and you didn't do it, why run?"

"Because all the evidence pointed to me doing it, and Patsy is in danger as we speak. If I allowed myself to be arrested it could take days before the forensics suggest that it might not have been me." He sipped his drink and pinched the bridge of his nose. "That is, of course, if there is any other forensic evidence. I need to find who did it, and I need to stop those pulling the strings. I can't do that if I'm banged up."

"How are you going to do that? It's not like you can waltz around flashing your warrant card."

"I don't know. But I can try; I have a few contacts who will help."

"Like these blokes in London? Not that I'm familiar with these situations, Merriwinkle, but it seems to me like they put you in this mess. They may not have known that whatshisname was going to be killed, but they haven't done much to help, have they?" Peggy's hands were back on her hips as Meredith rolled his eyes. "What?" she demanded.

"That was the point, Peggy. They had to feel as though they could trust me, which meant my men had to question my motives. I confess it has all gone tits up because now they've brought Patsy into the equation." He sighed and thumped the table. "And I didn't allow for that, it didn't even enter my mind, so keen was I to take on a different type of job." The lines on his brow deepened, his distress apparent.

Peggy leaned forward and patted his hand. "Merriwinkle, don't go all bloody soppy on me, I can't be doing with another of your household in floods of tears. You've warned Patsy, but maybe you should also warn someone you can trust to take care of her. What about her partner, that bossy woman's husband? Couldn't he help?"

"Chris? I don't think so, he's helped put us here. He's on my list of people to see, but not for help."

Peggy put her hands flat on the table and pushed herself to her feet. "This is like the plot of a thriller. Why didn't you stick to arresting the bad guys? You're not handsome enough to be a hero." She took the almost-empty bottle from the table, put it in a cupboard, and made a point of banging it shut. "Well, I need to sleep on all this and see if I can come up with some sort of cunning plan. I suggest you do the same." She pointed at the cupboard, "That's off limits. Come on, upstairs, I don't care if you sleep or not, but I need to, and I don't want you banging around down here."

Meredith helped Peggy make sure everything was locked up, and followed her up the stairs. He lay on the single bed that Patsy had occupied a few nights before and stared at the ceiling. Closing his eyes, he sighed as he listened to Peggy peeing in the bathroom next door, and concluded she had a bladder the size of a cow. Mentally exhausted, he still managed to work out how to obtain another phone and make contact with the people he needed to before he fell asleep.

18

Peggy climbed into her car, and, reaching awkwardly through the gap between the front seats, she placed a small package on the rear seat next to the large shopping bag.

"That was easy, although you now owe me a fair wad of cash, Merriwinkle. Useful that you can't use your own credit card." She smirked as Meredith grunted and lifted the package onto his lap. She pulled out into the traffic. "Next stop petrol, then London. Although I have to tell you, if you don't stop moaning about my driving, you'll be walking."

"Give me your phone," Meredith commanded as he shifted position in the rear footwell to put his hand through the gap in the seats.

"Did you forget something?" Peggy rummaged in her bag to locate her phone. The car swerved towards the opposite lane of traffic a little, and an oncoming van beeped its horn. Peggy slammed on the brakes, the car stalled, and Meredith let out a shout. Peggy shouted at the driver of the van, "Sod off! You could have got a bus through there with Concorde strapped on the side." She shook the hand now holding the phone at the driver, before restarting the engine. Looking at Meredith's waiting hand, she asked, "So are you going to ask nicely? I'm not one of your minions, you can't order me about. Although, I have to say, you're giving it your best shot." She pulled away and the impatient motorist who had begun to overtake hooted at her. "And you can bugger off too," she shouted over her shoulder.

"Peggy, give me the sodding phone. Please." Meredith caught the phone as Peggy released it. "Now, concentrate on driving and get us back to yours in one piece, otherwise it will be you that kills me, not the Russians!"

He fell silent as he inserted the pay as you go SIM car into the new phone and switched it on, hoping the battery would be full. It was, and he breathed a sigh of relief as he scrolled through Peggy's contacts and tapped Patsy's number into it. Hitting the call button, he adjusted the position of his back and settled down for the short journey home.

Patsy was sitting at her desk, her finger repeatedly clicking the mouse as she moved it in small circular motions. The Hatton brothers were holed up in Stephen's office with men from the MOD, and she was attempting to give the impression she was working in case Irene should start a conversation. Her mind was with Meredith. She glanced at her phone as it vibrated and the screen lit up. It was a withheld number and she hit the ignore button. This happened several times, and Irene leaned to one side and peered at Patsy.

"Who are you ignoring? Whoever it is, they seem pretty desperate to speak to you."

The penny dropped and Patsy lifted her phone and waved it at Irene. "It's an insurance salesman that wants me to take out a pension. I made the mistake of telling him I had bad reception at work. He doesn't give up easily." Sliding the phone into her trouser pocket, she stood and lifted her mug. "Do you want a coffee?"

"About time."

Irene held her mug out and watched as Patsy left the office. She doubted very much it was an insurance salesman. Patsy had probably had a row with her bloke and was ignoring his calls. She smiled. Patsy had taken the phone with her so perhaps she was going to call him. Irene followed her. When she arrived at the kitchen, the door was shut, but she could hear Patsy speaking. She leaned her head against the door.

"Where are you? No, no, it doesn't matter, but I'm being followed. Tom Seaton first and now some fresh-faced rookie is sitting at the gates awaiting my departure."

As Patsy paused for a response, Irene's eyebrows rose.

"I know that, strangely enough. I'm not even going to try and lose him. But I want you to tell me, just the once, that you didn't kill him. Louie and Tom believe you did, and there's a warrant out for you. So, wherever you are, be careful."

Irene's hand flew to her mouth and she held her breath as Patsy paused to listen to the response.

"Okay, I know I shouldn't have asked. Is there anything I can do?" She let out a sigh as Meredith responded. "I'm sorry, I gave the money to Louie, both envelopes. I was mad with you. I can get cash from my account, but it won't be in the thousands. Is there anything else?" Patsy listened to the list of names Meredith reeled off. "Okay, I can give you some of those, the others I'll find out. Chris is . . ."

"Would you like to tell me what you're doing?" Stephen Hatton had approached Irene from behind. She gave a yelp and jumped away from the door.

"Nothing, I was about to make coffee, would you like one?" Quite apart from the fact that Hatton had been watching her for a few minutes, the flush on her face revealed her guilt.

"Don't lie, Irene, I've been watching you. Who's in the kitchen?"

Knowing that further lies would be futile, the guilty Irene decided that attack was the best form of defence.

"Patsy. She's talking to a murderer, there's a warrant out for his arrest, and she's arranging to give him money. Lots of it, and she's being followed. Someone is sitting at the gate waiting for her." Watching the expression on Stephen Hatton's face, Irene held back the look of triumph, and pushing her luck, she added, "She's feeding him information now, so you see why I –"

"Shut up, Irene and go back to your desk. I'll deal with this, and I don't want you talking about it to anyone else." Hatton pointed towards the office.

Muttering silently, Irene walked away. It took all her willpower not to turn around when she heard Hatton tap on the door."

"I've got to go." Patsy hung up and forced a smile. "Stephen, I'm sorry, it was personal. Did you want something?"

"I did, but I've forgotten what, given the nature of your conversation. Shall we go somewhere more private to discuss this?" He smiled as Patsy's expression changed.

"Have you been eavesdropping? Really, I'd have –"

"Not me, Irene. I think we need to do some damage limitation, don't you?"

Turning away, he walked to a door a little further up the corridor. Patsy said nothing as she followed him, her mind racing as to how she could talk the conversation away from Meredith. She walked through the door he had opened, and found herself in a small room containing nothing but a desk and two chairs. It reminded her of a police interview room: the only thing missing was a recorder. She settled herself into one of the chairs. Stephen did the same.

"What does Irene think she heard?" Keeping her voice level, she watched Stephen closely.

"No messing, Patsy, I know your background. Tell me what's going on, if it affects my business, and who is in the car at the gate – who's following you?"

"It doesn't have anything to do with you, or the business." Patsy smiled, and hoped it would reassure him. "I promise you. There is nothing for you to worry about."

"I think I should be the judge of that. I've been told you're helping a wanted man . . . or woman. Who would I find in the car at the gate if I went to ask? Much as I like you, Patsy, and I do like you," his eyes held hers, "this business is too important to me to be led astray by a pretty face."

"I'm not leading you astray. The conversation was private, the matter was personal." Patsy had an edge to her voice and she got to her feet. "I have nothing to tell you, Stephen. If you don't believe me, which I understand, I'll clear my desk. Your project is almost there now, you don't need me. I don't think you ever did."

As she took a step towards the door, Stephen jumped to his feet and put a hand on her arm.

"I don't think so. Not without clearing it with the powers that be, anyway. Patsy, let me help you. If it is personal, and you're in some kind of trouble, I'm sure I can help. If, however, you're lying, let's call Benson and get confirmation one way or the other." Seeing the look of incredulity on her face, he added, "Don't take offence, this product is worth millions. Sit back down, please, and tell me the truth."

Patsy did as she was asked, calculating the risks of the two options for Meredith. Coming to the conclusion that she needed to tell the truth, if only in part, she nodded.

"It's Meredith. He's in trouble. Not of his own making; he's been set up, and I'm trying to help him clear his name. There is nothing you can do, but for obvious reasons I would ask you to keep this to yourself. Calling Benson would only make matters worse."

"So, he doesn't know." Despite the control of his facial features, Patsy saw the slight smile at the mention of Meredith being in trouble.

"I would've thought that if Meredith is indeed innocent, then his, or indeed your, superiors should be able to help?" Not waiting for an answer, he leaned forward. "We are talking about murder, aren't we?"

"Not by Meredith. But yes, there was a body. Meredith says he was dead when he got there, and I believe him. I'm asking you to believe me." She shrugged. "I think you should stay out of it. No good will come of your involvement, only more problems. You have to trust me on that."

Stephen Hatton leaned back in his chair and gave a short laugh. "Your loyalty to the man is touching, but I can't stay out of it, Patsy. It appears that a police officer is sitting at my gate. I have important clients coming in and out, clients with top security of their own, how are they going to respond to that? How will I explain that, because we both know that I'll be expected to explain?"

Glancing at his watch, he smiled at her. "Now I must get back to Jake and the others." He rose quickly and held his hand towards her. "I think we should discuss this in more detail over dinner, and then I can decide what's best." Watching Patsy consider this offer, and catching the slight nod of her head, he knew he had her. But instead of leaving it at that, he blew any chance he thought he might have by adding, "Good. Correct answer, you'll enjoy yourself. Much better than sitting at home alone."

Patsy closed her eyes momentarily. They were cold as they opened and found his. "The murdered man was Filipp Myshkin. Now, I know he was here, but I doubt very much whether your intended clients did, so why would you want to bring that to their attention? A very bad move I would have thought, given his underworld connections. Your evening would be better spent hoping that Meredith won't find a link back to you." Patsy stood. "Now if you'll excuse me, I'll go and clear my desk."

The look of horror on Hatton's face almost broke her stride. She'd certainly made her point. Recovering his composure, he stepped out into the corridor. He held his arm out to impede her progress.

"I have nothing to fear on that count, Patsy; I hope that wasn't some sort of threat."

Patsy tilted her head. "It wasn't, but as you bypassed me in arranging the men and paid them in cash, you were certainly hiding something from someone. I don't know what, and to be honest, right at this moment I don't much care. But," she pointed at him, "you did that for a reason. I was merely pointing out that, hopefully, it won't be connected with what Meredith has to do."

Hatton dropped his arm. "I'll keep my mouth shut about your call to him, and only because I don't need any distractions at the moment." He leaned a little closer. "Now leave, quietly. I can see you are having trouble coping today, and I'll call you later."

Patsy didn't answer but walked quickly back to her office, where she collected her things and left the building. She briefly considered calling Burt, but didn't want him speaking to Hatton. Mentally crossing her fingers that they wouldn't already be monitoring her phone, she waved to the young police officer as she drove through the gates, and hoped Meredith would call back soon: she had yet to give him the final contact he'd asked for. Startled, the young office started his engine. His tyres squealed as he pulled away in pursuit, and once on the main road, he called Trump to tell him Patsy knew she was being followed.

"Of course she does. She's not stupid. All you have to do is stay with her. It's not that difficult to understand, surely." With unaccustomed rudeness, Trump terminated the call.

~ ~ ~

Peggy smiled at the young receptionist as she asked to speak to Mr Andronikov.

"Is he expecting you? He doesn't have any appointments in his diary." A slight crease ruined the woman's otherwise perfect features.

"Good, then he'll be free to see me. Go on, tell him I'm here."

"Of course, Ms Biskop, one moment please."

She expected Peggy to step away, but to her surprise Peggy leaned closer. When Andronikov answered she leaned back as far as her chair would allow, and announced the request from a Ms Biskop.

Peggy grinned when, after a brief silence, Andronikov asked the receptionist to repeat herself. She didn't have the opportunity. Not wanting to be turned away, Peggy snatched the receiver. Stunned, the receptionist didn't attempt to recover it.

"Hello, Ivor, I'm here on behalf of our mutual friend. He needs to meet with you and has suggested the hotel where the photographs were taken. You know the ones, the fake pornos." A silence followed and Peggy added, "Do you understand? I really wouldn't mess him about, he's not in the best of moods, but he thinks you'll know that."

"I understand, but this matter is nothing to do with me, I –"

"Good, then no excuses. I know your diary is clear, we'll see you there in thirty minutes. Don't be late, you don't want to wind him up. Bye."

Peggy handed the receiver back to the receptionist, turned on her heel, and walked the half a mile back to her car with a spring in her step.

"That was easy," she grinned at Meredith as she fastened her seatbelt. "I didn't give him the opportunity to refuse."

"He came out to see you?" Meredith nodded his approval as he pulled out into the traffic.

"Didn't need to." Peggy recounted her visit to Andronikov's office, embellishing it a little as she went. "So, I said, as the hulk would say, 'Don't make him angry, you won't like him when he's angry,' and I left."

Meredith shook his head and a smile appeared as he glanced across at her. "He's seen me angry. He didn't like me much before that anyway. And just so you know, you won't be attending the meeting. I have another job for you. How are you at accents?"

Peggy rubbed her hands together. "Fair to middling, what do you want? I like it when you're in trouble, Merriwinkle, it gets me out of the house, and I get to play a copper." Her hand flew out and she pointed across the road. "Look, the *Lion King* is on at the Lyceum. Are we stopping the night? We might be able to get tickets."

"No, we're not stopping the night, and even if we were, you seem to forget that I am wanted for murder. Going to see some bloody musical about big cats would not be the top of my agenda."

"Shame, it would have taken your mind off it. Now, what accent have I got to do, and what do I have to say? We'd better start practising."

Twenty minutes later, Meredith stood at the side of the hotel foyer, looking at a rack of flyers for every type of activity in London imaginable. Above the rack was a mirror giving him a clear view of the entrance. He drew in a breath as Andronikov arrived. Turning quickly, he hurried across the foyer, and took Andronikov by the elbow.

"Keep walking, we're not stopping."

Andronikov nodded, and allowed Meredith to lead him through a door at the side of the reception area into a service lift, through the basement carpark and into a dimly lit pub on the other side of the road.

Meredith ordered two beers, and the men sat opposite each other at the far end of the bar.

Meredith faced the door, which he watched rather than look at Andronikov as he spoke. "Have you guessed why I'm here?"

"I'm assuming you think I can help you get away with killing Myshkin." Andronikov shrugged. "I can't, but I came because I am intrigued. What made you kill him, and in such a manner?"

"I didn't, I found him dead. I thought you could tell me who did it." Meredith's eyes left the door for a moment; Andronikov looked genuinely surprised.

"I hear you were the one found holding the gun, and I also hear you didn't give up the knife. Peter Myshkin has people looking for you, so you'd better hope the police find you first."

Meredith frowned, but not wanting to get side-tracked he responded, "I didn't do it. Wrong place, wrong time. While we're on the subject of the live Myshkin, when you next speak, tell him I know where the bodies are buried." He smiled as Andronikov flinched. "Never thought I'd say that. Did I touch a nerve?"

"I have no idea what you are talking about." Andronikov made to stand.

Meredith reached across the table and placed a hand on his shoulder. "Now, I could take that as an indication you don't want to hear what I have to say, but given the seriousness of the situation that can't be right. You should have made sure she was dead."

Andronikov lowered himself slowly back into his chair. He sighed as though bored with the conversation.

"Am I supposed to ask who *she* is? I know you don't mean Veronika – you've given me great detail about her demise."

"No, not Ronnie, her flatmate, Elena." Meredith allowed his gaze to stray from the door.

Andronikov pulled his head back as though slapped, a deep frown on his brow. He closed his eyes as though in contemplation, and when he opened them his face was impassive once more.

"I know the name, but I don't know the woman. I never went to Bristol once Veronika left. Why is this of interest to me, and why would I want her dead?" He gave a short laugh and tapped the table with his right index finger. "You know, Meredith, I think you have an overactive imagination and for some reason you want to make me into a murderer running up and down the country killing people." His shrug was nonchalant. "I never met the woman."

Meredith grinned. "Well, I'm glad we got that cleared up. I'm off to meet her now, and she's going to tell me where in Horovice the bodies of the massacred men were buried." He caught Andronikov's sharp intake of breath, but continued. "I'm guessing near the old chateau, but whether she knows exactly where, I have no idea . . . yet."

Andronikov's face screwed up, and his gums appeared as he snarled at Meredith. "Enough. I have no idea of what you speak, and no interest in it. You are a very stupid man; you need to be very careful with these false accusations."

Andronikov got to his feet, Meredith stood to join him.

"I take it you don't want to hear it from her?"

Andronikov stilled, only his head turning to look at Meredith, their noses inches apart.

"No more games, she is dead." He stepped away from the table.

"Please yourself." Meredith held his arm towards the door. "I'll let you get on."

From her position across the road, Peggy saw her cue and hit the call button. Meredith's new phone rang, and he fished it from his pocket.

"Elena, good timing, I'm leaving to meet you now. No, wait a moment," he interrupted Peggy's greeting, "I would like you to do something for me. Tell this chap what you told me."

Meredith proffered the phone to Andronikov, who snatched it from his hand. Witnessing the exchange, Peggy smiled and launched into her best Eastern European accent mid-conversation.

"What chap? I am frightened, Mr Meredith. If they find me this time they will kill me for sure. I know their secret. The old chateau holds the secret."

"Bitch! You should be dead. When we find you, I will do the job myself, properly, and you will wish you'd died the first time."

Andronikov opened his hand and let the phone drop. Peggy's screech of fear faded as it bounced on the carpet. Andronikov formed his hand into the shape of a gun and rested his fingers against the centre of Meredith's forehead.

Meredith grabbed his wrist. "Come on, Ivor, let's not be too hasty. I'll keep your secret, but in return you have to do one thing for me. It won't cost you a penny." He forced Andronikov's hand down.

"Ha! You think I believe you? I am not stupid, Meredith. You really think you have the power to stop your more honest police comrades from taking this further?" He snorted. "I don't think so; you are a dead man."

"You're the third man to tell me that, and one of the others is dead," Meredith smirked. "Ask yourself what you have to lose; you don't even know what I want. Are you not curious?" He sat back at the table and retrieved the phone, which he placed in his pocket. Andronikov studied him for a few moments before walking closer to the table.

"Tell me," he demanded simply.

Meredith pushed a stool towards him with his foot. "Good man, take a pew."

~ ~ ~

The phone was ringing as Patsy entered the house. She snatched up the receiver.

"Patsy, what's happening? I've still not heard from Chris – he's been gone hours. Do you know where he is?" Sharon Grainger demanded.

"I have no idea. I'm a bit more preoccupied with the whereabouts of Meredith, strangely enough."

"Yes, yes. But Chris has been poorly, and he always checks in, whatever is going on, and he hasn't. I'm very worried, Patsy. It hasn't helped that Linda has been coming up with all sorts of conspiracy theories today. She's beginning to sound sensible!"

"Let me make some calls and I'll get back to you."

Patsy dropped her phone onto the hall table. She had no such intention, but didn't have the energy for a long conversation with Sharon. She would keep her lines free for a call from Meredith. He'd called again on her journey home and she'd provided him with the other contact details. He'd also started telling her about Myshkin's demise, but for some reason had to terminate the call. Despite the early hour, she walked to the kitchen and poured herself a glass of wine. Sitting at the table, she ran over her brief conversation with Meredith. After a few moments, she jumped to her feet and hurried to collect her phone. She called Frankie Callaghan.

"Patsy, I was going to call but, to be blatantly honest, I had no idea what to say. But, I'm on your side, wherever that might be. You know that."

"I do, thanks, Frankie. Can we meet? I'll come to you. Are you at the hospital?"

"I am, but I'm stacked, Patsy, it'll have to be quick."

"It will be. I'll meet you by the coffee machine that steals your money."

"Why? Patsy, you're not helping him, are you?" Frankie sighed.

"Of course, because he didn't do it. I'll text you when I arrive."

Patsy was with Frankie in less than fifteen minutes. She explained quickly what she needed, and Frankie ushered her into his office. Pulling the report from the pile on his desk, he chewed his lip as she scanned the details. She gasped.

"Patsy, what is it? How does this help clear Meredith's name? There was little forensic evidence, and the scene had been contaminated by Trump and Seaton."

Patsy handed him back the report. "I know who did it, but I don't know why or how I can prove it." Patsy closed her eyes and pressed her fingertips against her forehead as she tried to work out the best way forward.

"If that's the case, surely it's a matter for the police. I know they have a warrant out for Meredith, but if you have new evidence, then surely it's —"

"Frankie, please, let me think. I have no idea who I can trust. I have to get this right first go!" Frankie raised his hands in apology, and she forced a smile. "I'm sorry. I will explain, but at the moment you're better off not knowing." Jumping to her feet, she placed a kiss on the top of his head, told him to keep her visit to himself and hurried from his office.

An hour later, Patsy stood in the lobby of the police station, her foot tapping out her impatience as she waited for Louie Trump. The desk sergeant had given up on small talk, and had returned his attention to the wad of papers in front of him.

Trump smiled warmly as he opened the door into the lobby. "Patsy, come through please." He held the door with his foot and swept his arm towards the corridor beyond.

"No thanks, Louie, I'd rather not do this here. There's a coffee shop around the corner, will you come?"

Trump shot a glance at the desk sergeant, who rolled his eyes.

Patsy chose a table in the corner of the café and sat facing the door while Trump ordered at the counter. When he returned, Patsy glanced around to ensure no one was listening and spoke quickly and quietly.

"Louie, can we trust you? Meredith and I, are we able to trust you?"

"Of course, but DCI Meredith really should come in, and –"

"He can't. But I can tell you I now know absolutely that he didn't kill that man. I believe I know who did, but not why. Meredith has either been very unlucky, or he's been set up. I have no option but to go to my handler with this, and I need you to promise me that if anything happens to me, or if he refuses to do anything, that you will take this up for me."

"Handler? What handler? Are you in danger, Patsy?" He watched the hesitant shrug. Pushing his cup to one side, he leaned forward. "I promise on all that I hold dear that I will help you in whatever way I can. But you are going to have to start at the beginning, explain exactly what you think has been going on, and then we will decide if you should speak to this *handler*." He raised his fingers and made speech marks around the word.

Giving a sigh of resignation, Patsy nodded. She had to trust someone, and Louie had come top of the list. Drawing in a deep breath, she composed herself and, as directed, she started where she thought it had all begun.

# 19

Pursing her lips, Peggy took in the appearance of the man sitting opposite her. "You don't look well."

"I'm not," he sighed. "Don't piss about, Peggy. Where is he? Why won't he meet with me?"

"He's in London, had a meeting with your friend Andronikov. He says it was interesting." She raised her eyebrows knowingly.

"A contact. Not a friend, a contact. What's that got to do with me?" He flinched at the high-pitched cackle that told of Peggy's amusement. "At least one of us is amused." His eyes were cold as Peggy shook her head.

"That's not the way I heard it. But we're wasting time, let's get down to business. Merriwinkle needs your help: he is willing to overlook the deception and sleight of hand you've employed, and ignore any . . . how did he put it?" She frowned and looked at the ceiling before returning her attention to her companion, "Ah yes, misdemeanours. That was it. He's prepared to ignore any misdemeanours, however serious, if you are willing to help. And you can wipe that smile off your face for starters. He is holding the trump card, after all."

"Really?" His tone was derisive. "Let me put you straight on a couple of things." He tapped the table. "First, there have been no 'misdemeanours', at least none that haven't been sanctioned anyway." He ignored her grunt and continued, "Second, there is no trump card, as this is not a game, and third, I'm offended that he felt he needed to bargain with me to get my help, and not face to face either. Not that I don't appreciate your company, but Meredith and I go back a long way, and I'm insulted." Pulling a handkerchief from his pocket he blew his nose. "You tell him to call me, or better still get his arse back to Bristol and sort this mess out."

"I'll let him explain that to you, if he speaks to you. Can I tell you what he wants you to do, or shall I explain to him that you are as bad as he feared?" Peggy held her hands palms up.

"Get on with it."

"He wants you to set up your boss." She smiled and nodded knowingly.

"I don't have a boss. I have no idea what he's talking about. So, get him to call me." Shoving the soggy handkerchief into his pocket, he stood up.

"Shall we call him a handler, rather than your boss?" Peggy looked at the man now towering above her. "I'll rephrase to keep it simple. Merriwinkle wants you to set up the bloke that's pulling the strings. He knows who he is, you know who he is, but for some reason he thinks I'm safer not knowing." She pointed back at the vacant chair. "Sit. I'll tell you what he wants."

She pulled her head back as he leaned forward, their noses a hair's breadth apart.

"I have no idea why he employed the services of an ex-bag lady, but I will not discuss this any further with you. If he wants my help, then he asks for it himself, in person." Having delivered his message through gritted teeth, he straightened up. "I'm pissed off now, so a phone call won't cut it."

He made to turn away and Peggy crossed her arms across her chest.

"As you like. My next visit will be to Sharon. For some reason, Merriwinkle thought that would hit the right button – more effective than any other threat he could conjure up." She grinned as Chris Grainger turned back to face her. "And he was right. Now sit down, people will stare. Let's try and get this thing started. My lodgers get back at the end of the week, and I don't want them thinking I'm some sort of spy, although I have to say . . ."

Chris Grainger sat heavily. "Shut up and get on with it," he commanded.

Peggy knew not to mess him about, and while she ran through Meredith's requirements as instructed, she wasn't at all convinced that Grainger wouldn't double-cross him in some way. However, when she finished relaying the message, he nodded and told her to tell Meredith he would put his plan in motion that afternoon.

"How do I let him know when I'm ready for him?"

"He said he'd be in touch." Peggy shrugged. "He didn't say how."

Chris closed his eyes and drew in a breath that caught in his throat, causing him to choke. He coughed and sputtered for several minutes. His face turned scarlet and beads of sweat joined together and began to trickle down from his temples.

Peggy pushed herself as far back in the chair as possible, holding her head at an uncomfortable angle. "You want to see a doctor about that," she advised, a look of distaste on her face.

"Thank you, I'll consider it."

Wiping away the sweat with the soiled handkerchief, he left her. She watched as he climbed into the car and drove off, and waited a further ten minutes before crossing the road and entering the gym opposite. Using Patsy's membership card, which Meredith had found in his car, she swiped it across the reader on the chrome turnstile and made her way to the locker room. Once there, she entered the code on locker seventy-three and withdrew the solitary mobile telephone. Walking to the showers she locked herself in a cubicle, and with the sound of running water and idle chit chat from the few others that were there, she called Meredith.

~ ~ ~

Louie Trump looked at his uncle as he entered the incident room. He gave a grim smile as Seaton called for quiet.

"Settle down now, the Super . . . sorry, sir, the Chief Super wants to address you."

Chief Superintendent David Ashworth nodded an acknowledgement and stood with his back towards the room as he surveyed the ever-increasingly detailed incident board. His eyes rested on the photograph of Meredith. He reached out his hand and placed a finger in the middle of Meredith's forehead. Leaving it in position, he turned to face the room.

"I've been brought back to Bristol to head up this escalating case. I am now the Officer in Charge. I'll keep this brief, so listen carefully: I will discipline anyone who fails to take heed of my instructions." He glanced back at Meredith's photo. "I, like you, never thought I would see John Meredith on this board either as a suspect or as a victim, but if I had a choice it would be the latter." He cleared his throat, "That's not the case, and now someone – I have yet to discover who – has leaked the fact to the press that there is a warrant out for Meredith's arrest. There were several reporters outside when I arrived, and with the discovery of Jan Liska's corpse and the fact that he was clutching a business card from Meredith, which was also leaked, it will soon become a circus."

He pulled his hand away from the photograph and made eye contact with each and every officer in the room. He spoke slowly and deliberately as his head turned and searched out the eyes of each officer. "You will not speak to the press, you will not discuss this case with your nearest and dearest, and you will not even discuss this with your colleagues unless they are assigned to the case and there is no one else in earshot. I will not supply fodder to the press. In addition, you will not attempt to contact Meredith or his partner Patsy Hodge, and should either of them contact you, you will direct them to me and report it immediately. I will not tolerate any breach of my orders. Am I understood?"

There was a murmur of agreement from Meredith's team, and Ashworth nodded acceptance. He didn't notice Louie Trump avert his eyes as he continued.

"Now, whilst John Meredith has not been found guilty of anything, his failure to surrender into custody, the compromising situation in which he was found and the fact that Liska seemed to be holding his card as a clue for us, make his situation dire. He may be guilty of murder, and he is certainly guilty of accepting money from known criminals, and that being the case he must be considered dangerous. Do not be misled by any misplaced loyalty you may feel: be professional, be honest, and do the right thing."

He paused and watched the conflict on the faces of some of Meredith's team. Dave Rawlings shot a glance at Tom Seaton, and Jo Adler bit her bottom lip. He saw their resolve kick in.

"Tough shout, I know, but if Meredith is innocent we will work tirelessly to prove that. We will have internal affairs fishing about," his dislike of the department was evident from his tone of voice, "so cooperate fully and give them no room to point fingers unnecessarily."

He rubbed his hands together. "Now, down to it. I want all key facts about each murder summarised and on my desk within the hour.

Seaton, you can take care of that; Adler, assist him please. I also want two of you to get down to the morgue and see what evidence, if any, has been secured from Liska's body. The rest carry on with whatever you were working on, and remember – mouths firmly shut. Any questions?" When none were forthcoming, he added, "I'll be using Meredith's office. Trump, I'll see you in five minutes."

~ ~ ~

Trump walked into the kitchen, his face like thunder.

Linda frowned. "What's happened now? You look like you could kill." She placed a hand on his arm, and felt him flinch.

"I could, as it happens. You. What on earth possessed you to invite Uncle David to stay here? Do you not think I have enough on my plate?" He loosened his tie, opened the fridge and pulled out a beer. "Linda, you should check with me first."

Opening the can, he took a long draft and banged it on the table to reinforce his irritation.

Linda grabbed his arm and spun him towards her. "Can I remind you that this is my house and I'll do as I please. And isn't the key word *uncle*? This man is your flesh and blood – we've been to stay with him, why would I not return the favour? It was clearly what he wanted, or he wouldn't have called here to ask. He'd have called your mobile." She prodded him in the chest. "I'm not impressed at being told off in my own home for being reasonable."

"He's my boss at the moment, and it compromises me, both here and at work. Surely you can see that?" Trump dropped onto a kitchen chair.

"No. You're being dramatic for the sake of it. The boys know it's not your fault if you have a bigwig uncle, and if you're worried about him talking shop at home, he'll hardly discuss the case in front of me. Now, I'm going to take a shower because we're taking *Uncle* David out to dinner, and when I come down I hope you'll be in a better frame of mind."

Leaning forward, she planted a noisy kiss on his head before slapping it lightly.

Trump listened to her go upstairs, the creak of the bathroom door and the hum of the shower motor. Content she was fully engaged, he pulled his phone from his pocket, opened the back door and stepped into the garden. He hit the call button.

"It's me. I'll be quick because Uncle David, the Chief Super, is staying with us. Linda's idea, not mine I hasten to add, he's now OIC. I've copied the documents you wanted and emailed them to the address provided, and tomorrow I plan to visit this chap Patsy thinks is involved. I'll name-drop, as discussed. It's not looking good at the moment, so the quicker we get to the bottom of this the better. Liska was holding one of your business cards."

Trump listened to Meredith's response and rolled his eyes. "I'd apologise but it wasn't me who invited him. Where will you stay?" Hearing a door slam somewhere behind him, Trump brought the call to an end. "Must go now, I'll call later if I can." Terminating the call, he turned to go back to the house. He paled as he saw his uncle standing on the threshold. "I can explain," he offered weakly.

"I doubt that, but you can try. Get in here." Chief Superintendent David Ashworth glared as he stepped to one side to allow his nephew entry. Unless there was an excellent explanation, he would have to explain the necessary result of such insubordination to his sister, not a task he relished.

The two men took a seat at the kitchen table and Trump waited until his uncle had also loosened his tie before he spoke.

"I believe DCI Meredith is innocent. The nature of Myshkin's murder and –"

"Stop talking before you dig a deeper hole, you idiot!" Ashworth banged the table with his fist. "I know you only spoke to Meredith in an attempt to bring him in, and that you would have reported it to me at the first opportunity. This is that opportunity – where is he?"

"I don't know. He doesn't trust me that much . . . but you're wrong, Uncle David, I was trying to help him prove –"

He was interrupted by a bang on the table; Ashworth's fist remained clenched.

"When I said stop talking, what I meant was stop incriminating yourself. I may be your uncle, but first and foremost I am a police officer, and I will do the right thing –" It was his turn to be interrupted.

"Which is exactly what I believe I am doing. It's why –"

"Louie, shut the fuck up!" Ashworth bellowed, and in the bedroom above Linda stopped brushing her wet hair mid-stroke. She crept onto the landing and leaned over the bannister to listen. "You are a police officer, so of course you should do what's right, and that means what's right within the law. That would be bringing Meredith in, and, if he's innocent, finding the evidence to prove it. Not agreeing to gather information for him, not giving him the heads-up on evidence we might have, and certainly not going to meet people that his latest shag thinks might be involved. Am I making myself clear?" Ashworth ran his thumb and forefinger along his lower lip, and pinching them together removed the spittle that had landed there. "Where is he?"

"I am not a liar, I have no idea. But I do believe he is innocent." Trump gazed defiantly at his uncle.

"I accept your word on that. Can I also have your undertaking to stop consorting with him, and if he calls again to convince him to give himself in?" His mouth clamped shut, his chin rose in challenge and Ashworth drew in a deep breath, his nostrils flaring.

"I am aware of your rules, sir." Trump blinked.

"I asked for your undertaking, your personal promise," Ashworth demanded.

"I can't give you that." Trump looked over his uncle's shoulder and watched Linda's hand sliding down the banister. He resisted the urge to demand she go back upstairs as she stepped into the hall wrapped only in a towel, her damp hair clinging to her face. He looked back at his uncle, and his head bowed slightly. "I'm sorry, but I have to do what is right, be that within the rules or not."

"Oh, for God's sake." Ashworth threw his arms into the air as Linda arrived in the doorway. She attempted to catch Trump's eye, but they remained fixed in challenge of his uncle. Running his fingers through his hair, Ashworth demanded, "Then tell me his side of the story, and explain why you believe him."

"What will you do with that information? Do you give me your word it will go no further?"

Trump spoke softly, unlike his uncle who exploded. Jumping to his feet, his chair falling noisily, he shouted, his shaking finger pointing at Trump. Linda jumped back in fright, her towel falling to the floor. She clamped her hands on her breasts, her mouth open.

"You make demands on me? You question my motives? I'll do what's right with the information you give me. Now tell me."

"I can't do that. Someone in a senior position is being less than honest, and whilst I don't believe that person is you, you may inadvertently give the game away, so to speak."

For a short while Chief Superintendent Ashworth was speechless.

He looked at the man he had previously thought of as a son, a protégée, and wondered how Meredith had managed to corrupt him so totally in such a short space of time.

"Sergeant Louie Trump, you are suspended from duty with immediate effect. You will not speak to or attempt to make contact with any other serving police officer. I will arrange a disciplinary hearing and you will be notified in due course when and where that is to be held. You will attend the station in the morning and speak only to me, where you will return any property belonging to the police department, and any evidence on this or any other case which may be in your possession. Do you understand?"

"Yes, sir. And I'm sure you'll also understand why you can't stay in this house any longer, but I hope one day, when the truth is out there, you will agree with my decision." Trump swallowed back the lump in his throat. "One day you will understand –"

"I understand nothing, I don't even know you anymore. One day? One day when? You may not have a job by this 'one day', you stupid, stupid man."

Turning abruptly, his intention to stride away, Ashworth almost bumped into Linda, who, mouth still open, cowered from him.

He looked her up and down. "His mother said you were mad." Without further comment, he sidestepped her and left the house.

She turned to watch, her hands lowering to rest on her hips. "He's supposed to be your uncle. What was all that about? What have you done?" she asked turning back to Trump.

Trump looked at her nakedness as he walked towards her. "I love you, Linda, and in any other circumstance I'd probably have peed myself laughing, but as it is I have to go out. I'll call you later, I promise. In the meantime, get some clothes on in case anyone calls." He pressed his lips to her wet hair, and once more the naked Linda turned to watch the departure.

"Well, that's it. That really takes the biscuit," she exclaimed once he'd gone. Running up the stairs she retrieved her phone and called Patsy. Patsy was not given time to greet her before she demanded, "Why has Meredith dragged poor Louie into this? He's been suspended because of Meredith, fallen out with his uncle *and* his mother thinks I'm mad."

Patsy hung up on the angry Linda. She had done little to calm her, so great was her concern for Meredith. Glancing at the clock, she sighed: it was almost an hour until Meredith was due to call.

Meredith pulled up the hood of his jacket and dropped the coins into the hand of the young girl manning the stall. Picking up the bottle of water and a bar of chocolate, he tucked the tabloid newspaper under his arm and walked back to the car, which had been hired in Peggy's name. As indicated by the small headline to the right of the main story, he turned to page five. He glanced only briefly at the photograph of himself striding angrily across Dave Rawlings' garden when he had been working on the case of Dave's missing daughter. His lips pursed as he looked at the credit given to the photographer, Tommy Sealy.

"You'll get yours, you bastard," he muttered before moving on to the stark passport photograph of Jan Liska. He bowed his head. So many innocent people drawn into a life of crime to line the pockets of the likes of Andronikov and Myshkin: he knew there were at least five murders, and top of that list for him was Jane Roscoe. If nothing else came of this situation he would avenge her death one way or another.

His eyes moved to the headline: *Top Cop Wanted in Relation to Russian Mafia Killing*.

"I wish," he muttered, "at least then this might be worth it." He continued to read.

*Sources have confirmed that Detective Chief Inspector John Meredith is wanted in connection with the brutal murder of two Russian Mafia lieutenants. It is unclear at present whether the police believe Meredith was personally involved or simply helping senior Mafia members to avoid arrest. Meredith has been suspended from duty in his absence.*

*Meredith is known for his violent temper and has had several altercations with staff members of this publication. Senior officers refused to be questioned on an on-going operation, and confirmed that a press conference will be held when appropriate to give full and frank information to the concerned citizens of Bristol. The murders of Jan Liska (pictured right), found with Meredith's business card in his hand, and Filipp Myshkin are the latest in a series of murders connected with the crime ring. An officer, who asked not to be named, indicated that it appeared that Meredith had been receiving payments from the group for quite some time.*

*Meredith's case is the latest in a long line of allegations concerning corruption throughout both the police force and the secret services. Last year senior operative . . .'*

Meredith stopped reading and screwed the paper into an unwieldy ball which he threw into the footwell of the passenger seat. He checked the time on the clock in the centre of the dashboard: it was still too early to call Patsy. Opening the chocolate, he took a bite, and wondered how Chris Grainger was getting on, if indeed he was making any attempt at all. His thoughts were disturbed as a large saloon pulled into the space next to him, and several highly excited children spilled out. He watched as they clambered over the small wooden fence, rather than go to the gate, before they ran off towards the playground. Becoming aware that an adult hadn't followed, he looked to his right. A woman in a brightly coloured anorak was looking at him. Her frown told him that either she had recognised him or that she thought a lone man sitting in a car overlooking a children's playground was suspicious. As she drew her phone from her pocket, he started the engine and reversed quickly towards her. She jumped to the side of her car to avoid him, and, as Meredith hoped, had not recovered her wits quickly enough to take down the registration of his car as he drove away.

Ten minutes later, he pulled into Temple Meads railway station and parked in the short-stay carpark. Walking briskly into the foyer, and ignoring the commuters side-stepping each other as they arrived at and left the station, he headed to the telephone kiosk where he slid Peggy's credit card into the slot and dialled Patsy on her newly-acquired pay-as-you-go mobile.

"I'm missing you, what news?" He placed his finger in his exposed ear in an attempt to drown out the sound of heels on marble and idle chatter that echoed around the iconic building.

"You too. No good news, I'm afraid. Chief Superintendent Ashworth overheard Louie speaking to you, and when he didn't play ball and tell him what he knew, he suspended him from duty. Don't panic though, he's on his way to see them now. They don't know he's suspended, and Ashworth didn't know who Louie was speaking about, so it may help."

"Bollocks! Chris still hasn't come back to me but he agreed to do as I asked. I can only hope all is well on that front. Have you got a pen handy?"

"Yes, what do you want me to do?"

"Some research, get your laptop out." Meredith gave his instructions on the research he wanted Patsy to undertake, and she repeated some of his instructions to ensure she had the names correct.

"That's it. I have to go, I've been here too long. I need to get ready for this meeting tonight."

"Be careful Meredith, stay safe."

"Don't I always? Love you, Hodge."

Patsy didn't respond as she heard the click of the receiver as Meredith hung up. Hurrying to the living room, she pulled her laptop from her bag. She'd only had time to type the first name into the search engine when the doorbell rang. Cursing, she balanced the laptop on the arm of the sofa and went to answer the door. As soon as she released the lock, the door was shoved forward and Burt stood in the hall looking very agitated.

"What's Meredith up to?" he demanded.

"I have no idea, and I'm well, thank you, how are you?" Patsy responded with a confidence she didn't feel. She walked into the kitchen, not wanting Burt to see her laptop. "I take it this isn't a social call, so I won't offer you a drink." She felt the closeness of Burt as he followed her, making her aware of the urgency of his visit. Once in the kitchen she took a seat at the table. "I know as much as you do, if not less. Perhaps if you'd tell me what's –"

"Don't waste my time. I heard your conversation with Meredith – your side of it anyway. What exactly does he want you to do, and who is Louie Trump going to see?"

"You've bugged me? How dare you? I'd like to see the warrant for that!" Patsy had jumped to her feet and was pointing at the door. "Get out! Or are you going to throw me into the back of your car again? No more, Burt, or whatever your real name is. I've had enough. I'm not playing your games any more. And for your information, I've jacked in the job with the Hattons!"

Burt grabbed her outstretched arm, pulled her towards him, the table legs scraping on the floor as her body jerked forward. With a grunt, he spun her round and, holding her arm up her back, he pressed her up against the wall.

"Stop fucking about, Patsy. I'm not leaving here until I have what I want. We can do it the easy way or the hard way, it makes little difference to me."

Patsy gritted her teeth against the pain, refusing to let him know how much discomfort she was in or her growing fear for the safety of Meredith. She shivered as she felt his hot breath against the back of her neck.

Burt spat out a laugh. "Ha! You like it rough, do you? Is this how he does it for you?" He lifted her wrist a little higher, causing her muscles to stretch into an unnatural shape.

She groaned in pain. "Get off me, you bastard. Perhaps if you'd been more open at the beginning I might be of a mind to help you now. Arghh." She groaned again as Burt increased the pressure.

"I work for the government. When you signed up you knew it was a need-to-know basis."

"You sound like Chris Grainger, and believe me, that wasn't a compliment." Patsy attempted to push herself away from the wall, but this served only to increase the pain.

"Grainger has chosen the wrong side – he'll get his in due course – but for now I need to know what Meredith is up to before he starts a war." He felt her body relax as she considered his words.

"What does that mean? Has Chris done something wrong?" She angled her head in an attempt to see his face, "I'm concerned about him too, maybe I can help?"

"Grainger backed the wrong horse. He's also gone off the radar, so unless you know where he is, let's stick with Meredith."

"I don't. All I know is that he's still missing. I've had his wife on the phone," she gave a short laugh, "but you know that, don't you?"

"Meredith. Stick to Meredith." He increased the pressure. Tears sprang to her eyes at the searing pain in her upper arm, but she refused to cooperate.

"Do your worst, I'll never betray Meredith, even if I did know where he was. He's guilty of nothing except to trust you lot." Patsy rested her head against the wall and attempted to regulate her breathing. "I'll do a deal with you," she added after a few seconds in the hope he would release the pressure a little.

"Correct me if I'm wrong, but you're in no position to make deals."

"And, nor it would seem, are you!" she spat back. "You wouldn't be here if you didn't need me." She felt his breath again as he sighed.

"I'm going to release you. When I do, you'll return to the table and take a seat. I'll take my gun out, and I warn you that I will shoot you if you try anything. Do you understand me? Because I'll make it look like Meredith did it once I've killed you. So think about your actions." His words were delivered slowly, his lips brushing her ear as he spoke.

"Let me go, I understand."

Once released, Patsy' arm fell limply to her side. She rubbed the muscle frantically, attempting to erase the pain as she walked to the table and kicked the chair back to its former position. Once seated, she watched as Burt drew his gun from the shoulder holster and, still holding it, place it on the table pointing her way.

"You go first," she instructed, holding his eye and determined not to look at the gun.

"What?" Burt laughed, genuinely amused.

"You tell me why I was placed with the Hattons – it certainly wasn't to be Stephen's gofer. Also, tell me what your problem with Chris Grainger is. Once you've done that, if I believe you I'll tell you all I know, including where both of them should be tonight." She watched his eyes widen.

"Why should I do that? What gives you the ability to call the shots?" He raised the barrel of the gun a little before returning it to its resting place, his amusement still evident.

"Because if you don't, your only other course of action is to kill me," Patsy shrugged, "so surely it's the lesser of two evils. And I promise you this: I will not lie to you or renege on my side of the bargain because I know Meredith is innocent and I'll do anything to help him."

Burt sniffed and looked at the ceiling, pondering her words. When he looked back any trace of amusement had vanished.

"Patsy, I'll tell you what I think you should know, but only that: if this goes tits up this might be put to use." He lifted the gun a little. "So, don't mess about. The stakes are high."

"I have no intention of messing about; I thought you'd know me better by now." Patsy watched him shrug indifferently.

"Perhaps." Leaving the gun lying on the table Burt relaxed a little. He watched her reaction closely as he spoke. "I think Benson is a double agent in some way." He nodded as Patsy gasped. "My suspicions began with Lyndon Ward. As you know it came to our attention that he appeared to be prepared to sell his skills to the highest bidder. Well, he got out of his depth and annoyed some seriously dangerous people. We took him under our wing, and gave him protection, but he's not trusted and is monitored twenty-four-seven." He gave a wry smile, "That's how we came into contact with you."

"But Meredith is trying to get evidence that the Russians are responsible for various murders, which is nothing to do with nuclear science, and besides, the Russians already have nuclear weapons, probably more than the rest of the world put together." Patsy's frown revealed her confusion.

"Shut up and let me talk." Burt ignored her eye roll and continued. "It became clear that Ward was working on something with his sister, Abigail. She was working with the Hattons, and the Hattons were trying to do a deal with the Ministry of Defence, so we started watching everyone. It's what we do."

"So, you think the magic formula for the personal armour the Hattons are making was the skill of Lyndon, and not Abigail? Why is that a problem? Surely the outcome is what matters?"

Burt shook his head and leaned forward. Resting an elbow either side of the gun, he held his face in his hands.

"This is going to take too long if you don't shut up."

Patsy mimicked zipping her mouth and looked duly contrite, but her mind was racing with the various possibilities that now presented themselves.

"What we discovered was a very complicated web of people, and what we didn't know was what the connection was. On one hand, we have the Hatton brothers trying to find, and making contact with, Russian crooks, in particular Filipp Myshkin. They were also dealing with a couple of our informants in Northern Ireland, attempting to track down a former IRA operative. This, added to the Wards' involvement, didn't make sense so we dug deeper, and we got a whisper that our counterparts in Prague were also watching Myshkin's cousin and his associate, Andronikov. So we needed to investigate and keep an eye on them too. Benson was summoned to a meeting at Whitehall to discuss our interest. They didn't reveal what the Prague outfit were interested in." He pursed his lips and blew out a frustrated breath.

"What did Benson think it was, and did you find how the Hatton brothers are connected with the Russians?"

"Benson said very little, and therein is my problem. Benson is a talker, likes the sound of his own voice, but on this occasion all he said was, we were to tread carefully. I knew something was amiss and I kept an ear out. I found that Benson was making enquiries via operatives outside our team, which was totally unnecessary since we had the manpower, and that he had several meetings with none other than your partner Grainger."

"You think the two of them are in cahoots somehow?" Patsy ran her fingers through her hair, and, pulling it into a ponytail, she rested her hands on the top of her head. "I'm pissed off with Chris right now, but I don't think he'd do anything against the greater good, so to speak." She wondered whether to tell Burt that Chris had agreed to assist Meredith, but her stomach lurched at the implication of making the wrong call. She decided to hold her tongue until she had more information. "What do you think they're up to?"

"I have no idea as yet. I'm not convinced Grainger is any more than a facilitator, but I could be wrong. Until this kicked off I thought Benson was sound; he still could be, but it's unlikely."

For the first time since she'd met him, Patsy saw a flicker of self-doubt. With a quick shake of the head he dismissed it and continued.

"Benson was recommended to use Meredith to re-open the murder enquiry, and –"

"Who recommended him?" Patsy forgot her promise to keep quiet. Burt shrugged.

"I wasn't told. On a need-to-know basis, and I didn't need to know." His smile was brief. "With Meredith signed up, Benson thought it a good idea to get you to sit and watch the Hattons. But, you're right, whatever it is it's nothing to do with nuclear weapons, or anything similar. I have no idea why a handful of Russian criminals are of so much interest to everyone. I tried to get answers from Prague, but nothing, although a very helpful agent told me Benson had full intel but had asked for it not to be provided to anyone else in the department. She didn't say why, but the inference was he had indicated there was someone he couldn't trust. When you add all this up, Benson is either working on something so top secret even I don't know about it, or is playing both ends against the middle." He leaned back against his chair. "Your turn."

"So, you know who killed Filipp Myshkin?" Patsy released her hair and tried not to sound irritated.

"Probably one of the Hattons, not sure why, but they went to a lot of trouble to track him down. A coincidence? I doubt it. What do you know? What's Meredith up to?"

"I think you're right it was one of the Hattons, probably Stephen. Myshkin was paid cash to act as a sniper to test the body armour. He shot Stephen in the foot, and when challenged he laughed at them. He told them they wanted to find a weakness, and there it was, and if he'd really wanted to hurt him, he'd have shot the feet to disable him and taken the time to kill him slowly . . . or words to that effect. I've seen the post-mortem report: Myshkin was shot in the feet and then sliced from throat to navel. He bled to death. Meredith didn't do that."

"Ah, hence your visit to Frankie Callaghan. So, you're favouring Stephen."

"If you know all this, why haven't you helped him?" Patsy had become irritated again.

Burt flapped his hand indicating she could calm down. "Because a desperate man gets results and Meredith is desperate. Benson was happy for him to be loose, but once he met with Andronikov, Benson became agitated and wanted him found."

"And you think I'll dish him up for you?"

"No, I think you'll work with me to find out why Benson changed his mind so suddenly, and if Meredith doesn't know, to find out exactly what the Russian connection is. I need to know what Meredith said to Andronikov, and in detail, and I need to see him face to face. We can help each other."

Patsy thought for a moment. She had no proof that Burt was telling the truth: it might be that he was the renegade and not Benson. Her stomach lurched to remind her how high the stakes were. To give herself more time to think she changed tack.

"Why did the Hattons go to Northern Ireland?"

"Now, that we do know," Burt nodded. "They murdered the men responsible for a bombing that killed thirteen people, including their adoptive parents." Burt shrugged as if that were a minor detail.

"And they haven't been arrested?" She raised her eyebrows as Burt snorted.

"The men who died were bad men – the Hattons provided a quicker and cheaper result than a trial and imprisonment, saving the taxpayer millions. Don't tell me you would rather that?"

Patsy ignored the question and made some assumptions. "So, the government knows about this?"

"Benson knew – he's the liaison with the minister. Not my job to tell them." He smirked at the look on Patsy's face.

"I can't believe I'm hearing this. You know the Hatton brothers are responsible for numerous deaths, and yet they are allowed to walk free. Why? Because it's cheaper than jailing them? Exactly who decides who gets arrested these days?"

"Don't be naïve, Patsy, it doesn't suit you. The Hattons are working on a project in which the government have invested a large sum of money, not to mention several careers, so it will do no harm to let them carry on. It may be that they are pulled in once the project has been completed and the government have what they want."

"Really! I can see the headlines now: Government's favoured contractors jailed for murders carried out whilst working with ministers on. . ." She let the sentence trail away. "Meanwhile, innocent men, good men like Meredith fall into a cesspit and are left to flounder. I bet you know who Critchton was too!"

"Don't be so dramatic. Meredith knew exactly what he was doing, more so than you, I reckon. He was briefed by Benson. And, yes, of course we know who Crichton was, you might get to meet him one day. He's one of Benson's men." Burt sat up straight. "Now, you tell me what you know. No more messing about." He moved his hand to cover the gun.

Patsy drew in a breath and nodded. She had to trust someone, and if her instinct was correct, despite the gun, his story was genuine. Her heart beat a little faster as she gave Burt all the information she thought was relevant, ending with the last conversation.

"I was about to start researching it when you appeared. Meredith is convinced something happened there that Andronikov and the Myshkins were involved with. Now you're telling me that the authorities in Prague were also interested in the Myshkins, it seems he was correct. Have you heard anything connected which may be useful?"

"Nope, but I think we'd better start looking." His eyes glanced around the kitchen, "Where's your laptop? Go and get it, and while we're looking you can tell me what Meredith is up to."

He smiled as Patsy nodded and got to her feet. She walked slowly, collecting her thoughts, and attempting to work out how much she should reveal about the meeting Meredith had planned. As she lifted the laptop a thought occurred to her and she hurried back to the kitchen. Sitting down, she typed a note and turned it to face Burt. He winked at her.

"Don't worry, no one is listening. Only I know you're being monitored."

"There was no warrant?" Patsy tutted, but a feeling of relief swept through her. This confirmed that Burt was working alone, and for some reason she couldn't explain, she believed it was for the right reasons. "Okay, the town in question is Horovice; I've got no further than that." She clicked on the top result. "Blah, blah, blah, local economic centre… nope, nothing obvious. Seems it's a pretty bohemian city, was once important but not anymore."

She returned to the search results and hit a different response. Her eyes quickly skimmed the words, and she read out the odd phrase.

"News. Look at the news." Burt reached over and turned the laptop to face himself. Tapping in the name of a Czech newspaper, he searched for Horovice. He gave a running commentary as he did so. The first yielded no obvious results and he typed in a second.

"You seem very familiar with Czech news," Patsy observed, and Burt tapped his head.

"A mine of information. Once I know it, it stays there until I need it again. Always been the same. It didn't . . ."

Something caught his attention and he stopped speaking. Patsy allowed him a moment's silence while he clicked through various screens. After several minutes, she became impatient.

"What have you found?"

Burt pushed the laptop away and drummed the table with his fingers, his hand brushing against the gun. He looked from it to Patsy before replacing it in the holster.

"I'm not sure, but this could be a link. Andronikov was part of a Russian army division that was apart from the main body of soldiers. Sort of trouble-shooters, and I use the term loosely – a special force. We don't know what their exact brief was, but according to this article they were in Horovice in the late seventies when some local dignitaries disappeared without trace. But what would that have to do with Benson?"

"The seventies? That was a lifetime ago. How old is Andronikov? And if you think it's relevant, first tie Andronikov in and then work on Benson. If we find that out, the rest will fall into place . . . eventually." She allowed herself a small smile, it seemed she had made the right call.

"Andronikov is fifty-seven so he would have been around twenty-two at the time, and the older Myshkin, Peter, is a year older. Hmm." He continued to drum his fingers as he considered this.

"Tell me what you're thinking?" Patsy demanded, and requisitioned the laptop and read the article that had caught Burt's attention.

Burt ignored her and continued to compute the various strands of information, only returning to Patsy once she'd given a small gasp.

"I need to phone Louie." Jumping to her feet, she picked up her phone.

Burt up held his hand. "Why?" he demanded frowning.

"Because one of the men who disappeared was Josef Hasek. Hasek was Jake's birth name. Jakub Hasek. A coincidence? I don't think so, what are the chances of that?" She waved the phone at Burt. "Are you sure the Myshkins were part of this group?" She now had Burt's full attention.

"Peter definitely was, not sure about Filipp. I can't remember reading that, and I would remember if I had." Now doubting his memory, he closed his eyes and tried to bring the detail of the Myshkins' past history to mind. "Filipp was in the army – all Russians had to serve," he shrugged, "I suppose it's possible we didn't know, or it wasn't noted he was part of the special unit. If this is part of it, then he would have had to be there, or surely the Hattons would have gone after Peter." He sighed. "But that element is irrelevant; we want to know about Andronikov and –"

"Not irrelevant, not coincidence. It is all connected, it has to be; we simply don't know why." Patsy interrupted as she raised the phone to her ear and listened to the ringing tone.

"Okay, I'll give you that, but why, other than the Hattons' probable revenge, has this all surfaced now?"

"I expect that's where Benson comes in, but let's deal with what we know first. We can deal with . . ." She held up a finger. "Louie, where are you?"

Louie's soft tones brought her little comfort – she was worried that she had placed him in danger.

"Hi, Patsy, I'm in reception awaiting an audience with the Hattons. They are in a meeting scheduled to break in ten minutes. I said I'd wait. What news at your end?"

"Too much to give you in detail, but listen to me carefully and don't say anything until I've finished."

"Okay, but make it quick. I've just seen a lot of well-dressed men file out of a door along the corridor."

"Shit! For reasons we don't know, the Russians have probably got something on one of the top guys in SIS, but more importantly the Myshkins and Andronikov were part of some elite army unit during the occupation of Czechoslovakia. During their time there some

Czechs went missing, one of them named Hasek – the same name as Jake Hatton before his adoption. The bodies were never found. Put that with the nature of Filipp Myshkin's demise and I think we have Jake in the frame and not Stephen. Be very, very careful, the Hattons are also responsible –"

"Speed up, Patsy, he's been told I'm waiting for him, now he's walking towards me." Trump smiled at the approaching Hatton brother and pointed to the phone with his free hand, shrugging an apology. Stephen Hatton slowed his pace and waited for him to finish at a respectable distance.

"Who, Stephen or Jake?" Patsy asked.

"The former, sir."

Trump pursed his lips and shook his head, as though irritated at what was being said.

"Okay, briefly, as far as I know, they have killed at least five men. Who did what to whom, I have no idea, but they are protected at the moment as the government want this project finished. So, be careful. Don't attempt to make any arrests until you get back-up. Just keep it light."

"Thank you, sir, I must go. I'll call you later." Trump hung up and stood up. "Mr Hatton, thank you for sparing me a few moments." Trump shook Hatton's hand and looked around. "Is your brother available? I need to speak to both of you – it may save you time."

Trump watched the frown develop and Stephen Hatton raised his hand and rubbed his forehead in irritation.

"About what? We are in the middle of a very important meeting. Couldn't this wait until tomorrow?"

"Not really, sir, and if you could ask your brother to join us, it would be much appreciated," Trump smiled.

"I repeat, about what?" Stephen Hatton's tone was commanding.

"Oh yes, I didn't say. The murder of Filipp Myshkin." Trump lifted his hand towards the corridor. "So, if you'd please, ten minutes of your time would be much appreciated."

"Filipp who?" Hatton shook his head as though he couldn't place the name.

Trump's smile fell away. "Myshkin. Filipp Myshkin. He was here a few days ago. He described in detail how he would kill you, and lo and behold, he dies in that exact same way. Now your meeting will be delayed longer than necessary if you insist on me arresting you to question you at the station." Trump found his smile. "Please call your brother."

Stephen Hatton remained cool and collected although his eyes had widened in surprise and he returned Trump's smile.

"Arrest me, you say. Now that will never do." He pulled a phone from his jacket pocket and called Jake. His call was answered on the second ring. "Jake, old chap, a police officer is here. He thinks we may have something to do with the murder of someone called Munchkin or similar. He says he will arrest us if we don't speak to him now. Excuse yourself please, and let's put the man straight. Meet us in the annexe, if you would." He terminated the call without allowing a response, and looked Trump in the eye. "This way, keep it brief: the minister will not like to be kept waiting."

A smile flickered at the corner of his mouth as he turned to lead the way to the annexe. Once there he offered Trump a seat at the highly polished oval table, and sat opposite him, drumming his fingers on the table gently as they awaited his brother's arrival.

When Jake arrived, it was clear to Trump that he didn't have the same control over his emotions as his brother. His hand was stiff as it returned the handshake, his shoulders tense, and having taken a seat, Trump could see Jake was barely restraining his temper.

"What murder? Why are you wasting our time?" he asked.

Trump looked from one to the other and considered his predicament and Patsy's warning. Drawing in a breath through his nose, he pulled his shoulders back: he had little to lose and a lot to gain. John Meredith was depending on his help.

Turning to face Jake directly, he asked, "I understand that your birth name was Hasek, am I correct?"

"That is relevant how?" Jake thumped the table to show his irritation, but his eyes shot to his brother momentarily.

"Because, as I understand it, Filipp Myshkin may be responsible for the death of one of your relatives, probably your grandfather, and now a few days after coming to this facility he is murdered in the way he described he would kill you . . . or your brother. What can you tell me about that?"

Jake fell against the back of his chair and laughed. His body had relaxed and he put his hands behind his head.

"You are barking up the wrong tree, officer. I never met my grandfather – he died before I was born. I was adopted when I was very young. I have no idea where you obtained such a fanciful theory, but I assure you, whoever this man was and whatever he did, it is of no consequence to me."

Trump smiled engagingly. "Well, that's good to hear. If you could let me have your movements of the night of the twelfth between eight thirty and ten," he turned his head towards Stephen Hatton briefly, "yours too, I'm sure I can be on my way."

He pulled his notebook from his breast pocket. "Oh yes, and the names of the others involved in the trial here, both staff and the men hired to take shots at you." From the corner of his eye he caught the brief lip movement as Stephen mouthed something to Jake. He turned to face him, "Shall we start with you sir?"

He hoped he didn't look startled as Stephen jumped to his feet.

"But of course. I'll have to get my diary — been so busy lately, wouldn't want to mislead you. I'm sure you're the same, Jake." He held the door for his brother who stepped out of the room. "We shouldn't be long, wait here please." He began to close the door and changed his mind. "Your name was?" He nodded, as Trump held out his warrant card and gave his rank and name. "Thank you, I shan't forget that."

The door closed behind them, and Trump blew out the breath he'd been holding. He wondered why his name had become relevant, and said a silent prayer in the hope that they wouldn't call on the minister to interfere, as that might reveal his suspension. And if he had even a slim chance of retaining his job at the moment, that would be blown into oblivion.

## 20

Meredith flicked his cigarette out of the window as he pulled into a parking space. He sat with his hands resting on the steering wheel, eyes closed, and ran through the various scenarios of the meeting he had set up. Most weren't good, and he knew that the chances of a positive outcome for all concerned were slim. He had to ensure that he didn't end up in a worse situation, or, given the circumstances, dead. For a fleeting moment, he wondered whether the best move would be to turn himself in and let the law take its course. A thought he dismissed quickly.

He climbed out of the car. He had another two hours before anyone was supposed to arrive, but he wanted to ensure the others had kept their word with regard to arriving alone. He needed to monitor their arrival, and, of course that of any uninvited parties. Walking briskly towards the stairwell, and running with light steps down to the ground floor, he took a quick look around to ensure he wasn't already being watched, and rapped on the flaking paint of the blue door of the parking attendant's office. The door opened as he lowered his hand.

"Afternoon, Mr Meredith, come on in, the kettle's on." Billy Jones stepped back, sweeping his hand forward in invitation. Meredith nodded and stepped in. Billy wasn't aging well. The creases on his pale face deepened as he smiled, revealing uneven teeth. He attempted to pull his sweatshirt over his increasing pot belly as he said, "You'll be pleased to hear we're almost empty. I love Wednesdays, most of the shops around here close by six. Only twenty cars to go at the last count. Tea or coffee."

"Coffee, black with two. Thanks for this, Billy, I owe you one."

"Don't be daft, you've sorted me out a few times, it's the least I can do." Billy put a large teaspoon of coffee into a chipped white mug and poured on the boiling water before emptying two sachets of sugar into it and stirring frantically. "Quite exciting for me. Since I've been going straight, life's become boring for the best part." He smirked as Meredith raised his eyebrows at the statement. "Don't look at me like that, I haven't been naughty for months."

"What about the cigarettes?" Meredith took the coffee and walked to the small bank of television monitors. "That nearly got you pleasuring Her Majesty."

He looked at the chair he had to use dubiously: it had one arm missing, and the original colour of the seat cover was lost beneath many stains.

Billy Jones blew out a dismissive breath. "Get on. That doesn't count. If we're part of Europe, our tax should be the same as the rest of them. Why have we got to pay more duty than them? If anyone can tell me that then I won't buy them, but until then, if I get a chance at some cheap fags then I'll not pass it up. Anyway, they were for personal use."

"You bought ten thousand of them in a pub." Meredith took the newspaper from the desk and placed it on the seat before sitting. "That's not personal use."

"It is. I'm a heavy smoker, everyone knows that." Billy waved his nicotine-stained fingers at Meredith and smiled. "Let's not argue over trivia. At least I didn't steal them. Good money I paid over before your mob confiscated them." He tapped the top left-hand screen. "Top level is already empty, coned it off hours ago; not that many go up that far."

Meredith glanced at the grainy black and white picture and nodded. White stickers were attached to each of the screens, except one, to correspond with the level number. The remaining one changed every thirty seconds to show the lift doors on each level. He looked down at the control panel, trying to ignore the grease from previous hands.

"How do I use this?"

"Easy. Hit the number of the level you want, and use the joystick to manoeuvre the camera. You can see most of the floor space, except on level three. That's got a blind spot," Billy tapped the appropriate screen. "Just to the left of the stairwell. There's a girder in the way, shouldn't be a problem for you though – not if you're on the top level."

Meredith shrugged; that depended on who might also know that.

Benson wasn't stupid enough to turn up without assessing the risks, and the opportunities. Hitting button one, he manoeuvred the camera and counted eleven cars.

"Office workers mainly," Billy advised. "They get here early, and leave late. They'll all be gone by six though."

"Do you know if any of them arrived recently?" Meredith repeated the process with the second level.

"No, they've all been there all day. I've had five arrivals since one o'clock. Two on the third level, the other three on the fifth, and there goes one now."

Meredith looked at screen five and watched a small red hatchback reverse out of a space. As it approached the exit ramp he could see a middle-aged female driver struggling to clip her seatbelt while steering the car. Movement on the fifth level caught his attention, and he watched a fresh-faced youth in an ill-fitting suit hurry to his car.

"Bet he's been to court. You can always tell, they rarely look comfortable suited and booted." He laughed as the lad unlocked a car. "Guaranteed. His tax expired eighteen months ago."

"You check that?" Meredith glanced at him.

"Sometimes when I'm bored I notice things like that, but today I've been keeping a special eye out."

"Appreciated." Meredith turned his attention back to checking the other levels. "Have you noticed anything else I might find useful?"

"Only if you want to make a few arrests, but you're not here for that, so no. Can I ask you something, you know, personal like?"

"What?" Meredith's tone was flat and, he hoped, discouraging.

"What've you done? Word has it that your lot are after you. I didn't believe it until you called me." There was amusement in his voice as he added, "And I'm guessing it's not because you didn't pay the duty on a stack of fags."

"No, it's not. I'll tell you, but you'll have to promise to keep it to yourself." Meredith swivelled to look Billy in the eye. Billy slapped his hand on his chest.

"On my mother's life, Mr Meredith." He smiled as Meredith nodded his acceptance.

"Murder," Meredith announced and swivelled back to the screens.

Billy huffed. "There's no need to take the piss, I was only asking." He sounded hurt at the lack of trust, especially as he'd helped Meredith set the meeting up.

"I'm not," Meredith confirmed as he leaned forward to look at the man exiting the lift on the second level.

Billy looked at the back of Meredith's head, unsure as to whether he was winding him up or not. He tilted his head. "Who did you kill?"

"A Russian crook. Now shut up and show me how your recording system works."

Billy had gone pale. "Not the one that was gutted at the Hammer and Sickle? Shit, Mr Meredith, that's serious."

"I had noticed. Now, back to the job in hand." As Billy opened his mouth Meredith held his hand up. "Hang on a minute, that's one of my guests." Meredith looked at Chris Grainger's face as he drove his car to the second level. "Quiet, while I watch him."

Grainger reversed into a space opposite the exit ramp.

"As a mouse, but first tell me, did you do it?" Billy nudged Meredith's shoulder.

"What do you think?" Meredith waved him away. "Actually, don't answer that. Just shut up and let me concentrate."

Billy walked away and refilled the kettle at the small basin in the toilet off the main office area. He cursed as water splashed onto his midriff.

"This can't be right under health and safety rules. This sink is too bleeding small to fill a mug let alone a kettle." Back in the office he switched on the kettle, and as the gurgling noises of the water heating got louder, he went to peer over Meredith's shoulder. "What's he up to?"

"Checking it out at the moment." Meredith pointed at the screen as Chris Grainger placed a hand on the bonnet of a car, and lifting one leg out behind him, as though performing an awkward ballet pose, he leaned forward and looked under the car. As he righted himself he glanced at the camera before turning and climbing the ramp to the next level. He repeated this process on each level until he was out in the open on level five. There were no cars there, and he walked the perimeter, pausing every couple of yards to peer through the safety barrier and down to the road below. As he made the journey back down to the second level, he paused several times to wipe his brow with the sleeve of his coat.

"He don't look well, Mr Meredith, who is he?" Billy asked turning away. "Do you want a top up?"

"No, I need a pee, and I need you to shut up and watch him. I want to know what he does, so come and sit here." Meredith kept his eyes on the screen as he stood and made room for Billy. "Everything, Billy, however innocent it looks. I'll be two seconds."

Content Billy was concentrating, Meredith strode quickly to the toilet. He didn't shut the door and asked Billy to give him a running commentary as he relieved himself.

"He's gone back to his car, he's opening the driver's door, and . . . he's taken out a bottle which he's swigging from. He's put it back." Billy followed Meredith's instructions to the letter. "Now he's wiping his head again, reckon he's got flu. Now he's unbuttoned his coat, he's going for the inside pocket, and . . . fuck me, he's got a gun!"

Meredith swung towards Billy, spraying urine over the seat and onto the floor. He cursed.

"Are you sure?" Finishing what he'd started, Meredith zipped his trousers as he hurried back.

"Yes, he's checking it, look."

Leaning over Billy's shoulder, Meredith watched Grainger slide the magazine back into the hand grip.

"Well, well. That's a semi-automatic; I wonder where he got that?" He pursed his lips watching Grainger replace the gun in the holster under his arm before readjusting his coat. "That's an interesting turn-up, he . . ."

He stopped speaking as Chris Grainger spun around. He watched a shopper open the boot of her car, place her shopping in it and drive away. She only gave Chris a cursory glance. Chris leaned against his car door and pulled his phone from his coat pocket. Looking at the large sign behind the pay and display board, he made a call. The harsh sound of ringing filled the air. Billy stretched out his hand to answer the phone, but Meredith clamped his own on the receiver. "Leave it. He's checking to see if there's anyone here." With his free hand, he pushed Billy out of the chair and sat down.

"But he will have seen the light on as he drove in, and he's got a fucking gun. I never signed up for this, Meredith." Fear had caused Billy to drop any title he would normally have afforded Meredith.

"Well, keep quiet . . . there, it's stopped." The phone fell silent and Meredith felt his own phone vibrate against his leg. He pulled it out and answered it. "Chris, what news?"

"Where are you? I'm at the carpark. I've checked it out and everything seems okay, but there are a few cars here." Grainger, observed by Meredith, glanced at his watch, "An hour to go before Benson should get here, but I thought you might want to meet first."

"I'm on my way, but I'll be at least another half an hour. Where will I find you?" Meredith responded.

"Second level, I'll be in my car." Grainger paused. "I'll see you soon. Hurry."

Grainger hung up and climbed into his car. Lifting the bottle from the pocket of the door, he took another swig.

"Is that alcohol, do you reckon? I don't want to be here, not if we've got a drunk with a gun running around." Billy was stepping from one foot to the other, clearly agitated.

Meredith looked at him. "Calm down, he's not going to hurt you."

"No?" Billy's tone was sarcastic. "How do you know that? He's going to hurt someone, especially drinking that much." Billy jabbed his finger at the screen, turned away, and lifting a jacket from a hook on the rear of the door, he added, "I'm off. If you survive, call me when you're done."

He stepped towards the door and Meredith sprang to his feet. Grabbing Billy by the arm he pushed him down into the chair.

"Don't start mucking about. It's not damage from him you should be worried about if you don't do as you're told."

Billy went pale, as tales of what had happened at the Hammer and Sickle came to mind. He swallowed, and unable to speak nodded his understanding. The contents of his stomach turned to liquid and he needed the toilet – urgently. A shaking finger pointed towards the door.

"Can I go? I have to go."

Meredith released his grip and nodded, and as Billy scuttled off towards the toilet he went to the door, turned the key in the lock, and slid it into his pocket. Returning to the desk, he smiled as Billy swore as he sat down on the now-wet seat.

"You peed on the seat, you could have lifted it," Billy said almost to himself as he emptied his bowels at an alarming velocity.

Billy remained sitting on the toilet long after he'd finished what he had gone to do. He decided he'd seen enough, and was better off not knowing what else was going on. If Meredith was bent, the less he knew the better. He didn't want to end up as a witness in some long, drawn-out court case or, worse, being found gutted by the side of some car. No, it was preferable to sit in Meredith's pee and contemplate how he always ended up in the wrong place despite his best intentions.

Meredith's thoughts were not dissimilar. He too was wondering for the umpteenth time how he came to be watching one of his oldest friends, unsure as to why that friend was armed, and dismayed that he was unable to call for support from anyone but the woman he loved. He closed his eyes and vowed that he would marry her as soon as he'd unravelled the mess he was in – assuming that he could unravel it. His thoughts still with Patsy, he opened his eyes, and as they darted to the fourth level where the final car was reversing out of its parking space, he hit the speed dial number on his phone.

Patsy answered immediately. She didn't allow him to speak and rushed straight into bringing him up to date with the developments regarding Burt. Rather than declare his love for her, Meredith exploded.

"You stupid, stupid woman. Which bit of don't trust anyone, don't speak to anyone, didn't you understand? I'm sat here watching an armed Chris Grainger waiting for me to turn up to a meeting. Some top fucking spook is on his way, also armed I'm sure, and you've decided to bring another one to the party. Well, how's that going to work? You don't think they might notice you in an empty carpark? You don't think that might piss them off a tad. I don't know how close you are, but back off. I don't need you here. Do you understand me?"

Patsy remained silent; her phone was on hands free and Burt had heard Meredith tear into her.

Burt cleared his throat. "Meredith, I'm on your side. Benson is in this up to his neck: pacify him until I get there. You're a big man and all that, but you can't handle this on your own."

"You have me on fucking loudspeaker?" Meredith thumped the desk. "Patsy, have you told him where the meeting is?" When she didn't respond quickly enough, he bellowed, "Answer me!"

"No! Meredith, listen to me, we know about the Czech town, we think –"

"Well, good for you. You carry on working on that, and drive wherever you like, but not here. I've got to go."

Meredith hung up and had to stop himself punching the screen in front of him.

In the toilet, Billy was zipping up his trousers. This was too much. A drunk with a gun outside, Meredith pissed off and shouting in there. As soon as Meredith was distracted he would make a quick but unannounced exit. As he closed the toilet door behind him, his eyes darted from Meredith to his escape route. His heart sank when he saw the key had gone.

"Bollocks," he muttered. "Why are you keeping me here? I can't be of any use to you." His slumped shoulders caused his pot belly to escape the ribbing on the bottom of his sweat shirt. Sighing, he made a half-hearted attempt to cover it.

"Shut up moaning and get over here." Meredith peered at the screen for the first level. "We have another visitor who seems to have settled down in his van. Do you know who this is?"

Billy placed his hand on the back of Meredith's chair and looked at the dark blue transit van. It appeared to be empty and Billy too squinted to check out the surrounding area.

"I can't see anyone, and I don't know the van. Why would I?"

"So you don't have a regular that might park here and bed down for the night in the back of a van? Even with the prices you charge, it's still cheaper than a hotel."

Billy shook his head. "Nope. Is he in the back?"

"He is. Parked up, walked round to the back, opened the door, climbed in and closed it. I didn't see his face – he was on the wrong side of the van. Been in there five minutes, and judging by the lack of movement he's not having a quickie with a local tom."

"What do you think he's doing?"

"My guess is waiting for me. You'll have to help me with him later."

"Help you how?" Billy's voice had risen an octave. "He might have a gun too."

"Which is why you will need to help me. Quiet now, another of my guests has arrived . . . Ahh, there you go . . . they must know each other." Meredith tapped the screen as the driver of the Range Rover flashed its lights as he drove past the van. "What a naughty boy."

Despite the lightness of his tone, Meredith was becoming concerned. Benson had brought company, Chris Grainger was carrying a gun, and the only person he had to watch his back was the increasingly nervous Billy Jones. After watching Benson park next to Grainger, and both men exit their vehicles to shake hands, he rubbed his hands over his face. "Billy, what I'm going to ask you to do is essential to my wellbeing: I need you to strap a pair on and step up a gear." He tore his eyes away from the screen to look at Billy. "Are you capable of that?"

"Depends what you want me to do, but I ain't going out there." Billy nodded at the screens. "I owe you, Mr Meredith, I know that, but I'm not getting involved out there. What is it you want me to do?"

"It's simple. Let me make a call and I'll fill you in." Meredith picked up his phone and paused before hitting the call button. Billy listened to Meredith asking someone he assumed to be another bent copper for help.

"It's me. I don't have much time. I'm in it up to my neck and I need someone to watch my back. My guests are armed." Billy watched Meredith's frown deepen as he listened to the response. "Good man, and don't tell Lucy, she'll only want to come." Meredith hung up, and placing the phone on the desk next to the joystick, he tapped it lightly.

"Bad news, Mr Meredith? Who's Lucy, his bird?"

Billy didn't care one way or another, but Meredith seemed to be in a trance. He sat there staring at the phone rather than the monitors, and as there were blokes with guns outside he needed Meredith to be at his best. Meredith looked at him and blinked.

"What?" he asked.

"Is Lucy his ball and chain, his girlfriend or wife? Sounds a right interfering madam." He shook his head as Meredith responded.

"No, that would be Linda."

"Who's Lucy?" Billy persisted.

"I have no idea." Meredith stood and insisted Billy sit down. "I need you to concentrate, Billy. The guest list to our little soiree just grew, and your role is now crucial if you and I are going to come out of this alive."

"But you told me I didn't need to go out there," Billy whined.

"You don't, but they'll know you helped and that you watched, so be careful. Don't do anything to draw attention to the office, and we'll be fine."

Meredith turned off the lights and the glow from the monitors increased as he explained what he wanted from Billy.

~ ~ ~

Patsy pulled over at a bus stop and turned to Burt. "Why would Chris Grainger have a gun?" She shifted in her seat to look at him.

"I'm guessing for protection; I didn't know he had one."

"If you didn't, can we assume it's illegal or do we think Benson gave him it?"

"He might be authorised." Burt shrugged nonchalantly. "He works for SIS, it's not a huge leap, Patsy."

"And that means you get issued with a gun? For God's sake, I'm working for them and I don't have a gun!" Patsy shook her head. "Surely they don't give them out like ties, do they? I'm checking this out."

Taking her phone from the dashboard Patsy called Jo Adler. Jo hit the answer button and on hearing Patsy's voice, she walked away from her desk and into the corridor.

"Two seconds, Patsy." She pushed open the door to the ladies' toilets and checked it was empty before speaking. "Okay, all clear, how are you? I'm not supposed to be speaking to you, you'll have to keep it brief."

"No problem, I want you to run a firearms check on Chris Grainger. Does he have a licence, and if so, what for? I know it's a big ask, but Meredith may be in danger."

"From Chris? Bloody hell, what's happening?"

"Far too long a story. Can you do it fairly quickly, Jo, time is of the essence." Jo heard the desperation in Patsy's voice.

"I'll try and do it now, but call me after eight. I'll be home then and will be able to speak. Would probably be best if you called Aaron's phone too. Leave it with me and I'll text you."

Patsy looked at Burt, who was shaking his head. "What now? At least we'll have more information," she snapped.

"To do what with? He could own five shotguns and a rocket launcher, but it doesn't help us, does it? Where are they meeting, Patsy? We need to get there irrespective of which side Chris is on. Stop fannying about and drive." Patsy didn't need to answer as a text caused her phone to vibrate. It was only two words and her heart sank. She shrugged. "No licence. It's either illegal, or Benson issued it." Biting her bottom lip, she started the engine but didn't drive away. "The thing is, if you and Chris are armed the chances are Benson is too. That's three guns, which means the chances of one of them being drawn is increasing. Perhaps we should just wait it out."

Burt tutted. "Drive," he ordered calmly. "No messing, simply drive to the location of the meeting. Now."

Patsy put the car into gear and pulled away, and minutes later pulled in opposite the entrance to the carpark.

"They're meeting in there. I don't think we should drive in, do you?" She turned to face Burt.

"I don't think *we* will be going in. I'll go in on my own, your emotions are running high. I won't risk you going all heroine on me. You wait here and I'll go and have a wander. With any luck, they'll have cameras and I can get into the office."

"And if they see you? What then? You will be putting Meredith in danger." Her temper was rising, as were the number of butterflies causing her breathing to become erratic.

Burt put his hand on the door handle and pulled it towards him. "Meredith is already in danger; my presence may lessen that." The lock clicked free and he pushed the door open, only to pull it closed again moments later. "Well, well. I wonder who invited them?"

Crossing the road, a hundred yards ahead was Louie Trump, followed by both Hatton brothers. Jake was walking very close to Louie, and Patsy guessed he had a gun pressed against Trump and she blew out a frustrated breath.

"Shit, they'll both be armed. The odds are becoming worse by the minute. What —" she shouted as Burt lunged towards her, wrapping one arm around her neck and pressing his face onto hers.

"Keep still and shut up. Pretend you like me for a second. Stephen was looking directly at us: if he sees you we'll be compromised." He released his hold a little. "Move your head to one side and tell me what you see."

Patsy did as she was asked.

"Nothing good. They're wearing their biking suits, but no head gear. It looks as though they feel that they need protection. They're made from the same material as the body armour. I guess they thought it would draw less attention than the suits they have for the MOD."

"Why would Trump bring them here, I wonder?" Burt resisted the urge to turn back. "What are they doing now?"

"They've reached the entrance to the carpark and the brothers are in conversation."

"What's Trump doing?"

"Looking worried." Patsy froze, "I think he's recognised me, or the car at least. Keep still a minute." Lifting one arm, she wrapped it around Burt's back. Then, as though it were a natural movement, she gave a brief thumbs-up signal, before laying her hand flat.

Her eyes remained fixed on Trump.

Trump listened to the Hatton brothers discussing the best way to access the top level, and whether it would be best to wait until the meeting had commenced. Concerned that he was becoming of little or no use to them, he was about to give them his opinion in the hope it might earn him some brownie points, when he spotted Patsy's car. At first, he thought she was dallying with a man, but quickly dismissed the thought as he could see it wasn't Meredith, and as Meredith was due to have a meeting here she wouldn't be so stupid. Their eyes locked briefly: he watched the movement of her arm and sighed with relief as he saw Patsy raise her thumb. His chances of surviving this situation had just doubled. He threw his arms wide and announced.

"Can I have a say in this? Because, unless you're planning on letting me go, I've got to go in there too." Having gained the Hattons' attention he gave Patsy a thumbs-up before dropping his arms back to the side.

"No." Jake Hatton looked at him with disgust and turned back to his brother. "I think we walk to the top level and check who's about. It's only Meredith who will recognise us, and with his sergeant in danger he's unlikely to give us any trouble." He shrugged. "It is almost certain that our time is up. Where would we run, and if we did, what would our chances of escape be? I must have Roper before we try. Are you with me, my brother?"

Trump looked from one to the other, wondering why they thought the mysterious Roper would be there. All DCI Meredith had said on the call, which Stephen had put on loudspeaker, was that he was in a spot of bother and the men he was meeting with were armed. He had asked Trump if he would attend to watch his back. Trump had responded by telling him that of course he would be there as promised, and asked if it were still at eight o'clock. He had not promised to be there, and knew the meeting was set for seven o'clock, and he was hoping that Meredith would realise the call was being monitored. He'd felt almost faint when Meredith indicated he'd got the message. Once the call had terminated, the brothers had asked who was meeting with Meredith, and when Trump had advised them as far as he knew it was SIS agents, he had hoped it would make them think about what they were doing. He was horrified to find that rather than concern the two men, it excited them. Jake in particular was delighted. He'd slapped Trump on the back and told him if he did as they asked, he had a fifty percent chance of surviving the day.

Nudging the gun against Trump's kidneys, Jake pushed him forward.

"Lead the way, Sergeant Trump, I think we'll get there early. Slowly does it, no sudden moves. I would hate to have to draw attention to ourselves."

Trump shot a glance at Patsy's car. She was still in a clinch with the man, but he felt better knowing she knew of his situation and could only hope she would call one of the team. So precarious was his situation, he wouldn't mind his uncle appearing with back-up. He stepped forward hesitantly.

"They're going in, and Jake does have a gun." Patsy waited until all three men had disappeared from view before pushing Burt away. "What now?"

"Same plan, you stay here and I'll go in."

"And do what?" Patsy's tone was derisory. "Unless a miracle has happened Meredith is unarmed, and assuming Stephen Hatton also has a gun you are outnumbered."

"Shut up. If things get out of control I'll signal and you can call the cavalry, but at the moment all we have is a meeting with a few uninvited guests, and we need to know why. Meredith needs to know why, if he's to clear his name. So, don't overreact, keep your eyes peeled and text me if anyone else turns up."

"But it's a carpark; you'll be seen. Meredith chose this location for a reason. I . . ." Patsy was at a loss for words. "If I don't hear from you in ten minutes, I'm calling this in."

Burt shook his head as though disappointed with her attitude. "Wait until I tell you to."

Knowing he could say no more, he climbed out of the car. Shoving his hands deep into his pockets, he whistled as he strode into the carpark.

~ ~ ~

"It's that simple, Billy, no more, no less. Ah, that's why he couldn't speak." Meredith watched Trump appear on the ramp leading to the first level. He tapped Billy on the shoulder. "Lock the door." Meredith stopped speaking and leaned forward, snarling at the screen as the lift doors opened on the third level and Burt stepped out. "Shit! She ignored me." Picking up his phone he punched in a number as he gave Billy the final instructions. "Answer this, then lock the door behind me and talk to me constantly: if you don't I'll have to come back and find out why, and that might attract the men with the guns." The telephone rang and Billy jumped with shock, and looked from the phone to Meredith. "Pick it up," he snapped wondering how on earth he ever thought he might come out of this on top.

"Hello?" Billy said quietly, the hand holding the receiver shaking as he raised it to his ear.

"It's me, you idiot." Meredith fitted the earpiece and dropped his phone into his shirt pocket. He took a stapler from the desk and slid it into his jacket pocket. Billy frowned. "I'd explain, but it would take too long. Lock me out and get back on the phone. I won't be responding so you keep talking. If I don't hear you et cetera, et cetera. Have you got that?"

Billy nodded frantically and had closed and locked the door before Meredith had time to drop into the shadows at the side of the office. He rushed back to the phone.

"Right, I'm locked in, can you hear me?" He waited for Meredith to answer. "I'm here Mr Meredith, I'm doing what you said." He paused again, and Meredith, who was still pressed against the wall outside, allowed his head to fall to his chest as he waited for the penny to drop. It did, and Billy gave a short laugh. "Sorry, Mr Meredith, don't come back, I've got it. Right, from the bottom . . . the three blokes that arrived a minute ago are moving towards the ramp leading to level two. The taller one has dropped back a little. No movement from the van, they just passed it. Level two, your mate with the gun and the one that flashed the van have started walking up the ramp to three. Oh, someone just got out of the lift on four." Billy paused and Meredith willed him to recommence the commentary, but the silence continued for a few seconds more. "Oh, it's okay. The final punter has got into the car on four and is leaving, your mates have hidden behind a pillar on three and . . . the car has passed them. The three blokes are now on the ramp to three and . . ."

Billy continued with the commentary which Meredith lost temporarily as he took the lift to the fifth level. Once there, he redialled Billy who snatched up the phone.

"Is that you?" He waited and saw the wave as Meredith slipped the phone back into his shirt pocket. "Thank God. The one that was hitting the bottle looks like he's having a coughing fit on four, a little before the ramp for five and . . ."

Billy was warming to his role and gabbled on, including each hand movement. Meredith stepped into the shadow cast by the lift shaft and watched the ramp. He had no idea what was going to happen, but he had to hope that Benson arriving with Chris Grainger was a good thing. What he couldn't work out was the interest from the Hatton brothers. He frowned as Chris Grainger mopped his brow on reaching the top of the ramp – he was clearly struggling – and Benson grabbed his elbow and led him to the opposite side of level five. Meredith wondered why he hadn't waited on level two as he had said he would, and waited for the arrival of the Hatton brothers and Burt. Trump appeared first and Grainger and Benson stepped forward.

"Louie Trump, is that you?" Grainger called, and Trump turned to him, raising a hand in recognition.

"Yes. I have company, I'm afraid."

"Is Meredith not with you?" Grainger asked as Trump stepped towards him.

"No, I am." Stephen Hatton took three quick strides and rested a pistol on Trump's shoulder.

"Hatton?" It was Benson's turn to sound confused.

"Indeed. A few loose ends to tidy up," Hatton smiled as he nudged Trump forward.

Meredith now knew that Jake had gone back to the lift shaft on three and was holding the door open, stopping anyone from using it. Burt had taken the stairs and should be exiting onto level five on the opposite side of the lift shaft from where Meredith stood. There was no movement from the van. While it was crucial for Meredith to have Billy's running commentary, it was proving difficult to hear the conversation between Hatton and Grainger, so he stepped forward a little and pulled the earpiece out.

"I think you might already have the answer to that question. Don't you think Mr . . ."

The rest of Stephen Hatton's words were lost on Meredith as the door from the stairwell opened slowly and Burt appeared to his left. Meredith put the earpiece back in and moved his hand to his pocket. Billy was speaking quickly, announcing Burt's arrival and confirming Jake was still holding the lift. Meredith froze as Stephen Hatton forced Trump to his knees and held the pistol against the back of his head.

He'd stopped speaking and was staring at Benson and Grainger. Burt stepped forward a few paces and drew his own gun. Benson was speaking and Burt leaned his body forward, his head cocked to one side in an attempt to catch the words. Unaware of Meredith moving slowly across the entrance to the lift, Burt crouched down and shuffled a little further towards the odd ensemble of men. As Meredith reached him, he flipped open the stapler, which made the appropriate sound, and placed it against Burt's neck.

"Don't speak, simply raise your hand and let me take the gun." Meredith's whisper was harsh, and his eyes darted from Burt to the group. They appeared to be in deadlock. Stephen Hatton was smiling while Benson shook his head. Burt blew out a relieved breath.

"Thank God for that. Meredith, I'm here to help." Bending his arm back awkwardly he handed Meredith the gun.

"I'm sure." Meredith pulled some wrist ties from his pocket. With the exception of the stapler they were his only weapons. "Very slowly hit the deck and put your hands behind your back. Keep it quiet."

Burt lay on the ground, but rolled onto his back, tapping his breast pocket.

"Patsy is outside and will call in the troops if I don't text her. Your shout," Burt whispered. Meredith pointed the gun at Burt and knelt down slowly, placing the stapler on the ground. Meredith held out his hand. Burt took out the phone and handed it to Meredith. The phone was protected by a code. "Double zero double seven," Burt whispered.

Meredith allowed a brief grin and wondered if Burt were embarrassed by having to share that information. He tapped in the code and opened the latest message from a contact labelled PH.

*Five minutes. Have you seen Meredith?*

"A stapler? You held me up with a stapler?" Burt ignored the gun in Meredith's hand and rolled silently on to his stomach. His eyes locked on the group. "We have to get closer. We need to rescue your colleague. The other brother is here but I have no idea what happened to him."

Meredith processed this statement quickly. There was no reason for Burt to share that information, and he had been with Patsy, so it was odds on the text was from her. Lowering himself slowly he lay next to Burt.

"He's holding the lift on level three for some reason." He pushed the gun across the tarmac until it was touching Burt's hand. "Here you go, you'd better have this. You're more likely to use it wisely."

Burt didn't respond. Benson had thrown his hands into the air and taken a step closer to Stephen Hatton. Hatton had released the safety on his gun and pushed it forward, causing Trump to fall forward and he was now on all fours. Benson raised his hands in surrender and stepped back. Burt's hand curled around the gun. He shot a sideways glance at Meredith.

"Thank you. This is a shit venue for this type of meeting. Nowhere to hide."

"That was the point, and actually there is. There's a bloke in the back of a transit on level two: he's still in there but Benson knows him. He flashed an acknowledgement when he arrived. I have to confess, I wasn't expecting the Hattons. I have no idea what that's about."

"Nice, someone in the office watching your back I take it." Burt nodded approval. "We have to get closer – we need to know what's being said. Slowly does it, another couple of yards and we'll be out in the light."

The two men crawled forward slowly, keeping their bellies on the ground and using their elbows and knees to propel them forward. They stopped slightly short of the overhead light which would have illuminated them.

"The van has just been vacated," Meredith whispered. "He's going to the lift."

"Well, that won't work if Jake Hatton is holding it, so he'll be appearing behind us if he takes the stairs."

"I need you to show yourself. Get up and walk confidently towards them, demand they release Trump or similar. While you distract them, I'll move back behind the door."

"Do I get the gun back? They need to know I'm serious. He's entered the stairwell."

Burt rolled onto his side and pulled a small revolver from an ankle holster.

"Take this. Be quick, we've only got seconds."

~ ~ ~

Down on the street Patsy looked up at the carpark and thumped the roof of her car.

"Why hasn't he answered me?" she muttered. She'd heard no

disturbance and had walked the perimeter of the carpark but her resolve to wait for Burt had dissipated and she pulled out her phone. It was answered quickly.

"I need your help, and quickly. You'll need an armed response team."

## 21

Meredith pushed himself to his feet, gave the front of his jacket a cursory brush, and walked briskly forward.

"And you have Trump here for what reason?" he demanded as he raised his arm and pointed the gun at Hatton. "And who invited Action Man?" The group all turned towards him, but no one answered. "I asked you a question," he hissed through clenched teeth. "I'm pissed off, confused and I expect a fucking answer. Now, who do I have to shoot to get one?"

Lifting the barrel a little, Meredith pulled the trigger. The group flinched, then, swinging his arm around he took aim at Benson. The bullet passed through the group and hit the barrier, causing concrete chips to fly into the air. Hatton raised the gun and pointed it at Meredith, the distraction allowing Benson and Chris Grainger to pull their weapons. Benson took aim at Meredith, and Grainger at Hatton. Meredith felt sick but managed to bellow out a laugh.

"You've got to be kidding me. Doesn't this only happen in films – who blinks first and all that?" He took another step forward and glanced at Louie Trump who had raised himself, and was sitting back on his heels. Meredith wondered which one of them was the most nervous. "I think we're all agreed that Trump is an unnecessary distraction. Trump, move away. Go and sit against the far wall." Meredith's gun pointed the way. He knew that it was unlikely they would allow Trump to leave, but he wanted him out of the line of fire. As Trump raised himself to his feet, Billy was screaming in Meredith's ear.

"The one on level three is coming up in the lift, the bloke in the van must be about to come out of the stairwell, and you didn't tell me you had a fucking gun! Where's your mate gone? Don't answer that, he's got the one from the van. I'm going to punch your fucking lights out if you survive this, my nerves . . ." Billy's fear had produced a false confidence.

Meredith stopped listening and without moving the gun he turned towards the lift, as did the others when they heard the noise.

"Jake Hatton about to arrive," he called in warning to Burt.

Burt lifted his gun and, using all his force, he bought it down against his captive's head. Unconscious, the man fell heavily, and Burt stepped back into the shadows as the lift door opened. Jake Hatton, pistol at the ready, stepped quietly out onto level five, unaware everyone awaited his arrival. He spotted the feet of the man sprawled on the ground. Content it wasn't his brother, he focused on the group of men all holding guns.

Stephen called out to him. "There's one behind you."

His warning came too late. Burt stepped up neatly behind him and placed the barrel of the gun against his head.

"Drop it," he snapped and Jake did as instructed. "Now, very slowly grab hold of him, and let's go and join the party." Burt pushed him towards the prostrate man. Jake grunted as he grasped hold of the man's jacket and heaved the top of his body from the ground. "Drag him, it'll be quicker." As they neared the group Burt shouted at Stephen. "Drop your weapon, Hatton, or I'll take him out."

"I doubt that very much," Stephen responded.

With no further warning, Burt lowered his aim and shot Jake Hatton through the foot. Jake dropped the man he was dragging, howled and sat to nurse his wound.

"I don't make promises, I don't keep. Now, drop the gun," Burt snarled as he stepped forward and placed the barrel against Jake's forehead.

Meredith blew out a sigh of relief as Stephen Hatton dropped his weapon. He took several steps forward and kicked it out of reach. With a tone of confidence, he didn't feel, he snapped, "This is getting very messy, can we have all the bodies in one place? Trump, drag whoever that is over there, and Hatton, you can join them. Help your brother." Using the gun to give direction he turned to Benson and Chris Grainger and lowered the gun to his side as Burt took position several feet away. "I want answers and I want them now."

"Shit, Mr Meredith, this is bad, man. What are you going to do now?"

Billy had been silent for a while, and Meredith winced at the whine in his voice. He returned his attention to Benson.

"Why don't you start the ball rolling by telling us who the bloke in the van is?"

"It's Peter Myshkin," Trump grunted as he placed Myshkin in a sitting position against the wall. "He's coming round, by the way."

"Burt, if you would." Meredith nodded towards Myshkin who groaned and let forth a string of expletives in his native tongue.

"I have him," Burt assured him. "I'm wondering why he was invited to the meeting. Perhaps that should be your next question." Burt and Meredith looked to Benson, who shook his head.

"He's an agent of the state, or was, but he'll be of no use now. He was supposed to have my back. Now, let's wrap this up and get back to civilisation before anyone else gets hurt." Benson gave a shrug as though that were the obvious thing to do.

"You chose a foreign agent as back up? BOLLOCKS!" Burt roared, and then added calmly, "Perhaps Mr Grainger would like to enlighten us."

He looked at Grainger who simply shrugged.

"I'm here because of Meredith," he responded.

Meredith looked at the man who had been his boss, his mentor and his friend for more than fifteen years. Beads of sweat covered his forehead, his cheeks were red, and his voice thick with emotion. His eyes, however, told Meredith that, despite his current condition, he was still in full control.

"Why am I here, Chris?" Meredith asked. "Who orchestrated this and why?" Meredith turned his head towards the row of men sitting against the wall as one of them snorted. Stephen Hatton was attempting to bandage his brother's foot with the tee-shirt he had removed and ripped into strips. Myshkin snorted as though Meredith were a dolt. "Something you'd like to share with us, Myshkin?"

"You still don't know? You are a stupid man, an impotent policeman." Myshkin laughed and winced at the pain as he nodded his head in amusement. "Some of us will die here today – you almost definitely – and you will die not knowing."

He said something in his native tongue.

"You called this meeting, John, but you are here because you didn't follow orders. You went out on a limb, and now it's time to put that right." Chris Grainger was one of the few people who ever used Meredith's first name. He had recovered his composure, and there was now a trace of irritation in his voice. "Benson is right, we need to go in. No one needs to die."

"Except, perhaps, this piece of shit." Meredith turned face to Myshkin. "Tell me why I'm here. You are clearly amused by the situation, so why not rub it in by telling me what I don't know?" Myshkin looked past Meredith and said something in Russian. Meredith inclined his head. "Who are you speaking to? God? He isn't going to help us now."

"He is speaking to Roper, you idiot. He is right about you – you know nothing." Jake Hatton's words were clipped as he battled to ignore the pain in his foot. Meredith turned his head.

"Roper?" Meredith lifted his gun and turned full circle looking at the faces around him. "Roper is here?"

"That's why the brothers are here, sir." Trump jerked his thumb towards the Hattons. "They wanted to deal with him before they got arrested for killing Filipp Myshkin."

Peter Myshkin roared and stopped mid-lunge as Burt fired at the ground in front of him. He cursed and spat at the Hattons. Meredith waited until everyone was settled and caught Stephen's eye.

"Which one is Roper?" he asked.

It was Jake who responded. "Give me your gun and I'll show you."

"I might just do that, but first let's give Benson a chance to explain."

Meredith turned to face Benson. Myshkin took advantage and lunged at Stephen Hatton: with no weapon he used his teeth, sinking them into Hatton's chin. Stephen fell backward letting out a bellow of anger and pain. Despite his injuries, Jake threw himself forward, and locking his arm around Myshkin's neck he began to throttle him. Knowing he was more likely to get information from Myshkin than any of the others, Meredith rushed forward and pressed his gun onto the centre of Jake Hatton's forehead.

"Let him go. Nobody dies until I get answers."

Jake ignored him. Grinning, he increased the pressure until Myshkin's thrashing began to subside. Meredith took a step to the side and aimed at Stephen Hatton.

"You may not care if you die, but what about Stephen? Do you care about him?" To his surprise, Stephen nodded permission to his brother.

"Do it. Maybe he'll shoot me or maybe not, but either way we got another one." He grinned at his brother. "We almost made it."

Jake returned the grin but, unable to take the risk, he released his grip. Myshkin rolled away gasping for breath and massaging his throat. Meredith told Trump to move him further away, and turned to Chris Grainger.

"I won't insult you by pointing this at you, but you start talking now. I know you know who Roper is, and how all this joins up." Meredith swung his arm wide around the sorry-looking group.

"There's not much to tell, but I'm not doing it here. Listen Meredith, we should . . ."

Billy was laughing in Meredith's ear. "Well, thank God for that. The cavalry have arrived Mr Meredith, there are . . . Oi!" Billy shouted as the receiver was pulled from his hand.

"Meredith, are you okay?" Patsy's voice sounded in Meredith's ear. Meredith heard Billy tell her he wouldn't answer. "I can see you. Hold on, there are armed officers on the ground floor – they're working their way up. Don't get hurt before they get to you."

Meredith growled and returned his attention to Stephen Hatton.

"Start talking before your brother bleeds to death. What are you doing here, who's Roper, and what do you want with him?"

Stephen glanced at his brother's foot. He knew the injury shouldn't be life-threatening but his recent movement had dislodged the shirt he had wrapped around it, and a puddle of blood was forming below it. He weighed up their options. His best guess was that either or both Meredith and Trump would survive this meeting, and if they knew the truth, perhaps Jake would get his revenge in another way.

"Roper was an undercover agent. He had supposedly defected to the Russians, and he served as an adviser to the army in occupied Czechoslovakia. A small group was stationed in the town of Horovice. During the war, a group of fleeing Jews had hidden their wealth there and the unit found out. They took the men away in the dead of night, forced them to reveal where the treasure was and then executed them. Roper was part of that group, as were the Myshkins and Andronikov. They took the treasure, whatever that was, and the men never returned. Their bodies were never found." He looked at his brother and winked.

"Revenge one way or another, my friend, my brother."

Stephen smiled as Jake gave a brief nod of permission.

"So, who is Roper?" Meredith demanded, and spun round as Myshkin bellowed out a laugh.

"Roper is the man who will kill you today. Roper is the man who told our troupe of the treasure and organised its collection. He is . . . what do you English call it?" He scratched his head as though confused. "Ah yes, he is a pillar of society, he is –"

A shot rang out and Myshkin lay dead, feet away from Meredith. Not knowing where the shot came from, Meredith spun round.

"No more!" Burt shouted and stepped forward. Meredith lowered his gun.

"You are Roper?" he asked quietly, not expecting an answer but his eyes challenging the man. A movement to his left caught his attention. Jake threw himself into a roll towards the gun his brother had dropped. Grasping it in his hand, he expertly released the safety as he rolled onto his stomach and took aim.

"He is Roper," Jake snarled.

Another shot was fired and hit Jake in the shoulder, but he retained the weapon and pulled the trigger several times as armed officers stormed through the door of the stairwell screaming at the top of their voices. One of the bullets hit Roper in the centre of his forehead and he dropped to his knees, his unseeing eyes looking at Meredith as he fell forward, but Jake had hit another person who fell forward, landing on Roper. Seconds later, Meredith joined them face down on the cold ground as armed officers secured his arms. He heard Trump shouting that he was innocent before a heavy boot met the side of his head. He was unconscious when Patsy reached him.

## 22

After an informal reprimand from Chief Superintendent David Ashworth, it was decided that Meredith's and Trump's actions would be overlooked given the final outcome, and the detail of their suspension was removed from their records. Ashworth was bitterly disappointed that the money Benson had authorised Meredith to accept from Andronikov was to be handed over to the SIS.

Meredith and Trump spent the following days being debriefed in London. Neither was surprised that the identity of Roper and his involvement in the Horovice murders was to remain top secret. The authorities in Prague were already working on the site where Meredith thought the bodies were buried. The Foreign Secretary had attended a meeting with the Czech and Russian Ambassadors and had given his understanding of what had happened in Horovice, and confirmed that the men responsible had been killed by Jake Hatton taking revenge for his grandfather's death.

He reported that only one of the Russian soldiers remained alive, and would spend the rest of his life in prison due to his activities in the UK. In return for confirming this to be the case, and not mentioning Roper's involvement or his later identity, the brothers would be charged with manslaughter and their barrister would plead self-defence. They would serve only a minimal sentence, if any time at all. There was to be no mention of their possible involvement in the murders in Northern Ireland, and it was decided that the murder of Filipp Myshkin was the responsibility of his cousin, Peter, who had confessed shortly before his death.

Billy Jones, who had no idea who was who, was relieved to hear that it wouldn't be necessary for him to attend court as it was felt that the recordings made by the CCTV system would be sufficient. Two days later a clerk took early retirement when the only copy of the recordings was lost. Benson was buried the same day: Meredith heard it was a simple affair with only a handful of mourners.

Meredith and Trump were given permission to sit in on the interviews with the Hatton brothers, and given documents detailing the parts of the interviews, which could be used to wrap up the inquiry.

Trump was quiet on the return journey to Bristol.

"It doesn't sit well, does it?" Meredith commented. Trump sighed.

"No, sir, it doesn't. I can see the bigger picture, and the fact that the minister in charge at that time is dead and buried, as are the majority of the others involved, and it does beg the question what does it matter . . . But the Hattons." He shook his head slowly. "I will abide by my undertaking, but still . . ." He allowed the sentence to drift away.

A few minutes later he turned to Meredith. "What about you, sir? Your involvement was far deeper than mine. I mean –"

Meredith interrupted him. "I think we should move on. Get this bastard case put to bed, for Jane Roscoe if nothing else, and move on."

"Are we speaking literally, sir?"

Meredith caught the concern in Trump's voice and shrugged. "Possibly. Now get your wallet out; there's the service station, I'm starving."

~ ~ ~

Almost a week after the events in the carpark, Meredith walked to his familiar spot in front of the incident board. His face was grave, the ugly bruise which had shadowed the left side of his face had almost gone, and there was no sense of urgency in his movements.

"Listen up. This case is almost done, but we need to tie up the loose ends to ensure the paperwork is watertight." He turned to Seaton. "What news on Andronikov?"

"He's still talking non-stop, more detail is coming through as we speak. Now that he knows he's going to be tried for the murder of the men in Horovice, he's attempting to plea-bargain. He would rather do his time here than in the Czech Republic, or worse, Russia. It won't get him anywhere but it is adding facts to the case against him. His operation in London, the meat factory and all the spin-off businesses have been closed down. The blokes from London are dealing with the arrests from that little lot." Seaton pointed at the board. "So how did the Hattons get involved?"

"It was the Hattons that started the ball moving." Meredith sighed and sat on the edge of the table. "It's a long story. I'll keep it as short as possible, so hold questions until I'm done. The Hattons set off a chain of events that resulted in at least eleven murders, probably more. Jake and Stephen Hatton had a sorry start in life. Stephen Hatton's mother was in a relationship with Jimmy Ridgeway: she fell pregnant, and to get her over her post-natal depression he started feeding her drugs. One day she overdosed. Stephen was alone with her body for over twenty-four hours, and when Ridgeway returned he dumped his child with his mother in Ireland. Stephen was adopted by the Hattons at the age of seven when his grandmother died, and his father didn't want him. Despite her addiction, she'd been a good mother apparently. Stephen never forgot her, and only stopped having nightmares about her death when the Hattons adopted Jake.

"Jake had not been born when his grandfather was killed, but his death overshadowed the whole of Jake's life. His mother died giving birth to him, shortly after both his grandfathers disappeared during the Russian occupation: his father was convinced this loss caused her death. Two brothers were left behind to raise young Jakub Hasek, and although the bond they built with him was strong, his formative years were spent listening to tales of revenge and being dragged along to various meetings as they attempted to uncover what had happened to the men who had gone missing. When Jake's father was killed in a car accident on the way to Prague, Jake was left alone with his uncle. He got hit by depression and so gave Jake up for adoption at the age of seven. He spent a year in an orphanage, which has since been closed, before being adopted by the Hattons. Together the Hatton brothers thrived: they were bright, and they loved each other and their adopted parents. Life was good for the brothers until their parents were killed by a terrorist bomb."

"Is that when they started their quest for revenge?" Jo Adler asked. "How did they find out what happened when the security services couldn't?"

Meredith shook his head, and Jo saw the sadness in his eyes and looked away.

"Nope, they started planning revenge when they hit fourteen. Jake's uncle had his illness under control and married a Portuguese girl. Once they were settled, he went back to get Jake and found he had been adopted. He contacted the Hattons, but realising Jake was better off with them, he left well alone. They maintained contact, and he only lit that touch paper when he knew he had months to live. It was then he gave Jake a recording of his grandfather's execution. The uncle had not managed to get revenge, or even bury his father, but he had found and tortured a Russian soldier he knew was in town at that time of the disappearance and got the truth from him. The murder of the townspeople had been recorded on an old camcorder, and the soldier had kept a copy of the tape as security against taking any blame for the murders. The soldier had told how things had got out of hand, and Filipp Myshkin had executed one of the older men in a fit of temper when he refused to give up the secret of where the treasure was buried. That had never been part of the plan, but now they were all implicated. The other members of the troop had no option but to kill the other civilians who were witness to the crime, but only after they had revealed the secret, believing it would save them. They executed them one by one, military style."

"So why record it? Why would you risk it being uncovered?" Confused, Dave Rawlings shook his head.

"I don't know, I wasn't there." Meredith looked irritated. "Andronikov didn't know it had been recorded at the time. His fear arose from the fact that Hasek pulled his identity tags off while he was readying him for execution. He forgot to recover them, and they were buried along with Hasek in a mass grave."

"So, how did Andronikov find out about it? I know it was something to do with their MOD contract, but not what or how." Dave was used to irritating Meredith, and continued his questions regardless.

"They found the Myshkins quite by chance. Jimmy, Stephen's father, dished them up on a plate."

"So, Stephen killed his own father?" Jo sounded surprised, but little shocked Meredith anymore and he pursed his lips and looked at the floor to curb his irritation. "Gov, are you okay?" Jo was concerned for Meredith and she softened her tone, which only irritated Meredith further.

"I would be if you lot stopped interrupting. Shall I continue, or is there anything else you would like to know about before I get there?" There were a few grins but the team remained silent.

"Stephen tried to develop a relationship with his father when he first traced him, but he quickly realised that they had little in common except the odd gene, and he lost interest, preferring to concentrate on his adoptive parents. When they were killed he tried again. By now Ridgeway had stepped up a grade and was working with the Russians. He bragged about the Mafia types he was working for, and described in detail what they did and how they achieved results. He found the carving of a hammer and sickle into their victims' skin of particular amusement. Stephen said he wasn't sure if his father was trying to impress or frighten him, but the mention of the name Myshkin excited Jake, and he strung him along long enough to check out the Myshkins. And then his father disappeared. He was pleased to hear he'd been tortured, given Ridgeway's former amusement."

"I almost had him down for doing it," Tom Seaton frowned. "Do we know who killed Ridgeway?"

Meredith exchanged glances with Trump. "Lock the door," he instructed.

Trump was about to argue, but thought better of it and did as ordered. Meredith gave a carefully worded version of the Hattons' involvement and that they would be tried for the murders of the Myshkin cousins. He warned his team that they would have to be content that the outcome of that trial would also include any other activities which involved the Hattons.

"Did the Russians know it was Hatton?"

"Oh, they knew. Jake took stills from the Horovice film and sent both the Myshkins and Andronikov copies, together with a photo of the body of Ridgeway. The only message was 'You're next'. That caused a flurry of activity, as they all circled each other in an attempt to work out who had sent the message. Peter Myshkin thought it was Andronikov and vice-versa. Andronikov went to his contact in SIS – Roper." Meredith sighed and rubbed his fingers on his forehead. "Roper didn't know who was sending the messages, but given his involvement in the Horovice murders he used his position to keep a close eye on the Russians."

"What was Roper's involvement?"

"I know that – it was one of the first things they asked Andronikov."

Jo was surprised when Seaton answered, and turned to face him.

"Roper was ordered to tell the rest of the troop about the Jewish treasure: it was considered to be a payment for their future loyalty, something to hold over them. They were never supposed to kill anyone. Andronikov says that was all down to Filipp Myshkin and his lack of control. But, once the first man had been killed it spiralled out of control. Andronikov said that neither he nor Roper killed anyone, but Roper did supervise the disposal of the bodies, which was also recorded. Roper was pulled out and the others were used as agents as originally intended. Andronikov thinks there must have been a storm, albeit minor, as Roper emerged as someone else."

"I didn't know that." Meredith's tone was clipped as though accusing Seaton of withholding something from him.

"I've only read the first couple of pages myself, Gov, they're on your desk."

"But how did the Hattons trace Roper? New identity, new job, relocation once he'd come out of Czechoslovakia – even we couldn't find out who he was." Jo was keen to hear more.

Meredith raised his eyebrows. "Fluke. Simple as that: pure fluke. The Hattons' involvement with the MOD, and their efforts to find Filipp Myshkin, were monitored by the SIS. At that stage, Roper didn't know it was the Hattons who had sent the photographs, so he made contact with them on the pretence of it being connected with their project, but it was really to monitor their interest in the Russians. I know that much. The Hattons had everyone they wanted, except the Irish of course, all ready to take out. It was . . ."

Meredith tutted as Jo Adler pointed her pencil at him.

"But that's another thing I can't get my head around. If the SIS, or some of them, or even just Roper knew what they were planning, why not stop it? Although, I suppose until the deed was done they couldn't touch them, but they certainly could after the event. Why were they left alone? Why are they not answering to that? Because of the body armour? Surely our government can't be that shallow." Jo looked around the rest of the team for support in that statement.

"Don't be naïve, Jo," Meredith snapped. "Of course they are that shallow! Don't forget we have no idea who knew what was going on. Roper must have, and Patsy told me Burt knew, but did any of that information get to a minister?" Meredith shrugged, "I doubt we'll ever know. Their motto should be, 'Need to Know'. Apparently, we don't."

"Can I summarise what we have, Gov?" Rawlings asked. "This is a lot of information."

"If you must." The familiar smile twitched at the corners of Meredith's mouth. Dave started counting on his fingers.

"For various reasons, the Hatton bothers have killed both Myshkin cousins, Jimmy Ridgeway, five Irish terrorists and Roper, as far as we know, although officially they will only be charged with the Myshkins. Who killed Jane Roscoe, Veronika Biskop, Elena and Jan Liska?"

"Veronika was almost certainly murdered by Filipp Myshkin, but as to the others I have no idea. With only Andronikov left alive, unless we get some evidence they may remain unsolved." Meredith looked despondent for a moment. "The only straw we have to grasp at is that due to all his other misdemeanours Andronikov will never be a free man again."

He shook his head as though to clear his thoughts. "So today, get on to Sherlock's office and see if anything else has turned up on the forensic front, pull in all those connected with the Myshkins here in Bristol and see if any of them will talk. Now the cousins have both departed, their tongues might be loosened since the threat of violence has been removed. Any more?" Meredith looked around his team, "Good, because I have yet another meeting with the powers that be, and no doubt another bollocking, so go get some more evidence and make me look good."

He nodded curtly. Pausing only to pick up a file from his desk, he left the incident room in search of the Chief Superintendent.

~ ~ ~

Patsy poured the wine as she listened to Meredith moving about above her, and carried it through to the sitting room, Meredith appeared seconds later. He looked washed out; the shower had done nothing to improve his demeanour. She patted the sofa.

"You look crap. Come and sit down, talk about it or not, but I need a hug."

"Move over." Meredith dropped down next to her and pulled her close. "I've lost interest, Patsy. Once this is tied up I need to consider my options. I've got a few years behind me, the pension won't be that bad – I simply need to find something to do." He closed his eyes and rested his head on the back of the sofa. "I think after the episode in the carpark, I really can say been there, done that, and I don't want the tee-shirt: I want out."

Patsy stroked his chest. "I can understand that. I have no idea how you must have felt . . . be feeling, but after tomorrow it's over for the best part. I know you have to put in the paperwork and tie up a few loose ends, but the others are more than capable of doing that. Why don't you take a few weeks off, a month even, then you can decide? There's no point in rushing into it, because once done, you can't go back. I've got tons on at work – Linda has booked a couple of new cases which I must get started on." Patsy sighed. "So I can't fly off to the sunshine with you for a while, I'm afraid. Perhaps you can take up a hobby, or decorate the bedroom."

"Perhaps." Meredith pecked the top of her head before returning to his previous position. Patsy remained silent. Meredith hadn't argued or been horrified at the mention of decorating, which was unusual. Things may be worse than she thought. When he'd been silent for some minutes, she assumed he had gone to sleep and attempted to move from under his arm.

"Stay. I have something I want to say."

"Go on." She relaxed back into his embrace.

"I want to get married as soon as we can. I don't want us to find anything else to delay it, or fall out about. If we go to the registry office we only have to wait fifteen days before we can get on with it." Meredith paused, giving her time to respond. It was Patsy's turn to remain silent. He nudged her. "Should I be worried about your silence?"

Rather than his usual irritation or anger, Meredith sounded resigned to defeat. Patsy thumped his chest.

"Of course not. I was processing that information. After all, it does mean I could be Mrs Meredith within three weeks, but am I ready for that? Could we organise it that quickly? Do I care where it is, or who comes? Will –"

"Okay, okay, I get the gist. What are the answers?" Meredith opened his eyes and looked down at her. He was already smiling.

"I think I'd cope." Patsy returned his smile. "Patsy Meredith has a nice ring to it."

"We'll go and see the registrar tomorrow afternoon."

"Tomorrow? Are you sure?" Patsy was shocked.

"I am. Something good has to happen tomorrow, I need that."

Patsy twisted and released herself from his grip. Taking his face in her hands she kissed him gently.

"Then tomorrow afternoon it will be." Her smile was soft. "We got there in the end."

"We did. Are we eating first or second?" His eyes answered his question for her. Patsy stood and held out her hand.

"Second, of course."

Meredith looked at his phone, which had been set to silent, and dropped Patsy's hand.

"I must take this, sorry."

He winked as she nodded approval and moved away to answer.

Patsy walked over to Sharon. "You're sure you don't mind?" she asked.

Sharon shook her head as she blew her nose. "Get on with it. Get him off that bloody phone and do it. And about time." Sharon's voice broke, and taking Patsy by the shoulders she spun her to face Meredith. "Go. Now, before he gets called away."

Patsy twisted back and hugged Sharon. "I will. I'll call you later and let you know how we get on, and hopefully give you a date."

"You do that. I want to speak to Meredith anyway, and now is not the time. Look, he's beckoning you. Go quickly before that phone rings again." Pulling Patsy into another hug she whispered in her ear. Patsy's eyes widened, she opened her mouth, but Sharon had rendered her speechless. "Go." Sharon gave her a push.

"Everything okay?" Meredith queried as Patsy reached him.

"Yes, fine. Well, I think so. Give me five minutes to get with it." Patsy opened the door and climbed into the car.

Meredith left it a whole three minutes before he tried again. "Come on, spit it out. What did she say?"

Patsy turned to face him, unsure whether it was irritation or concern she'd heard in his tone.

"Did that call upset you, or is it Sharon?"

"It was only Peggy, making sure I remembered to book the wedding and to say that she'd had an idea for the reception, but I'll tell you about that later. Sharon said something that threw you, so much so you needed to get with it before telling me. What was it? Sharon hasn't upset me." There was the irritation again.

"Well, you didn't say goodbye to her, which was a little rude. Not that she'll mind as she's so pleased for us. Who was on the phone? Clearly someone who made you forget your manners."

"I didn't . . ." Meredith stopped himself. "The call was to let me know that Andronikov ordered the murder of Jane Roscoe, but it was Roper who dealt with Jan Liska, bastards the both." Meredith tried again. "What did she say? Why won't you tell me?"

Irritation gone, Meredith now sounded concerned.

"She'll tell you later. I have to phone her. What's wrong, you sound worried?"

"Tell me what?"

"For goodness sake, Meredith, later," she snapped.

Meredith pursed his lips and stared at the road ahead. Patsy clearly wasn't worried about whatever it was or she would have said. He resolved to leave well alone, at least until after they'd set a date. His resolve didn't last long.

"Patsy, I need to know, it could be important. Was it about Chris? Bloody cyclists!" Meredith hit the horn as he swerved around the bike in front of him.

"Stop the car before you hit someone! That was your lack of concentration, not his. What on earth is going on? Why is this so important?" Patsy gripped the dashboard to steady herself as Meredith swerved onto a bus stop and braked sharply. He turned to face her.

"Tell me. Please."

Patsy opened and shut her mouth several times as she sought the right words. Meredith was barking up the wrong tree, and she needed to set his mind at rest.

"If I tell you, when you speak to Sharon you have to act surprised. And don't jump at an answer because . . . well, because of many reasons. Promise."

"Answer? What's the question?" Meredith's finger drummed a tattoo on the steering wheel. Patsy drew in a breath.

"Sharon has decided what she is giving us for a wedding present."

"Present? What present? That was why you looked like you'd been hit by a bus?"

"You don't know what it is yet," Patsy frowned as Meredith visibly relaxed, and hitting the indicator he pulled back into the traffic. "Don't you want to know?"

"Of course." Meredith threw her a smile. "What is it?"

It was Patsy's turn to be irritated. She was bursting to tell him, and yet now he seemed to have lost interest. She was going to press him on what he'd thought it might be, but thought better of it. Instead, she blurted out the answer.

"Grainger and Co." She smiled as the same shock she'd felt registered with Meredith. This time he didn't wait for a bus stop: he stopped at the side of the road. Instead of shock, Patsy saw a sadness in his expression.

"You're kidding, right." He shook his head. "I can't accept Chris's business . . . Apart from anything else, I have a job."

"Why not? I'm not suggesting you should jump in – after all, we need to discuss how it would affect us – but why such an absolute answer without considering it?"

"She can't do it, that's all. Bloody ridiculous."

"Why?"

"Because it is. Now, shall we get this wedding booked?" Meredith pulled away without indicating.

"Obviously, but why?"

"Because she's just buried her husband. Because she's not thinking straight. Because I don't think it's what Chris would have wanted." Meredith was angry and spittle collected at the corner of his mouth. He wiped it away.

"Why? She said it's what she thinks Chris would have wanted. Their son has no interest in the business. So explain, Meredith; the way you're talking it's like she's insulted you, not paid you a huge bloody compliment and offering you shares in a business worth hundreds of thousands of pounds. What is it?"

Meredith blew out a frustrated breath. He mumbled something Patsy didn't catch and she demanded he repeat it. Meredith shook his head.

"Later, we're here." Meredith circled the carpark and eventually found a space. Glancing at his watch, he fed the ticket machine. "I want to park for an hour, not buy the bloody place." Forcing a smile, he held out his hand. "Come on, let's get this done."

"Very romantic, I'm sure." Patsy took his hand and leaned against his arm. "Something's bothering you, I don't know what, but if it's about Chris, it wasn't your fault, you know."

She looked up as Meredith snorted.

"I know that!" he snapped. "Chris died because he had one secret too many, and he should have trusted me."

They had reached the door of the registry office and Meredith stepped to one side to allow Patsy to enter.

"He did trust you, he was trying to help you. The SIS stuff wasn't his fault, it snowballed out of control, but Chris . . ."

Meredith stopped abruptly, turned and walked quickly towards the exit.

"I can't do this now," he announced as Patsy rushed after him.

Striding out into the courtyard, he sat on the edge of a raised flower bed and lit a cigarette. Patsy joined him and took the cigarette from his hand. She took a puff and looked at him as she blew the smoke away and returned the cigarette.

"What's going on? You have to explain this."

Meredith looked at her for a moment, and, dropping his chin to his chest, he closed his eyes.

"His whole life was a lie. Sharon didn't know . . . I didn't know." He paused and opened his eyes. "I didn't know him. I won't take his business." Flicking the cigarette away he stood and took a step away. "I won't discuss this further. Let's go home – we can do this another time."

"Because he was SIS and didn't tell you, we postpone again?" Patsy was exasperated. "Meredith, you are taking this far too personally. He was your friend! It was a good friend you buried today. Please, Meredith, don't you walk away from me!"

Patsy stopped walking, Meredith didn't. She was about to call out an insult when, without stopping, he turned his head.

"Chris Grainger was Roper."

Shoving his hands into his pockets, he increased his pace.

# ABOUT THE AUTHOR

Having worked in the property industry for most of my adult life, latterly at a senior level, I finally escaped in 2010. I now dedicate the bulk of my time to writing and, of course, reading, although there are still not enough hours in the day.

I began writing quite by chance when a friend commented, "They wouldn't believe it if you wrote it down!" So I did. I enjoyed the plotting and scheming, creating the characters, and watching them develop with the story. I kept on writing, and Meredith and Hodge arrived. In 2017 the Bearing women took hold of my imagination, and the Bearing Witness series was created. I should confess at this point that although I have the basic outline when I start a new story, it never develops the way I expect, and I rarely know 'who did it' myself until I've nearly finished.

I am married with two children, two grandchildren, two German Shepherds and a Bichon Frise. We live in Bristol, UK.

I can be contacted here, and would love to hear from you:

Website: http://mkturnerbooks.co.uk/

www.ingramcontent.com/pod-product-compliance
Lightning Source LLC
Chambersburg PA
CBHW061541170626
46811CB00001B/43